Acclaim for

Kendy Pearson brings t............................ explosive Civil War history in this multi-faceted jewel of a tale inspired by true events. Endurance, faith, and love shine through *When the Mountains Wept*, the first book in what is sure to be a stellar series.

Laura Frantz,
Christy Award-winning
author of *The Rose and the Thistle*

As West Virginia sat perched between the Union and the Confederacy, neighbors were forced to make difficult choices and kinfolk found themselves across from one another in battle. Gifted storyteller Kendy Pearson makes this scene spring to life with her vivid storytelling, every character so expertly sculpted that I found myself missing them when I closed the cover. Augusta and James stole my heart, and I rooted for them from page one until the very end. Don't miss *When the Mountains Wept*, and I can't wait to see what Pearson writes next.

Karen Barnett,
Award winning author of *When Stone Wings Fly*
and the Vintage National Park Novels

Kendy Pearson's debut is a stirring look at the people who lived, loved, and lost during the darkest period in our country's existence. *When the Mountains Wept* is a heart-rending romance between Augusta and James that reveals the God who is always there...even when we think all is lost. A story to savor and an author to watch!

Tara Johnson,
author of *To Speak His Name*

Kendy Pearson plunges the reader into life in western Virginia just before and moving into the Civil War. With excellent attention to details of life in the 1860s and historical accuracy, the story brings the reader face to face with the personal struggles of Southerners in an untenable situation. It's not a story to be rushed through, and I highly recommend "living" in this book for a while.

Susan Pope Sloan,
Award-winning author of
"Rescued Hearts of the Civil War" series

When the Mountains Wept takes readers on an emotionally-layered journey, both heart-stirring and redemptive. Pearson pens a moving tale of family loyalty, complex devotions, and hope amid the turmoil. A delight historical fiction fans won't want to miss!

Stephenia H. McGee,
Award-winning author of
"The Accidental Spy" series

West Virginia: Born of Rebellion's Storm 1

WHEN THE
MOUNTAINS
WEPT

KENDY PEARSON

Heart of History
an imprint of
PEAR BLOSSOM BOOKS

When the Mountains Wept

Copyright © 2024 by Kendy Pearson

All rights reserved.

No portion of this book may be reproduced in any form without written permission from the publisher or author, except as permitted by U.S. copyright law. No part of this publication may be stored in a retrieval system or transmitted in any form or by any means—for example, electronic, photocopy, recording—without the prior written permission of the publisher. The only exception is brief quotations in printed reviews.

Published by Pear Blossom Books in the United States of America.

Scripture quotations are taken from the King James Version of the Bible

Publishers Note: This novel is a work of fiction. Names, characters, places, and incidents are either products of the author's imagination or used fictitiously. Because this is a work of historical reconstruction; the appearance of certain historical figures, places, and incidents are therefore inevitable.

ISBN 979-8-9899317-0-5 (print)

Library of Congress Cataloging in Publication Data

Cover Design by Mountain Creek Books LLC

Subjects: Novel / Historical Fiction / Christian Historical Fiction / American Civil War / West Virginia breaks from Virginia / Christian Historical Fiction inspired by true events

In memory of my father-in-law, Dr. Harris Pearson, who shared my love of historical novels, devoured every one I owned, and encouraged me at every turn.

It is not the light that we need, but the fire.
It is not the gentle shower, but the thunder.
We need the storm,
the whirlwind,
and the earthquake.

Frederick Douglass
July 5, 1852

1861-1865

Rebellion's tempest swept the land
and a state was born of a nation torn.
West Virginia: a Child of the Storm

One

FAYETTE COUNTY, VIRGINIA

February 1861

"We can do this, Daisy. Just don't you kick me." Augusta puffed a wisp of hair away and wiped blood from her arm as a new contraction sent ripples through the cow's coppery hide. Daisy's brown eyes widened as she let go a rafter-shaking bawl. Poor ol' gal. "You just hold on, now. It'll all be over soon."

Movement caught Augusta's eye as a woolly spider descended on a single thread. It plunged, paused, plunged again, and settled on the floor. A familiar ache wrenched her already bruised heart. She wasn't so different from that little wire-legged creeper, was she? She had abandoned her dreams only to plunge into an impossible situation.

Two days—forty-eight agonizing hours—until she'd have her answer.

"Did you do it, Gus?"

Augusta's head snapped up. "What, Will?" Twelve-year-old Willamina had been planted at Daisy's other end for the last half hour.

"Can the calf come now?" Her sister slapped at a fly tangled in her unruly curls. "There now, Daisy," Will crooned as she caressed the jersey's blocky head. "You go ahead and birth that little one of yours." She winked at Augusta. "Gus will take care of you."

The cow huffed through inflamed nostrils, raising tiny clouds that vanished in the chilly stall.

"Could be there's something wrong here besides this little fellow not being right where he oughta be." Augusta sorted her tangled thoughts, separating tomorrow's worries from the task at hand as hay and manure odors mingled with the metallic scent of blood.

In the next seconds, one hoof and then another emerged, followed by a bony forehead and flat nose. She dragged the calf into the fresh straw and scraped away the mucous sack with her fingers. Always a beautiful thing—new life.

She massaged the moist nose of the stirring newborn. "Well, I guess the good Lord wanted the Dabneys to have another bull. Not much for milk and butter, but I reckon come time to butcher, we'll be thankful for the roasts."

If they weren't forced to sell the little guy before then. Surely, the Almighty had a plan. He just wasn't sharing it with *her*.

"Aww, I was wantin' a heifer this time." Will snagged her worn hat and stood, shaking straw from her britches.

"You can want all you want, but it won't make it happen. We've got two more due to calve in the spring. Maybe you'll get your heifer then. Now, go set the table and ring for supper."

"That's woman's work," Will grumbled.

"Willamina Dabney! I will not have you complaining. You be thankful you've got family to call to supper and food to put on the table." She swatted the girl's behind. "Now scoot!"

Once the newborn discovered its first meal, Augusta stretched weary muscles and quit the barn, aiming to see to Pap's meal, already simmering on the stove.

She dipped broth from a steaming kettle and made her way to his bedroom. Glad to find him awake, she set aside the cup and brushed grizzled hair from his drawn face. He was fretting, and she knew why. "I'll be fine, Pap. Don't you worry about me. I'll be back from Charleston afore you know it."

"I just wish I was the one going." He wheezed and caught his breath. Moist pewter eyes wrapped her in love. "If we can't get the bank to work with us—"

"I won't let you down, Pap." She'd do anything to keep her family together. Anything to keep their farm. "Zander's coming with. We'll stay with the Carmichaels. You remember my friend, Maudie Carmichael, don't you? From Mrs. Munday's School for Young Ladies?" She stirred the hot broth, refusing to pine for happier times just now. "And Melinda Jane will take fine care of you whilst I'm gone. I wouldn't be surprised if Izzy didn't come sit a spell. Maybe play some checkers, too." She was rambling now, but she'd see him rest from his worrisome talk.

Her dearest friend would watch over Pap, but Augusta still cringed at the thought of leaving him like this. Every day, she thanked the Lord for a little more time. She wasn't ready to see him go on to be with Mama and Jesus. Not just yet.

Pressing a kiss to his hairline, she squeezed his mottled hand. "I'll look in on you later." Grief stole her voice, so she nodded and softly closed the door.

Her sweet Pap. Would he even see Christmas this year?

൦ൈ

Charleston, Virginia

Marble columns towered above Augusta's head, testing her mettle. Her hand hesitated on the cold, brass handle of the door as something contrary to peace sluiced through her. Bold script etched the smooth, stone façade to her left–CENTRAL BANK OF CHARLESTON. She hated this place. It was an edifice to the financial ruin of farmers everywhere—plain folk struggling to eke out a living from the land, only to lose it all to the snobbish coat-and-tail types in their hilltop mansions.

But all she held dear was precariously perched upon the shoulders of one Thaddeus Fontaine, Bank President.

"I'm here to see Mr. Fontaine," she told the window clerk. "I'm Augusta Dabney. I believe I have an appointment."

The white-haired gentleman glanced at a schedule and flipped over the tiny OPEN sign. "Right this way, ma'am."

She followed the crisp black suit through the lobby and up a gleaming staircase with the scent of lemon oil hovering in the air. She paused an instant to admire the flawless shine of the floor. Quickening her steps, she caught up to the clerk once more. A carved door loomed at the end of the hall; the transom bedecked with flashy gold lettering—PRESIDENT.

"He'll be with you in a moment, Mrs. Dabney."

"It's *Miss* Dabney," she corrected as the clerk walked away. Drawing a deep breath, she pulled back her shoulders and lifted her chin. She could do this. The door opened and two men stood shaking hands. Her stomach lurched as a jumble of memories frayed her courage in an instant. *Dear Lord, please don't let him be the bank president.*

"I hope I'll be meeting you over at the Pattons' place soon, James. Good to see you again."

The visiting gentleman whirled without warning, knocking her off-kilter. His hand moved to steady her, then recoiled. "Excuse me, ma'am." Half a smile did nothing to soften the stern edges of his handsome face.

"Ah, my next appointment." The banker's eyes fixed on Augusta. His familiar, enthusiastic smile unsettled her. "Dr. James Hill, may I introduce to you Miss Augusta Dabney?"

One eyebrow arched below carved lines on the doctor's forehead. "Are you, by any chance, related to the Dabneys of King William County?"

"Why yes, I am. My father—"

"Good day then." A shadow darkened striking brown eyes before he spun and marched down the hall.

How rude! But she couldn't afford to be rattled.

"Where is Mr. Fontaine?" She frowned, looking past the enormous leather wing chairs for a glimpse of the gray-haired man. Gripping the front of her dress, she pressed down the whirlwind in her middle. If only Fin weren't away on business. Her brother should be here.

"I believe you are looking for Uncle Thaddeus. *I* am now the acting Bank President." His coy expression only sickened her stomach. "I do hope you remember me, Augusta."

She remembered him all right—from her one year at finishing school. After a brief acquaintance and a healthy dose of youthful infatuation, she had agreed to accompany him to a coming-out ball. He had been overbearing and much too familiar. The recollection burned her cheeks.

"I see you *do* remember. It was the Hansford House, was it not? A lovely gala, with quite a collection of beautiful women, as I recall. Ah, but I was fortunate to accompany a particular auburn-haired lass that evening. Was it so long ago, Augusta? You've changed." His fingers touched a tendril fallen from her hat. "More . . . beautiful."

Drawing back just enough, she narrowed her eyes. "And do you recall that particular lass slapping you for being boorish?" She stepped around him and took a seat. "If you don't mind, *Mister* Fontaine, I'd like to talk business."

He chuckled and settled into an oversized Empire chair behind the mahogany desk. "Now, what can I do for you?" He folded his hands and glanced down, seeming to admire his reflection on the polished desktop.

"I've come about the note on our farm. I'd like to talk to you about modifying the terms." She sat a little straighter. Her family needed this.

"I see. What kind of modification do you have in mind, *Miss Dabney?*"

"As you know, we haven't missed a payment in five years on that note. There's not much more owing, and I was wondering if you would accept smaller payments—or perhaps an installment every *other* month." Hoping she sounded business-like, she clutched her reticule to steady her quivering hands.

He leaned back into the tufted leather. "That's quite a modification. It would be highly unusual for me to allow such an arrangement." He paused for seconds that felt like minutes, tapping a finger on the desktop. "Is there anything of value you can leverage against this loan to lower your balance? Livestock or horses?"

"Not right now, but later perhaps, after the spring calving." *I will not grovel.* She lifted her head a bit higher.

More tapping. At last, he retrieved a page of paper and blotter from the top drawer and dipped a pen. "Perhaps we can arrive at a solution that would work for both of us—I mean, for your father and the bank, of course. Mmm?"

"I would be obliged. What do you have in mind, Mr. Fontaine?" A crumb of relief. This was going to work. It had to.

"Why don't we start with an agreement for the bank to accept whatever amount you feel you can afford for now? I will need to draw up a temporary deferment for the full payments. However, you must realize there is still interest. The bank will allow you until August to bring the payments current. Is that agreeable?"

August? So soon. "I appreciate your willingness to work with us, Mr. Fontaine. Might you allow us until the end of the year to bring the note current?"

His bare upper lip twitched into a brief smile. "A shrewd proposal, Miss Dabney."

The mantle clock's second hand thumped its advance. Her confidence wilted.

He scratched several sentences on the paper before glancing up—all business. "Let us say October, then. Is *that* agreeable to you?"

Did she have a choice? "Yes. It will surely have to be, won't it? Thank you for your time, Mr. Fontaine." She stood, conscious of every tenacious corset stay squeezing her ribs. Only God knew how they would make this work.

"I'll have the documents for you by noon," he said, standing.

Her heart clung to a frail hope. She had won only the first battle of the war—a war against a formidable foe. She offered her hand to conclude their business. He looked at it for a moment, chuckled, and clasped it. But when he didn't release his grip, she attempted to pull her hand free—until his eyes pinned her in place.

"I hope to see you soon, then . . . Augusta." One side of his mouth slithered upward as her heart thundered a warning. Finally, he nodded, releasing her hand.

The air shifted in the room, and she bit her lip. This would've gone so much better with the senior Fontaine.

What had she gotten herself into?

Two

Charleston

James plucked a piece of candy from the tall glass jar, offering it to the timid child. Wide eyes glittered, and her mouth rounded to a perfect *O* as she studied the store-bought confection.

"Go ahead," he encouraged, ducking his face to her eye level.

The girl's skinny legs dangled over the edge of the examination table, twin pendulums swinging back and forth. Finally, she reached for the strumpet candy with a Christmas-morning smile sprouting across her cheeks.

James chuckled. The best part of an office call—*after* the unpleasantries.

"Doctor, how can I ever thank you?" The round woman smothered her daughter's face against an ample bosom, her hand flattening a mass of unruly golden curls.

"I believe the fee for my services today, Mrs. Pratt, is one mincemeat pie. But if you don't have a whole pie available, I'll take it in installments." He grinned at the girl and touched her chin with his thumb. "And no more attempting to eat peanuts through your nose, Beth Ann. Understood?"

"Yes, sir." One hand clung to a tattered doll while the other slipped the candy stick in and out of her mouth. "Can you check my dolly too, Dr. Hill?"

The child had stolen his heart in the course of five minutes. Hazel-gold eyes studied him eagerly, still shimmering from spent tears.

He positioned the end of his stethoscope on the doll's tiny, grubby chest and tilted his ear to the tube. "Sounds healthy as a horse. I prescribe lots of love and attention for your little one."

"Thank you, Doctor." She giggled as he lifted her from the table and set her gently on the floor.

"You are very welcome, Beth Ann." He turned to the mother. "Good day, Mrs. Pratt."

"Thank you again, Doctor Hill. I'll be keeping a closer eye on this one." Rosy cheeks beaming her thanks, she turned, tugging her daughter along behind.

"Mrs. O'Donell, are there any other patients out there?" Some days, the parlor-turned-waiting room sat empty. Today, however, patients trickled in like ants to a picnic.

Mrs. O'Donell's portly figure filled the doorway. Her motherly concern for him, a grown man, never ceased to tug at his senses. Whatever had he done to deserve such a delightful assistant? He was much too stern with her at times. Perhaps because he resented the sad truth of it all—in many ways, she had been more of a mother to him than his own.

Growing up wealthy had its benefits, but the affection of adoring parents wasn't one of them. He could count on one hand the number of times his mother had said she loved him. No appendages needed to tally his father's favorable remarks.

"Well, Mrs. O'Donell? Are there others?"

"Oh my, yes." She wrung her hands, glancing over her shoulder. "Tis Mrs. Taylor, sir. Havin' a bit of the vapors." Her face soured, and she lowered her voice. "So, she says."

"Well, what are you waiting for? Send her in."

"It's just that—beggin' yer pardon, James—she's got a swarm of servants buzzin' about her. Sure'n, she insists they accompany her, too."

"She does, does she?" Of all days. First that Dabney woman at the bank. Now this. Obviously, starting his practice on this side of the mountains wasn't far enough from home.

"She's bent on the two of ya having tea while *discussing* her *condition.*" Her jowls shook as her Irish brogue coiled around the words.

Was he amused or put out? Indulging the hypochondriasis of Charleston's upper crust was—among other duties—part and parcel to his station as a physician in this city. And the requisite charge *did* serve to remind him of why he became a doctor.

Mrs. Taylor and the likes of her represented all that was wrong with this country—this world. *His* world. The people who needed him most didn't have servants to dress them, cook for them, and drive their spit-shined carriages.

Smiling deliberately through his disdain, he instructed Mrs. O'Donell, "Please send her—uh—them in, Mrs. O'Donell. And would you be kind enough to prepare a tea tray for us?"

"Yes sir, Doctor." She rolled her eyes as she backed across the threshold.

"Thank you." He sighed, wishing for a quick end to the day.

Mrs. Hamlin Taylor III soon wilted in the chair opposite, a purple feather from her outrageous bonnet drooping over one eye. A white porcelain tea set and six petite pumpkin cakes set on the low table between them. To the right, a slender Negro woman in a crisp-collared black dress and white apron waited. Next to her, a tall, lighter-skinned footman stood at attention, dressed in impeccable black and white livery.

"Really, Mrs. Taylor, your servants can most certainly wait outside. This is, after all, a personal office call. Is it not?" James lifted a cup to his lips. Addressing the situation seemed pointless, yet he had to try.

"Oh, mine go with me everywhere, Dr. Hill. What would I do without them? They're no bother, really." She flipped her hanky at the servants as if batting flies.

Well, he tried. He placed the dainty cup back on its saucer. "What brings you here today, Mrs. Taylor?"

She dismissed the footman with a wave of her hand. When the door clicked shut behind him, she turned to James. "Oh Doctor, I'm just not myself these days." She brushed at her brow with the back of her hand.

"Please, go on. Can you list your symptoms for me?" He reached for a notepad and scribbled nonsense on the paper while she continued. He chewed the inside of his cheek to affect a sober countenance.

"I seem to be too weary to get out of bed in the morning." She reached for another cake. "And certainly, I'm finding it most difficult these days to enjoy the company of others. Why, I have not even entertained in a fortnight. What must the ladies think of me?" Wagging her head woefully, she pressed her fingers to her lips. "I confess I find myself more and more relishing the idea of a nap most days—even in lieu of dining at the Kanawha House.

"I fear there are few days in my future remaining. Life as I've known it is winding down, and my demise is near. Oh, Doctor, you must do something. I simply am not ready to die. I'm too young." She dabbed the embroidered hanky to teary eyes. "Whatever would my Hamlin do without me?"

"Mmm . . . I see." James continued writing for a moment. Rising slowly, he crossed the room to a wall-mounted glass and oak cupboard. He removed ten tiny blue pills from a round tin and inserted them into a small brown envelope.

"Mrs. Taylor, I do believe we can avert this disaster—for the time being. I am prescribing these pills. You will take one upon waking and another upon retiring for the next five days. I am confident that your symptoms will dissipate after a time." He handed her the envelope. "I'm advising a particular course of treatment for you as well."

She straightened, biting her lip, apparently assessing the *grave* situation. "Treatment. Certainly, Doctor. I will follow your instructions in perfect detail." Stuffing the hanky into her sleeve, she leaned forward, eyes wide.

"Mrs. Taylor, I am prescribing a brisk walk for a twenty-minute duration upon rising each morning. I am also prescribing two teaspoons of cider vinegar in a glass of water before each meal."

"A . . . a brisk walk, you say? Where would I walk? What if people see me?" Her countenance fell once again as she fidgeted with the cameo broach at her throat.

"Walk where you will, Mrs. Taylor. This is my prescription for you, which, if you want to put off your demise a while longer, you must certainly follow. I'm confident you will feel better by this time next week. Dare I say I do not wish to see you in my office again for such a serious matter?" He forced a smile.

"Oh, I do hope not, Doctor. I will adhere to your course of treatment beginning this very evening. Thank you, Dr. Hill. You've been most kind." She tucked the pills away, and he helped her to her feet.

"Good day, Mrs. Taylor."

The moment the front door closed behind the woman and her servant, Mrs. O'Donell peered around the doorpost, eyes shifting. "Is the coast clear?" A slice of mirth bespoke her ever-present cheerful nature.

"You may come out now, Mrs. O'Donell. She is gone."

"Blue Mass?" A knowing smile bloomed across her ruddy cheeks.

"Blue Mass, Mrs. O'Donell. The lovely blue pill for every woman who is her own worst disease." They shared a laugh as he retrieved the tea tray and carried it to the kitchen.

"Now, James, ya needn't do that. I can manage it meself." She shuffled after him.

"Yes, yes, I know. You can *always* manage. And I can always help myself." He turned and winked to preclude any ruffled feathers. "Have we another patient today?"

"Little Gerald Cooper is coming in for ya to be checking on his splint. But, that's not until two o'clock, so you've a bit of free time for lunch today, ya have. Will ya be wantin' to stay in or go out?"

The bell above the front door jingled, announcing another patron.

"So much for lunch," James lamented as Mrs. O'Donell ambled to the parlor to welcome the unexpected visitor.

"Is James busy, Mrs. O'Donell?"

At the sound of the familiar voice, James strode into the parlor. "Austin, what brings you here? Neither for the services of a doctor nor in the duties of a solicitor, I hope."

Austin Kennedy removed his tall hat and tapped two fingers to the brim. Perfectly waved black hair and an impeccably groomed beard evidenced a recent trip to the barber.

James extended a hand to his friend and raked fingers through his own beard. When was the last time *he* visited a barber?

"On the contrary, I came by to see if you have a break in your schedule and would care to join me for lunch at the Kanawha House?"

"Food sounds wonderful, but what say we sup at Miss Molly's Eatery? They've got the best fried chicken this side of Richmond." He retrieved his hat and frock coat from the hall tree.

"Always the Puritan, James." Austin's mouth tipped in a teasing smirk as he held the door.

Miss Molly's was like an extended family at mealtime. Not that James had experienced anything like this as a boy. The checkered tablecloths, homey atmosphere, and smiling calico-clad waitresses suited him just fine. The simple fare was much more to his liking than the bouillabaisse of the aristocracy or the two-pound steaks of the mining moguls at the Kanawha House.

"I want you to talk to George Patton, James."

Austin directed a flirtatious smile at the approaching waitress, who balanced two water glasses in one hand and two steaming plates of fried chicken and mashed potatoes in the other.

"We've been through this, Austin."

"I know, I know. Just come with me on Saturday evening and talk to him. It's an honor to be invited to be a Kanawha Rifleman. If your answer is still no, at least give the man a reason." Austin winked at the woman as she served their food. She promptly blushed and scurried away.

"Is no woman safe around you?" James shook his head. "I dare say you can't leave your office without dispensing a dose of trifling with some unsuspecting woman."

"God made women beautiful just for the joys and follies of men, wouldn't you say?"

"I can't say I agree with that, old man. In fact, as I recall, woman was made to be a helpmeet for man." *Where did that come from?* He stroked his chin, schooling his expression. Well, of course, he knew *where* it came from, but why did he say it aloud?

One eyebrow cocked, and Austin leaned closer. "Does Victoria know you don't rank beauty above your desire for a *helpmeet* in your quest for a wife?"

"I don't have a 'quest for a wife'. I've no desire to marry." Certainly not Victoria Jamison. "Building my practice—that's what's important to me. Joining the Kanawha Riflemen is not something I deem productive."

"But the Riflemen include the most prominent members of the Charleston community. Why, the most highly regarded doctors and attorneys are all members. You'll be in company, and the connections you make will allow you to advance your practice in more ways than you can imagine. The people of Charleston will look at Dr. James Hill through fresh eyes."

He wiped the last of the grease from his fingers. Under Austin's scrutiny, he sucked in a long breath and let it out. He downed a glass of water and tossed his napkin on the table. "Might as well get this over with. I'll go with you to speak with Captain Patton. But this is the last I want to hear of it. Are we agreed?"

Austin reached across the table and pumped his hand. "You got it. Not another word."

As they exited the eatery, Austin turned sharply. "Oh, and I *might* have mentioned to Victoria that she would look lovely on your arm at the Pattons' gala Saturday evening."

"Austin . . ." He growled, crossing his arms, thoroughly perturbed by the presumptuous intrusion.

Austin whirled and started down the street at a clipped pace. He spun once and waved. "See you Saturday, Dr. Hill." Laughter drifted behind his words.

James cringed at the prospect—once again roped into one of Austin's schemes. And his own best intentions entirely dismissed.

Three

Fayette County

Invigorated by the tang of mud and chill, Augusta struck out across the yard. She snugged the woolen wrap tighter around her shoulders as she made her way across the pasture and over the rise to her special place.

Bare earth poked through the gray-white carpet of snow, melted away in sporadic patches by an unexpected thaw. A raccoon scurried across the field—a sure sign of an early spring. With the edge of her shawl, she scattered icy crumbles of snow from the rough board swing and hoisted herself up.

Here, in her *thinkin' spot* beneath the giant cedar, she could forget about the future, remember the past, and pray for today. Surely her God was bigger than the snarled knot within her heart. And bigger than the fear that peeked around the corner and stared her in the eye. But a feeling she couldn't shake—a shadow of something beyond today—darkened even this sovereign haven beneath the stately tree.

She'd find herself daring to dream. Dream of a family of her own, a husband to love, a future. But it was no use. Her life was here, caring for the young'uns. She'd promised Mama.

"Halloo to the tree!" A familiar voice rescued her from her pensive mood.

Through all her years on this earth, that voice had reproved her, counseled her, and teased her. Ol' Izzy's little cabin at the edge of the grove had ever been a source of laughter and story-telling.

"You in yer thinkin' spot, missy. Something bothering you?" He stooped low and his brown hand brushed snow from a wild crocus shoot. "We gots to help them that needs helping," he said with a snicker. "Not that this here bit o' shoot is depending on Ol' Izzy's help to spring up and blossom. Good Lord see to that."

"Izzy, you always could lift my spirits."

"There's that smile I like to see. I come by to take a look at that new calf I heard tell of."

"Gus! Gus! Where are you?" Will's crumpled slouch hat popped over the hill before the rest of her barreled down to the swing, arms flailing like a baby bird tumbled from its nest. She skidded to a stop, hooking Augusta's arm as an anchor.

"Whoa, there. First of all, a lady doesn't holler like that. And secondly, a lady doesn't run." Augusta used her sternest voice.

"Well, first, I ain't a lady—at least not yet—and second, I'm in a hurry!"

"What is so all-fired important, Willamina?" She hid a smile beneath her *mean face*, as her brother Bertie liked to call it.

"The boys are going twilight huntin'. Can I go with them?"

"And *ladies* don't hunt." She sighed, assenting. "But, yes, you can go with your brothers. Because *ladies* do what needs to be done." Augusta staggered as Will's flannel-clad arms squeezed her middle.

"Thanks. And thank you too, Izzy." Will started a lazy jog up the hill.

"What'd I do, missy?" Izzy shouted after her.

Will spun to face him, continuing up the hill backward. "You always put Gus in a good mood. See ya later—with meat, I hope."

"Heh, heh, heh. Like a rabbit on the run, that one." An impish grin peeked through Izzy's white beard, a striking contrast to his dark terra cotta skin. He stretched out a wrinkled hand. "Now, what say we take a gander at that calf?"

∽

"Supper's ready, Pap." Augusta's voice was little more than a whisper as she knelt beside the bed. His cough was better today. Didn't his lungs sound a bit clearer? Jonathan Dabney was a force to be reckoned with just a year ago. Now consumption pitilessly drained him of life, just as it had Mama.

Life hoed a rocky row for him before Mama died—months at the sanatorium up in Grafton, endless trips to the doctors in Wheeling, a bank loan for all the bills. And how he had suffered. Months of grieving even before Mama passed. He told her once that the best part of him had died with Mama.

Pap frowned, gingerly clearing his throat. "Can you get the boys to help me to the table?"

"They'll be here shortly. It's been a week since you joined us for a meal, Pap. I'm real thankful you're up to it tonight."

Moments later, chairs bumped and scraped on the floor until all the Dabneys and Melinda Jane settled at the table. Augusta scanned the cherished faces. Her flock. And she was the mother hen. Hadn't she raised Bertie like her own?

If only Mama could see the beauty Will had become—and Zander, practically a man at just sixteen. Not a day went by Augusta didn't ask God to show her what Mama would've done about this or that.

Her gaze moved to Fin. Just a year older than her own twenty years, he stood tall and muscular like Pap. A fully grown man, but she even felt like *his* mother.

"Lord," Pap began softly, "I thank You for this bounty and the hands that worked hard to prepare it. It is Your gift to us, and we thank You." He sucked in a rattly breath. "And Lord, I ask You to take care of this family, whatever may come. We trust You, Lord. Amen."

"Talked with Jimmy Lee Campbell this morning, Pap." Fin set a pork chop bone on his plate, wiping at his chestnut beard with a napkin. "He got himself a *Kanawha Valley Star*. Gave it to me to read. News doesn't sound good."

"Pap don't wanna hear no news." Six-year-old Bertie pushed his straight, blond hair from his eyes. "Ain't that right, Gus? Ain't that what you always say?"

"It's '*doesn't* want to hear *any* news'—and I don't always say it." Minding Pap's schooling gaze, she shifted her attention to Zander, who was already shoveling up second helpings. Hollow legs, that one.

Pap nodded to Fin. "Go ahead, son. Let's hear it." His usual smile dipped as he reached down to rub the graying head of the old hound, Coot.

"Well, for starters"—Fin straightened and wedged his back against the chair—"six more states have seceded, and they've gone and composed a constitution, calling themselves the Confederate States of America. They even voted themselves a president, Mr. Jefferson Davis."

"Can they do that?" Will's glances bounced between Pap and Augusta. "Can they just up and pick a new president?"

Zander halted the bite aimed for his mouth. "I guess they figure they can, 'cause they did." He turned to his older brother. "Dirch Sizemore says Virginny's got to choose up sides."

"He's right." Fin rapped his fingers on the tabletop, setting his jaw hard. "They're choosing up county delegates for a convention in Richmond this month to decide whether Virginia's gonna stay with the Union or join the Confederacy. I even read the Choctaws and some other tribes are joining in with the South if there's a war."

Augusta's stomach quivered at the mention of war. How she prayed it wouldn't come to that. Didn't folks see the horrors it would reap? Surely it would slash a wound through this nation so deep it'd never heal.

Pap combed his fingers through a gray-flecked beard. "Seems to me that nothing's been the same since that John Brown incident up at Harper's Ferry." He muffled a vicious cough with his napkin, then grimaced at the cloth. Stealing a peek at Augusta, he promptly folded it and took a drink. "War is an ugly thing. I don't want my boys fighting some war that's not ours." Furrows piled like storm clouds across his forehead. "*Our* business is our family and our land. The good Lord watches over His own, and He always will. No sense inviting trouble."

༄

Augusta dumped another bucket of water over the boy, sending soapy gray waves splashing over the washtub sides. "Bertram Eliakim Dabney! Sure had better be the last time I have to deal with this. Makes two years running that you and Coot got yourselves sprayed by a polecat."

She rolled her stinging eyes at Melinda Jane, who merely grinned, ignoring the foul odor. If only a clothespin on the nose truly did work. Grabbing up the brush again, Augusta rubbed it onto the chunk of lye soap and scrubbed his skin red.

He was surely trying, but how she loved this little brother of hers—his innocent antics and the way he bounded into each day as if all the wonders of the world waited just for him. Likely, Mama was laughing at all this from heaven right now.

She tossed her friend a frustrated look. "Honey, will you please fetch some tomatoes from the cellar?" Sweat trickled from Augusta's hairline, no doubt calling forth the dreaded crimson blotches on her cheeks. How she envied Melinda Jane's velvety complexion, as flawless as her perfect white teeth. And her hair, a striking mix of wheat, sand, and copper.

Melinda Jane laughed at the shivering boy and flashed Augusta a knowing smile. "Boys will be boys. Isn't that what you're always telling me, Gus?"

Augusta snorted, then flicked water across her friend's apron.

"Hey! I'm not the one in need of a good scrubbin'!" Melinda Jane's doe eyes sparkled with mischief. She made an exaggerated *to-do* over her wet apron before scooting off to get the tomatoes.

Augusta frowned, wishing there was a way around what she had to say. "There's not much can be done for old Coot, Bertie. I am not wasting my tomatoes on him. He'll just have to stay out of the house 'til summer, I reckon."

He scowled, none too happy about the edict. Bertie was more attached to that old hound than a tick to a wildcat.

Melinda Jane emerged from the house; arms laden with canning jars. "I'll do the tomatoes for you Gus. Seems this is usually the part I'm best at."

Bertie gasped, indignation flushing his cheeks and creasing his chin. "Last year you shoved some in my mouth!" He pooched out his lower lip. "You know I don't like maters, Melinda Jane. Never have in all my years."

"Hah! In all your six years, you mean. You're an old man for sure."

He scrunched his eyes shut as she dumped the first jar over his trembling, shrinking body. Melinda Jane squished and rubbed the fruit into his now pink hair. Her smile gave way to laughter as seeds squirted through her fingers, splattering Augusta's face.

Augusta dabbed at the juice on her cheek and licked her finger. Bertie's irate scowl ignited a spark of hilarity, contagious and welcomed. Seconds later, she was holding her bouncing middle, tears streaming from her eyes.

She'd forgotten how good it felt to laugh. And how delightful it was to set aside thoughts of banknotes and war and Pap's illness—if only for a short time.

∞

Pressing her head against Daisy's side, Augusta's hands moved with practiced rhythm. This was serenity—the music of the milk striking the tin bucket, the sweet smell of hay, and the occasional lowing of the cows. If she couldn't be at her *thinkin' spot*, she'd aspire to be right here. Here, the world didn't invade. Here, no one cried for attention, or needed to be bandaged, fed, or read to.

She felt fifty, not twenty—already considered an old maid by some. But she didn't need a family of her own. She had this one. The very words she told herself every day. Every time her heart ached for something more than God's chosen portion.

The wide door creaked as Zander pushed through with his back, a saddle hugged to his chest and tack over one shoulder. "Gus, I didn't know you were in here."

"I'm just finishing up. Did you have a nice ride?"

Riding was Zander's thinkin' spot. And my, could he ride—bareback like a wild Indian, his straight yellow hair blowing in the wind. Pap always said there wasn't a horse in the county that could throw him. For sure, Zander has a special way with horses—a gift, Pap calls it.

An instant later, Fin burst through the barn door fit to be tied. "I think you better talk to Will. That sister of yours says she's not putting any food on. I've been mending fences all day, and I'm hungry as a March bear."

"That *sister* of mine is your sister, too. I'll be in to deal with her shortly." She poured the last of the milk into another pail and headed for the house.

"Will? Where are you?" Finding the kitchen empty, she traipsed up the stairs. "Willamina Dabney, you open this door right now and tell me why the supper table isn't set!" Listening at the door, she worried her bottom lip. Would Mama be this harsh? Will was a good girl, just high-spirited. And sometimes she had a habit of kicking against the goads of propriety. She mostly played with just boys at school, sorely lacking the companionship of other girls.

"You can come in." Will sat on the edge of the bed; a slouch hat mashed tight over her ears. On the braided rug, clumps of hair lay in small heaps. *Her* hair.

"What have you done?" Augusta knelt, looking into her sister's damp, green eyes. Eyes so much like her own. Seldom did Will let anyone see her cry. She was always strong, so unconcerned about what anyone thought.

"I hate being a girl!" She wrenched off the hat, slinging it to the floor. Uneven hanks of honey-colored hair covered her head like a rag mop.

Augusta fought the urge to scold. This was serious—serious enough, at least, for Will to have done something so drastic. She sat on the bed and folded the young hands into her own. "What caused you to do such a thing, honey? What happened?"

"Leroy Franklin tried to kiss me!" She spat the words like blinked milk.

"Well, I declare. It's not the first time a boy tried to steal a kiss from a twelve-year-old girl. Why'd you have to go and cut your hair?"

Will harrumphed, crossing her arms over her chest. "Leroy Franklin has stringy hair and smells like year-old butter. Once he was layin' on the ground, he said he only did it 'cause I was so pretty."

"On the *ground*? Oh, Will, you didn't! Did you wallop that poor boy?" She shook her head, dreading what she must do. *Miss*

Norris. This wasn't the first time she would have to deal with the schoolmarm. Oh, no.

Her sister merely shrugged.

"Listen, Will. I was on your side when you caught those boys swiping Bertie's slingshot and made them regret it. And that time you beat the Dorton twins in a foot race and shamed them in front of all their friends—I guess you could've handled that differently—but this!"

Sore losers didn't sit well with Will, and she'd never been one with the wisdom to back down from a fight.

"I only hit him once. Then I ran. I was afraid somebody saw what he did." She hung her head, and a single, fat tear splashed onto her arm.

"Oh, Will. You *are* a pretty girl." Augusta ran her hand through the shaggy hair. Was there a deeper problem here? She lifted Will's chin, searching out the truth. "Is that why you cut your hair? So no more Leroys will try to kiss you?"

"I guess." Her lips twitched to one side. "I maybe should've waited a spell until I cooled off, though, huh?" She scrubbed her tousled scalp, and a pool of regret spilled from her eyes, snaking fresh tears over her freckles.

Augusta hugged her little sister, and for the first time in a long time remembered what it was like to be a girl on the cusp of womanhood. Before her fanciful dreams had evaporated like morning mist in a holler.

Four

Fayette County

Augusta closed the bedroom door, careful not to wake Pap from his third cat nap of the day. How she wished and prayed things could be different. Wished she could turn back the years.

"Pap's not joining us tonight," she told the boys, seating herself at the table. "I'll give him some broth in a little bit." She had invited Izzy for supper too, hoping he'd sit a spell with Pap and lift his spirits some. "Fin, will you please pray?" She reached across Pap's place and squeezed Bertie's fingers.

The usual chatter at the Dabney supper table warmed the room like a welcomed winter fire. Izzy regaled the women with his habitual compliments as the conversation turned from the garden to the weather to the hubbub of rebellion.

"More news from down at Gauley today," Fin said, chewing his last bite of shoofly pie. "Jimmy Lee lent me the paper. I thought maybe Pap would like to take a gander at it."

"Can he read some to us?" Bertie asked, looking to Gus.

"I guess, since we're pretty much done with the meal." She stood to gather plates.

"Says here that Abraham Lincoln was inaugurated on March the fourth."

Bertie tugged on Augusta's work dress, his brows crumpled, lips in a peculiar twist. "What's eggnog-or-ate-it?"

"*Inaugurated*. It means a special ceremony where Mr. Lincoln is now President Lincoln." She patted his shoulder. "Now listen. Go on, Fin."

"This is a portion of his speech printed in the paper here: 'I have no purpose, directly or indirectly, to interfere with the institution of slavery in the states where it exists.'"

"So, why's Dirch saying that Virginny's gonna have to set their slaves free if there's a war and the Union wins?" Zander tapped the handle of his fork against the oak tabletop. "Sounds to me like President Lincoln doesn't care about setting the slaves free."

Fin eyed their dear friend. "What do you make of all this, Izzy?"

Izzy pulled wrinkled fingers through his white beard. "Seems to me that what folks be thinking is that since there's no slavery in those states up north—that's where them runaways head to, up north—that things can't stay the way they is less'n the slave states band together."

Will cleared her throat, waiting until all eyes were on her. "Miss Norris taught us that the southern states need their slaves for the tobacco, cotton, and rice crops. And since the North uses those things, the South needs slaves."

"Well then, Miss Norris is teaching nonsense, and I'll have words with her. No one *needs* slaves. They may need human beings for their labor force, but not *slaves*!" Augusta didn't like the sound of her harsh words, but anger could rise so sudden-like when she considered the way some of her neighbors treated their slaves.

A couple of years back, Melinda Jane brought a runaway to their home for doctoring. Pap was strong then. He didn't care they were breaking the law. They were just helping out that poor woman, whose back looked to be but straps of meat.

Augusta doctored the woman for a week, then one day she just up and disappeared. Melinda Jane claimed she didn't know where the woman could've gone. Augusta knew better. Ever since Melinda Jane was a tot, she could no more lie to Augusta than a stag sidestep Pap's buckshot.

"Jimmy Lee says there's no difference betwixt those factory workers up north and our slaves in Virginny," Fin was saying. "Seems to me the factory workers get paid something for their labor, at least. He says they've got slaves up north, too. They're just called by some other fancy name."

"They're indentured servants, and it's not the same. Jimmy Lee and all those other slave-holders are just looking to find some excuse to justify what they're doing." Augusta frowned and shifted her gaze to Izzy. His head down, eyes closed, a low hum vibrated from his chest. Soon, every eye was fixed on him.

"I'm sorry, Izzy. We haven't been very considerate of our conversation manners tonight." Augusta's irritation melted into compassion. All this talk must bring back memories of his slave days. She loved Izzy and would never want to cause him pain. Catching Fin's attention, she raised her eyebrows.

"You're all excused," Fin said, sliding his chair out.

Her older brother was gradually stepping up to act as head of the family. With Pap's sickness, Fin's workload had doubled on the farm, and he still managed to add to the family's income with his leather tooling business. That boy would make somebody a mighty fine husband one day.

Slumped over the sink and working at a snail's pace, Will scraped slivers of soap into the dishpan as Augusta poured hot water over the plates.

"How about I trade you? I'll wash while you put the food away." Augusta added a dipper of cool water and started washing.

Will straightened as a familiar spark returned to her eyes. "Fair enough." She spun into action like a tornado, gathering the serving platters.

There never was much left after a Dabney family meal. Usually, just a few biscuits they'd eat for breakfast with some lard gravy and bacon. The egg count had been down a bit lately. She blamed that old rooster, Rupert, for that.

Melinda Jane hummed a mountain song, pulling a broom across the floorboards, its strokes keeping time with the melody. Contentment wrapped its powerful arms around Augusta. What a blessing it was to have her very best friend living with them these past few years.

"Gus, can we talk?" Fin pulled on his coat for evening chores as his eyes followed Melinda Jane around the room.

"Of course." Augusta wiped wet hands on her apron.

Melinda Jane flashed a broad smile at first Fin, then Augusta. "I'll finish up here. Go on, you two."

"Thank you, sister."

The parlor's single lantern cast a golden glow over the tasteful furniture. It wasn't a genuine parlor. Just an inviting room to entertain guests and a place for the family to spend their evenings together. Augusta often read books aloud, while Will and the boys whittled a bit or played checkers. Sometimes, Melinda Jane would lead them all in a song or two. Now and then, even Pap was up to joining them in the evenings.

Fin poked at the fire, then motioned for Augusta to sit. She ran her hands along the carved walnut arms of the soft brocade chair.

"What's on your mind, Fin?"

His brow furrowed. "I'm just busting to talk to somebody. If what they're saying is true, a war is coming. It's coming sure as shootin' and Virginny will be smack dab in the middle of it."

"Now Fin, we can't be living our lives according to what might be."

"But folks are talking. They're sayin' Fayette County is siding with the Confederacy. I know how you feel—and how Pap feels. What do I do when I'm expected to fight for the South? Like it or not, we Dabneys may be the only ones around these parts who don't see this thing so black and white. We've got to be choosing up sides, and I don't expect it'll go well with our neighbors if that side is North."

"I tell you what we do—we pray. Pap says this isn't our war. He says the only thing that concerns us is protecting our land. Right now, I'm more concerned with that land remaining ours to protect."

◦∞◦

"Hold him still now, Bertie. This has got to hurt." Augusta pressed the pliers close to the dog's skin and grasped the porcupine quill. In one quick motion, she pulled it through. Coot let out a whimper. But those trusting brown eyes fixed on Augusta's own.

She pulled five good-sized quills from his muzzle and smaller ones from his gums and between his toes, laying each on a rag, spread across the porch boards. She studied her little brother's face, wanting to smooth away the shiny, red furrows in his brow. Was this harder on Coot or Bertie?

"It's okay, boy. Gus'll fix you up good as new. You're the bravest coon dog in the county. There ain't no more skunks or porky-pines ever gonna mess with you again." Bertie swiped at an escaped tear. "Ain't that right, Gus?"

Izzy stood behind the boy, his calloused hand squeezing Bertie's shoulder.

Augusta dribbled honey over Coot's snout, carefully working it into the open pits of flesh left by the barbs. She wrapped a length of cotton around the dog's muzzle. "He'll have to wait until tonight for a drink of water, but at least this'll give the honey some time to work before he tries to lick it off. You keep him around home. I'd hate to see him get in that muddy crick and make matters worse."

"Thank you, Gus." Bertie looped his short arms around her waist and squeezed.

Love surged like a wave, its force hugging him tight against her heart. She shuffled her fingers through his straw-colored mop, pressing a kiss to the top of his head. Would that she could spare him all the bruises of life.

Turning back to Coot, he smacked his thigh. "Come on, boy." Minus his usual jog, he led his four-legged companion off to the barn.

"What you won't do for that young'un," Izzy said, shaking his head. "The Lord surely blessed you with the gift of healing, missy. He give you the gift of compassion, too."

"Aw, now Izzy. I recognize your butterin'-up voice."

Augusta smiled when crinkles sprouted from the corners of his eyes. Long years had carved in him a character of sincerity and goodness—something a soul was hard-up to find these days. Izzy was her reminder of God's grace and mercy in a world so torn by hatred that it threatened to completely unravel.

"Missy, you remember when I become acquainted with a needy family along about last fall?"

"I do. Are you wanting to help out another family?"

"I am. If you could spare some of them apples you wintered over plus anything else, I'd be beholdin'." His eyes twinkled above thick, white whiskers.

"Well, let's just see what we've got in the root cellar." She took his hand, leading him into the house. "The Lord always provides for the hungry. Did you notice? The peas are already sprouting in the garden." Augusta reached for the heavy iron ring in the floor.

"Let Me." Izzy pulled on the ring, and the cellar door dropped open with a thud.

Thirty minutes later, Augusta watched as Izzy made his way down the porch steps, a sagging potato sack in each hand. She grinned as he talked to himself, pausing with each measured step.

"Thank Ye Lord," he whispered. "You just keeps blessin' and a-blessin'. For everyone who asks, gets. And him who seeks, he finds. And him who knocks, it opens. This son of yours asks for bread, Lord, but you done blessed yo little ones with corn and beans and flour and maters and apples. Lord, You good to yo children! Bless this food, Lord, to fill bellies that soon be free."

His voice faded as he shuffled off. It was just his way, always communing with the Almighty. And one of the many things she loved about him. Drawing her work apron ties into a bow, she pushed through the kitchen door and started for the garden. She halted at the edge of the large plot, her cheerful mood scythed and trampled.

Instead of rows with tender green pea shoots, the ground along the fence-line looked churned as if someone had just worked it. Only a few feet of peas remained and there, snout to the ground, was the culprit. A wild sable sow raised its head and looked square in her direction.

"Oh, no you don't!" Augusta hitched up her skirt, and ran back into the kitchen. She lifted the Belgian shotgun from its place on the wall and snatched two percussion caps from a leather possibles bag on a peg.

She strutted out the door, but her prey wasn't where she'd left it.

By now, the sow decided an audience did not bode well and had sauntered off toward the trees. Pulling the hammers to half-cocked, Augusta settled a cap on each of the nipples. She bit her lip, her thumb pulling hard against first one hammer, then the other.

With only the sow's backside in her sights, Augusta aimed and fired. When its hind legs dropped, it turned just enough, and she emptied the other barrel into the pig's neck.

"That'll take care of you *and* our Easter dinner."

Fin glanced around the main street of the small town of Gauley Bridge, then secured the buckboard to a post in front of the blacksmith shed. He dipped a wooden bucket into a water barrel just outside the door and watered the horses.

Hauling a wheel out of the wagon's bed, he rolled it around to the back of the building. When he didn't see his friend, he leaned the wheel against the woodpile. "Hey Tiny, you about?"

"I's here, Fin. What you needing today?" Tiny wasn't so tiny. He stood a head taller than Fin's six feet. Black skin glistened over bulging muscles that might have been hidden by sleeves, if there'd been any. A sweat-drenched homespun shirt clung to his mounded chest. He dragged a rag across his face with one hand and extended the other to Fin.

"Howdy, Tiny." Fin shook his hand. "Keeping real busy, I see."

"Busy is a blessing from the Lord, friend. Yo family doin' well?"

"We're all about the same."

"How's Ol' Izzy? I owe my life to that one."

"Izzy's doing fine, too."

"And that fine granddaughter of his?" Tiny sure could push his buttons.

Fin shuffled his feet. "Melinda Jane is *very* fine."

Tiny roared, kindling a rush of heat that scaled Fin's neck and blistered his ears. He glanced around to make sure they were alone. Seemed his friend just couldn't pass up a chance to tease him—not when Tiny was the only one privy to the truth.

"So, what you got for me, Fin?"

"This wagon wheel is outa-round. I tried to fix it, but I'm thinking it's in need of a forge." Fin hefted the wheel onto an old table. Covered in burn scars and gouges, the table looked to carry a hundred tales of hard work.

An hour later, the repaired wheel sat in the back of the wagon. Fin gathered the reins to head out.

"Fin. Wait up!" Jimmy Lee Campbell trotted his black gelding up to the wagon. "I was just thinking on heading up to your place. Mind if I tag along?"

"Sure. Tie Midnight to the back and climb on up here. I'm heading straight home anyways."

∞

Just as Fin pulled the horses to a stop in the yard, Zander rounded the corner of the house. Gus followed close behind, a shotgun in her hands and a smile on her face. *What...* He shook his head and set the brake. There was definitely a story to be had here.

Jimmy Lee aimed a toothy grin at Gus and doffed his hat. "Well, now. I don't suppose you heard I was coming and felt the need to arm yourself against my charm and good looks?" He winked and bolted from the wagon seat.

"It's not your charm she needs protecting from," Fin groused. "It's your tomfool blatherin'." He eyed his brother and sister. "What's going on?"

Zander headed for the barn. "Gus shot a sow in the garden. I'm gonna go finish what I was doing."

Fin hollered after, "You best get back up to the house as soon as you can so we can gut that sow. Gus shot it. The least we can do is clean it if we want to eat it." That brother of his always had a way of disappearing when there was game to be dressed.

"Why, that's proper kind of you, Fin." His sister smiled sweetly, tipping her head.

Jimmy Lee placed his hat over his heart. "When you smile like that, Gus—why, you just set my heart a flutter." Sweat flattened his mop of brown hair as he lifted his chin in the air like he was reciting in a school pageant. "Would you consider taking a stroll down the lane with me, Miss uh . . . Gus?"

"Thank you for the compliment, Jimmy Lee—and the offer. I'm sorry to disappoint, but I have work to do. Good day to you." She whirled and walked to the house, soundly shutting the door behind her.

Fin thumped his friend on the back. "Jimmy Lee, I told you—you're barking up the wrong tree and there's not a coon around for miles. I know you see the two of you sparking, but it just ain't gonna happen."

"Aww. She'll come around. Just give her time."

"*Time?* Gus has known you all her life. I think it's the *time* thing that's got her convinced otherwise."

"Whose side you on anyway, Fin?"

"That's something I've been thinking on, Jimmy Lee. Something I've been thinking on." Fin led the horses to the barn, his mind a mishmash of notions. A heaviness weighed on him, an uncertainty that clamored for attention, for decision.

Five

CHARLESTON

James slowed his horse, wending unnoticed among meager dwellings. Coal fires burned in pitted buckets as blackened pots steamed above their glowing heat. He pulled to a stop, eyes fixed on a tiny Negro woman, her face awash in the rain of cruel years. She squatted low, stirring the contents of a pot with a broken wooden spoon. Dried Virginia mud caked the edge of her faded homespun skirt.

He dismounted and untied his black bag from the leather thongs.

The old woman looked up. "Glory be!" The Good Lord knowed we was in need of a doctorin' visit today. He surely did draw you to come by here today, Dr. Hill. You be the Lord's servant. That what you be."

"Good morning, Hanna. How is everyone?" James reached to help the woman as she painstakingly rose from her position.

"I be good today, Dr. Hill. Ain't no rain today. These creaky bones don't be shoutin' at me so much less'n it be rainin'. I's sure frettin' over Olive, though. She been off her feed nigh on three days now." The old woman clutched her skirt, using it to grab hold of the hot pan. "She in there." She motioned toward a ramshackle hut.

Hobbled-together broken bricks comprised the bottom of the dwelling's walls, and mud-chinked stick bundles made up the upper part. The withered sod roof dipped here and there, no doubt a poor hindrance to rain. James followed Hanna into the house, ducking his head to clear the threshold.

The musty air reeked of sweat and sickness. In the corner of the one small room, a slight form lay wrapped in a tattered quilt. Hanna lit a tallow candle and set it on a roughhewn stool beside the pallet.

"She been feverish off and on, too." The old woman's trembling hand brushed at something unseen on the girl's forehead.

James knelt, pulling the stethoscope from his bag. "Would you please fetch her a cup of water, Hanna?"

"Yessir. I be right back. Gots a bucket from the crick this morning that I boiled up."

When Hanna returned, James was already closing up his bag. "This is quinine, Hanna. I want you to give her a few drops in water three times a day." He pulled the cork from a small green bottle. "Like this." He dripped a couple of drops of the liquid into the cup. The woman nodded, her serious eyes bouncing from the bottle to the cup.

He lifted her leathery hand and set the cup in it. "I'll be back to check on her in a few days. If she's out of her right mind or goes into fits, please send someone for me right away."

"Is this here medicine gonna get her well?" The old woman stared at the bottle. "I been givin' her some fever root tea, but it don't appear to be doing her no good."

"You keep giving her the tea, it may still help. You're taking fine care of her, Hanna. If you can get some soup and this medicine down her, I think she'll pull through." He clasped her shoulder, taken aback by the sharpness of her bones and the yellowness of her eyes. He smiled his most reassuring smile for this angel in her disguise of rags and neglect. "You be sure to boil the drinking water real good in that black kettle you've got out there, you hear?"

"Yessir. I's goin' to do everthin' I can for this po child. She got no one but Ol' Hanna. The Good Lord and me watch over her day and night."

⁂

The bank teller laid a small stack of bills on the polished counter with a smile. "Thank you for your business, Dr. Hill." James didn't return the smile, his mind already on his next mission of the day. Retrieving the leather wallet from his inside coat pocket, he promptly stashed the money and turned to leave. Just as he exited the bank, a familiar voice caught his ear.

"James?" A dainty hand captured his forearm, and he turned.

Victoria Jamison, daughter of Charleston's wealthy steamship mogul, Phillip R. Jamison. His vessels cruised the Ohio, transporting the cotton and tobacco of the South and human cargo. Part of that cargo didn't wear the striped vest of a dandy, but the iron manacles of a man, woman, or even child, considered human chattel by some. The familiar gall scraped at his senses, but with practiced control he gathered the foul lesions in his fists and calmed his voice.

"Hello Victoria." He just couldn't do it right now. He couldn't paste on a smile and be polite. But he was still a gentleman—so he forced an ambivalent expression.

"James, dear. I've not been formally asked, of course, but I assume you are simply so caught up in your duties to the fine people of Charleston that you are dilatory in your invitation. We *are* going to the gala at the Patton's tomorrow, are we not?" She pooched her lower lip out beyond the plane of her nose—most unattractively—and batted her eyes.

Victoria was not a plain woman. She was beautiful. It was the young and wealthy part of her vitae that he found most distasteful. She was much too young. Her feigned knowledge of current affairs only proved she valued her latest choice in yard goods more than news of a country on the verge of war.

Her father—men like him had surrounded James the first twenty years of his life. As far as the wealthy were concerned, the world was their footstool, and the common populace was an insult to their sense of rectitude.

James cleared his throat and bowed, bringing her gloved hand to his lips, kissing her knuckles. "I'm sorry, Victoria. I'm rather in a rush. And yes, I'll be by to collect you for the gala tomorrow at eight." He hoped this exchange would be sufficient as to allow him to continue with his agenda for the day.

"Oh James, dear, I know just what to wear. You won't be disappointed." She batted her eyes again. "Will you spare a moment to walk me to the Kanawha House? I'm meeting Papa there for a quick bite before he is off to Parkersburg."

"Certainly." He'd been hooked. There was no escaping. He offered his arm in escort and steered her toward the large brick hotel one block farther down Back Street.

༄

"I'll have my boy load your wagon, Dr. Hill." The squat mercantile owner pulled on a ribbon, ringing a bell somewhere behind a curtained doorway as his face plumped up like a ripe, red tomato. James wondered how long it would be before the man succumbed to apoplexy.

"Thank you, sir, but I believe I will load it myself."

James hoisted a flour sack onto his shoulder just as a Negro boy, about ten years of age, walked through the faded curtain.

"But . . . but, Doctor. There's no need. This boy will do that for you." He aimed the boy toward the stack of goods on the counter, shoving him roughly. "See what happens when you're too slow, boy? Now get this—" The front door slammed, halting the tirade.

"Sir, I will tend to my purchases." With that, James lifted a smaller bag of cornmeal to his hip. Mrs. O'Donell opened wide the door she'd let *slip* from her hands, smiled at James and followed him out.

"Mrs. O'Donell, your timing is impeccable." He offered her one of his rare, sincere smiles, then settled his load into the carriage. "I'll just be a moment. Only a case of canned goods is left." He turned and strode back into the mercantile.

∾

James eyed the dark clouds off to the west as he and Mrs. O'Donell made their way to the outskirts of town. While he was without opinion on the subject of weather, today he'd certainly opt for sunshine.

The carriage rolled to a stop, continuing to rock from the rutted road that led to Kanawha County's poorhouse. James helped Mrs. O'Donell down, then proceeded to unload the food stuffs he'd purchased.

Big-eyed children, flocked to him, their calloused feet bare and their clothes resembling rags. He patted one little fellow on the head and looked around for another familiar face.

"Doctor Hill, yer a sight fer sore eyes!" The slight, gray-bearded keeper shook James's hand. The mountain man's stature reminded him of a leprechaun—or at least what he fancied one would look like if they existed.

"I'd like to make my rounds, if you don't mind, Mr. Howard. Mrs. O'Donell will see to the food distribution."

"You go right ahead, Doc. You might wanna start with Stubby over in the first cabin. He feathered into a soul, and his eye's so swelled-up he cain't see nothin'." The old man winked at Mrs. O'Donell. "Good day, ma'am." His smile was broad and several dark gaps betrayed his long, simple life.

"Gidday to ya, sir. Now, if you'd be getting outa me way, I'll be seeing to the needs of these growling stomachs." Mrs. O'Donell busied herself with the cargo as an animated audience surrounded the carriage.

James pulled a handful of licorice sticks from a bag, stuffed the candy into his shirt pocket, and headed off toward the far cabin to check on Stubby.

By the time James finished with his patients, a single piece of licorice peeked out of his pocket. He snapped his medical bag closed in the dusky room, amazed at how fast his time always seemed to pass when he was here. This was where he was truly needed.

"Doctor Hill! Doctor Hill!" A woman's panicked screams sounded outside the cabin. He snatched up his bag and charged out into the road. A young woman ran toward him, sand-colored tangles matting her cheeks and a child's limp body in her arms. "My baby! My baby!" She choked out the words, gulping air as she staggered the last few yards.

James rushed to meet her, taking in the child's face—an angelic face. Wet blond locks lay across full cheeks. Pale cheeks. And blue lips.

His heart sank.

"Here, let me take her." It was too late. Misery struck with such force his nose stung.

"I was doing the washing at the crick. Lost track of her just for a minute. I called to her . . . and . . . and she didn't answer." The mother's hiccupped sobs came faster. "Tell me she's gonna be all right. Tell me my baby's gonna be all right, Doctor." She fell to her knees, clutching her belly.

"I'm sorry." He knelt beside the woman with the girl's body in his arms. An old ache clenched his gut—a helplessness swollen by a fury that simmered nearly unchecked. He waited for the mother. He'd wait as long as necessary.

After a time, she lifted her head. Her swollen eyes took in her daughter's form.

He gentled his voice. "Do you want to hold her?"

She nodded, the utter agony in her gaze wrenching him as he tenderly transferred the girl to her mother's arms.

It's not fair! He ground his teeth to slake the urge to scream. To cry out. But he'd learned over the years that no amount of cursing or tirade could speak to his weighted spirit. Only silence could do that. And he'd learned to do silence well. He rose from the dirt, willing each movement, willing every step forward.

The woman rocked on her haunches; the body of her precious child wrapped in her embrace for the last time. A mother's fierce keen arose, and a miasma of grief permeated the air, settling on everything it touched, drawing the mourners. Ragamuffin children. Grannies toting babies. Hobbled old men in oakum-hung overalls. They all came.

A single voice raised heartfelt words to a familiar melody, garnering hums and sobs and *amens.*

> *While I draw this fleeting breath,*
> *when mine eyes shall close in death,*
> *when I soar to worlds unknown,*
> *see thee on thy judgment throne,*
> *Rock of Ages, cleft for me,*
> *let me hide myself in thee.*

Faces. A dark face, runnels of tears down dusty cheeks, stark eyes, glistening wide in terror. A pallid face, small and angelic, curly amber hair. Blood. Dirt. The crack of a whip.

A mother's wail split the room, and James bolted upright, heart pounding against his ribs, limbs tangled in sweat-soaked bedding. He clenched his eyes as the wraiths of his memory receded to the tombs where he had locked them away. Heaving, he fell back to his pillow. A pillow now wet by tears whose only escape was the blackness of his dreams.

Six

Charleston

April 13, 1861

James pushed down the irritation that threatened to rob him of what could well prove to be an interesting evening. Setting aside a frown, his gaze slid briefly to his passenger

"Honestly, James. Couldn't you have hired a brougham and driver for this one special occasion?" Victoria lifted the tiny mirror in her hand higher. Pursing her lips, she turned her head from side to side. An exasperated sigh spoke volumes for her attitude as she snapped it shut, returning it to her French-beaded reticule.

"This buggy is perfectly fit, and *I* am perfectly fit to drive it, Victoria. Driving my conveyance does not make me less of a gentleman. I promise I won't leave you on your own to disembark." If she found him so lacking, why did she insist on keeping his company?

The buggy rolled smoothly down Back Street as the Patton house came into view. James pulled the horse to a stop in front of the white, Greek revival style home known as Elm Grove. Not an opulent mansion, its four pillars and enormous stone foundation still spoke of the Pattons' integral role in Charleston society.

Although a citizen of Charleston a mere five years, the captain garnered respect among the wealthy and military alike. The inviting veranda overlooked the Kanawha River. No doubt the calming music of its rushing waters was the antithesis of the gregarious clamor within the stately house.

"James, must you be so dramatic? Do smile a bit tonight. I'd hate for the other women to assume you are melancholy." Victoria pouted her lips as James's hands grasped her petite waist, delivering her to the ground. She brushed at her burgundy cottage cloak and gave the stiff crinoline a bounce to arrange the voluminous fabric over her gray satin skirt.

Entirely against his will, James managed a polite smile. This evening could not end soon enough.

Furniture lined the perimeter of the two main rooms of the home. Ladies in full skirts of taffeta and lace stood in small groups. Their counterparts likewise huddled in conversation.

Though a few of the men wore black tails, as did James, by far the majority sported the impressive uniform of the Kanawha Riflemen with their high collars and embroidery-trimmed coats. Gold buttons lined up like soldiers marching two-by-two down the front of each gray jacket, accented by a gold stripe down each dark green trouser leg. Every officer wore white Berlin gloves, one hand holding a drink, the other on the hilt of a sword, the scabbard complementing the flashy ensemble.

"Over here, James." Austin looked no different from the other marbles in the bag.

Austin lifted Victoria's gloved hand to his lips as he bowed. "You look lovely tonight, Victoria, but I'm sure James has regaled you with that compliment more than once this evening."

Victoria giggled behind a lace fan and fluttered her eyes. "Why thank you, kind sir. I don't believe I recall such a compliment from the doctor this evening, however." James ignored the jab, his interest claimed by a group of men in an enlivening discussion.

Austin cleared his throat, and James snapped from his diversion, abruptly aware of Austin's outstretched hand. "I'm glad you made it, James. I have someone I want you to meet."

Flashing his most indulging smile, Austin addressed Victoria. "I know you've only just arrived, Victoria dear, but would you be kind enough to allow me to steal away your escort for some man talk?"

"I will allow that, Mr. Kennedy—so long as you promise me a dance, should we be here long enough to enjoy the delightful entertainment." Victoria dipped in a curtsy and flashed a daring smile in James's direction.

"A promise it is. And I thank you, Miss Jamison." Austin bowed slightly and clicked his heels.

"Don't let that fancy uniform go to your head." James elbowed his friend and followed him across the room to the very clique of men that had garnered his attention earlier.

"Captain Patton, sir, I'd like you to meet my friend, Dr. James Hill, previously of King William County." As usual, Austin's flare for the dramatic captured the attention of several bystanders. The captain's pristinely oiled brunette hair waved from a side part. Intelligent brown eyes sparked above a neatly trimmed mustache and beard.

"It's a privilege to meet you, Captain Patton. I've ridden past your law office on many occasion." James nodded, suddenly wanting to know more about the man who stood before him.

"A pleasure, Doctor." He pumped James's hand with vigor. Patton lifted the lid of a polished walnut humidor atop a round table. He retrieved a cigar and inserted the tip into the brass cutter mounted on the box. After offering one to each of his immediate guests, he continued.

"Fine professionals like yourself and other outstanding Charleston citizens have joined the ranks of the Kanawha Riflemen, Doctor. I hope you might consider such an investment of your time. Lieutenant Kennedy here tells me you have a successful medical practice in the north part of the city. Virginia needs men like yourself."

James waited as a valet lit the captain's cigar. "Yes sir. I've done well for myself."

"I understand you are considering marriage to Phillip Jamison's daughter?"

"Y... your information is incorrect, sir," he stammered, hoping his expression didn't betray the mixture of shock and near horror assaulting him. "Miss Victoria Jamison is merely an acquaintance of mine, sir."

"I see. Well..." The captain brushed an invisible hair from his gold-embellished jacket sleeve. "This country is heading into dangerous waters at more than a mere canter. Confederate forces have fired on a Federal schooner; they are preventing the provisioning of troops at Fort Sumter.

"As I speak, Confederates have positioned a floating battery to take on multiple Federal naval vessels awaiting orders to attack in Charleston Harbor. Whether the Federalists abandon their station or fight, I fear any action at this point will ignite a fire whose heat will be felt throughout this great country of ours."

"If indeed what you say is true, Captain, I will be far more valuable in a medical capacity than I could ever be in a military effort." The air in the room had become stifling. James glanced around for an open window.

"I understand you to be a virtuous, respectable physician, James. You have obviously put thought into this. You deem the healing weightier than the killing. I respect that. Not to sound trite, and I do not want to appear to be a warmonger, but I do believe it is important from time to time for men to engage in war to bring us to a remembrance of the value of one's liberty." The captain took a long drag, seeming to plan his next words as he exhaled a lazy wisp of smoke. "Without war, there is no freedom. The entirety of the freedoms we covet in these United States have, every one, been purchased with the blood of a soldier, Dr. Hill."

Possibly no more than two years James's senior, Captain Patton, at this moment, appeared to be a man beyond his years. A man of great passion, fortitude, and a fierce sense of loyalty. And the nature of that loyalty muddled James's thinking with uncertainty.

"I applaud your ardor and value your candor, Captain Patton. I will take into consideration what you have presented to me." James caught a nod from Austin out of the corner of his eye.

His friend clapped James on the back. "James will come around, sir. It's just a matter of time."

A young soldier appeared at the captain's side and saluted. He wore the sharp uniform of the Kanawha Riflemen, but with a black stripe down his leg.

"What is it, Private?" Captain Patton's voice nearly barked the request, commanding the attention of the surrounding officers.

The private handed him a telegram. "It's marked urgent, Captain, sir."

The captain discreetly read the message. His mouth and mustache melded into a taut line, and his eyes closed for a moment. He folded the paper, tucking it into his pocket, then solemnly scanned his guests. "Lieutenant Kennedy, will you please secure the attention of the room?"

"Yes, sir." Austin lifted an empty glass in the air and tapped it repeatedly with an hors d'oeuvre fork. "May I have your attention?" His voice projected over the crowd, and in seconds, the room quieted.

"Ladies, gentlemen, and officers, I have just received an important telegram." The captain cleared his voice and dropped his cigar into an ashtray. "At four thirty p.m. yesterday, under the command of Brigadier General G.T. Beauregard, Confederate troops opened fire on the Federal garrison, Fort Sumter.

"This directly resulted from the refusal of the Union army to evacuate the facility on lands belonging to the sovereign state of South Carolina. At two thirty p.m. *this* day, the Federalists occupying Fort Sumter have surrendered to the Confederacy."

The captain held up one hand to abate a wave of escalating discussion. "As we have arrived at this somber juncture, poised to affect our very lives, fortunes, and homeland, I suggest we terminate this gathering to seriously consider what this means for each of us. Godspeed." He nodded. "Ladies, gentlemen, officers . . . good night."

∞

James snugged the suture, knotted it, and then snipped it close to the puffy little hand. The boy's blue eyes met his, tears still flowing down fleshy red cheeks. "I was brave, wasn't I?" He took a deep breath and let it out, swiping at his face with his hand.

"You were the bravest patient I've ever had the pleasure to stitch up, Georgie. I know this was painful, but you did a fine job of holding still. I didn't even call for Mrs. O'Donell to sit on you—as is sometimes the case with a cut like this." James roughed up the sandy hair of the eldest Patton child. He retrieved a striped candy stick from the jar on the table.

"You're joshin' with me, ain't you, Doctor? You'll tell Papa I was brave, won't you? Riflemen are brave, and I want to be a Kanawha Rifleman, just like my papa." The boy flinched as James wrapped his hand. "That didn't hurt," he blurted.

"My husband insisted I bring Georgie to you when he cut himself. He said you were a good man, Dr. Hill, and I believe he speaks the truth. I hope we can use your services in the future?" Susan Patton was a handsome woman who stood no taller than James's shoulder. She withdrew several coins and a slingshot from her reticule. The coins she gave to James and the weapon to Georgie.

"So that's where that went!" Georgie shoved the candy stick into his mouth and reached for the slingshot.

"Thank you, Doctor, we'll be going now. Come along, Georgie." Mrs. Patton caught her son's arm as he jumped from the examination table.

James patted the boy's shoulder just as the bell on the front door sounded. "Good day to you, Mrs. Patton. And, Georgie—no more sticking your hand into tin cans."

"No sir, I won't." Georgie managed to hold his slingshot with his bandaged hand. With one eye shut and the candy stick jutting from his mouth, he shot imaginary ammunition into a waste receptacle across the room.

Mrs. O'Donell materialized next to James. She stood on her toes and whispered, "Mr. Kennedy is here for ya, sir. Says 'tis important. Looks to me to be a mite het up." She smiled at Mrs. Patton and then escorted her and little Georgie from the exam room.

"Austin, what is it, man? Is something wrong?" James ushered him into his private office.

James held his tongue. This was a different Austin—not the man whose fervor rarely ventured beyond whatever plan he'd concoct for his next female conquest.

Floorboards creaked as his friend paced the length of the small office. "Haven't you been reading the papers? Droves of those West Pointers resigned their commission and joined up with the Confederacy. Colonel Robert E. Lee was appointed Commanding General of the Confederate army."

"So, it's really begun, has it? There's no going back." James sank into the high-back chair. The weight of all his twenty-six years, twice over, settled on his body with a groan.

"That it has." Austin tapped his pipe against his palm, a frown darkening his face. "Union naval vessels are blockading ports all up and down the coast—even in the gulf. Do you know what that means for the South, James? Do you?

"I'll tell you what it means—only with a great deal of trouble will food and supplies of any kind find their way into the South to help fight this war. What are the people going to eat? Tobacco? Cotton? Where are we going to get the supplies to arm the forces to make this a fair fight?"

Austin pressed tobacco into the polished pipe. He held a match to the bowl and puffed. Leaning one hand on the window sash, his somber gaze wandered back and forth along the street outside.

"You seem to think only of the South, Austin. What about the men who will die? The women without husbands? The countless children who will grow up without a father? This war will wreak havoc on every person. And think of . . ."

Austin whirled on James—lips pressed in a sneer. "Always the idealist, aren't you, James? There is a bigger picture here you don't see." In three strides, he was across the room. His pipe in one, he leaned both hands on the desktop, drilling James with blazing eyes. "Every state is sovereign. Each one joined the Union of its own accord and, by thunder, each one has a right to pull out of its own accord. We won't be bullied by a Union we helped build!

"What do you think has made these United States so wealthy? So successful? I'll tell you what"—Austin's fist pounded the desk—"the South, that's what. If we didn't provide the labor and land to grow the cotton, what do you think the North would do with those big factories of theirs? Where would their people work? There'd be thousands of immigrants cluttering the streets.

"The North's textile industry will come to a screeching halt. Mark my words. Even those high-minded Washington types will suffer at the hands of Great Britain's prices to keep them in their silks and fancy living. Without the South, the North will wither up and die. They're cutting off their nose to spite their face. They just don't know it yet."

Austin pulled himself up to his full height. "The Kanawha Riflemen have cast their lot with the Confederacy. So, I ask you—are you in or out?" He slid a hand into the gap of his waistcoat, cupping the bowl of his pipe with the other. Conviction etched the fight on his hardened features. "You can't sit on the fence and not get knocked to the ground on this one, James."

"Austin, please sit down. There's more to this—"

"In or out, James?"

"I . . ."

Austin's jaw twitched. "That's it, then. I suppose I expected as much. I just didn't want to accept it." As he pulled his hat from the hall tree, the bell sounded on the front door.

James stood and crossed the room. "I'm sorry, Austin." He extended his hand, a gesture of peace.

Austin's eyes shuttered. He ignored James's effort entirely, and with a nearly imperceptible shake of his head, quit the room. "Goodbye James."

James stared at his outstretched hand. A piece of his determination and a chunk of his heart followed his friend out the door.

Blast this rebellion! Here was only a friendship torn apart. How many families and lives would be ripped asunder before this whole affair was over?

Seven

Fayette County

Augusta let the last few beans fall through her fingers into the furrow. Will followed her with the hoe, sweeping waves of yellow-brown soil over the seed.

"You did a proper job with my hair, Gus. Mamie Dorton says it looks like one of those new hairstyles in *Harper's Weekly*. Her mama says"—Will propped hands on hips—"'That's no way for a young lady to wear her hair.'" She mimicked Maude Dorton so well. "Hah. I say, that's good, cuz I ain't no lady!" She guffawed and swatted her knee. When she finally gasped for a breath, her eyes collided with the glower of Augusta's *mean* face. Her outburst froze, mouth still agape.

"Will, what *am* I going to do with you? Someday you're going to realize that God made you a beautiful young woman and somewhere out there He's already got a handsome young man just waiting to marry you—someday."

"I was just joshin' with you, Gus. You gotta laugh more and work less. You know I don't like any of them boys at school."

"*Those* boys. Besides, maybe you won't fall in love with a Fayette County boy you've known all your life. Maybe when you go off to finishing school, you'll—"

"I ain't going off to no finishing school. Pap won't make me if I don't want to, and I don't want to. Besides, I got a couple more years before I'm old enough, so I got that long to build my case against going."

Will huffed dramatically, whirled, and trudged to the pump for another bucket of water. Most folks in these parts still just got their water from a well with a bucket, but Pap had the pump installed just before Mama took sick. It sure made life easier.

Augusta plopped down on the dirt. What would Mama say to Will? She'd not bother Pap about her sister. He had enough worries—with the mortgage loan and all. Fin and Zander worked hard to keep the farm running, but she knew her pap felt bad not helping. Some men would be venting their gall, being laid up like he was, so sick and all. But not Pap. He was kind and even-tempered as the day was long.

Looking over the plantings of the day, she envisioned the string beans climbing the fence that surrounded the half-acre garden patch, their white-petaled blossoms against the green heart-shaped leaves. She always marveled at the way the squash stretched its gangly vines away from the banked hills, sometimes growing a foot a day. Not long now, and she'd have most all the early spring garden planted.

The tinkle of the bell beside Pap's bed invaded her reflections. Dropping the seed packet, Augusta hitched up her wincey skirt and ran to the house. She burst into Pap's room, her chest pounding. He didn't ring that bell very often, and every time he did, she'd conjure up images of Pap on the floor, or Pap covered in blood . . .

"Pap?"

"Don't you get riled up, now Gus, I'm fine. I just decided that I'm sick and tired of being sick and tired. I'm going to take a walk. This is the day the Lord has made, and it looks to be a dandy! Where are my britches and a walking cane?" Pap sat upright, his bare feet planted on the braided rug, the likeness of a little boy in a nightshirt. He hadn't donned britches for over a week, and he'd not seen the outside of the house in nearly a month.

Augusta massaged her temples, relaxing her face and her breathing. "I'll get them for you, Pap. Don't you overdo it, though. I don't want to have to call one of the boys to pick you up off the barnyard ground."

"Away with you, daughter." A grin betrayed his bossy tone as Pap swatted in her direction.

○○

Folks filed into the one-room, white clapboard building. During the week, it served as the Gauley Bridge School, but on Sundays, it was the Gauley Bridge Methodist Church. Augusta and her family sidestepped into the Dabney family *pew*. A more affluent church would've had a pew, but in this case, it was a splintery bench. Most of the womenfolk brought a piece of fabric or pillow to sit on so as not to snag their Sunday go-to-meetin' clothes. For many of the residents of Fayette County, their only change of clothes *was* their Sunday attire.

Preacher Coulter approached the narrow pine pulpit. On its front hung a fancy carved walnut cross, looking out of place in the otherwise plain room. The stout preacher clasped a black Bible in one hand and a hymnal in the other.

Lifting both books to the heavens, his voice fairly vibrated the dust off the rafters. "May the Lord God Almighty, Ruler of all things created, cause us to hear Him this day. To seek Him on this day. To beseech *His* favor this day and not the favor of man." He thumped the hymnal onto the pulpit and set the Bible on top of it.

Retrieving his spectacles from his pocket, he positioned them halfway down his hooked nose. A short, gray beard brushed his collar as he swiveled his head, making eye contact with his flock.

His voice boomed in the tiny building, "Blessed is the man that endureth temptation; for when he is tried, he shall receive the Crown of Life, which the Lord hath promised to them that love Him. St. James, the first chapter, twelfth verse." Children sat straighter and wives grasped the hands of their husbands.

Preacher Coulter was not usually one prone to so much emotion on a given Sunday. Him not introducing a hymn was enough of a shock to the congregation—and now this.

"You may wonder why we have not begun our time together this Lord's Day in song. I feel I must be faithful to yield to Almighty God and speak to you with a heavy heart of the dark trials that lay ahead. It has come to my hearing just this morning that the Federal schooner, the *Rhoda H. Shannon,* has been fired upon by the Confederacy."

Gasps, then immediate shouts and approving yips from the younger men pierced the stillness. The preacher silenced the rowdiness with a raised palm. "Gentlemen . . . men, this is still the house of God."

In a few moments, silence ensued, although tense glances continued to bounce among the audience. "I have chosen this Scripture today because I feel it is fitting that we should be reminded that—even though a man may serve God, love Him, and do right by his neighbors and family—there will come a time of testing. That time of dire testing is upon us this day.

"There is great anxiety amid such circumstances, which are bound to provoke the bitterest of passions. This nation stands in need of right counsel, thoughtful reflection, and heartfelt dependence upon God for guidance and strength as we, with earnest purpose, do our duty."

He leaned forward, a scowl carved into his darkening face. "We stand eye to eye with an evil. A calamity. A war. How we conduct ourselves hereafter must be the very trace upon which the Almighty rides."

Brother Coulter stepped to one side of the pulpit and clasped his hands together. The room was photo-still as his lips curled into a smile. "Now, it is obvious the South has had no hand in precipitating this calamity before us. We can stand without bloodguilt, and know that at least the South is in the right and garnishes the favor of Almighty God." Murmurs of "amen" sprinkled over the audience.

"The South is on the defensive. We ask only to be left alone. The Union that once was, has dissolved. As Cain slew his brother, Abel. Abel, the innocent party. Abel, who did not provoke his brother, but only strove to please God."

Beads of sweat dotted his forehead as he moved back behind the pulpit. He stretched his neck like a bird, and his lips puckered, then pressed together. "The Federalists Cain is the party with the bloodguilt. We ask for peace. 'Leave us alone!' we shout." His hand pounded the pine surface. "But they will not. That they should choose war over peaceful separation is an abomination to Almighty God."

The bench groaned as Augusta shifted her weight, clutching her Bible to her chest. Anxiety and trepidation pressed against her stomach, pulling her heart lower. She glanced in Fin's direction and their eyes met. A flame simmered in his.

"When a man's way pleases the Lord, He maketh even his enemies to be at peace with him. Proverbs, the sixteenth chapter, verse seven. Let us then seek earnestly the favor of Almighty God, without Whose blessing we cannot triumph.

"Yes, blessed is the man who endureth temptation. Some of you will fail in this, brothers. An awful time of temptation is upon us. Will some of you sacrifice your Christian character to the passions of the moment? Will others of you emerge purified by the fiery trials, thereby securing for yourself a brighter crown? Ask yourself this day, oh Christian, which will you be? Will you cast your crown away, or will you hold fast your resolution as never before? Will you be stronger for the battle?"

Clearing his throat, he wiped his brow with a white handkerchief. Preacher Coulter's piercing gaze scrutinized the reaction of his flock. Long seconds ticked by as silence hung within the four walls like the morning fog on Kanawha Gap.

"Please turn to hymn number forty-three as we dismiss," he said at last. Pages rustled and voices lifted:

> *"Nearer, my God, to Thee, nearer to Thee!*
> *Though like the wanderer, the sun goes down.*
> *Darkness be over me, my rest a stone.*
> *Yet in my dreams, I'd be nearer my God to Thee."*

Moments later, the churchyard buzzed with uncharacteristic activity. Women huddled together, babies on hips. Mothers and sweethearts dabbing at tears with frayed hankies while the older men shook their heads in hushed exchanges. Augusta hurried through *goodbyes,* then rushed past a spirited group of young men. They pounded one another on the back, sharing chaws and puffing out their chests.

Fin lifted her onto the buckboard seat, then helped Melinda Jane up next to her. The Dabneys—except for Zander, who had stayed home with Pap—loaded into the wagon, and Fin guided the horses away from the church. Long after the voices faded behind them, only the grind of wooden wheels on the road stirred the somber silence as the team plodded ahead.

"I told you this was coming, Gus. It's just like I said." Fin chucked the reins, and the horses started into a trot. Deep furrows marked his brow as he trained his eyes on the road.

"There's gonna be a war, ain't there?" Even Will's voice was subdued as she tossed straw into Bertie's neatly combed hair.

"I reckon it's true, Will." A jumble of fearful imaginings seemed to pull Augusta right down to the ground, and she slumped with the weight of it. She looked up when Melinda Jane grasped her hand. A trail glistened where a single tear had runneled down her cheek.

"Izzy says the South is fighting to keep their slaves. Others are saying the South is fightin' because no one can make them do what they don't want to," Melinda Jane said, her troubled gaze intent on the road ahead.

Will tossed a pebble over the side of the wagon and watched it bounce. "Listening to the preacher, sounds to me like the South is the one with God's blessings. Preacher Coulter called the Federals the enemy."

"You be careful now, Willamina Dabney. Don't you take every man's word as Gospel—not even Preacher Coulter's. I'll bet there's a northern preacher saying those same words to his congregation this morning. I don't believe God's on anyone's side. War's just man's foolish pride puffed up in a giant twister, fixin' to take out whatever lies in its path." Augusta touched Fin's arm. "We'll pray, and we'll trust the Lord. I hope Pap is up to talking just as soon as we get home."

"Even King David went to war, Gus. Why, the Old Testament is plum full of war. God told who to wipe out who, if you recall." Fin glanced over at Melinda Jane. Eyes closed; she hummed an ancient Sottish tune of the mountain folk.

"Do you hear something?" Will asked of no one in particular. Melinda Jane's eyes opened with a start.

"Look. Over there!" Bertie pointed to a roan mare grazing under a red oak tree.

"Whoa." Fin pulled the team to a stop. "That's Tiny's horse. Something ain't right." He reached beneath the wagon's seat, producing a cowhide-wrapped parcel. "You stay here."

Eight

Fayette County

Fin cocked the Colt Navy revolver as he approached the horse. Reins hung loose on the ground. A rope trailed from the saddle horn into the weeds. The mare nickered as Fin drew closer, blood glistening on the long welts that striped her rump and withers.

His gaze searched the scraggly patches of chickweed before advancing with guarded steps, following the rope. There, at the end of its length, lay Tiny Gwinn—hands bound, unconscious, and crumpled in a fetal position. Dust coated his black skin, giving it a ghostly appearance. Shreds of pink flesh peeked through the gravel that clung to his bare torso. Dirt and blood were caked between his toes and across the tops of his feet.

Fin eased the revolver hammer back into place and dropped to his knees, pressing down a wash of rage. "Gus, over here, it's Tiny. He's hurt real bad!" He pulled out his knife, cut Tiny's hands free, and gently rolled him onto his back.

"Dear Lord, no." Augusta closed her eyes as tears squeezed past. How could anyone be so cruel?

Melinda Jane dropped to the ground next to her. "Oh Tiny, what have they done to you?" She covered her trembling lips with her fingers and choked back a sob.

Augusta laid her hand on Tiny's chest then lifted the swollen lid of one eye. "He's still alive. We need to get him into the wagon and back to the house."

"Tiny's a big man, Gus. How are we gonna do that?" Fin stood and coiled the rope, untying it from the saddle horn.

"His horse dragged him here. Maybe we can use the mare to tow him into the wagon."

"There's a couple of planks in the buckboard that'll work just fine for a travois and ramp. I'll move the wagon close as I can get, then mayhap we can run that rope, rear to front, over the seat. The horse can do the work to hoist Tiny into the wagon bed."

Fin went to work, explaining his plan to the others as he tossed the line over the wagon seat.

With the plank tied to the rope, Fin and Augusta cautiously rolled Tiny onto the travois. The mare, still skittish from her wounds, seemed to sense Tiny needed her help. She gave way to Fin's lead, and the rope groaned as it hauled the injured man up the makeshift ramp and into the wagon. Melinda Jane folded an old blanket and placed it under his head. A low moan rumbled from deep within his chest.

"He's waking up, Gus. It's gonna to be mighty uncomfortable for him jarring all the way home. Anything we can do for him?" Melinda Jane dabbed at Tiny's brow with her hanky.

Augusta climbed onto the seat. "There's not much more we can do until we get him to the house. It'd be a blessing if he stays unconscious until then. Just try to keep him still."

Tears stung as Augusta buried her face in her hands. *Father, what evil sort of men do this kind of thing?* Tiny never hurt anybody. First the warmongers at church, now this. What is spreading through this valley? *God, we need you. Give us wisdom. And should the days grow darker than this, please, oh please protect my family.*

The crunch of wagon wheels filled her ears, seeming to roar louder with each mile. And for all the wagon's racket, it couldn't wake her from this nightmare that she feared had only begun.

☙

Augusta dropped another rug onto the porch at Melinda Jane's feet, retracing her steps in her head. *Look every place three times before you get flustered.* She could hear her mama's voice saying it even now.

Stretching over the porch railing, Melinda Jane gave the rag rug another vigorous shake. "You know, we've passed a completely peaceful week since finding Tiny, but I still prickle at every little sound. Thinking it might mean unwanted visitors, I reckon."

"You're not alone. I keep wondering when something else awful is going to happen."

Melinda Jane smiled, draping the rug over the railing as she watched a tall figure dismount a bay gelding. "Duke is a fine-looking horse, wouldn't you say?"

"Uh-huh . . . but I'd guess it's Duke's handsome rider that's really catching that eye of yours." She bumped her friend with an elbow.

Melinda Jane turned, claiming another rug for shaking. "And why not? I've known him all my life. You'd think that'd give me enough time to catch *his* eye." Her bottom lip rolled into a pout.

Her friend had been inseparable from the Dabneys pretty much since forever. She and Fin had swum the crick together, fished the lake downstream of Gauley Bridge, and played tag until candle-lighting. Augusta smiled, remembering how Fin was kind enough to let himself get caught by a certain skinny girl, two heads shorter. That boy had best come to his senses. And soon.

Augusta stepped through the door, leaving it open behind her. "Melinda Jane, do you know where those clean bandages went to?" She searched the lowest shelf of the dry sink, then stood, hands on her hips. "I was just sure I folded them and put the stack on that shelf. Right there."

"You did. I saw you. There's more in the trunk. I'll get them for you." Fin reached the door an instant before Melinda Jane and beamed down at her. She punched his chest to make him move. "You make a mighty poor door, Fin!"

So much like a sister and brother, those two. Maybe that was the problem.

Augusta turned as Tiny's giant frame filled the kitchen doorway. "This body don't need no more bandages. You got me wrapped so tight now I can hardly draw breath."

"Tiny Gwinn! You get back in that bed this instant. I'll say when you are no longer in need of medical attention. Your wounds are healing well enough, but they still need clean bandages. Those ribs ought to be braced another few weeks yet."

She tried to redirect him, steering him back to the porch and his bed. They'd had a hard enough time getting him into the house, let alone up the stairs to a bedroom. It was better this way, anyway. Here, she could keep a close eye on him. Cleaning the dirt and rocks out of his wounds had been mighty painful, and the laudanum she'd given him had helped him sleep for days. Now he was faunching at the bit to get out of the house and back to his blacksmith shop.

"Aw, Miss Gus, you been real kind—doctorin' me and all—but I got to be gettin' back to my shop. Got me a bad feelin' about the men who done this to me. They be just evil enough to burn my place down. I don't know who they are, but they be doing the devil's work, that's for sure."

Fin tossed his hat on a wall peg. "Those men were cowards, Tiny. They didn't even have the guts to let you see who they were. What kind of vermin clobbers a man unconscious from behind that way? They weren't even man enough to fight fair."

"What's fair about evil?" Augusta's temper sparked. "I can feel it. It's like the folks around here are anticipating a fine parade, not the slaughtering of innocents, as is bound to happen if this conflict doesn't burn itself out real fast like."

"You're dreaming, sister. There's news in town, and there isn't a lick of it that good. Is Pap awake?" Fin snatched two biscuits from beneath a towel on the sideboard and tossed one to Tiny.

"He's sleeping now, but he says he's gonna join us for supper tonight. Says he wants to talk to all of us." Augusta tucked the towel back around the biscuits. "Will you ask Bertie to go get Izzy? Ask him to sup with us tonight, too?"

"I'll go tell him for you, Gus." Melinda Jane reached for the screen door, but Fin was faster. He smiled and pushed the door open. "Why thank you, Phineas." With a coy smile, she winked and sashayed past.

Tiny seemed to choke on a bite of biscuit. "Phineas?" His laughter boomed. "If that don't beat all." He smacked his thigh with his hand and winced.

Fin scowled at his friend. "I hope that hurt!" He stomped through the kitchen into the parlor, staring straight ahead, ears red as strawberries.

༄

"Maude Dorton informed me there was a certain group of boys dangling from the rafters of the Gauley Bridge this morning. Now, Maude is a might nearsighted, mind you, but she says one of those boys looked very much like someone sitting here at this table."

Augusta had said plenty. All eyes diverted to Bertie—even Ol' Izzy's—but a twinkle in their warm depths betrayed a poor excuse for a frown.

Pap set his spoon down with a *CLINK*, knocking the knife from his plate. "Son, we've had this discussion before. What was the occasion this time?" The weakness of his voice tempered his scolding words.

Bertie hung his head. Silence. Silence at the Dabney table was never a good thing, and this time, he was the center of everyone's attention. "Well . . . sir. I guess there was some cattle takin' the bridge."

Fin's head jerked up. "Buster Crawford's cattle?"

"Maybe." Bertie's gaze flitted from his plate to Pap and back to his plate.

"Buster Crawford drove more than a hundred head across that bridge this morning. Bertie, do you know where one slip of your foot could've gotten you? Dead, that's where!" Fin struck the table with his fork handle.

Bertie seemed to shrink in his seat. "I'm sorry, Pap, really. I won't do it no more. Those Dorton twins dared me to. I didn't want them thinking I was *yella*. They started calling me a baby and claimed I couldn't brave those rafters while the herd passed through." A tear leaked from Bertie's eye and he swiped it away, but not before Augusta spotted it. She wanted to take him on her lap and wrap her arms protectively around him, but this was serious.

Pap cleared his throat, masking a cough in his napkin. "Well, Bertie, I can forgive you, but you got to know that it seems to me you haven't learned how to say no to temptation yet, son. Those Dorton twins were tempting you to do what you knew to be wrong, and you let your pride get in the way of doing the right thing." Pap took a swallow of water and a spoonful of soup that Augusta had made just for him. "You'll be taking the early milking until the end of summer, Bertie. You'd best get used to getting up real early."

"Yes, sir." Bertie nodded to Pap, his face fallen as he leaned on his elbow—pulling it from the tabletop an instant later, sheepishly tucking his hands in his lap.

"Well, now. Does anyone have anything entertaining to say tonight?" Pap's eyebrows lifted with his weary smile as he looked around the table. "It doesn't do anybody's digestion any good to get all melancholy at the table."

"I picked up a *Valley Star* in town this morning, Pap. I could read you some, but the news isn't good," Pap nodded his consent, and Fin leaned to one side, tugging a folded newspaper from his back pocket.

"Says here: 'After a formal surrender ceremony regarding the Federal Garrison, Ft. Sumter, at Charleston, South Carolina, Union Major Robert Anderson and his men proceeded northward by sea. During the evacuation, Union casualties were sustained when a stockpile of ammunition was inadvertently detonated. They included two dead and four injured.'"

"You want me to read some more?" Fin looked over the top of the paper.

"Go ahead. We might as well have it." Although sickness had diminished Pap's once-robust frame, he seemed to shrink even more just now.

"Yes, sir. 'President Lincoln has issued a public proclamation calling for seventy-five thousand militia to still the insurrection in South Carolina. As discontent rises within the Border States, the legislature of the state of New York has committed three million dollars in aid for the Northern cause. While at a secessionist meeting in Baltimore, Missouri, and Tennessee decided against meeting Lincoln's requests for volunteers. And at Richmond, the State Convention has passed a secession ordinance, eighty-eight to fifty-five. The northwestern counties of Virginia represented all nay votes. A public referendum is to be held for Virginia citizens on May the twenty-third.'"

"What's a ref-er-an-dum?" Bertie looked at Augusta.

"It means there's going to be a vote," Will chimed in. "Isn't that right, Gus?"

"What are they going to vote for?" asked Bertie.

Zander halted his glass, just inches from his mouth. "Whether to join the Confederacy."

"Huh?" Bertie screwed up his face, tipping his head.

"It means, most likely, Virginia is going to leave the Union. There will be another vote by the people, but it's pretty much decided already." Augusta glanced at Izzy. With his gaze fixed on his plate, she didn't miss the almost imperceptible shake of his head.

Pap's throat growled, starting up his voice. "I'd say it's pretty obvious, based on the vote, that a good many folks in western Virginia aren't going to take kindly to being forced into secession."

"That's not all," Fin said, giving the paper a shake. "Says here that Lincoln is calling for men to volunteer to fight for the Union for a period of ninety days." Fin looked up from the paper. "That doesn't sound so bad."

Bushy white eyebrows shadowed Izzy's hard gaze. "War means killin', Fin. You ready to go killin' another man?"

"Izzy's right, son. Ninety days of war is long enough to turn a man into a killer and haunt him for the rest of his days. You don't want that." Pap's solemn eyes bore into Fin's. "There may come a time to fight, but for the Dabneys, it's not today."

Pap rose slowly from his chair, and Izzy stood to help him to his room.

With the last dish dried and put up, Augusta headed to the parlor in search of Fin. Finding the room empty, the next best place to check was the front porch. Sure enough, there in the old rush-seated chair, Fin sat, deftly whittling on a stick of pine. His deliberate strokes kept time to the rhythm of the creaking rockers.

"You're not really thinking of volunteering, are you, Fin?" She leaned her backside against the railing.

"Don't rightly know, little sister."

"I'm praying you don't. We need you here, Fin. I've got this feeling that Pap won't see Christmas this year."

Fin stood. "Don't be talking like that. He'll come around. I know he will. He just needs a month or two of sunshine. You'll see. He'll be feelin' his oats by summer's end."

"You didn't answer my question, brother."

"No, I didn't." Fin sheathed his knife, slapped his hat against his hand, and headed into the house.

Nine

FAYETTE COUNTY

Augusta's heart swelled as she gazed down at the bed through misted eyes. Jonathan Dabney fought his illness with courage, but some days more than others evidenced a battle lost to retreat. Today was such a day. She wiped a dribble of soup from the corner of his mouth. "Let's get you lying down a bit more now, Pap."

She clung to him with a fierce love, but something else invisible held him here. Her faith told her God would take her father home in His timing and nothing was going to change that. These days, most of the time, Pap lay swaddled in sweet sleep. For that, she was thankful. At least when he was sleeping, he wasn't coughing or struggling for breath.

"Izzy'll come sit with you, Pap. And Zander will be about whilst I'm gone to the bank. Will and Fin are going with me into Charleston this time, and Melinda Jane will keep an eye on Bertie."

She washed Pap's face, arms, and hands. Dropping the rag into the basin, she stood to take the soup cup to the kitchen.

His weak voice ground like boots on gravel. "Gussy? Sit with me a bit longer, will you, honey?" A quivery smile stretched his lips, and he reached for her hand. "You take such good care of your pap. And you are a mighty fine mama to your brothers and sister, daughter." He pulled in a ragged breath to continue. "I'm real sorry life has dropped all this on you. You should've found yourself a husband and birthed children of your own by now. Promise me—" a cough erupted, jagged and sharp. Spittles of blood dotted his beard and the linen napkin spread across his chest.

"Pap, you just rest now and don't you be fretting over what the Lord's got control of." She'd worked so hard to take those same words into her own heart. She kissed his forehead and smiled. "Besides," she whispered as his eyes closed in sleep, "I've got the best man God ever put on this earth, right here in front of me." Tears squeezed from her eyes, and she wiped them away. *Not now.* She'd be strong for the days ahead. Strong for those who needed her.

∞

Melinda Jane stood in the yard, eyes closed as she breathed in the clean air. Last night's downpour had ignited a sweet scent throughout the green hills. A sharp bark cut through the moment, and her eyes popped open to see Coot running full-out from the far side of the barn. He slowed to a prance when he neared the house, a stick gripped in his jaws.

Bertie rounded the corner at a jog and slipped on a patch of gumbo. "Hey you, bring back my arrow!" One hand clutched a homemade willow bow, the other a mangled straw hat. Coot rolled in the mud as he waited for his master to catch up. "Now what'd you go and do that for?" Bertie tugged the stick from the dog's teeth. As if in answer to his question, Coot sat and offered a paw to his master in a truce.

Melinda Jane set a fresh bucket of water on the ground. "Well now, what was that all about? You weren't shooting at something you oughtn't to be. Were you now, Bertram Dabney?" She settled on her haunches to give Coot an ear-rubbing.

"Aw . . . never mind that." Bertie brushed his wind-blown hair out of his eyes, but the cowlick on his forehead forced much of it right back. No answer would be forthcoming—that was obvious. His shoulders straightened. He twitched his lips to one side and back. "Can you and me go down to the crick and catch crawdads whilst the others go to town?"

She never could resist his six-year-old charm. His eyes smiled up at her, and he tugged on her hand. "You can just watch me catch 'em."

"Bertie, Bertie . . . what *am* I gonna do with you?" She tucked a string of hair the color of dried grass behind his ear. "We'll *both* go huntin' up crawdads. But only after you help me hunt up some ramps. I want them for my soup kettle tonight."

The clap of the screen door snatched her attention, drawing her eyes to Fin like a bee to honey. She watched him take the steps two at a time, then head for the barn. He glanced her way and stopped in his tracks.

Sauntering in their direction, Fin cocked his head to one side, eyebrows scrunched in suspicion. "You two look like you're plotting something."

"We're gonna catch us a mess of crawdads whilst you all are in town," Bertie said. He attempted a wink at Melinda Jane. "Ain't that right?"

"*Isn't* that right!" Melinda Jane and Fin corrected the boy in unison. She stared at him and he stared back. A tick later, they both burst out laughing, matching the mirth in her heart. She covered her mouth, failing in an attempt to act more lady-like.

Bertie just shrugged. "Come on, Coot. We'll go find us some buckets." He patted his leg and bounded off to the barn, the dog close on his heels.

"You reckon on being back Wednesday morning?" Melinda Jane asked, fingering a strand of curly hair. She flashed her sweetest, demure smile.

"Yeah, I figure we'll be back by n . . . noon." Fin's gaze fell to the ground. The toe of his boot drew a line in the mud. An awkward silence hung in the air until at last he turned toward the barn. When he reached the entrance, he glanced back. Their eyes locked, and when her smile widened, he stumbled into the barn.

She pressed back a giggle with her fingertips. *That boy.*

༄

The morning sun still hid behind the hills when Augusta stepped off the porch, a packed basket over each arm. Fin stood by the wagon, waiting to help her up to the seat.

He reached for the baskets. "Where's Will?"

"She said she'd be along in a minute."

The door clattered, and she turned to see her sister bounding down the stairs. "Don't leave without me!"

Augusta set her jaw. "Oh, no you don't, young lady. You get back in that house right this minute and change into a dress—and make sure you pack nothing but lady's habiliments. Or do you wish to stay here?"

"But, Gus . . ."

"No *buts*. If you're wanting to go, you will go as a young lady."

In a short time, the buckboard rumbled down the Dabneys' lane. After a while, Augusta pulled mending from a basket to keep her fingers busy. "All right with you, Fin, if we stop and check on Tiny before heading up to Charleston?"

"Sure thing." His elbows rested on his knees, holding the reins loosely. "You packed us lunch and supper, didn't you, Gus?"

"Melinda Jane packed some vittles for us while I was tending to Pap." She caught the way the corners of his mouth curled upward. He had it bad, poor boy. She poked him in the ribs. "I know you're sweet on that girl, Fin. Why don't you just admit it? Every girl in Fayette County who's tried to catch your eye goes home disappointed. I reckon they haven't come to the notion they've got competition."

"Aw, the gals 'round here are all caught up in themselves. They flirt with just about any feller that returns a look. Seems to me they're all just playing a game with us men. When I'm good and ready, I'll"—he scowled—"When I' good and ready, you'll be the second person to know, Gus." He sat straighter and gave the reins a jerk.

"The *second* person to know? And who will be the *first* person, brother?" She couldn't hide the grin that threatened a giggle. How she loved to tease him. Despite his tough talk, this brother of hers was gentle as an old mare.

The wagon rattled over the planks of the Gauley Bridge. Rafters high above their heads supported the wooden roof that blocked the morning light. When they exited the bridge, two riders, dressed in the gray uniform of the Confederacy, waited.

"Good day, sir, ma'am." The stockier of the two tipped his army-issued kepi. "Mighty fine day, isn't it?"

"Yes, it is." Augusta offered a polite nod. "What brings the Army to Gauley Bridge?"

The other soldier, one hand on the hilt of a sword, answered, "We're riding a circuit, ma'am, to promote the raising of levy monies for a militia from each county."

"And have you met with success on your mission?" she asked, but his attention had fled elsewhere, and she followed his gaze. His lips curved as he leered at Will, who was gaping from the back of the wagon.

"Why yes, ma'am, we have." He flashed a broad smile at Will. She promptly tugged on her bonnet ribbons and turned her back to him.

Fin frowned. He clicked his tongue and jostled on the reins. "Good day, then."

The wagon lumbered into town as the fading *clip-clop* of the soldiers' mounts echoed across the bridge.

In front of his shop, Tiny loaded a crate of barrel bands into the rear of an old wagon. He waved a greeting as the Dabneys slowed to a stop.

"What brings ya by this early in the mornin'?" Tiny wiped his hands on his britches and approached the Dabney's wagon.

"You know Gus, she's always checking on her patients." Fin's easy grin played from Tiny to Augusta.

"Aw now, Miss Gus, don't you worry yer head none about Ol' Tiny. I be just as ornery and strong as ever—thanks to yo good doctorin'." Tiny ran his sizable hand beneath the trace and along the withers of the nearest horse.

"How are those ribs, Tiny? You still keeping them wrapped tight?" If only she'd talked him into spending a couple more weeks at the farm so she could see to his injuries.

"Yes, ma'am. I's doin' just as the doctor ordered." He chuckled. "Takes a whole heap-o-somethin' to keep me down."

"You know, the more you take it easy, the faster those ribs will heal."

"Yes, ma'am." Tiny's toothy smile warmed her heart. This gentle giant had been a constant source of encouragement to Fin these many years. Even through the hard times of Mama's illness, then death, Tiny had been a faithful friend.

Fin grunted. "We just saw two Confederate soldiers over at the bridge. You know of any trouble they're causing around these parts?"

"Not that I hear of."

"Just the same, if you could check on everything at the home place tonight, I'd be appreciative. Izzy's keeping company with Pap, and Zander is at the farm." Fin's eyebrows sank, and his voice hushed. "But there really isn't a man around that's able-bodied enough to stand up to soldiers looking to cause trouble."

"Happy to, Fin. I'll ride on over there just after supper."

"Much obliged, Tiny. We best be heading on up the road. With this mud, we'll be pulling into Charleston well after dark unless we camp on the road." Fin signaled the horses, and the wagon rolled forward.

Augusta hadn't considered those two soldiers might be a problem. But then again, she should've learned something from Tiny's beating. Evil palaver riles all men. Some are apt to do what they normally wouldn't. And such men are dangerous.

"Fin, do you really think those soldiers will stir up trouble?" Will asked from the wagon bed.

"Soldiers usually do mean trouble for somebody."

Ten

∞

Charleston

James fit a cork to each of the tiny bottles, restocking his medicinal supplies. He didn't mind the menial task. It gave him time alone with his thoughts. Uninterrupted. And he quite preferred it to making polite conversation with a patient whose greatest need was a healthy dose of castor oil.

"Mrs. Orr is here for ya, James." Mrs. O'Donell stood in the office doorway. "She's a bit out of sorts."

James shoved his ponderings back for the moment. "Am I available?"

She nodded. "I'll put her in the examining room straight off."

"Thank you, Mrs. O'Donell." James treated a Henry Orr for syphilis a few months back. He remembered him well. A large man dressed in an outdated suit two sizes too small. He smelled of scotch and sweat and possessed a most indignant disposition. Surely that ogre couldn't be married? Perhaps his mother?

A plump, gray-haired woman fidgeted in the center of the room, her bonnet toppled a bit to one side. "How can I help you, Mrs. Orr?" James motioned to a chair as he lifted a new medical chart from the counter. "Please, have a seat."

"Oh dear, it's not me who's needing your help, Doctor, it's my house girl, Nan. She's in a way, you see. My husband went on a drunk and beat her bad. I don't dare bring her here. Could be someone would see."

He eyed a small black box in the woman's hand. She lifted the ornate lid and pinched a bit of snuff. It wasn't until she returned it to her woven reticule that she spoke again. "Could you come to our place and have a look at her before my husband wakes? I'm sure he'll be none too aware for the rest of the day."

"Your husband's name wouldn't be Henry, would it, Mrs. Orr?"

"Why yes, Doctor. Do you know my Henry?" She glanced from the window to the door of the room, fidgeting with her bonnet as her smile twitched.

"I don't know him well personally, ma'am. I would be pleased to follow you to your home." James ushered the woman out of the office and Mrs. O'Donell held open the front door. She handed James his hat, shaking her head. A sad knowing dimmed her eyes and weighed on the lines of her ruddy face.

∞

The Orr home was a simple brick house, but the sloping porch and a missing shutter spoke of better bygone years. James retrieved his medical bag and dismounted his own carriage. Before he could assist Mrs. Orr, her driver helped her to the ground.

Just off the kitchen, in a closet no more than five feet square, a young Negro woman lay curled on a mat. Fresh bloodstains streaked the faded quilt, covering most of her body. She was unconscious and her arm lay at an odd angle.

Anger surged as James knelt beside her. He placed two fingers on her neck, checking her pulse. "How long has she been this way?"

"Didn't show up to empty my slosh pot and bring me breakfast this morning. I knew right away something was amiss. I had to dress *myself*. Then I found her this way. She's been a bargain for us, this one. Says nary a word and does her work real well." The woman batted the air with her hand. "Oh dear, I do believe I shall sit down. All of this has been most trying."

The creaky complaint of the wood told him she'd plopped into a chair in the kitchen. Within seconds, she was yelling for her *boy* to make her tea.

James leaned close to the girl's battered face, lifting one eyelid. Purple, swollen tissue buried the other eye. "Nan? Nan, can you hear me?" He watched for signs of movement. A low moan made its way to her throat, but her eye remained closed.

"Don't move. You have a broken arm. I'm going to have to examine you. I need you to tell me where you are hurt." Gently, he felt for broken ribs first, relieved when the young woman didn't respond in pain. Finding no other major injuries, he cautiously checked the arm that lay over her chest. Bloody stripes cut into her forearm as if she'd blocked strike after strike from a leather belt. He gingerly lifted the arm cocked off to one side, already discolored and swollen. Nan cried out in pain, and, now fully aware, began to sob.

"I'm going to give you something to help with the pain, Nan. I'll have to set that arm. I won't lie to you; it's going to hurt." He uncorked a tiny green bottle. Lifting her head, he dribbled the full amount into her mouth.

Had there been another slave woman in this small household to treat Nan, James was certain he would never have been called. Although he feared his efforts might come to naught, he had to do right by the young woman. She could easily lose the function of her arm if someone did not set it properly—and right now. He knew firsthand what masters did with slaves who could no longer perform their duties.

James snapped his bag shut and stepped into the kitchen. "Mrs. Orr, I'd like to take Nan back to my office. Her broken arm and lacerations will require a certain amount of recovery time."

"I should say not, Doctor Hill!" Mrs. Orr had her feet propped on a chair—something he'd never seen a woman do. She sloshed sherry into her cup of tea. "Please see to whatever you can, then leave her to herself. I expect her back to her duties by supper. It won't do to have her laid up once Mr. Orr wakes."

He closed his eyes at the sudden spectral remembrance of a familiar teen-aged face streaked with dried rivulets and blood. Still, deep brown eyes, seeing nothing but eternity. James shook his head, loathing his past with clenched fists as he returned to the closet, only to find Nan barely conscious.

Her lips moved, and he dipped his ear close to her mouth.

Two raspy words: "My baby."

James swallowed hard. *Lord, have mercy!* He scanned the tiny room, and again her body. This time, he noticed blood pooling beside the old quilt. He shoved aside hair fallen over his right eye. Why didn't he see this before? The quilt must've absorbed it.

In the tiny, dusky closet, the reality of the situation sharpened. James ground his teeth to squash a rush of loathing. Vaporous spots assaulted his vision. The father could only be the miserable recreant he'd treated in his office.

"I must set this arm, Nan, before the swelling gets worse. This will be painful, but try to let sleep carry you." He found three adequate sticks in a fagot of kindling, and then searched his bag for a roll of cotton and cut four lengths.

Firmly grasping her upper arm with one hand and just above the wrist with the other, James took a deep breath. If only he could do this in one motion. He expelled his breath and steadily pulled on the lower arm until he felt it give, then released it to slide back against the elbow. Nan cried out, but her eyes remained closed. She tossed her head twice, then merciful sleep engulfed her.

Positioning the sticks along the sides of Nan's arm, James tied them together in four places before wrapping the entire arm. He requested a pail of warm water from Mrs. Orr's servant and proceeded to wash away what blood he could from the girl's limp body. He placed tight rolls of bandages to absorb the bleeding from the miscarriage. At last, he mopped up the floor.

An idea was taking shape. "God," he whispered, "I ask little from You, and I know I don't talk to You very often, but if You *are* there, help me get her out of here."

"Mrs. Orr," James said, startling the dozing woman, "I will return within the hour. Nan is resting comfortably, but she is not to be moved. Am I clear on this?"

"No need to come back, Doctor. I'm certain she'll be up to start the evening meal after she rests a bit. She's usually not down more than a day." The harridan positively sickened him.

"I *will* return." James thrust his hat atop his head and strode to his carriage. His plan had to work.

Eleven

CHARLESTON

"I'll walk to the mercantile when I'm done here. I don't expect to be long." Augusta straightened her bonnet and waited for Fin to help her down.

"Thank you for doing this, Gus. It's just not something I'm cut out for." Fin looked at the ground. "It's just better this way."

She squeezed his hand. "Don't give it another thought, brother. I'm just thankful for your last leather job so we could make this payment." She waited as he drove off, her fingers fidgeting with the yellow reticule she'd sewn to match the gingham dress she wore. This visit to the bank had to be more pleasant than the last. Could she possibly be lucky enough to find Mr. Edward Fontaine Jr. *out* of his office for the day?

The bustling bank lobby evidenced its popularity with the Charleston set. Customers sat across from sharp-suited bankers at two heavy desks. Patrons waited in three lines to conduct their business with bank tellers. One of those figures in a line looked familiar. As she stared at the back of his head, the tall, rather handsome gentleman turned.

The ash-colored hair. The russet beard. He was the doctor introduced to her by Edward Fontaine. Ah yes, the *rude* doctor. What was his name?

As if reading her mind, their eyes met. He looked kinder somehow, but the illusion was short-lived. A shadow of recognition crossed his eyes, and that quick, his pleasant mouth crouched in a frown. He turned his back to her.

Still rude.

Augusta lifted the front hem of her dress and followed the curved stairs up to the second floor. Walking the length of the long hall, she prayed for God's favor and calmness for her anxious thoughts. The heavy door loomed before her like the entrance of a cave, sheltering unknown villainy. *Thou preparest a table before me in the presence of mine enemies.* Augusta knocked lightly.

"Come in." The sound of his voice bolstered her resolve.

She filled her lungs as she turned the doorknob. *He will not rattle me.* She would simply make the payment and be off. Edward Fontaine, Jr. stood behind the massive desk. His impeccable attire and handsome face caught her off guard, distracting from her mission for an instant.

"My dear Augusta, how wonderful to see you again. Please, won't you have a seat?" He gestured to one of the wing-backed chairs and positioned himself to sit in the chair adjacent instead of behind the desk.

"I believe I will stand. Thank you." She decided indifference would be the best attitude she could afford.

He frowned, then walked behind the desk. "Since then, dear lady, you insist on standing, the vestiges of my stature as a gentleman require that I stand, as well."

"All right, Mr. Fontaine, I believe I will be seated, but my business will be brief." Augusta sat at once and produced an envelope. She slid it across the desk. "I hope the amount will suffice for this month, per our previous agreement."

"Tell me, Augusta, how is your family? Your father?" The envelope remained untouched.

"My family is not your concern, sir, but they are all faring well., thank you." She would give him no excuse to call in the loan.

"I see." He gestured toward the envelope. "You know, I'm sure the money in that envelope could be put to use on that farm of yours. Why don't you just keep that payment and know that I'll make sure everything works out for you?" He tented his fingers, but they did not hide the crooked smile on his face.

Whatever the man's intent, Augusta's stomach curdled. Everything within her wanted to jump from the chair and scurry out the door like a wild rabbit.

"I would prefer you accept my payment, Mr. Fontaine—as previously agreed."

His features softened, and she noticed the way his flaxen mustache followed the curve of his mouth as his smile broadened. "Please, Augusta, I insist you call me Edward when we are alone. Perhaps we got off to a bad start." She reached to slide the envelope closer, and he placed his hands atop her own before she could pull them back. "Would you do me the pleasure of having dinner with me? At the Kanawha House, perhaps?"

"*Mr.* Fontaine. Edward." She hoped she sounded more polite than she felt. Her indifference was swiftly melting into disdain. "My family is waiting for me, and I must be off. Please, do me the favor of accepting my payment and providing me with a receipt." In a swift movement, she pulled her hands free, placing them firmly in her lap. Even a polite smile would betray her sensibility.

"Very well." Edward picked up the envelope, counted the money, then jerked open the top desk drawer and scrawled a receipt for her. She reached across the desk for the piece of paper, but he stood, holding it aloft with two fingers. "I sincerely hope, Augusta, that your next payment will be delivered with a bit more, shall we say, consideration for your predicament."

A moment later, with the receipt tucked safely in her bag, Augusta stood as Edward opened the office door.

"I'm not the enemy, Augusta." Sincerity colored his voice, and his hand raised briefly as if to touch her arm, then lowered again. "I'm here to help—in any way I can. If there is anything at all you need, just send a telegram. I assure you—my intentions are most honorable."

"Thank you, Edward. I'll see myself downstairs." Augusta's heels clicked at a brisk pace on the polished floor. She slowed her breathing. Another battle won.

∽

As if what James was about to do wasn't distasteful enough, his day had soured even more when he set eyes on that Dabney woman again at the bank. But no matter, he'd been able to get what he needed.

He knocked on the Orr's front door and stepped back, waiting. A curtain moved, so he knocked again. Minutes ticked by before Mr. Orr opened the door. It was him, all right. The pernicious excuse of a man he had met in his examination room.

"Good day, Mr. Orr, I am Dr. Hill. I assume you remember our previous acquaintance some time ago?"

Mr. Orr scrubbed his unshaven face with a meaty hand. His rumpled mass of graying hair tumbled over his ears and his breath reeked of liquor and rot. He squinted at James for a moment, then recognition dawned. "Yes, Doctor, what can I do for you?"

"I'd like to make you a business proposition, Mr. Orr. One I believe will allow a shrewd deal on your part."

"A business deal, huh? What kind of business deal?" Orr stood a little straighter and narrowed his eyes.

"I'd like to buy your slave, Nan." How James loathed the sound of his own words.

"She ain't for sale." Orr attempted to slam the door closed, but James blocked the action with his foot.

"But, sir, I think you'll find my offer most generous." He was counting on Orr to suggest a price—one he was prepared to pay. "What do you want for her?"

The middle-aged man seemed to reconsider. He opened the door again, but this time, his eyes lit up. "Well, Doctor, that one's a fine one, she is. Young and feisty, but yields to a strong hand, if you get my drift." He licked his lips and wiped his hand over a lascivious smirk. James's anger roiled, but he tamped it down behind a feigned smirk of his own.

"Replacing that one will be hard, for sure." Orr tugged a hunk of gray hair from his ear and examined it before letting it drop to the floor. "I couldn't let her go for less than, say . . . two hundred dollars."

Two hundred? He was not quite prepared for that amount. "Two hundred would buy two strong young bucks, Mr. Orr." James turned to leave, hoping to call the man's bluff. Either the man's debased nature or his greed would win out. He counted on the latter.

"Suit yourself, then."

James pivoted and reached for his breast pocket. "I'll give you one seventy-five cash, Mr. Orr. Take it or leave it." James was not a card player, and now he knew why. This dalliance of wills was like plucking a splinter from your foot. Most unpleasant, albeit necessary. He held his breath, trying to appear casual. Was he actually offering to purchase a human being?

"Sold!" Orr roared and reached for the money.

Relief flooded through James, but he must continue the ruse. He simply nodded. "Very well," he said, snatching the money before Orr could touch it. "In the interest of proper business, I should like a receipt and papers at the moment of our transaction, sir."

"Fine, fine. Come in then," the man growled.

Moments later, Orr handed James the ownership papers. "I'll go fetch the wench."

"If you don't mind, I'd like to retrieve her myself." James formed a wicked smile, shifting his eyebrows for effect. If the ogre thought his intentions base, perhaps he would be allowed to move the girl himself, with care.

Mr. Orr guffawed. "You're a slick one, Doc. Go ahead. What do I care? She's yorn now." Mr. Orr strode into another room and slammed the door behind him—no doubt to count his money.

※

James stood at the foot of the bed as Mrs. O'Donell fussed over their new houseguest. He had properly set her arm and seen to her other delicate situation just after arriving home. Now, Nan lay beneath fresh sheets, her body washed and wearing clean dishabille. With a room right across the hall, Mrs. O'Donell would care for the girl like a newborn babe. Of that, he was certain.

"Poor, poor dear." The older woman caressed the girl's forehead, pushing back a loose tress of coal-black hair. "What ya done for this lass was a fine thing, to be sure. You've a heart of gold, me boy." She picked up Nan's clothes and tossed them into an empty bucket. "I'll burn these in the stove. She'll be in need of proper clothes afore long."

"I'll get you some money from my office for clothing, Mrs. O'Donell. Would you mind seeing to that, please?"

She nodded. "Ya know ya don't need to be askin', James."

He looked down at the sleeping young woman. But it was not Nan's face that filled his vision just now. No. The face before him was from the past, but every bit as real as this young woman here. Right now. In this room.

Twelve

CHARLESTON

May, 1861

James slipped the polished monocle from a velvet bag as the toddler slumped on his mother's lap. His cheeks glowed pink and a pudgy, wet finger slipped in and out of his mouth.

Mrs. Patton held the child close, rocking him back and forth. "Can you do anything for him, Doctor?"

After an examination of the boy's ears, James was fairly certain of the tot's problem. "I believe he has an earache, Mrs. Patton. We'll get that cleared up in no time. It won't take long to prepare the treatment."

"Thank you so much, Doctor. This is our second visit to you in a month. I feel like we've suddenly become quite a regular customer for you."

James smiled at the loving scene before him. He placed the back of his hand against the damp cheek of the child, then brushed away a curled lock of brown hair. "You have two active boys, Mrs. Patton. I am confident a reason for them to visit me will pop up more frequently than you'd like."

At the worktable, James opened a miniature trunk. It held all manner of envelopes, tin containers, bottles of tinctures, and even jars of twigs and dried leaves.

He placed several small leaves from a tin into a mortar and worked them with the pestle. After grinding the contents to a fine powder, he added a measure of quinine. Taking pinches of the thick paste, James formed twenty small pills.

Next, he selected a singular dried leaf from a different tin and crushed it into a powder. He added a bit of bacon grease and mixed it. Scooping up the concoction with a knife, he wiped it into a tiny tin and tapped a cap in place.

"I want you to give him one of these pills every evening. The Veritria salve is to rub on the outer ear. It will help ease the discomfort." James wrapped the medicines in brown paper and turned to the regal man standing near the door. "Captain Patton, I assure you, your fine son will be feeling better by this time tomorrow."

"Thank you, James. I cannot tell you what it means to us to know the boys are in such good hands. Susan has gained the utmost confidence in your skills." Captain Patton was not a tall man, but he commanded a presence in the room as if he towered above James's head.

"I'm certainly happy to be of service."

"Susan, would you mind leaving us to talk for a moment?" Captain Patton opened the examination room door.

"Certainly, Dear. Thank you again, Doctor." She re-situated the now sleeping toddler on her arm and left the room.

"President Davis has declared a State of War." Captain Patton crossed to the window. "There are different faces of war, James. Some fight for the right to live their lives unhindered, as they have for generations. Lincoln offered Robert Lee the command of the Union Forces, but he refused, believing himself to be a Virginian first and an American second. He believes that when Virginia joined this Union back in 1776, she did not give up her sovereignty.

I concur with Colonel Lee, and I now will serve under him as my Commanding General."

He turned back to James. "I'm enlisting tomorrow in the Confederate Army and taking my men with me. We will dispatch under General Henry Wise's Army of the Kanawha. I want you with me on this noble quest, James. In the capacity of a doctor *and* a soldier. I'll have a uniform for you by this evening. What do you say?"

James searched the floor for the answer that best represented his convictions. He, too, believed Virginia was sovereign. But along with that, independence rode an ugly black horse called slavery. He didn't want to fight. Did that make him a coward? If he were more honest with himself—would he lay down his life for folks like Nan? Like Ezra? Blackness squeezed his heart. He couldn't breathe as Ezra's face stole into his vision. *I would've gladly taken your place.*

James met the captain's gaze. "I understand what you are saying, sir—what you believe to be a noble quest for which you will bear arms. I, too, support Virginia's right to her independence. But unlike you, sir, the face of this war—for me—wears chains and cowers to an overseer's whip."

He opened the door, standing to one side to permit his guest to exit.

"I see." The captain directed an intense gaze at James, yet without rebuke. "I believe I understand your heart on this matter. I respect a man who stands by his convictions."

The captain walked through the door, then turned. "James, I hope when next we meet, it will not be on the battlefield. Good day."

"I share that hope. Good day, sir." James slowly closed the door. The conversation kindled a fire in his belly. Its purpose was yet unknown, but he sensed he'd know before long.

Fayette County

Augusta pulled the brush through her hip-length copper waves, wove her hair into a thick braid as she did every morning, then wrapped it into a flat bun. She'd need to buy some new hair pins on the next trip to town. Even for a special occasion, all she'd ever done was pull a few strands loose to frame her face. She never quite knew what to do with the excessive length.

The image in the mirror grabbed her attention. The days had become warmer, and the sun had coaxed her freckles from their winter sleep. Though her green eyes were striking, her reflection was ordinary. She wasn't beautiful, like Will. Her sister's freckles were sparse and her hair a softer hue of auburn. And now that her hair had grown a little, adorable, wispy waves framed her face—unless she stuffed them under that old slouch hat.

The gray of dawn filtered in through the kitchen window. Still time before breakfast for a quick walk. She'd wake Bertie to do the milking if he wasn't already in the barn with Fin. Since she made cornpone last night, breakfast would go quickly this morning.

Beside the basket of eggs on the worktable sat a ham. That sow she'd shot didn't just offer up a good rendering. They'd gotten some fine hams out of it. Fin figured the old girl had been into some farmer's grain store for some time before she wandered into the garden.

Augusta donned her straw hat for the brisk walk down to Izzy's. She placed the ham in a tow sack, envisioning the pleased look on Izzy's face when she presented it to him.

A gossamer fog rose from the green of the pasture, cloaking the treetops of the holler to the south—a sure sign of a sunny day. She'd always admired the beauty of this rugged land—the rolling meadows and farmland held prisoner by the steep rise and fall of the earth, the high cliffs of the river, and streams that darned their way through the hills. She liked to imagine God's smile as he formed the Appalachian Mountains and the lands that would attend them.

"Hallo to the cabin!" Augusta shouted as she approached Izzy's little one-room hovel. She couldn't wait to see the twinkle in his eye when he spied her gift.

Izzy appeared at the door, pulling his galluses over each shoulder, then trotted out to meet her. "Why, missy, you didn't have to come away down here." He fidgeted, glancing behind him to the cabin. "What's you got there?"

"I brought you a ham. I thought you could eat on this most of the month." She started for the cabin door, but he took hold of the burlap bag.

"Woo-wee. This be good eatin' fo sure. Thank you kindly, missy. Now you best be gettin' on back to cookin' up some breakfast fo that family of yorn." He guided her in a little circle until she was facing back the way she'd come.

"It was just such a nice day for a morning walk—"

"Yes, yes, that's fo sure. I'll be seeing you later when I comes up to see yo pap. Thank you again, missy." The old man headed back toward his cabin, but looked over his shoulder in Augusta's direction. With a little shrug and a wave, she started back up to the house.

She'd not let a bit of disappointment taint this perfect morning. Nor would she spend a mite of reflection on the odd scenario that had just played out. Her mood climbed again as she thanked God for Izzy and Melinda Jane and the rest of her family.

An hour later, with breakfast past, Augusta leaned on the porch rail. She took a deep breath of the morning air. The colored clouds over the Alleghenies off to the east could paint such a startling picture. Sometimes it brought a tear to her eye. *Thank you, Father, for the beauty of Your creation; for Your handiwork displayed for all to see.* Her smile gave way to the joy in her heart. This was her home. She loved every inch of this farm and every soul that lived here.

Augusta strolled to the chicken house, swinging the egg basket. Just like *Little Red Riding Hood*. She chuckled at her frivolous thoughts.

The door to the henhouse creaked open, and she stood on the threshold, letting her eyes adjust to the dimness. In a noisy instant, a fluttering mass of feathers bushwhacked her. Her arms shielded her face to block the attacker. She stumbled backwards to make her escape, but not before Rupert caught her with his spurs.

Blood trickled off her elbow into the dirt. She slipped a rag from her pocket and wiped her arm. She'd have to tend to that later. With all the chickens out of the shed now, she went about gathering the eggs.

Why had they kept that mean old rooster around, anyway? Maybe if they tossed him in the stew pot, the other cockerels would feel more like tending to their duty.

Rupert ruffled his white feathers and trotted past her to the yard. He stood two heads taller than all the hens and age had coaxed his bright red comb to flop so far to one side, it covered one eye.

―

Augusta sighed in resignation as her sister pulled the tattered slouch hat over her uncombed hair and bounded down the steps toward the barn. With school out for the summer, Will had extra chores. It was an ongoing battle to get her to help with housework, so Augusta had bargained with her sister to weed the garden in place of doing the wash. Augusta would rather be in the garden any day herself, but Will was like a caged bear in the house when the sun was shining.

The rhythmic click of hooves sounded in the distance and grew louder. Visitors. Augusta smoothed her apron as she walked to the front porch to greet them. Four mounted Confederate soldiers entered the yard. Fin stepped from the barn, a rifle in his hand. Augusta hid her shock when Zander rounded the chicken house with a shotgun pressed to his shoulder.

"Whoa now, brother, there's no need for weapons." The officer in front motioned for Fin to lower his gun. The men accompanying him sat tall in their saddles, each with a hand on the pistol in his belt. "We aren't looking for any trouble. We're just patrolling these parts and wondered if you'd be kind enough to share some of that sweet, cool well water with us."

Hospitality. Augusta's mother had drilled it into her. Mrs. Munday had drilled it into the girls. Why was it something she had no desire to muster at the moment? She let out a breath. "Certainly, gentlemen. I suppose you'd be wanting something to eat besides?" Her own forced smile gained one in return from the lead soldier.

Fin gaped at his sister. He walked over to stand beside her as the men dismounted. "What are you doing?" he whispered. "We don't need to make friends with these soldiers."

"You catch more flies with honey, Fin. If they view us as friendly, they'll find no cause for trouble." While the men helped themselves to water from the pump, Augusta returned to the house.

Several minutes later, she presented a plate of cold ham sandwiches to the soldiers. Fin still stood in the yard, rifle in the crook of his elbow. He eyed the men as they splashed water on their faces and donned their hats over dripping hair.

"That's mighty kind of you, ma'am." The men helped themselves to the proffered sandwiches. The officer signaled the others to mount up. His eyes pinned Fin. "I expect you'll be joining the

Fayette County Militia before long." It wasn't a question, more of a statement.

Fin looked hard at the man, but held his tongue as his arm muscle flexed, threatening to lift his rifle. A twitch in his set jaw didn't escape Augusta's notice.

The soldiers swung their horses around. The officer tipped his hat to Augusta, and they trotted off again.

"Don't you be making enemies now, Fin." Augusta laid her hand on the barrel of the rifle and stared into her brother's eyes until she held his gaze. "This isn't our war."

Just then, a volley of shots rang through the air. Fin took off running in the direction the soldiers had gone. Zander came barreling out of the barn on Rampart, past his brother.

"No! Zander, come back!" Augusta yelled, running as fast as her legs could carry her. She called over her shoulder, "Will, you stay here!"

Fin's angry shout filtered back to her. "Zander, get back here!"

Augusta slammed to a stop, fighting back tears and breathing hard from the run. At the juncture of their lane and the road into Gauley, a lone horse lay dead on the ground. Ten feet away, its rider sprawled in the dirt, blood pooled on his chest. His eyes stared vacantly at the bright May sun.

"Over here!" Zander's disembodied voice rang out.

Augusta and Fin rounded a large oak to discover the three other Confederate soldiers—all dead. She dropped to the ground, heaving for breath. *Lord have mercy. What evil had come to her home?*

"There must've been a Union patrol in the area." Fin shook his head. "I didn't think they would come clear down here to Fayette County. I read they're doing all their training up north near Wheeling and mostly patrolling the upper regions." He yanked off his hat, scowling. "What did these men prove by dying?"

"What are we going to do with the bodies?" Zander asked. "We can't just leave them here."

Augusta was torn. And sickened. Should she protect her frail father from this grief or lean on his wisdom? The latter would likely be her choice so long as he breathed. "Let's get some blankets back at the house and cover them up for now, boys. We'll talk to Pap and see what he says."

Thirteen

CHARLESTON

May, 1861

The yeasty aroma of fresh baked bread still hung in the kitchen as James set his napkin on the table. "A magnificent meal, Mrs. O'Donell—par excellence." He lifted a glass for one last gulp of water.

"I'm thinking betwixt the fancy words, there's a compliment in there—to which I say, Yer most welcome." Mrs. O'Donell chuckled and turned to Nan. "Are ya finished, las?"

"Yessum, ma'am. I ain't never eat this good before. This body o' mine gonna blow up like a dead possum on a trace." Nan stood to help clear the table. "Ya'll been mighty kind to me. Ain't no way I can never repay your kindness. I'm feelin' well enough to do my duties now, Massa Hill. No need for Miz O'Donell here to keep cooking and cleaning."

James slid a look to Mrs. O'Donell, then directed his gaze to Nan. "Sit down, please, Nan."

She sat again, fussing with the back of her headscarf as she chewed her bottom lip.

"I believe you are right about one thing, Nan. You are indeed well enough to be getting on with your life. You are not correct, however, about the cooking and cleaning part."

A shadow swept across her face like a storm cloud, shriveling her posture, freezing her in place but for a slight quiver of her chin. "I's sorry, Massa Hill. I done spoke outta turn." Panic clung to each word as she stared at the floor. The cup and saucer in her fingers began to rattle.

James stood, promptly wanting to assuage her fear. He touched her slight shoulder with practiced gentleness. "Nan, I want you to look at me."

The young woman lifted her gaze. James's heart plummeted when he marked the sheer terror in those wide eyes. Nan appeared to sink into herself. What had he done? "I'm sorry I didn't explain something to you before now, Nan. I aspired to be sure you were well on the mend. You needn't lift your hand or callous your knees to do another lick of work for someone else unless you want to."

A guarded interest creased her expression. Why had he waited so long?

James left a confused Nan standing alone while he rushed to the office to retrieve an envelope. He returned to find Mrs. O'Donell, her face streaked with tears, and her arms encircling the girl in a tight embrace. James spoke at first, but the ache behind his throat snatched away his words.

Lifting her hand, he placed the stiff, yellowed envelope in her palm. One corner of his mouth twitched as he claimed control of his emotions. Ever so tenderly, he encased the envelope and her rough hands in his own, willing her eyes to meet his.

"You are free, Nan. I didn't buy you from Mr. Orr to make you my s . . . slave." He swallowed hard. The thought of the duties required of her at the Orr home—*all* the duties—made what he had to say all the sweeter. "I bought you to give you your freedom."

Nan's legs gave way, and he and Mrs. O'Donell lowered her to a chair.

"Nan is free? Nan is free?" The young woman echoed the three words over and over, as great wet drops coursed down her dark cheeks. Her eyes stared at the envelope, blinking, as if waking from a dream.

Mrs. O'Donell snatched up a napkin from the table to catch her own tears, then pushed another into Nan's open hand. The girl's thin fingers gripped the cloth, but she let the tears fall unabated. She rocked back and forth, like a mama soothing her tiny babe. "I ain't never knowed a free colored folk afore, Massa Hill."

James knelt beside the chair, finding the beauty in her watery brown eyes spectacular. His voice rasped, "Don't you ever call another man 'massa' from this day forward, Nan. Do you hear me?" He blinked away unshed tears. "You are free now—the same as me, the same as Mrs. O'Donell—and we call no man 'massa.'"

He caught his breath as a rhapsodic truth overtook the doubt in her eyes. She tipped her face heavenward, searching something unseen. A soft, throaty melody groaned through her chapped lips—from her very soul. At first, it a was a whisper of disbelief. Then the song gained a life of its own, filling the kitchen and swelling like the first sunrise over God's new creation.

"Oh! Freedom! Oh! Freedom Oh! Freedom Over Me!
But before I be a slave, I be buried in my grave,
And go home to my Lord and be free.
No mo runnin', no mo runnin', no mo runnin' over me!
But before I be a slave, I be buried in my grave,
And go home to my Lord and be free."

James lingered in the restaurant entry, sizing up his noon appointment and wondering what was about to transpire.

"Thank you for meeting with me, Doctor Hill." The man was a full head shorter than James, but posed a commanding presence in the blue and brass ensemble of the Union Army. He extended his hand. "I'm Captain Gerald Canton. I'm with the Regiment of the Kanawha under the command of General Jacob Cox. Please, be seated." He motioned to the rosewood chair, half hidden beneath the linen tablecloth.

"I got your telegram, Captain, but I haven't a clue as to the nature of our meeting." Tantalizing wafts of unknown culinary delights distracted James. The odors coaxed a growl from his stomach, and he glanced at the captain, hoping his hunger had not proven embarrassing fodder.

"Let's order first, if you don't mind. Then we'll get down to the reason I'm here."

The captain signaled to the liveried waiter, who promptly took their order. In the corner of the spacious, chandeliered dining room, a stocky bald man ran his fingers over the keys of a square grand piano. The soothing atmosphere of the Kanawha House dining room was only one of the fine amenities of the pricey hotel—touted as the finest lodging in all of western Virginia.

"Now, what is this about?" James's fingers twitched with the urge to fidget, so he reached for his water glass.

"I'll be most direct, Dr. Hill," the captain replied. "You may or may not be aware that President Lincoln has ordered that each Union Regiment be provided a surgeon and surgeon's assistant from the area in which the regiment is formed. I am here to ask you, on behalf of the United States Army, to serve as the surgeon for the Kanawha Regiment."

Not what James expected. Two Charleston doctors of his acquaintance now served as officers with the Kanawha Riflemen. But he understood that the Riflemen—now officially Company I of the Confederate Army—held them in the capacity of soldier, not physician.

"What would the station of a Regimental Surgeon entail, Captain?" Along the edges of James's mind, a dim light waxed brighter. Something was unfolding within his thoughts, still too out of focus to see clearly.

"You would attend a few weeks of military training, since you would be on the battlefield. In the throes of conflict, we would need you to tend to the wounded, primarily at the rear of the engagement. An agreement has been reached with the Army of the Confederacy that medical personnel on the field may, under a green flag, tend the wounded unmolested. When possible, other medical assistants on the battlefield will attend medical situations."

"When possible?"

"Yes. We wouldn't want our surgeon taking a bullet when he's so essential to the injured. In addition to battlefield triage, you would be in charge of setting up a field hospital. Should the situation require it, you would have the authority to commandeer a building from civilians."

With grace and attention to detail, a cheerful, yet professional garcon placed the food before them. James returned the man's smile with a weak one of his own, welcoming the interruption.

As they ate, thoughts that had evaded James until now found momentum during the stall in conversation. He silently conjured all manner of questions while the captain chewed his food for a time before continuing. "It is not possible to fully predict the nature of circumstances you may encounter, Doctor."

"Are you aware I turned down Captain Patton's invitation to join with him?"

"Yes. We are quite aware of that fact." The captain lifted his glass to signal for a refill. "A mutual acquaintance of ours inadvertently made it known while imbibing at a social event."

"And who would that be, sir?"

The captain grunted, then forked a piece of meat. "Austin Kennedy."

"I see. And did Mr. Kennedy also tell you I am averse to the taking of lives? My call is to sustain life; to repair the damage inflicted on the less fortunate, maimed, or lying by the way—or on the battlefield." His mouth instantly a desert, James gulped the rest of his water and blotted his beard with a napkin.

The captain's eyebrows arched as he acknowledged James's concern with a nod. "He did. You would be granted a commission as major, Doctor. Regardless of your lack of military expertise, you will be afforded every responsibility and respect of the rank. As the Regimental Surgeon, your priority will be to the wounded, not the conflict."

The captain sat straighter and tugged at the edge of his mustache, his face somber. "However, and let me be clear on this point, if you indeed were to see yourself unable to protect one of your fellow soldiers—whether that required taking the life of another or the giving of your own—then, Doctor Hill, you are not worthy of this uniform."

Captain Canton stood, placed a dollar bill on the table, and extended a calling card. "I have presented you this proposition in all sincere candor, Doctor. Please consider it with equally serious deliberation. I require your answer by five o'clock tomorrow afternoon."

James rotated the card in his fingers. His eyes stalled on the embossed lettering until the sound of polished boots on the wooden floor faded away.

∞

James pounded the pillow and flopped onto his back. Seemed so little about life was simple anymore. He longed for his mind to approach this decision with sound reasoning, with consideration to the outcome and consequences.

What was this pressure in his chest? What was the yearning that whined from his gut like a puppy crying for his mother? A tumultuous slurry of angst and ire threatened the soundness of his thinking. He rolled to his side. Confound it! Why couldn't he think this through?

Sleep came long after midnight, but rode a pike sullied by battlefield clashes and the thunder of cannons. Faceless bodies in Union blue—and gray-black smoke. Thick smoke. Choking smoke. His lungs felt close to bursting. Eventually, it dissipated into gauzy puffs, a familiar countenance emerging from the chaos. Eyes crinkled in merriment and full lips curved into a smile across the dark face of one not yet a man.

James jumped to his feet—sleep thrown off like a stinging bee. The *what* and the *why* made their way to his senses. He knew what he must do.

∞

James halted between trips outside, intrigued at the mixture of concern and love on his housekeeper's face as she fussed with Nan. She had scooped up this girl with the widest motherly wings he'd ever seen. What if he'd had a mother dote on him like that? Of course, Mrs. O'Donell did well to make up for it. But seeing them there like this, seeing the joy in her glistening eyes—his heart swelled all the more with not just appreciation, but a genuine love for the woman. He was going to miss her.

Mrs. O'Donell hugged Nan to her chest, then straightened the girl's bonnet and retied the ribbons. "Just as soon as ya get settled, be about finding someone to write and tell me yer safe, lass. I've tucked me address into the pocket of yer bag. Keep a close hold on those papers and ticket, now. Tis yer new life right there."

"She'll be just fine, Mrs. O'Donell." James jostled a small wooden chest at his side. "The Fords are a wonderful family, and they'll treat her kindly." While he attended college in Maryland, the Fords had taken him under their wing like the lost son he was. Over the years, they had become the family he needed.

He returned to the carriage to load his medicine chest. The army would supply much of whatever he needed, but he doubted they would provide the herbs he depended on for certain treatments. His pace slowed as he entered the house for the last time. He hated goodbyes.

"Yous been like a mammy to me, Miz O'Donell," Nan said. "I's goin' to miss you. The good Lord has surely blessed this girl. I gonna learn me to read an' write, jes like Massa—Doctor Hill say. Then I write you long letters all about my new life up North." A tear escaped and Nan didn't bother to wipe it away.

The older woman's bottom lip quivered as she hugged the girl one last time, then turned her sad eyes on James.

"Mrs. O'Donell, I leave you as caretaker of my entire estate," James said dramatically, indicating the house with a sweeping motion of his arm. "Such as it is. I've left an envelope of money for you in the top desk drawer. I hope it will be enough to see you through the next few months until I return."

"Oh, James, me boy. God go with ya." She patted his cheek with one hand and grasped his arm with the other. "Don't ya go gettin' yerself killed." She fluttered her eyes and released him, turning toward the kitchen. "Always so much to be done . . . tsk, tsk, tsk

. . . always so much to be done . . ." The chant trailed behind her until the door bounced shut.

Before continuing onward for his duties in the Union Army, James wanted to see Nan safely off. Silence hung over them as they rode toward the river, and he contemplated if, and when, he'd see her again.

They disembarked at the docks of the Kanawha River. The smell of fish mingled with burning wood as it wafted on the crisp breeze. Thick, black smoke already belched from the tall stacks of the vessel as travelers presented their tickets and boarded the flashy steamer.

"You'll be safe as long as you keep your papers and ticket on you, Nan. Just show your ticket to that man in the brown and gold cap. He'll see that you board the correct steamer in Pt. Pleasant."

He handed her the carpetbag Mrs. O'Donell had purchased for her. "The ticket shows which train you'll transfer to in Parkersburg. From there, you'll just stay in your seat until the Fords greet you at your first stop in Maryland. It's all right there on your ticket."

He cleared his throat, then smiled, hoping to infuse her with confidence. "You'll do just fine, Nan. You're a smart young woman. Try to remember everything we talked about."

"Yessir, Doctor Hill. I remember." She worried her bottom lip and clutched the bag to her stomach. "Ain't no way in this life, on this earth, I be able to thank you."

The loud blast of the ship's horn startled Nan, and her hand flew to cover her ear. James released her elbow and stepped back. He wanted to blaze that sweet face into his memory. His desire for her future pressed against his heart, straining his voice. "Goodbye, Nan."

Brown eyes, shimmering with tears, held his gaze.
Godspeed, little one.

Fourteen

Fayette County

June 1861

"Gus?"

"I'm here, Fin." Augusta dried her hands and headed toward the front door.

"You be wanting anything in town? Zander and I are heading into Gauley. I want to see if Tiny can make me a hinge to match this other one." He stood just outside the threshold, holding up a rusty hinge.

Her eyes fell to his mud-caked boots.

"I could use some more nails from Jackson's while I'm at it."

At least he hadn't tracked in the mud. Last night's rain was a blessing, but it sure made a mess of the barnyard. She untied her apron and thought to look in the mirror. "All right if I ride along? I'm in need of a few staples, and I'd surely like to get out of this kitchen today." She would check on Pap before leaving. He'd had a fitful night, and she wanted to make sure he was resting. "Will can stay with Pap."

"I'll bring the wagon around for you."

∽

When they turned onto Gauley Road, Augusta trained her eyes forward as they drove past the section of pasture where they'd buried the dead soldiers. She didn't need reminding about the heartbreaking mess. One week after the terrible incident, several more soldiers had arrived to claim the bodies. Now, uneven, weed-covered mounds of dirt were all that remained to tell the tale.

Not three miles down the road, they came across six mounted Confederate soldiers on the side of the road. One of the men wore a Duckett hat instead of the gray kepi of the confederacy. Another squinted at a map as his yellow teeth gnawed a piece of straw. He glanced up and signaled for Fin to stop the wagon. Stringy, gray hair covered one eye until he pushed it aside.

"Howdy folks, I hope you can tell us how much farther it is to Gauley Bridge." A stream of tobacco juice squirted from the corner of his lips.

"Just another two miles up this road. You'll cross over the bridge, then the town's just a mite farther." Fin's hand hovered over the pistol in the gun belt he'd taken to wearing.

"Much obliged." The soldier clicked his tongue and launched into a gallop. The others followed, sending chunks of mud into the air.

"They're in a mighty big hurry," Zander said. "I wonder what's got into them."

Fin started the team moving again. "From the looks of those boys, I doubt it's anything good."

∞

Tiny pounded the flattened iron with a few more licks on the anvil. Soon, he'd fashion it into another cultivator tine, but right now it was too cool to work further. He set the iron tine back into the fire, then pulled the bellows rope several times. Grabbing up the empty bucket to add water to the barrel, he headed out to the back.

Water sloshed as Tiny worked the old pump handle and an old tune found its way out by way of a whistle. He didn't remember learning the melody. It seemed he'd known it all his life. The sound of horses on the road caught his attention, so he walked around to the front of the shop.

Confederate soldiers pulled up their mounts from a dead-out gallop. One dismounted, then pulled a paper from his coat. "Where's your master, boy?" He directed his question to Tiny, but his eyes watched the door of the shop.

"I got no master, sir. I'm the blacksmith here." Tiny stood tall. The thick muscles in his arms flexed as he clenched and relaxed his fists. He'd dealt with men like this all his life.

The soldier laughed and turned to the others. "He got no master," he said, mimicking Tiny's bass voice. The men snickered and two more of them dismounted. "Well, I reckon there are different masters, *boy*. Your master is the Confederate States of America now."

"I want no trouble. Jackson's is down the street a ways. Has supplies you most likely lookin' for." Tiny pointed toward the mercantile and glanced at the two soldiers, now taking positions on each side of him.

"I have here an order for two dozen standard horseshoes. The confederacy will pay a penny a piece for them." He threw the paper at Tiny, and it drifted to the ground. "We'll be back to retrieve them in two hours." He held his stirrup, lifting his foot to mount up.

"I can't help you, sirs." Bile climbed Tiny's throat, but he choked it back. *Lord, I'm a-needin' Your help here.*

The soldier whirled and pinned Tiny with a hard glare. "What did you say?" He sneered and took a step closer to the big man. The rest of the soldiers dismounted, tying their horses to the post.

"I say I cannot help you. These hands will not make one horseshoe for the Confederate Army."

The ranking soldier snatched off his hat and smoothed back his straight hair. It shimmered a greasy silver in the sunshine as he nonchalantly glanced up and down the alley. "Let's take this buck inside here and teach him to respect this uniform, shall we, boys?"

∞

As Fin brought the wagon to a stop in front of Jackson's Mercantile, Augusta tucked several stray hairs into her bonnet. "Pap isn't doing as well today as yesterday. I thought I might see if Mr. Jackson has any camphor. I'm thinking that could help relax his breathing some."

In the store, Augusta fingered a measure of green fabric, deliberating on the purchase.

After a lengthy conversation with Mr. Jackson, Fin finally retrieved the nails. "Zander and I are heading to Tiny's, sister. Want me to come back for you, or do you want to walk on down there?"

"I'll take my time here and meet you there in a while. That'll give you men some time to jaw."

∞

A soldier on each side grasped Tiny's thick arms while the leader pulled a pistol and shoved it into his gut. They forced him backwards through the door. The rest of the soldiers followed, slamming it shut behind them.

"Maybe you just need a little convincing, *boy*!" The one with the Duckett hat threw a punch directly to Tiny's jaw. His head snapped to the side for an instant before he fired an undaunted glare at his shocked attacker.

The Rebel took a step back, his eyes betraying a trace of fear.

Another belted him in the midsection, then hooted like a child, grabbing his hand. "His belly's hard as the ground!" Anger drove the soldier to throw a punch with the other fist—this time lower.

Tiny grunted. *Lord, I need ya now.*

A different Rebel attempted to kick his legs out from under him, but he stood strong. The silver-haired leader grabbed at his neck and Tiny head-butted him.

The no-good shook his head like a wet dog. His eyes sparked wild. He squirted brown juice to one side. "Take him, boys!"

As one, the soldiers mounted a vicious assault on Tiny. He took the punches, his anger mounting. *Lord, you my Helper . . . I will not fear what man shall do unto me.* He returned every blow with a mighty one of his own, sending each attacker to the ground.

The altercation stalled, so the soldiers started in on his vulnerable face. They took turns jabbing mercilessly at his eyes. His nose. His mouth.

Tiny gave it right back, but each time a man hit the floor, there were four more anchoring his arms.

He shook two loose at once and rammed his fist into the leader's face. The crunch of cartilage hung in the air as the leader spun and stumbled into the forge. When his face hit the fire, he screamed in agony and clutched his head, howling like a wildcat. He groped and clawed, tripping over firewood and knocking tools to the ground. One of his men helped him to the water barrel. Profanities and the acrid odor of burned flesh permeated the air. The water level was so low he fairly toppled into the barrel, trying to ease his agony.

Tiny heaved for breath and staggered. Blood from his slit eye blinded him and streamed into his open mouth. Working a tongue that felt like a raw potato, he spit out the thick fluid that threatened to choke him, sending with it two teeth and the tip of his tongue. The room spun. Mocking faces distorted, growing fuzzy.

All the smells he'd grown to love—the forge, hay, firewood, hot iron—intensified with the throbbing in his temple. The soldiers backed away, two of them still gripping his arms, struggling to keep him upright.

Tiny watched through a tunneled haze as one soldier wiped blood from his lip and leaned against a barrel. Another held his ear, blood streaming into his shirt collar.

"I reckon you'll be reconsidering your answer now, *boy*. Ain't that right?" The leader gasped for air; his yellow teeth bared in a malevolent sneer. Dark leathery bubbles covered most of one cheek and the corner of his eye. "You'll make them horseshoes, then you'll pay *us* for the privilege. You done passed the point of no return, *boy*!"

Tiny hung his throbbing head. This had to stop. And *he* was going to have to stop it. He sucked in air through his mouth, gagged, then spit. In a scratchy whisper, he pled his case, "Father, forgive them, for they know not what they do."

A foreign fury quaked. A low growl rose deep in his throat. In one movement, Tiny wrenched on the two soldiers holding his arms. A sickening thud sounded as their heads crashed together. Bodies crumpled to the ground like marionettes. The rest of his attackers lunged at him in tandem—one on his back, one on each arm.

The leader kicked him in the groin, but Tiny managed to grab the man's leg, twist it and yank hard. He leaned forward and began to spin. The men clung to his head and arms, flying about like the petals of a spinning dandelion in the hand of a child. A bear-like roar vibrated the building as Tiny shook off first one attacker, then another and another.

His vision fogged, he staggered toward where he figured the door to be. His foot tripped over the arm of an unconscious soldier, and he dropped to his knees, his head ricocheting off the hard floor.

A howl like the north wind whined loud and long. He watched through a red haze as the leader hobbled over to the forge.

Covering his hand with his sleeve, the Rebel picked the white-hot tine from the fire. "Hold him still, boys!" He extended the tine in front of him, its end glowing like a branding iron.

The three still-conscious soldiers hovered over Tiny's body. They jabbed their boots into his side, into his back. Over and over, they kicked him. His neck, his mid-section, his groin—until he lay helpless, curled on the floor.

The burning in his body dulled, and the pounding in his head abated. Sweet numbness washed over him. Like the dusk seeping over the hills on a clear summer evening, a cocoon of peace settled over him. He embraced the sweet relief. His fight was over. Wispy words caressed his mind, coiling around his very soul—a tender voice breathing his name, a father to a beloved child. It urged him, *"Come home."*

Six hands pinned him to the dirt floor as the glowing iron plunged deep into his chest. Only a soft groan escaped Tiny's throat. The leader pulled out his pistol and fired.

A report shattered the quiet of the little town. A blaze of thoughts shot through Fin's mind as he met his brother's eyes. They bounded up onto the buckboard. "Giddap!"

"Sounded like it came from the edge of town." Zander clutched his hat with one hand and the seat of the wagon with the other.

Fin pulled the team to a hard stop. Mounted Rebel soldiers circled their horses just outside of Tiny's shop. The same six he'd seen on the way to town. The gray-haired Rebel looked at Fin. Their eyes locked. The soldier's nose was a mangled collection of skin and blood. Blistered flesh veiled one cheek. His horse sprang from its haunches, and the others followed, racing wildly out of town.

An unseen boulder weighted Fin's chest. *Tiny!*

He leaped from the wagon and burst into the shop. There, on the floor, lay his friend, his face unrecognizable. Fin dropped to the ground and gently lifted the battered head into his lap. His mind swam in clouded reality, as if viewing the scene in slow motion. He watched his hand, detached from his will, reach forward to remove the iron tine from the lifeless body.

For the first time since his mama's funeral, Fin wept.

Time held him captive as wave after wave of grief and fury assailed him. A hand touched his shoulder. How long had his sister been standing there?

Tears wet her face, but they could not mask the anger that burned in her eyes. "Let's get him home. We're all the family he's got."

∞

Augusta headed to the wagon to retrieve a blanket and found Zander bent over the bushes at the corner of the building. "You all right?"

Breathing hard, face pallid and wet, he pulled his sleeve across his mouth. "I don't reckon I'll ever be all right again." He stood, and she saw the anguish in his eyes. "Why'd those men do that to Tiny, Gus? He never hurt no one."

She wrapped her arm around his waist and walked him to the wagon. "There's evil all around us, Zander. This war is bringing it out in some more than others, I reckon." She shook her head, then pulled herself up tall. "We'll be taking Tiny back to the farm. You run on and see if you can find us some help."

∞

Augusta watched, almost numb, as the wagon lumbered across the field with Pap propped on a cushion of quilts in the back. Her brothers unloaded him, settling him in a chair between her and Izzy.

She embraced the ache in her heart and drew a deep breath of spring blossoms mingled with the scent of wet earth. Passing her gaze across her family, she made contact with each of her siblings. Grasping Pap's hand, her eyes fell to the rough coffin settled in the depths of the freshly dug grave.

The heaviness of loss hung in the air until Melinda Jane's rich voice quenched the parched silence. Her words took flight, swelling their hearts: "Swing low, sweet chariot, comin' for to carry me home." She lifted her face to the cloudless morning sky as if singing to God Himself.

As the last note died away, Pap motioned for Augusta to take the Bible from his lap. It was opened to the twenty-third Psalm, so she read it aloud, her voice faltering toward the end.

Izzy kneaded his ragged hat with his fingers. "Lord, we delivering to You one of Your own. A good man. A God-fearin' man. And a redeemed man. Tiny knew Yo mercy and grace and blessings all his life long." He paused and looked heavenward.

"Oh, I know he already be sittin' at Jesus' knee, Lord. But this thing we do here today—it be for us more than anything. Thank You for the blessing of knowin' this kind, bear of a man.

"Lord, some of us havin' trouble lettin' go of our anger." Izzy's eyes slid to the left. Fin stood with his back rigid and jaw set, eyes staring at the coffin. "We need Yo help, Lord—to forgive. We know if'n we don't forgive them that sins against us, there's no forgiveness for *us*. Help us to forgive, lest that unforgiveness grab hold of our lives and pull us down so low we can't never get up." Izzy blinked several times and nodded. "Amen."

"Amen," voices echoed.

Augusta's gaze traveled to the small, engraved headstone that marked her mother's grave. She'd planted bluebells the year before and they had re-seeded, blanketing the sunken earth with an azure sea. How her heart ached for Mama right now. She supposed all death brought a person to recollect other deaths.

Fin scooped up a handful of the fresh soil and handed it to Pap, who tossed it onto the casket. One after the other, the mourners threw dirt into the grave. Augusta watched her older brother, his face hard like granite. He blew out a long breath, then nodding to Zander, the two of them began shoveling the loose dirt over their friend's body.

But for the scratch of a blade and the thud of clods against the pine casket, silence reigned. Even the birds in the trees ceased their medley of song and chatter to mourn the loss of this gentle giant of a man.

PART TWO

*My tears have been my meat day and night,
while they continually say unto me,
Where is thy God?*

Psalm 42:3

PART TWO

Fifteen

GUYANDOTTE, VIRGINIA

July 1861

Ash scattered as James tossed a birch twig into the smoldering fire. His new assistant, Seamus McLaughlin, balanced on a nearby campstool, filling a canteen with buttermilk. Buttermilk! The burly Irishman was crazy about the stuff. When James saw him take a swig from his Bullseye canteen for the first time, it was a shock. Thick, white liquid collected on his red mustache with every gulp, like wax to a wick, until he finally wiped it away with his sleeve.

With his military training behind him, James held more than a little trepidation about the coming weeks and months. But he'd met good men willing to lay down their lives. He'd set his sights on making a difference for as many soldiers as he could. He'd give his all to send sons and fathers home to their families. And he'd give his all to set others free.

"Best be turning in, Doc. 'Tis a two-day march to Charleston, with resistance all the way. I'm not expecting those Johnnies to just throw up their hands and let us cross through. General Wise's troops are all over these parts." Seamus rose and kicked dirt over the fire.

Other campfires glowed, dimming throughout the evening, disappearing one by one as the moon shone through the smoky haze over the Union camp.

∞

Barboursville, July 14, 1861

James squinted, watching the galloping riders in the distance. He took a draw from his canteen and cast a glance over his shoulder at Seamus. "What do you make of that? Scouts?"

General Cox's forces had been marching since daylight, and now the sun rode high in the sky. Mounted troops and those on foot stretched out in orderly file over a quarter of a mile. Since they were medics, the Army had issued him and Seamus fine horses. For that, he was truly thankful.

"Looks to be something important that's got them in such a hurry. Wanna go see?" Seamus eyed him with a spark of curiosity.

At James's nod, they galloped to the front of the column, hoping to garner some information.

The scouts saluted General Cox as their horses skidded to a halt. The general returned in kind. "Your report, Private."

"Sir, the Rebels are dug in along the far ridge overlooking the Mud River. Looks to be about five or six hundred militia. They got a real clear shot at the bridge from there, General."

"We have to cross that bridge." Brigadier General Jacob D. Cox scrubbed his beard with long fingers. Though only a few years James's senior, the man carried with him the respect afforded men twice his age. His reputation preceded him as an avid abolitionist and man of great conviction.

The general turned a somber face to the officer on his left. "Colonel Woodruff, you will take five companies to traverse that bridge and tear down those rebel forces."

"Yes, sir." The colonel saluted and took off to sprint the length of the column.

"Major Hill, I want you and your assistant to hold steady. There will be casualties. The men on that bridge will be sitting ducks until they can get across." General Cox removed a kerchief from his coat pocket and mopped his face.

The bulk of the troops followed behind the advance companies, halting 200 yards shy of the bridge. Infantrymen from the 2nd Kentucky Regiment fell in six men abreast, before approaching the bridge. Holding formation, they fixed bayonets.

The hair on James's arms rose as if a lightning storm threatened instead of hundreds of Confederate troops. He took in the faces of those in the formation. Many held focused determination, but more showed eyes that darted about, sparking of fear. He'd been told that most of these men were raw recruits, never having seen battle. Even the horses danced against the tension that floated through the men.

On order, they advanced double-quick to cross the covered bridge. As Union troops emerged on the other side of the Mud River, the Confederate militia opened fire.

James watched in horror as first one, then more Federals fell. Both armies exchanged fire, Woodruff's men suffering heavy casualties. Smoke blurred the scene for a moment, then the repeated command to charge carried across the river.

Union troops pushed up the hill, stumbling on the rough shrub and tree-speckled terrain. Those with unspent ammunition returned fire, continuing the charge all the way to the ridge, bayonets leading the way.

When the first two Rebel militiamen fell, the rest disappeared from view. Immediately, the Confederates retreated and conceded the ridge to Woodruff's men.

James and Seamus kicked their horses into a full run, crossing the bridge. James dismounted, pulled his supply bag from the saddle, and sprinted to the first body. It was no use. Vacant eyes stared up from a face yet to see a razor.

He rushed to another fallen soldier. The man was stirring, and in James's assessment, appeared unharmed. A dark-haired private clutched his thigh, writhing in pain. James tore the blue fabric of his pant leg to expose a fist-sized, jagged divot of flesh. He yanked a bandage roll from his bag and tightly wrapped the wound to staunch the bleeding for now.

"You'll be fine, Private. Take this." James handed him a canteen and a dose of morphine. He motioned to the wagon of wounded and it came to a stop. "Over here!" Two privates jogged to his position to carry the injured man to the conveyance.

Seamus's voice filtered through the chaos, calling to him. "James, this one's needin' you. I don't know what else to do." He looked down at the soldier, prostrate on a lush patch of clover. "He's alive, but I cannot stop the bleeding." A swipe of crimson colored Seamus's brow and blood painted both arms up to the elbows.

The soldier coughed feebly, gasping ragged breaths as blood bubbled from the corner of his mouth. James knelt on the ground, but before he could see to the flow of blood, with a violent shudder, the private expelled the dark, choking liquid. A metallic scent brushed the air. In the next instant, the man stilled.

James stretched his hand to close the young man's eyes. Sorrow twisted his heart as he imagined a mother back in Ohio, penning her son a letter, oblivious that, even before she put ink to paper, death had already claimed him.

Minutes blurred into more than an hour as James and Seamus triaged and managed the loading of wagons carrying the wounded. The subtle symptoms of shock numbed James's mind as his body continued working. Earlier, he had battled the need to vomit. Now this.

Soldiers eventually loaded the dead atop the caissons to be transported to the next fortification for a proper burial. Five deaths, eighteen wounded. James vowed never to forget those two numbers. In the months to follow, his logic told him, there would soon be too many to remember.

Seamus and James tended to the wounded the best they could in the wagon as it rocked and bounced down the uneven road toward Charleston. In just a few hours, the Kanawha Brigade would make camp with plans to continue on in the morning.

Once at camp, Seamus cleaned wounds while James proceeded with treatment. He had no training in the care of gunshot wounds, so he greatly appreciated the army-issued medical volume, which now lay open on a nearby trunk. An apprentice again, he was confident he would find himself consulting the pages of this tome with regularity.

"I'm thanking the Lord we've not come to lose another soul this evening." Seamus tossed bloody water from a basin into the weeds and refilled it with clean water for his hands. "This whole affair would've been a far bit worse if those Rebs had stood their ground to fight after our men charged that ridge."

"I'll be happy when we can get these boys to a hospital." James adjusted the mosquito netting over the last of the wounded. Mosquitos thrived in the sweltering heat of a Virginia summer and the acrid scent of blood attracted them in swarms.

James's thoughts begrudgingly transported him to a time in his youth. He was again sitting at the supper table with his family. A house girl, less than his own young age of ten, stood nearby, waving a large frond to circulate the stifling air in the room. Her skinny arms lifted the giant leaf rhythmically for the entirety of the family meal, even throughout dessert. He remembered because as he ate the blackberry cobbler with clotted cream; he watched a tear trickle down her glistening cheek. A single tear.

When her eyes found him looking, she jerked to attention, fear shading her flushed face. At that moment, all he could do was wonder why they didn't just eat outside, where the cool breeze made the heat tolerable. Then that little girl wouldn't have to keep waving that big frond.

"Major Hill?" General Cox's voice roused him. James and Seamus saluted, and the General waved them off. "How do our wounded fare, Doctor?"

"We are fortunate to have sustained no additional fatalities this evening, sir." James closed the book and returned it to his knapsack.

"I understand this was your first engagement?"

"Yes sir, that is correct."

"Might I have a word with you, Major?"

James walked from the pallets of wounded toward the campfire. The General plucked a glowing twig from the fire and lit his pipe. He puffed several times before a coughing spell seized him.

"Are you well, General?" Concern drew James a step closer.

"Never mind that." He swatted at a mosquito and then puffed on the pipe. "I dare say none of this"—he motioned to the wounded—"is something that you or I would have chosen, if given the choice, Major. I'm a lawyer and a politician. I belong on the Ohio State Senate floor by day, and by night, in my home, surrounded by family.

"The thing is, there is no choice for me in this. As a father, it is my duty to make this world a better place for my six children, and a united country without the blight of slavery is just that—a better place."

"I couldn't agree with you more on slavery, General. Although, I fear, we may not agree on the right of a sovereign state to remain sovereign, if its citizens so desire." Had he overstepped his bounds? "I do, however, believe that freedom for all people, regardless of skin color, trumps the Secesh's desire to be left unmolested."

"I see." The General cast his gaze into the night sky. His cheeks undulated until his lips lifted from the pipe stem and a cloud of smoke vanished into the darkness. Cupping the bowl with his fingers, he angled the pipe to one side, clenching it in his teeth. "I have a degree in theology from Oberlin College, Doctor. Were you aware of that?"

"No, sir, I was not."

"The reason I did not pursue ministry, but a different course of service to my fellow clutch of humanity is not simple. In any capacity I've served—whether it be as a lawyer, school superintendent, or senator—I've endeavored to seek God's purpose for my life. Sometimes, it has seemed that purpose lies unmoving, beneath a wilted pile of blossoms that once heralded the oncoming rush of spring—its identity unknown for a season." He removed the pipe and his shoulders sagged in tandem with a sigh.

"This is one of those times, Doctor. Instead of blossoms, however, I fear this time the purpose lies sleeping beneath piles of young bodies, bloodied by the ages-old collusion of piety and willfulness."

James stood unmoving, not knowing how to respond and not wanting to interrupt the General's reflection.

"Psalm thirty-six, eleven: Let not the foot of pride come against me, and let not the hand of the wicked remove me." The General faced James. "We will win this war. It may take three months or three years, but we will win it. As God empowers me, I will be a force to be reckoned with. And, amidst the repercussions of that force, Doctor, you are in a position to herald a reminder of its purpose, though for a season it lies unmoving, beneath the bodies of our brave men."

"Yes, sir." A weight of understanding pressed James's deliberation. An enormous burden indeed was cast upon this man's shoulders.

"Get your sleep, Major. We have a long march ahead of us tomorrow."

"Yes, sir. Goodnight, General."

∞

Fayette County

Augusta ripped off another strip of an old shirt and handed it to Melinda Jane. Together, they worked to tie up the gangly arms of the tomato plants. Best get it done while the dew still supples the plants.

"Looks like this year's crop is gonna be better than in a long while." Melinda Jane straightened the maple branches she'd stuck into the moist ground.

"I just wished old Rupert hadn't led the hens to forage on the lettuce. It's time to keep them penned until the garden's bolted." Augusta shook her head. It seemed like something was always working against her. The chickens had done a fine job of keeping down the weeds, but now the harder work of everyday hoeing would have to be a priority.

Will picked another pea pod and dropped it into a bowl.

Her little sister refused to wear an apron, so she didn't have a readymade pouch for picking. Augusta pushed back a smile and shook her head. She'd not make a mountain out of that mole hill.

The sound of horses reached their ears. Before the riders even came into view, Fin and Zander were in the barnyard, each of them armed.

"That's far enough!" Fin shouted.

The two riders pulled up short. One stranger sported a black hat and vest, looking something like a dandy. His horse pranced as his eyes scanned the farm. The other wore a cowhide jacket with uneven fringes dangling from its stained yoke. His jaws pumped beneath a scraggly black beard as he worked a chaw, keeping one hand on his gun belt.

Augusta shooed her sister into the house and whispered for Melinda Jane to bring the pistol. Her friend followed Will through the back door.

She stood at the rear corner of the house, watching, praying there'd be no cause for trouble.

"Not very neighborly of you folks," the dandy said, presenting his palms in surrender. "May I dismount?" He flashed a painted-on smile.

Augusta sucked in a breath, eyeing the pearled handle protruding from his gun belt.

"I don't recollect you being a neighbor of ours, mister. State your business." Fin trained his gun on the dandy as he dismounted. The barrel of Zander's gun was still focused on the other rider.

"Robert Billett is the name, sir," the dandy said, "and this is my associate, Mr. Laurence Marsh. I have assigned us the noble task of procurement for our men in arms against the Yankees—to preserve our fair and sovereign state of Virginia."

"Is that right?" Fin's aim held steady. The dandy lowered his hands a mite, but Fin cut off the motion with a threatening glower.

Melinda Jane appeared and handed Augusta Pap's old single-shot pistol. "I sure hope you won't need this," she whispered.

"I am prepared to offer good Confederate money for able horses and meat cattle. May I reach into my pocket, sir, to show my sincerity?" The man lowered one hand, and Fin moved two strides closer.

"If you want to keep that pretty little face of yours from looking like it was caught in a bear trap, you'd best get back on that horse and ride away."

The dandy reached for his gun and Fin clipped his chin hard with the butt of the shotgun. The man staggered. A shot rang out, and his partner screamed in pain, clutching his hand as his revolver fell to the ground.

Augusta lowered her pap's smoking pistol.

As the first man staggered off-balance, Zander seized the opportunity to land a punch to his gut. And a right cross to his chin. He hit the ground hard, his face dredging the mud.

"Help me get this varmint into his saddle." Fin seized the dandy's arm. Zander grabbed the legs and together they hoisted him over his saddle. They handed the reins to his partner, who was still gripping his hand to his chest.

"Get on out of here, and don't be coming back. I see you on our land again, I'll kill you!" Fin spit the last words with venom as hatred flamed in his eyes.

Augusta flinched at her brother's words. What was this war doing to her family?

Fin scowled, watching until the two strangers disappeared at the bend in the lane.

Two pistols lay in the dirt. Zander picked them up. "We might be needing these," he said as nonchalantly as if he were gathering eggs.

"This is only the beginning." Fin inhaled a long breath and let it out.

The screen door banged shut, and Bertie stepped onto the porch. "W . . . what happened?" His mouth dropped as his eyes froze on the firearms.

"I reckon I'll be sleeping in the barn for some time to come," Zander said, handing the guns to Fin.

Fin ruffled the boy's hair. "We both will. No one's laying a hand on Rampart, don't you worry."

Sixteen

SCARY CREEK, VIRGINIA

July 17, 1861

James scratched his beard, shaking away the lingering grogginess. He stood to stretch, easing himself to his full height as muscles and tendons complained. The night had been long, filled with specters from his past. All much too real. He made his way to a bucket, picked up the dipper, and poured water over the back of his neck. A delightful shiver purged the last bit of sleep from mind and body. Today, he would transition into a different nightmare.

Yesterday, a detachment had returned from an altercation with Rebel lookouts at the mouth of the Poca River. Scary Creek, on the west side of the Kanawha River, was occupied by Patton's Kanawha Riflemen, now Company I. This morning, General Cox's forces would advance to the mouth of Scary Creek.

"You ready, Doc?" Seamus asked, stuffing provisions into his knapsack. "The wounded are already loaded. We'll see them to Camp Pocatallico after we cross that bridge this morning."

James pulled his gear together and checked his medical bag. He grabbed a couple more fists of bandages and stuffed them into his pockets. "I don't think a body can ever be prepared for this, Seamus, my man." As the cavalry moved out ahead of the main force, James and Seamus mounted and galloped toward the rapidly forming column.

James could do nothing but wait. He was a reluctant observer to a tragic scene. Command ordered Captain George's Ironton Cavalry to secure the ridge while infantry prepared to take the fortified bridge.

Men painstakingly rolled batteries into place. James's stomach churned in anticipation of the canister and shot that would soon rain down on the Rebels who were dug into the opposite side of the creek. Confederate artillery was already positioned to block a Union advance.

Colonel Sedgewick of the Kentucky Volunteers bellowed orders. Both sides exchanged shots. As bullets found their mark, muffled grunts of the fallen plucked a chord of grim reality—with or without him, men would die here today. The rattle of musket fire intensified, driving Rebel pickets back from their position on Scary Creek.

When the Union Cavalry appeared, it drew enemy cannon fire, then vanished again. Long-range cannonade dotted the banks, pitching dirt high into the air. Cox's men were not fairing as well, having had less time to position their artillery.

The leading regiments charged the bridge, spirited shouts urging them forward only to be beaten back by heavy Rebel fire. James watched with rapt attention as once more they tried. Forced back again, they sustained heavy losses.

He recognized the flashy green of Captain Patton's Riflemen as the altercation grew and casualties mounted. Col. Lowe of the 12th Ohio Infantry ordered more men into the fray. The sheer number of Federal fighters forced back the Rebels.

But Rebel reinforcements soon offset their retreat. Hours of fighting ensued, with little ground relinquished.

James and Seamus had at first hung back, out of the range of enemy fire. It wasn't long before soldiers were dragging fallen comrades to the rear of the fighting for treatment. Soon, however, the artillery fire pinned down many of the medics attempting to retrieve those in need of medical attention.

James grabbed up the green flag, pitching it to Seamus. "Let's go!" As he sprinted into the black powder fog, his stomach protested the reek of burning sulfur. He soon reached the bridge where the injured were dragged onto the bank in full view of the Confederate guns.

Seamus stabbed the flag into the rugged earth, then grabbed bandages from his knapsack.

James rolled one soldier to his side to examine his bloodied back. No use—the wound was too invasive. Thankfully, he didn't seem in pain. The hair on the back of James's neck bristled at the rush of a bullet which pelted the mud in front of him.

He moved in an awkward crouch to the next soldier, who clutched his arm in pain. Blood oozed between splayed fingers, feeding the flow down to his wrist. James wrapped the arm, moving the man's hand in increments as the bandage pressed into the wound.

A cacophony of wild yells filled the air, and James looked up to see the bold green coats and gold buttons of the Kanawha Riflemen. They charged as one body. Swords clashed. Screams pierced the air as bayonets found their marks. Pistol shots perforated the din, and James glimpsed a familiar figure crumple to the ground.

Movement snagged the corner of his sight, and James turned. Two Rebels had waded into the water, approaching the bank where Seamus and James squatted in the mud. He glanced up at the green flag. Wasn't it supposed to offer protection?

Time stalled. A Rebel aimed at Seamus's back.

"We're medics, man!" James screamed as the nightmare unfolded.

Seamus turned, pulled his pistol, and fired. His bullet pierced the man's neck. The other Rebel, his site on Seamus, pulled back the flintlock. At once, James's hand clasped his revolver. He squeezed the trigger, mesmerized by the shock in the man's eyes just before he fell face-first into the murky water. James stared, unblinking, as the water turned red, then charcoal.

Just as an order sounded for the third charge across the bridge, voices lifted above the din. A rhythmic shouting in the distance. No. *Singing?* Red-clad Confederates marched into the fray—a fighting chorus of men belting the words to *Bullets and Steel*.

Their spirited tune rallied the Rebels as they regained momentum to once more crush against the Federals. James's attention was drawn to the Confederate ground. There, like ants emerging from an anthill, reinforcements appeared three and four at a time, zigzagging through the trees, their numbers multiplying as they barreled toward the creek.

"Fall Back! Fall Back!"

James and Seamus scrabbled up the bank. In one swift movement, Seamus hoisted a man onto his back, and his thick legs propelled him toward the stream of retreat. James knelt on the ground and turned over a green-coated body. Dirt tarnished the gold braids that decorated the sleeves. Austin Kennedy's blank eyes stared into the sky, his chest crimson.

"No!"

James raked trembling fingers over his friend's eyes. His breath came in waves. He pounded his fist into the ground. Jagged rocks clung to his hand. One sliced deep, oozing red drops.

Still clutching the green flag, he stood and sprinted toward the rear with the rest of his infantry.

After four hours of fighting, they'd been out-manned and gained no ground. *Senseless!* Senseless. The word repeated in his mind, claiming a pulse of its own.

Camp Pocatallico, Kanawha River

"You all right, Doc?"

James looked up at Seamus, blinking his vision into focus. He pinched the bridge of his nose with two fingers. "I'm sorry. Did you say something?"

"You're not looking to be so bushy-tailed this mornin'. We'd best be checking on our boys. The General's calling a meeting at nine o'clock."

Seamus lifted the entry flap on the hospital tent for James to enter, but he just stood there, waiting for his eyes to adjust to the dim interior. He hadn't slept at all last night. Visions of the dead soldier face down in the water haunted him. Austin's unseeing eyes and a familiar dark face stole into the mix of cannon and musket fire, smoke, blood, the sound of a whip, his finger squeezing the trigger. He'd vomited twice during the night. Now he looked down at his hands. Hands committed to healing, not killing. He'd told himself, "*Never Again!*" But he did it. He'd pulled the trigger. If he hadn't, Seamus would be dead. He had to—didn't he?

"Doc! Off gatherin' wool, are ya?" Seamus's freckled hand rested on James's shoulder.

He looked up to find his friend's compassionate eyes shaded with concern. "I'm fine, Seamus. Let's get this done."

James stopped at the first cot, recognizing the face of the young man with a bandaged head. He looked over the neat rows of beds and the folded stacks of linens. Steamers coming down from the Ohio River supplied the camp regularly, and now a resident surgeon would tend the patients. James was confident these boys would have good care. He finished his examinations and left Seamus to carry out his instructions.

The whiff of boiled coffee made his stomach growl as he walked past cook fires. Clusters of men shared stories while they dipped from a common bucket to wash their muskets. They stacked them neatly, muzzles together forming a cone. He paused at a heavily guarded tent. It housed only prisoners who required medical attention.

Inside, a dozen Rebels lay on cots, affording him little more than walking room between them. One very familiar Confederate officer sat upright, arm in a sling.

James wished it hadn't come to this, but the situation certainly could've been worse. "Captain Patton, it seems we did not meet on the battlefield exactly, but here you are."

"Doctor Hill, I heard you'd accepted a position with General Cox's Army. Mark my words, you'll soon wish you'd accepted *my* offer. My men fought well, as I'm sure you Federals noticed while retreating." Captain Patton chuckled, but then grew serious. "How many did we lose, do you know?"

"I'm not privy to that information, Captain."

Seamus poked his head into the prisoner tent. "You're wanted for a meeting, Major Hill."

"Thank you, Corporal." James returned his attention to Captain Patton. "I don't know where you go from here, Captain. In all sincerity, whether now or at the conclusion of this ugly business, I hope you return healthy and whole to your wife and children."

"Thank you, Doctor, my hope also."

∞

James nodded to a nearby captain and sat down on the end of a splintery bench. He was out of his element like a sparrow among owls. Did he genuinely think he could make any kind of difference in this war? He was a doctor, not a soldier. It took more than a few weeks of training for a man to think the way these men think.

General Cox ordered those officers standing to be seated. "Men, as some of you already know, Captain Allen was one of the fallen at Scary. We've also confirmed that Colonels Norton, De Villiers, Neff, and Woodruff have been taken captive. That unfortunately leaves us dreadfully lacking in field grade officers, but I am hopeful we can arrange a prisoner exchange in the coming days."

The general turned his attention to a map tacked to a plank leaning against the wall behind him.

"On a brighter note, I am pleased to announce that General McClellan has thoroughly routed the Rebels at Rich Mountain, Laurel Hill, and along the line of the Baltimore and Ohio Railroad in the northern counties." He tapped the map and then motioned with a pencil as he spoke.

"General Rosecrans is now marching southward with a portion of his command to the valley of the Kanawha. Wise has begun a retreat back through the valley toward Lewisburg. Rosecrans's troops will enter the valley here, near Gauley Bridge. This flank movement will hem in Wise's Legion, cutting off his retreat. General Wise's troops will have no choice but to surrender or throw down their weapons and scatter to the hills.

"Captain George, I want you to immediately dispatch ten of your men to accompany Major Hill and Corporal McLaughlin to Gauley Bridge. Major Hill, you will commandeer a facility there to be used as a field hospital in the vicinity north of Gauley Bridge." He circled the tip of a pencil over the map. "We will remain here at the camp for a few days, then the bulk of our regiment will continue to follow Wise to ensure his retreat into McClellan's grip. Are there questions?" The General paused. "Dismissed, then."

The officers stood to disperse.

"Major Hill."

"Yes, General." James stepped aside, allowing the others to pass.

"Major, you will no doubt encounter Rebel activity, as my report shows that much of Wise's force is not retreating in orderly fashion. Many have taken to the wayside, molesting Union sympathizers and stealing what they need. Be watchful." The General extended his hand to James. "I hope to see you on the other side."

"Thank you, sir." James saluted and headed for his tent. So, his time had come. And he was on his own from here on. Only twelve men. How hard could it be to set up a field hospital in the path of enemy retreat?

∽

Fayette County

The dawn painted the barn in misty light as Fin tucked his bedroll into the corner stall. Extra arms and ammunition lay hidden nearby under a mound of straw—for just in case. He kicked Zander's foot. "Rise and shine there, sunshine." Zander flopped to his belly and moaned.

"Hallo to the barn!" A familiar voice. He shushed Coot and grabbed his rifle as had become his habit. He heaved the barn door open, its hinges groaning in reluctance. Fin squinted into the bright sliver that edged the horizon. Jimmy Lee Campbell sat tall on his horse, Midnight. Wearing a Confederate jacket.

"I've done it, Fin. I've gone and joined up with the Fayette County Mountain Cove Guards."

"Jimmy Lee, those boys aren't playing around. You're like-ta-git yourself killed," Fin jabbed good-naturedly—the way he and Jimmy Lee always bantered and joked. But this time he wasn't joking. Temper and gloom rose in a dance, tapping out a pang of regret. What could he say to make his friend understand the very real consequences of this decision?

"Aww shucks, Fin. Don't you got no more confidence in me than that? I'll come back a hero, you'll see. They'll pin medals on my chest whilst I be wearing a full uniform." He wiggled his eyebrows. "The gals like war heroes."

"I don't think you're taking this whole fighting thing serious."

Jimmy Lee dismounted. His gaze slid from the house to Fin, his expression earnest. "I came to say goodbye, Fin. And I was wondering..." He shuffled his feet, all awkward-like. At the sound of the front screen door, they turned. Gus trotted down the front steps. Her face looked freshly scrubbed, and one long, coppery braid trailed down her back.

"I thought I heard something out here." She joined her brother and his friend. Her smile faded as she noticed Jimmy Lee's jacket.

He snatched off his slouch hat. "Good morning, Gus. I just come by to say goodbye. I'm going off to fight the Yankees. Mm ... might I have a word with you?" He glanced at Fin, then back to Gus. "In private?"

"Certainly, Jimmy Lee." She took the arm he offered and strolled several paces away from Fin. They conversed within earshot, and Fin strained to hear their conversation. He silently scolded himself for not allowing them privacy, but kept his eyes and ears on the exchange anyway.

"I wonder if you'll do me the honor of allowing me to write to you whilst I'm away fighting them Yankees, Miss Gus ... Augusta?" Jimmy Lee scuffed the dirt with the toe of his boot, then looked into her eyes. The seriousness was unnerving. "Chances are good I won't be coming back, but it'd bring me great joy to get a letter from you now and then. Maybe keep me remembering the folks back home and what I'm fighting for."

Augusta. Jimmy Lee has never, ever called her Augusta.

Different emotions played across Gus's face. His sister would sacrifice her own desires before she'd dash the hopes of someone else. Even if that someone was Jimmy Lee. She smiled at his friend.

The same sad, knowing kind of smile he'd seen on her face when she'd soothe Bertie after a scolding—hurting right along with him. She'd see through Jimmy Lee's false bravado to the insecure bumpkin that he was.

"Of course, I'll write to you, Jimmy Lee." She squeezed his hand with both of hers. "God keep you safe." As she headed back toward the house, Jimmy Lee silently *whooped* and punched the air. He whirled and met Fin's eyes.

With no little difficulty, Fin kept a straight face. A mishmash of irritation and amusement coursed through him. You'd think the hobbadehoy had just proposed!

"You take care now, Jimmy Lee. I'll pray the good Lord keeps your fool head on those shoulders."

They shook hands, then Fin pulled his friend into a hug, clapping him sharply on the back. Jimmy Lee swung onto Midnight and trotted on down the lane.

Fin watched the dust filter through the air and settle back. The heaviness of his heart seemed to anchor his feet. Would he ever lay eyes on that corny grin again? *Lord, please keep that boy alive. I doubt he can see his way to do that himself.* At last, he returned to the barn. Zander had better be at his chores.

Seventeen

Fayette County

Augusta closed the worn Bible and set it on the bedside table. She brushed Pap's hair from his brow with care and pulled the bedsheet up to his neck. He'd fallen asleep again as he often did when she read him the Scriptures. Their music lulled him into a peaceful respite most every time. Hopefully, he'd rest for the next couple of hours before he'd need another vapor treatment.

"We've got company." Melinda Jane appeared in the doorway, a basket of radishes and greens under her arm.

Augusta lifted her Pap's shotgun from the pegs on the wall. With it loaded and primed, she pushed through the front door. Fin and Zander already stood in the barnyard. A single rider, their neighbor, pulled his old nag to a stop. To look at the horse, you'd expect her to drop dead any minute. Hector Dorton was a simple man with a small farm over towards Gauley Bridge.

Coot recognized him, stopped barking, and padded over to sit next to Bertie at the barn entrance.

Fin strode out to meet his neighbor and hooked his fingers over the mare's bridle. "Is something wrong, Mr. Dorton? Where's your gelding?"

Augusta lowered her firearm and joined them. Seemed the unexpected was just part of life these days. Seeing Mr. Dorton like this kicked up a cloud of curiosity and concern inside her.

"I came to warn you," Mr. Dorton said. "A group of Rebel soldiers showed up at my place earlier." He pulled off his hat and swiped an arm across his forehead. "They stole my horse, helped themselves to our foodstuffs, and near cleaned out the garden." Urgency tinged his voice and fire sparked his gray eyes. "I thank the Almighty that my Mamie was here with your Will, or heaven only knows what them soldiers might've done."

He crunched his hat back onto his balding head. "Don't you take chances, you hear? Keep your family close to home. Word has it that Wise's Legion is on the run from the Federals and his men have taken to the hills hereabouts."

"We're much obliged for the warning, Mr. Dorton," Fin said with a nod.

Augusta forced a smile through new concern about the girls' whereabouts. "Can I get you some cool water?"

"Thank you, but I'm gonna ride on up the road a-ways and warn a few more folks. Then I'm gettin' myself back home and stay put. No telling what a bunch of high-spirited soldiers looking to cause trouble might do." He waved his hat and kicked the old mare into a trot.

Fin wagged his head. "I doubt that old nag could be coaxed into a run if her tail was afire."

"Did he say Mamie was here? I haven't seen her. Come to think of it, I haven't seen Will for a couple of hours." Augusta returned to the house and knocked on her sister's door. No answer.

Inside the room, nothing looked out of the ordinary. Fear pricked the back of her neck and snaked its way to her belly. *Dear Lord, please let Will and Mamie be somewhere close by.*

Augusta and Melinda Jane searched around outside, calling for Will. They checked the barn, the chicken coop, the garden. They even walked out and checked the corncrib. There was no sign of the girls, and Augusta's uneasy feeling ripened to a panic.

"I'll see if they're down to Izzy's." Melinda Jane hitched up her skirt and took off running through the green field toward the little cabin over the rise.

Fin trotted out of the barn on his bay gelding, followed by Zander on Rampart. "We'll check the main road and see if the neighbors have seen them. We'll find them, Gus." Fin galloped off with Rampart a nose behind.

༺༻

Melinda Jane found Izzy sound asleep in his rocking chair on the front porch of his little one-room cabin. She opened the door and peeked inside, looking for Will. A small, spindled table had been pushed to one side, along with a wadded rag rug that normally covered the puncheon floor. Two simple chairs set at odd angles near the hearth. How strange . . .

"What yo doin' here, child?"

She startled at Izzy's voice and whirled.

"Yo nearly frightened this old man to death." He frowned for an instant, glancing into the disheveled room, then guided her by the arm, urging her back onto the porch, closing the door behind him.

No time to probe him with questions. "I'm looking for Will. Have you seen her?"

Izzy sat back down in the rocker. "Can't say I have. I been a-studying the insides of these eyelids for some time now."

"Poor night's sleep?"

"When you get to be as old as I is, you just sleep when you feels like it."

"If you see that girl, you tell her to skedaddle on home. Mr. Dorton came by and warned us about Rebels roaming around—stealing from people and causing trouble."

"I'll take me a little walk around—see if I see any sign of her. I'll be praying for protection for that girl. I loves her like my own." Izzy grinned and squeezed her hand. His gappy smile melted away the peculiar questions poking her thoughts.

She kissed him on the forehead. "I know you do."

∞

James, Seamus, and their escort kept to the dusty Kanawha turnpike most of the way from Charleston, knowing the Rebel army would likely avoid the open arteries. They'd been fired upon twice, the shooters hastily retreating into the trees.

If Wise's Legion was looking to make their way to the safety of Lewisburg, as General Cox had said, any altercations along the way would only slow them down. Just as reported, James witnessed signs of the Rebels' retreat all along the way.

At one point, James and his men had come upon a campsite—the fire and coffee still warm. The Rebels had fled in such a hurry that they left their tents and food behind. Seamus insisted they take advantage of the hospitality, so they spent a bit of time there, eating their fill and resting the horses.

James took in the main street of Gauley Bridge. No sign of General Rosecrans's men. So, his small contingent was the first Union presence in the sleepy little town. A few citizens meandered between buildings before scurrying out of sight. Only the clip clop of their Federal mounts broke the stillness of the suddenly deserted streets.

While the horses drank from the town watering trough, James visited the mercantile. It was one of only a few businesses at the tiny stop, but he was sure that in a town this size, where everybody knew everybody's business, the store owner would be the one to supply the information he sought.

James approached the counter of Jackson's Mercantile, wishing he wasn't wearing a Union uniform. Sentiments in this part of Virginia leaned overwhelmingly toward the Confederate cause.

"What can I do for you, officer?" The gray-haired man in the yellowed apron didn't smile at first. Abruptly, his eyebrows lifted. "Why, you're a Yankee, ain't you?" His lips curved into a welcome as he offered his hand to James. "The name's Jackson."

"I'm Major Hill." James removed his glove to shake the man's hand.

"Are you boys here to stop those Confederate raiders? They come in and near cleaned me out. Would've given them some food if they'd asked, but they just poked a gun into my face and took plumb near all of it. You're welcomed to what's left." The store owner pulled a small sack of rice from behind the counter.

"That won't be necessary, Mr. Jackson, but thank you for your kind offer. I'm actually after some information." James tossed a penny on the counter and took the last piece of licorice from a jar. "I'm a doctor with the Kanawha Brigade, and I've come to set up a field hospital. Might you know of a farm north of here with a good-sized barn I could utilize?"

The man rubbed his chin. "I don't know now. Most folks around these parts have kin fighting with the Confederacy."

"Most of the western counties of Virginia are in Union hands now, sir. I daresay the balance of the counties west of the Alleghenies will be overtaken by summer's end." James pulled at the licorice and chewed for a moment. If only he could say the same for this whole miserable affair.

"Can you think of a family, perhaps, that is neutral in their leaning and would have a heart for the wounded of either side?" James slid two U.S. dollar bills across the marred wood counter.

The man's eyes widened. "You just won me over, Major. I ain't seen nothing but graybacks since this whole affair started, and I'll take United States currency over a Confederate promise any day of the week." He snatched up the bills and jabbed them into his apron pocket.

"Go on out this way," he gestured to the east, "over the bridge and head on up the road going north along about five miles. There'll be a big weeping willow tree off to the left. Turn right up that lane. Two-story white house, with a beauty of a barn. You can't miss it. Just ask to talk to Fin or Gus."

After watering the horses, James's men mounted, preparing to leave. Mr. Jackson emerged from the store with two bulging flour sacks. "Take these with you. I'm heading up north to my brother's place in Wheeling until all this is over."

"Much obliged." James said, signaling the soldiers to take the bags. He headed off toward the bridge, hoping the man's recommendation proved feasible.

He breathed in the woodsy scent. Surely this had to be the prettiest part of the entire state of Virginia. Streams and gaps crisscrossed the lush hills. Views from the high ground revealed massive groves of maple and hemlock. They painted the foreground of the rising Alleghenies to the east. Natural rock formations poked out from the verdant foothills. The original flat terrain near the river had changed as they followed the winding road, so they'd been riding a gentle roller coaster for the last mile.

"What the . . ." One of the men ducked his head, drawing his pistol. He pranced his horse in a circle.

The unit pulled up, drawing their carbines. James braced for the report of a rifle. The sound of a bullet cracking against bone. The thud of a body falling to the ground. His quickened senses burst on alert.

A second soldier flinched, grabbing his head. While others searched the side of the trace, James looked up. Something rock-hard pelted him on the cheek, and he winced. Two other soldiers clutched their heads and cursed. Following James's gaze, they aimed into the trees.

"Hold your fire, men!"

Green butternuts dotted the ground and laid scattered across the road. In the branches, a boy grasped a tree limb with one hand, aiming to pitch a handful of the walnuts with his other.

"Hold it right there!" James aimed his pistol.

"Well, I'll be doggoned," Seamus said. "If that don't beat all. The mighty Union cavalry attacked by a mere boy. I'll teach you a thing or two, boy-o!"

"Come down now, and no one will hurt you," James ordered. "What's your name, son?"

"Will," came the reply as the lithe figure crouched on the branch partially hidden by the leaves. In one swift movement, he dangled from the branch on which he'd been standing and then dropped the last five feet to the ground.

Seamus dismounted and snatched him up by the arm. "I got a mind to paddle you all the way up the road, me boy-o!" The lad clamped his mouth shut and set his jaw, but a tear trickled from one eye.

Seamus fidgeted. "Aww . . . Get up on that horse, you." He gave the boy a kick in the backside to get him started in the right direction. Seamus mounted first, then swung Will up behind him. "You give me a lick of trouble, and I'll be hauling you over me knee." Seamus wagged his head, his lips tight. "Hugger-mugger milksop," he muttered.

The Union detachment turned their mounts up the lane at the big willow tree. The place looked deserted. James took in the buildings. It was the right farm all right, just as Mr. Jackson had described. Not even so much as a dog bark broke the stillness.

The riders came to a halt when the front door of the house opened. A young woman wielding a shotgun stepped onto the porch. A white apron covered part of a red gingham dress. Another young woman appeared from the side of the house with a pistol.

"State your business," the woman on the porch hollered.

"I'm looking for Fin or Gus." James raised his hands in a gesture of peace. "I'd simply like to speak with them."

The young woman approached, tipping her head as if trying to get a better look at him.

The Dabney woman from the bank! "You?"

"I thought I recognized you—the rude doctor from Charleston. I see you're a Federal officer now." She eyed the other soldiers.

"Rude?" His mind bounced back to the bank meeting. He was rude? "I won't be a bother to you, Miss Dabney. I simply would like to speak with Fin or Gus."

"Well now, let me see . . ." She lowered the shotgun. "Fin isn't available at the moment, so I reckon you'll have to deal with Gus."

"All right then, where can I find him?" The less he had dealings with a Dabney, the better. The name alone scraped at his bitter bone and plunged his mind into a vat of unwelcome memories.

Seamus was the last rider to pull into the yard. Without warning, his disgruntled passenger slid from the still-moving horse to the ground. "Gus!"

"Gus? *You're* Gus?" James looked from Miss Dabney to the boy, then back again. He scowled as the pieces of the puzzle fell into place. *This is the Dabneys' farm?*

"Will? What are you doing with these soldiers?" Now Miss Dabney aimed her gun at Seamus, her eyebrows puckered above blistering green eyes. "If you so much as touched a hair on Will's head, you'll be dismounting head first."

Seamus raised his hands. "I'm not the offender here, ma'am. 'Tis the boy who attacked us."

"What is he talking about, Will?" The woman lowered the barrel again.

The boy hitched up his britches, hung his head, and tromped up to stand next to Miss Dabney.

"Explain. Now," the woman demanded.

"Mamie and I went picking wild berries, and when we got back to her place, her mama said there'd been trouble." The boy's words tumbled out in one long string. "Rebels had come to their farm and stole Mamie's pap's horse and a bunch of food from the house." He seemed to run out of steam.

"And?"

"Well . . . er . . . I sorta picked a heap of butternuts and planted myself up in a tree down the road so I could sabotage those Rebels if they rode by. I thought these soldiers was them." Lower lip protruded and shoulders slumped, Will rammed each hand into a pocket and fixed his eyes on the ground.

"In the house. Now. I'll deal with you later, Willamina Dabney!"

James jerked his head back, then glared at a slack-jawed Seamus.

Seamus stuttered, "W . . . Willamina? You mean *he's* a *she*?" He whisked off his hat and scratched at his unruly hair.

"I believe you may owe that young lady an apology, Corporal McLaughlin." James struggled to school a grin, then wiped it clear with his hand.

"I still haven't heard why you're here, Doctor," Miss Dabney said. "Why don't your men water their horses? We can talk over here." She motioned to the two rockers on the front porch.

James looked at this woman afresh. Her hair wasn't the bright red-orange of Seamus's. It was darker, richer—and a lot of it, twisted up onto and behind her head like a thick length of rope. A spray of freckles dotted her face. She laid the shotgun on the porch floor, then claimed a rocker.

James took the second chair. "General Cox of the Kanawha Brigade has sent me ahead of the main body of troops. He's tasked me with finding a structure of sorts to be used as a field hospital in these parts—should the need arise."

"What does that have to do with us?"

James surveyed the barn. The vertical board structure with a stone foundation was impressive, much larger than most. "Your barn would be perfect, Miss Dabney. Your family would be doing a great service for the Union Army and your countrymen." James waited, afraid to say more, hoping to keep a hasty "no" at bay. Truth be told, he'd already made up his mind. He'd rather take it with permission than commandeer the building. Her silence was a hopeful sign.

"I'll have to talk to Pap about this." She indicated the house with a tip of her head, then stood.

He jumped up. "I'd be happy to explain the situation to your father."

"I noticed you didn't mention the 'why' behind this location for your hospital, Doctor." She tipped her head to the side, hands on her hips, her eyes studying James as if searching for a hidden snare in the grass.

She has grit. He'd give her that.

"I can't lie to you, Miss Dabney. Wise's Legion is in full retreat, and they're headed this way. General Rosecrans's troops are in route to head off the Rebels at Gauley Bridge. These hills are already littered with Confederate guerillas and deserters. It is possible that things around here could get ugly.

"I might also mention, as I seem to be spilling all the 'whys,' that there will be armed Union soldiers here at your farm day and night. I can't think of a safer place to be if Rebels are scattered about the countryside." There, he'd said it. All there was to say. Now, if the Dabney clan would just listen to reason so he wouldn't have to take the barn by force.

Two riders galloped into the barnyard, both wielding rifles. They skidded to a stop, eyeing the soldiers.

He needed no more surprises today.

Eighteen

Fayette County

Alarm sluiced through Augusta, raising all of her fears in an instant as she ran to meet her brothers. Whatever it was, riled Fin up good.

Fin swung down from his horse. "We saw tracks heading up our lane and got worried. Are you all right? Is there a problem?" He aimed his question at Gus, but his eyes bore into the doctor.

Zander fingered his rifle. When his brother signaled, he put it back in his saddle scabbard. He ruffled his brows in protest and continued to eye the soldiers.

Having followed her brothers in, Coot's full attention settled on the interlopers, hackles raised like a stand of wheat, and a low growl vibrating from his throat.

"There's no problem," Augusta assured him. "Will is in her room—I'll explain later." She motioned to the officer. "This is Doctor . . . uh, Major Hill, from Charleston. Major, these are my brothers, Fin, and Zander."

"Pleased to meet you, Mr. Dabney. I was just explaining to Miss Dabney here that the Union Army would be most appreciative of the use of your fine barn to serve as a hospital."

"I don't see any wounded, Major Hill."

The doctor explained the inevitable collision of forces and, yes, there would be wounded. "I'd like to speak with your father, if I may."

Fin's eyes shifted to his sister in unspoken communication. He was willing to trust her on this, for that she was thankful.

"Fin and I will discuss your proposition with our pap in time, Doctor Hill. Why don't you and your men make yourselves comfortable in the barn for now? I'm sure you could use the rest. We can't squeeze all of you into the house, but I can bring a pot of ham and beans out for your men. You are welcome to join us at the table."

∞

Augusta balanced a tray in one hand and carried neatly folded cloths in the other. She looked up at this brother of hers with irritation. If only he'd stop his fussing.

Fin's voice was hushed. "Are you really going to burden Pap with this, Gus?" He pushed open the bedroom door and his sister entered first.

"It *is* his barn, Fin."

She set the tray on the bedside table, then gently touched her father's hand. "Are you awake, Pap?"

"I'm awake, daughter." Pap's words ruckled before sipping from a proffered cup of water. "What was the commotion earlier? Bertie said something about soldiers."

Fin removed his hat and dropped into the chair on the opposite side of the bed. "The long and the short of it is this, Pap. The Confederates are backing out of Western Virginia, coming right through here, and the Union Army is planning to cut them off. From the sound of things, there's liable to be a goodly amount of fighting hereabouts. There's a Union doctor out there who wants the use of our barn for a hospital."

"I see." Pap's voice was rough, but whisper soft.

Augusta squeezed water from a fresh rag and placed it across his brow. "The doctor says that with all the conflict bound to be in the area, we'd be real safe with Union soldiers here guarding the patients."

"What do *you* think, Fin?" Pap closed his eyes, taking a slow breath. Furrows of pain rolled over his eyebrows before he opened one eye. "Well?"

"I don't know what I think, Pap. On the one hand, it might be safer here for you and the young'uns, but I can't say I like having the barn turned over to the Yankees."

Augusta cocked her head, searching Fin's eyes for a clue as to what he was thinking. Surely there was a compromise to be had here. "Can't we put most of the livestock in one corner of the barn, using just a few box stalls? Then there'd be room to set up cots and such for the injured."

Fin stood; his face unreadable. He tapped his hat against his worn jeans. "Whatever you decide, Pap, I'll abide by." He hesitated, then walked out of the room, closing the door behind him.

"He's working at finding his way, you know," Pap said, squeezing Augusta's hand. "I think he's torn between joining the cause and protecting this family. Protecting your own is a powerful force for a man to wrangle."

"I reckon you're right." She knew Fin had been struggling, and apparently, so did Pap. "So, what do I tell Major Hill, the doctor?"

"I believe the war has come to our doorstep, daughter. I believe, too, that God will guide us through. Could be God brought those Federals here. I suppose we best oblige them."

"I'll tell the doctor at supper then, Pap. Are you feeling up to joining us?" Augusta paused at the door, but Pap's eyes were already closed, his breathing shallower.

∞

Hinges moaned as Melinda Jane pulled on the stove door, then let it drop with a thump. She gathered her apron in her hands and carefully lifted the first heavy skillet of cornbread from the oven and onto the worktable.

Will balanced a blue and white bowl overflowing with fresh string beans and set it on the table. Picking up two that had toppled out, she poked them into her mouth before her sister could see.

Augusta had already divided up the large pot of ham and beans, setting aside a larger portion for the soldiers. She set a pitcher of milk on the table and looked to her sister. "I think that about does it. Go ahead and call for supper, Will."

Melinda Jane hummed, trying to add just one more piece to the platter she'd piled high with wedges of cornbread. She nonchalantly followed Will out to the porch.

She kept to the edge of the front door so Will wouldn't catch her spying. Yes, sir. She'd find entertainment where she could get it.

The iron rod grasped in both hands, Will spread her stance wide. She took an exaggerated breath, stuck her tongue out the side of her mouth, and walloped that thing for all it was worth. No one could ring a call to supper like that girl. After a full minute, she relaxed her stance, dropping her hands. She waited until the tinny clatter of the triangle faded before silencing it with her fingers.

Will sucked in another breath, cupping her hands to her mouth and yelled loud enough to wake the hills, "COME . . . AAAND . . . GET IT!"

With a satisfied smile lighting her face, Will trotted into the house, right past Melinda Jane. Yep, nothing quite like it for amusement. She chuckled and followed Will back into the kitchen.

Melinda Jane lifted the bale of the heavy kettle. "Will, you follow with that platter of cornbread, and I'll wrestle this pot of beans out to the barn."

As she neared the barn, a soldier rescued the heavy pot from her, his smile friendly and disarming. "You didn't have to go to all that work, Miss."

She returned his smile with a bright one of her own. "You boys might be around these parts for some time to come, but tonight, anyway, you're our guests."

༄

Seated at the table with the rest of the Dabney family—nearly the rest, anyway—James shifted uncomfortably. The odors wafting from the dishes set before him coaxed a growl from his stomach. He glanced at the others self-consciously. It appeared everyone was waiting for something. Then Fin and his brother stood, their eyes on the doorway.

Only then did he realize that Willamina and a lovely young woman about Miss Dabney's age had entered the kitchen. He stood quickly. The young boy stood too, a frown on his face. It likely had something to do with the sharp nudge from Miss Dabney. The unknown young woman stifled a giggle with her hand.

"This is our friend, Melinda Jane Minard, Doctor Hill. She lives with us," Miss Dabney said.

"A pleasure to meet you, Miss Minard." James bowed slightly, then seated himself along with the others. Fin gave thanks, and Augusta offered the first platter of cornbread to James.

"Might your father be joining us, Miss Dabney?" He slid a wedge onto his plate, noting the perfect, dark golden crust, then passed the plate on.

"Not tonight, I'm afraid." She lowered her gaze. "Pap is sick, Dr. Hill. I believe it's the consumption. Our mama died from it a few years back, and this looks to be the same thing."

"I'd consider it an honor to look in on him when we're finished eating, Miss Dabney. And I look forward to meeting him."

"I would truly appreciate that, Doctor. And you'll be happy to know that Pap has given his permission for the use of our barn as a hospital." She smiled and shifted her gaze to her older brother.

Before her eyes left his, just for an instant, James glimpsed a spark of gold in their green depths. He'd seen nothing like it in all his years. A phenomenon? Deafening silence intruded on his moment of reflection. Heat crept up his neck as he realized every eye at the table was on him—including Miss Dabney's.

The corner of her mouth curled. "Dr. Hill? Please pass the string beans. You seem to be holding up the line." A giggle from the youngest brother hung in the air.

Food made its way around the long oak table, accompanied by recent news. Melinda Jane slapped at the young boy's hand for reaching across the table, and Willamina and Zander shared some silent joke between them, snickering about something.

James had names to match up with all the Dabney faces except the youngest—a boy he'd already found to be curiously entertaining. He had a look of mischief in his eye. James addressed the child. "I believe I've not been introduced to this young man. Your name is . . . ?"

"Bertie, sir."

"I suppose *Bertie* is short for Albert?"

"No, sir." Bertie sat straighter; his chin raised. "I am Bertram Eliakim—Bert. E. But you can call me *Bertie*." Laughter sprang from everyone around the table, save one. The fork froze in James's hand. He hadn't heard that name in years.

Bertie hung his head in mock disgrace. "There ain't nothing funny about a person's name."

That name. It pressed painfully on his bruised past. The food no longer appealed to him. He set down his fork too abruptly, and the laughter stopped. "I'm acquainted with another person by the name of Bertram Eliakim Dabney."

"Yes, sir, that would be our uncle, my pap's oldest brother," Zander said.

James stood numbly and dropped his napkin beside his plate. His supper sat like an anvil in his stomach. "Thank you kindly for the delicious meal, hospitality, and conversation. I shall take my leave now and retire to the barn with my men." He left the house in silence. He'd have to check on the senior Dabney another time.

∞

The *whoop whoop* of a whip-poor-will accompanied the steady rhythm of hooves as James's detachment of Union soldiers ventured toward Gauley Bridge. He and Seamus took up the rear, discussing the supplies needed to equip the hospital at the Dabney barn.

Confederates had scuttled several steamers, carrying supplies and coal. Hopefully, the provisions for the hospital had made their way from the Ohio down the Kanawha—at least far enough to be hauled by wagon the rest of the way.

A rifle blast disrupted the calm. The soldier directly in front of Seamus crumpled. He slid from his horse, striking the ground with a dusty thud.

"They're in the trees!" shouted one man. Another returned fire.

James held his mount to a tight circle, looking for the enemy. Another shot rang out, but this time he saw the powder flash and took aim with his revolver—a show of gold catching his eye before he squeezed the trigger.

The nicker and thrashing of horses, just beyond a thicket, gave away the position of more ambushers. Two of the Union soldiers advanced on the thicket, firing on three mounted Confederates who wove their way through the dense brush in retreat.

James dismounted and tended to his injured man. He was alive, but unconscious. A bullet had grazed him just above the ear. James reached into his pocket. Sure enough, he still had a roll of bandages. He staunched the flow of blood and bandaged the soldier's head.

The man's limp body was hoisted into a saddle, and Seamus swung up behind him. He managed the reins with one hand while holding the soldier upright against his chest.

"You return to the farm and take care of him, Seamus. I'll continue on to make sure we get all the supplies we need." James addressed a gangly blond soldier. "Hanley, you go with them. These woods are probably crawling with Rebels. Be careful. And Hanley—when you get to the Dabney farm, stand guard. Now, off with you."

What was it about those Rebels? The thought niggled at him. James kicked his horse into a trot and continued with the rest of the detachment toward Gauley Bridge. Then it struck him. Just after the muzzle flash, he'd seen the ornate gold stitching of a Kanawha Riflemen uniform.

∞

Fin wiped at his face with the yellow kerchief his mama had made for him. Finally, the last stall was clean. Now there were four box stalls, swept and ready for use by the Union Soldiers, plus the area along the west wall of the barn.

He'd kept much of the livestock inside of late, hoping to keep them from the hands of the Confederates roaming the area. They'd slaughtered the Meyers' heifer and pilfered eggs from most all the neighbors over the past couple of weeks.

Coot's frantic bark erupted from the yard. The kind of bark that meant trouble. Fin grabbed his rifle from the corner and headed out the door.

Three Confederate soldiers galloped up the lane. "Hold it right there!" Fin set his sight on the first one as they approached.

"We mean no harm, son. As you can see, we have a man in need of medical attention." Dirt streaked the officer's face. He sat tall in a high collared, gold trimmed coat. The man next to him gripped his upper arm with one hand, blood staining the length of his sleeve.

Gus approached, shotgun to her shoulder, her steps slow and eyes hooded with suspicion.

A lazy smile replaced the officer's sober expression. "Well, I do believe we have stumbled onto the Dabney farm, boys. You may lower your weapon, Augusta. Certainly, you know I hold no ill will toward you or your family."

"You know this Johnny?" Fin shot his sister a look that held a thousand questions.

Gus lowered the shotgun. Her lips pressed into a firm line. Regret, then resignation, painted her eyes. "I'll see to your wounded man, Mr. Fontaine. Bring him into the house."

Irritation chapped Fin's hide, and he wasn't afraid to let it show. "Gus?" He lowered his rifle, but only a couple of inches.

"This is Mr. Fontaine from the bank in Charleston, Fin. Since he holds our loan, I reckon we're obliged to see to his request." She turned and fairly marched into the house.

"This one stays outside." Fin pointed the barrel of his gun at the third Rebel. Fontaine nodded to the soldier.

"We will not lift a finger to one of our own, Mr. Dabney. You have my word as a gentleman," Fontaine said, signaling a dismount.

One of his own? Fin scowled, prodding the soldier toward the porch, where Zander stood, Pap's pistol in hand.

The injured man and Fontaine followed Gus into the house, and Fin trailed close behind. "Keep an eye on that one," he said to Zander, motioning for the third soldier to sit in the rocker on the porch.

Just this morning, the girls had started rolling bandages, piling them in a willow basket. Gus took a roll and placed it on the table. She passed a look to Melinda Jane, whose eyes gaped wide with questions.

Setting a bowl of warm water on the table, she dipped a rag and wrung it out. "Take off your shirt, please." She handed the soldier a second damp rag to wipe the blood from his fingers.

Once the wound was cleansed, she narrowed her gaze at the intruding piece of lead. The soldier grunted through gritted teeth as she used a sharp penknife to coax it out. She quickly pressed lint into the wound to staunch the bleeding.

Gus shook her head slightly, lifting her gaze to meet Fontaine's. "This is going to require some stitches. I'm sorry I don't have any painkiller."

Fin thought of the laudanum his sister kept for Pap. A spark of guilt was quickly snuffed. He shifted his stance, adjusting the hold on his rifle. Pap needed it far more than this Rebel. Fin figured if he could endure the removal of the bullet, he could endure the stitching.

Fontaine pulled a brass flask from his pocket and offered it to the soldier, who took several swigs. "You may proceed now, Augusta." He smiled at her and then chuckled when her brows dipped and she looked away. Fin checked a growl.

Melinda Jane tipped her head in a nearly imperceptible act of encouragement as Gus took a needle and thread from her outstretched hand. His sister measured a length, biting it off with her teeth, and then threaded the needle. Gently pulling the skin together, she stitched and Melinda Jane dabbed at the blood. At last, she knotted the thread and clipped it with the scissors.

With her usual smile long gone, Melinda Jane held the soldier's arm while Augusta wrapped it with the bandage.

The soldier stood. "Much obliged, ma'am." Desire colored his gaze as he took in the full length of Melinda Jane, though she didn't notice. Fin wanted to knock his tobacco-stained teeth clear through the back of his skull.

Fontaine gripped Gus's elbow. "I'd like to have a word with you, Augusta." He shot a look in Fin's direction. "Privately," he whispered in her ear—not soft enough for Fin to ignore, however.

∞

An uncomfortable shiver trickled down Augusta's spine when Edward whispered in her ear. *Who does he think he is?* She caught Fin's concerned expression. "Very well Mr. Fontaine." She turned to Fin and Melinda Jane. "Family, if you'll excuse us for a moment." She led the way into the sitting room.

Edward combed fingers through his dark beard, then reached for Augusta's hands. She relinquished only one. "Augusta, we both know you cannot hang onto this farm much longer. Have you produced a recent payment?"

"No, sir, I have not. With God's blessing, I will though, by the end of the month."

"I won't beat around the bush, Augusta." His hands cupped her shoulders. A smoldering desire darkened his eyes as they sought hers. "From the moment you walked into my office, you've laid siege to my heart. I regret the manner in which we parted ways all those years ago, but we've both done some growing up since. Wouldn't you say?" His eyes rippled over her body in an instant, then found hers. "I know you cared for me once, and you will again, in time."

"I was young." *Very* young.

He moved closer, and it struck her that he was quite handsome in his fancy uniform.

"Young and foolish, Edward." What did she know about things of the heart all those years ago? She took a step back.

"I can make all of your financial problems disappear. Say you'll be my wife and your family can live out the rest of their lives right here on this farm. I'll tear up the mortgage agreement."

A tangle of emotions squeezed Augusta's heart. She was repulsed by this bully and, at the same time, intrigued by his obvious attraction to her. Did he genuinely possess a certain compassion for her family? Was Edward Fontaine God's answer to her prayer to keep this farm and her family together?

"I . . . I can't give you my answer now, Edward. You must give me time." Her ears heard her voice say the words, but uncertainty covered her heart like a prickly blanket. A familiar sadness crept into the corners of her spirit. She pulled away from him and walked to the window.

"I'll return for you, Augusta. You *will* come to see that I have your family's best interest at heart."

Clutching the front of her dress with one hand, she leaned her head against the glass. The staccato in her chest matched the determined cadence of his boots on the wooden floor as he retreated through the hall and out the front door. She closed her eyes, unwilling to look beyond the glass to the land she loved, spread like a magnificent quilt, stitched with a generation of love and sacrifice.

Wasn't her own happiness a small price to pay for her family's future?

"Bertie? You want to tell me where you were and why?" Augusta's hands perched on her hips. Did she have the *mean look* on her face just now?

Bertie scratched at his cheek, then his chin. "I was chasing a ring-necked on account of Zander sayin' it's a Confederate snake. I figured if I caught one, I could say I caught me a Johnny Reb."

"Now how's a snake supposed to be a Confederate?" Will challenged, folding her arms across her chest.

Bertie reached into his pocket. "See? It's gray on the back with a yeller belly." Ten inches of headless snake body dangled from two fingers. His grin stretched his cheeks as he scratched at his face with his free hand.

Augusta angled away momentarily to hide her smile, then painted on her *mean face* again. "Bertram Eliakim Dabney, did you or did you not disobey and leave sight of the barn?" She pressed her lips together, then cocked her head to one side, mystified by the red blotches appearing across her brother's cheek and down his neck.

"Yes, ma'am." Bertie lowered the snake along with his eyes, fixing his disappointed gaze on the ground. His dirty fingernails scraped a white path down the side of his neck.

"Well, put that Confederate snake in the manure pile and come back into the house. I'd say you found yourself more than just a snake. I'd say you found yourself some poison ivy."

Izzy's uneven gait carried him from the direction of the barn. "Did I hear you call that a Confederate snake?"

Melinda Jane looped her arm through Izzy's. "You never heard of a Confederate snake? Has a gray back and a yeller belly." She grinned up at him, then shot a wink in Bertie's direction.

Augusta pointed to a bushel basket sitting on the ground piled high with red and yellow tomatoes. "How's your garden doing this year, Izzy? You want any of these tomatoes? We've got plenty for canning already."

"I believe I *will* take some of them home with me. There's always someone needin' the Lord's bounty."

"I declare, Izzy, you always know hungry people here abouts. You take whatever you can to help those in need." Augusta snagged Izzy's other arm and curled hers around it. "How about I get you some buttermilk and shoofly pie, and you can see if Pap is up to a visit?"

"Woo-hoo-wee! Lord, I got two lovely ladies on my arms. Ol' Izzy's done died and gone to heaven!" He chuckled, and the women pulled him closer, their laughter bubbling up to drown out his own.

∞

The wagon of supplies rolled into the barnyard, with men sprawling atop the cargo. Two horses followed along, tethered to the rear. James and his men guided their horses to the watering trough, then dismounted.

"Where's Corporal McLaughlin?" James asked Zander, who stood just outside the barn, rifle in hand.

"I'm here, Doc." Seamus strode from the barn, wiping his hands with a rag. "Been seeing to our boy." Seamus looked over the wagon, then let out a low whistle. "What you got there?"

"We ran into some trouble, I'm afraid. A few miles back down the road." James turned to the rest of the troops. "Let's get these men settled and the supplies unloaded."

Bertie ran from the house and raced over to James. A white paste dotted his face and painted his neck and arms.

"Well, what happened to you, soldier?"

Bertie snapped to with a serious salute. "I was wounded app . . . appre . . . catching me a Confederate snake, sir."

James eyed Miss Dabney. She had tried to stop Bertie before the boy reached him, and now her hands snagged him by the shoulders. She failed in her attempt to suppress a grin.

James raised one eyebrow. "Dare I inquire regarding said Confederate snake?"

"Yessir." Bertie still held his hand in salute. "It was gray on the back and had a yeller belly, sir—just like the Confederates."

Stifled snickers sounded from the men. James squatted down, eye to eye with Bertie. "Well done, soldier. Stand at ease." James glanced up at Miss Dabney. Her eyes drilled into Zander, who coughed back a laugh, then shrugged his shoulders. The teenager artfully averted his sister's gaze. Smart boy.

While Seamus saw to the unloading of the wagon, James turned his attention to the Rebel positioned on the tarp in the back. "We have wounded to deal with, Miss Dabney. Is there a family here about by the name of Sizemore?"

"Why yes, why do you ask, Doctor?"

"Because I have a young man over here who needs to go home."

Her brow furrowed. "Dear Lord," she whispered, rushing to the injured confederate. "Dirch? What did you go and do?" Her face fell, and she moved her hands over the boy's head and arms, searching frantically for an injury.

"I can't feel my legs, Gus. I can't feel a thing." Fear etched the young man's face. "Is Zander around?"

"I'm here, Dirch." Zander looked at his older sister, panic rolling across his features.

"Take me home, Zander. I wanna go home." Dirch's lower lip quivered. He squeezed his eyes closed, then opened them again. Zander seemed to crumble as he stretched his hand out to his friend. His trembling fingers sprawled across the top of the young Rebel's head. Soundless words filled the space of regret between the two boys, as both failed miserably to squelch the flow of tears.

James clasped Zander's shoulder with one hand. "You can use this wagon as soon as it's unloaded. Take this boy to his mama, Zander. I'm sorry, there's nothing I can do for him.

The tears in Zander's eyes tugged at James's heart. Another mother's son. This time, a friend of the Dabneys. A hand pressed his forearm, and he lifted his head. The pain in Miss Dabney's moist eyes and the weak curve of her lips spoke volumes. *Zander's friend.*

James pictured a very young Zander running through the grass with the boy, chased by a younger version of his sister. If only he could wipe away her grief. He covered her hand with his own.

His throat constricted. "I'm sorry." He could only mouth the words.

"He's in God's hands now." She offered a brave, quivery smile, then returned to her brother's side.

༄

James stood near the workbench-turned-operating table. It had been scrubbed clean with lye and moved to a spot directly beneath a beam from which to hang lanterns. On a smaller, nearby table, a book lay open—*The Practice of Surgery* by Samuel Cooper.

James lifted the tray from a varnished wooden box. It contained various sizes of knives—some with serration and some without—forceps, and a tourniquet. The bottom portion of the box held a saw, pliers, and a substantial clamp with a worm drive.

Like soldiers on parade—scissors, scalpel, suture, and needle awaited duty on a clean white field of linen.

"Are you ready, Doc?" Seamus adjusted the chloroform cone. Private Jürgen lay unconscious, his mangled arm washed clean.

"As ready as I'll ever be, Corporal. I need someone to hold the light."

"I can do that for you." Miss Dabney stood at the door and walked forward; a napkin-covered platter of fried chicken in her hands. "Here's something to eat. I assumed you were pretty busy. I guess I was right."

She set the platter down and tucked a couple of stray hairs into her auburn crown of braids. Lifting the lantern, she frowned at the patient's arm. "I'll keep the light on your hands as best I can."

"This is no task for a lady, Miss Dabney." James scowled.

"I'd say you can use all the help you can get, Doctor. I'd hate to see this poor man suffer a moment longer than necessary because you refused help from a lady. Now, shall we get started?"

"Let's slide him over this way a bit more, Seamus. I need you to hold his arm." They shifted the patient, and Seamus pulled the arm out away from the table, positioning the shoulder on the edge.

"Miss Dabney, should the patient begin to rouse, please put the lantern down momentarily and administer a few more drops of chloroform onto the cone." Seamus had rigged up a band to hold the cone near Jürgen's mouth and nose.

"Yes sir, Doctor." She nodded and checked the location of the chloroform bottle.

James referred to the book on the table for another moment, then sucked in a deep breath. "Here we go, folks."

Good. "The artery tie from the field is holding fine. Still looks secure." He positioned a tourniquet just below the shoulder, then proceeded to make a circular incision as close to the damaged tissue as possible. He peeled back the skin almost to the shoulder, then clipped what muscle attachments remained—first in the back of the arm, then the front.

"You're not going to remove the bullet, Doc?" Seamus asked.

"No need. That part will come off."

James lifted the detached muscles up over the turned-back skin to reveal the bone. Jagged edges completely separated the upper and lower part of the bone, and a bullet lodged in its sharp teeth.

He blinked several times to avert the drop of sweat that threatened his eyesight. Selecting the saw, he positioned its rough blade about three inches above the ragged end.

James squinted. "More light, please, Miss Dabney." She brought the lantern closer.

He sucked in a slow breath, his mind reciting the procedure details he'd read in the book. Forgetting even one step could cause ultimate failure. He pulled the saw across the bone, slowly at first, then with more purpose. With each stroke, the blade cut deeper into the bone.

Jürgen groaned and turned his head. Miss Dabney set the lantern down and administered a few more drops of chloroform onto the paper cone. She waited for several seconds until the patient was under again and then grabbed up the lantern and returned to her place.

James glanced at her momentarily, her face partially hidden by shadow. He wished he could know her thoughts just now. He admired her mettle. But he had other business to tend to.

The cut was complete. Seamus gingerly gripped the severed limb and laid it on the floor beneath the table. He worked with James to pull the skin and muscle together to create a flap over the stump of the bone. The needle worked in and out of the flesh with practiced rhythm as James stitched the flap to the backside of the arm. He re-threaded the needle three times during the process, aspiring to be thorough, leaving no gaps.

At last, he exhaled a long breath, relishing the ebb of the ordeal. "Well, that's that." Victory. Now, to clean up. Knots of tension squeezed his shoulders. He twisted, stretching his back.

The two basins of water were dark with bloodied cloths, so he looked for a third in which to wash his hands. Miss Dabney pulled a basin from a stack on a chair and filled it with fresh water from a pitcher. How did she know what he was looking for? Her efficient, but graceful movements diverted his attention from the task at hand.

Without a word, she gathered up the two bloodied basins and took them outside. She returned in a few minutes with both pans emptied. The used cloths rung out, looking to be nearly clean.

Jürgen rolled his head to one side, his eyes still closed. "Let's get him to a bed," James said. Working together, he and Seamus lifted the tall man onto a cot.

Miss Dabney covered him with a blanket, placing her hand on his forehead. Like a mother caring for her child. She turned to James; her face a mirror of concern. "Will he fever?"

"Quite possibly. I've not much experience with this procedure, I'm afraid."

"Not much experience? How many amputations have you performed, Doctor?" She tipped her head to one side. Her tone wasn't judgmental, just curious.

There's that golden spark again. His amusement invoked half a grin. "Counting Jürgen here?" He paused. "One." He anticipated a look of outrage, but a smile crept across her pretty face and laced its way through her eyes.

"You did a fine job, Doctor. A fine job." She walked to the door, then pointed to the platter of chicken. "Enjoy your midnight snack, Doctor. Goodnight."

James stared at the barn door long after she disappeared. He'd never met a woman like this one. Something foreign stirred within his chest, akin to desire. But he knew it couldn't be that. *She's a Dabney. He could never care for a Dabney.*

Twenty

Fayette County

Augusta blotted sudsy hands on her apron and bustled to answer the knock at the front door. She ran her fingers over her hair, smoothing the fly-aways that always managed to break loose as she worked. Seemed with all the buzzing about the farm and unrest in the county, she never knew who would be waiting on the other side of that door these days.

Dr. Hill stood on the porch. "I realize everything has been a bit hectic lately. I would like to take a look at your father now, if that's all right."

"Certainly, Doctor, come in." Continuing to coax a few stray hairs into her braided bun, she led the way to Pap's room. Reaching the bedroom, she turned to the doctor, nearly colliding with his chest. "Oh."

Warmth crept up her neck and her words tumbled to intercept the rise of color she feared was obvious. "He drank a cup of broth about an hour ago."

The door hummed on its hinges as she pushed it open. "Pap?" She stepped into the darkened room. "Pap, the doctor's here to see you. Are you awake?" His lips formed a word, but a coughing fit interrupted his attempts to communicate. Augusta rushed to his side. A sip of water would soothe the spasm.

Dr. Hill moved nearer to the bed. With his full attention on Pap, his visage was kind, even compassionate. She preferred this James Hill to the somber, near melancholy man he seemed away from his patients.

"Hello, Mr. Dabney. I'm Doctor Hill. Would you mind if I examined you, sir?" Pap's chin barely registered a nod, but his face relaxed, and the pain-etched lines softened.

The doctor removed his stethoscope from his medical bag and positioned the flared end on Pap's chest. Was this the same man who had bolted for the door after supper? His large hands carefully tilted Pap forward to listen to his back. *He's so gentle with him.*

"How long has he been ill?" He looked up from the patient.

"It's been over a year now. I started treating him with skunk cabbage after the first month, when he just couldn't seem to shake this thing."

"Skunk cabbage, huh? That might explain why he's held on this long. Has his cough been productive?"

She set the glass down. "He goes in spurts. After he's coughed up a bunch of phlegm, he breathes easier and rests better. Then he gets worse, and the cycle starts anew."

"How's his appetite?"

"He doesn't have one. I've been fairly forcing broth and soup down him for days now."

"I recommend cod liver oil, about one tablespoon three times a day, if you can get him to keep it down." His eyes locked with hers for an awkward instant, then he lowered his gaze to his bag as he arranged its contents. "You can start him on a teaspoon dose each time, then increase it. If need be, I can make up some capsules for him. It will provide some additional nourishment as well. Does he have night sweats?"

"Yes, he does. They really just started the last week or so."

"Do you have alum, Miss Dabney?"

"I do." Of course, she has alum. How could she get along without it?

"Good. Mix it with alcohol and sponge it over his skin before he goes to sleep each night. I'll also prepare a mixture of aromatic sulfuric acid and sulfate of quinine. You should give it to him in water each evening." Although he directed his queries at her, she felt as though he purposely avoided eye contact. He looked everywhere except at her. "Have you been thumping him on the back to help release congestion?"

"I've been doing it since he took to his bed, but lately it gives him such coughing spells he nearly passes out. He's just gotten so weak, Doctor." Augusta stroked a lock of graying hair at her father's temple.

"I'd like to speak with you outside, if I may, Miss Dabney."

"Certainly." Augusta patted her father's hand. "We'll leave you be now, Pap, but I'll be back in a little bit." Her spirit was heavy as she noted his pallor. More and more lately, she'd taken to daydreaming about the robust father who used to swing her in circles until she was too dizzy to stand. About the man who'd held this family together with strong arms and undying love when her mama passed. *Please stay with us longer, Pap.*

∞

"Can I get you some coffee, Doctor?"

"Please." James followed Miss Dabney into the kitchen. She was different, this woman. And intriguing. "Your Pap is a very sick man, Miss Dabney." Finally, he let his eyes meet hers. Green. He liked green.

"I insist you call me Augusta . . . or Gus if you'd like. And I'm aware just how ill my father is, Doctor." She busied herself pouring coffee. "I saw my mother through to the end, and I'll see my Pap through to meet his Savior, too." She placed two steaming cups on the table, then sat in the chair he pulled out for her.

"Fair enough. Then I insist you call me James. Not Major or Doctor—James." He claimed the chair on the opposite side of the table. "It's apparent you've given your father excellent care, Augusta, Gus..." He tipped his head and squinted, thinking aloud. "An *Augusta* wouldn't have done what you did last night—assisting with that surgery and all. An *Augusta* would've been mortified at the thought of the procedure and fainted dead away. I believe I will call you *Gus* then, if you don't mind."

"I don't mind, James." She smiled timidly, then grew serious. "How long do you think he has?" She motioned toward Pap's room.

"It's hard to say. Once he becomes too weak to cough, all we can do is give him a sedative to make him more comfortable. When that time comes, I'll mix up—"

"Will syrup made from wild cherries help? It's real relaxing."

"You read my mind. I was about to say a mixture of paregoric and wild cherry syrup. The two together will offer him adequate comfort until the end. You'll have to give it to him every hour or two." James took in the spray of freckles across her nose, wondering if he could count them without her knowledge. What an utterly ridiculous notion.

The back door opened in the kitchen, and an easy smile showed through white whiskers on a face the color of tanned leather. The old man's fist gripped an empty flour sack.

"Hello, Izzy. Would you like to join us for a cup of coffee?" She was already picking a cup from the cupboard.

"I don't wanna be no bother to the two of you now. You just go right ahead. I just stopped by to see if'n I could snag me a few more of them maters from the garden."

"Izzy, this is Doctor James Hill. He's with the Union army. The army will be using our barn as a hospital for a while." She filled another cup with coffee, then set it on the table. "Surely you can spare a few minutes for some hospitality now, can't you?"

"Now Gus, you know I can't say no to you. Nice to make your acquaintance, Doctor." Izzy doffed his misshapen straw hat and joined them at the table. He took a long, cautious drink. "That's mighty good coffee, that is." He patted her hand, which rested on his shoulder. In a swift movement, she placed a peck on his scruffy cheek.

"Only the best for you, Izzy." They shared a soft chuckle.

James's senses started. He'd never seen such a thing. There were parts of this country where that little daughterly peck on the cheek would call for a lynching. This place never ceased to amaze him. No, it wasn't the place, it was the people. This family. This *Dabney* family.

"Izzy's been Pap's best friend since before Fin came along." Gus reclaimed her seat, then sipped her own coffee. "He has a cabin and a little patch of land down by the maple grove on the far side of the pasture."

"I'm pleased to make your acquaintance, Izzy." James reached across the table and shook the man's hand. He turned his attention to Gus. "Something has been bothering me ever since I came here. Do you recollect I told you I knew another Bertram Eliakim Dabney?"

"I do."

"Yo talkin' about Jonathan's brother over in King William County, I 'spect," Izzy said, shaking his head. "What you know about that man?"

"I know of the family. They are somewhat . . . ahh . . . quite—"

"Wealthy." Gus tapped her index finger on the rim of her cup. "You can say it. They're rich and they own one of the biggest plantations in all of Virginia." Her eyes grew somber as she studied the dark liquid inside. "And they own, *own* over a hundred human beings." She rose abruptly and set her coffee cup on the sideboard with a thud.

"Now, Gus. There ain't no sense getting' all worked up. They's yo kin, after all." Izzy stood. "I best be gettin' to picking me some of them ripe maters out there. Nice to meet you, Doctor."

"An honor, sir." James stood as Izzy made his way out the door. He set his cup next to Gus's. "I see you heartily disapprove of the lifestyle led by your father's kin. I take it you don't have any contact with them?"

"Once in a while, a cousin will come by, but mostly we get ignored. Pap's always saying he's the black sheep of the family because he chose a different road."

"A *different* road?"

"There were five Dabney brothers—Bertram being the eldest, and Pap the youngest. Pap didn't want to follow in his brothers' footsteps. He took his inheritance—which wasn't much compared to all the money floating around that place—and he set out to find himself a beautiful little piece of God's creation. Along about that time, he found Jesus at a revival meeting. That's where he met the other two most important people in my life."

"Your mother being one, I assume. And the other?" He smiled at the faraway look in her eyes.

"That would be Izzy. And that's a whole other story on its own."

"Izzy?"

"Uh-huh." Her face fairly glowed. There's that spark again. "He and my pap came to be tight as brothers and went to clearing this land. They built this place—the barn and house—up from nothing. That's why Pap gave him a few acres of his own and a cabin."

"Your pap seems like a fine man. I hope I can get to know him."

The door swung open and Miss Minard stepped into the room. She halted, looking from James to Gus. "I hope I'm not interrupting something, but I think you're needed outside, Doctor Hill."

James stood. "Thank you, Miss Minard."

"Shoot. You can call me Melinda Jane." Her smile lit the entire room.

"Melinda Jane." He nodded, then downed the rest of his cup. "Thank you for the coffee, *Gus*." His cheek twitched. Picking up his bag, he hurried out the door.

Sergeant Mallory sat atop his horse, one hand gripping the reins of another mount. Its rider drooped over the saddle; hands and feet tied. "I bagged me a Johnny, Major Hill. What do you want me to do with him?"

James approached the man, seeing his eyes closed. "Is he injured?" The stranger's eyes snapped open, and he hurled a wad of spit in James's direction. Stepping back, James wiped the glop from his jacket. He suppressed a rise of anger, recognizing it was the uniform that sparked the insult. "If he's not in need of medical attention, we can't keep him here. I expect some of General Rosecrans's men to come by in the next day or two. They can take him off our hands."

"I'll tie him up in the barn." Mallory dismounted and pulled his pistol. He slipped a long knife from a leg sheath and cut the soldier loose. Holding the gun to the prisoner's ribs, he escorted him to the barn.

Before following Mallory, James glanced back at the house. Regret for the interruption nagged him for a moment. It seemed each encounter with Miss Dabney nudged a mysterious door a bit more ajar—a door that somehow connected his heart to the discordant thunder of his past.

In the barn, Seamus looked up from tending to Jürgen. "Looks to be another guest at the Dabney Hotel. He doesn't look wounded."

"He's not." Mallory grabbed a coil of rope from a pile of supplies in one corner of a stall and marched the Confederate soldier to a support post. "Sit down and put your hands behind your back!"

Cutting a section of rope, he fixed a slipknot, sliding it over one of the Rebel's hands. Then he jerked the other hand around and secured them both on the opposite side of the post. Mallory kicked a stool back and grunted as he shoved some supply sacks out of the prisoner's reach.

"This one here thought he could jump me. I was just riding along minding my own business, and down he drops from the trees. Tried to give me a close shave with a skinnin' knife, too." Mallory lifted his head to reveal fresh blood under his chin.

Seamus approached, tipping his head to get a look at his neck. He shot a scowl at James. "Looks to be you got the better of 'im."

"That I did."

∞

Augusta twisted and stretched her back before lifting the pail of milk. The cows had given less milk the last few days. Most likely, they were a mite nervous with all the extra activity in the barn. Turning to take the milk to the house, she glimpsed James tending to one of his patients. Curiosity lured her nearer.

"How is Jürgen doing?" She asked, setting the pail on the floor and spying over James's shoulder.

"I don't think the bruising and swelling is beyond what's to be expected." He tied off a clean bandage on the stump of the amputated arm.

"He is running a fever, I see." Augusta placed her hand on his brow, then reached for a cloth. She dipped it into a nearby basin of water and squeezed out the excess. Just as she laid the damp cloth on Jürgen's head, James placed his hand on hers.

"You don't have to do that, you know."

Taken aback by the sudden contact, Augusta pulled away. "I know I don't. I *want* to." She moved over to the Rebel's cot.

"That one was more pleasant when he was still unconscious." James motioned to the cot. "Name's Miller. He's from Tennessee."

"I can speak for myself, Doc." Miller drawled. He struggled to sit up. A bandage swaddled his shoulder, and his bare chest bore the scars of a brawler. "Seems to me the Union Army went out of their way to recruit pretty nurses. What's yer name, honey?" His gaze roamed over Augusta as he licked his lips. "I could sure do with a cup of cool water." Four brown teeth bared in his crooked grin.

James raised his voice. "That's no way to talk to a lady, Miller. You may be a patient, but you're still a prisoner."

"I can take care of myself, Doctor." Augusta smiled sweetly. "I suspect this poor man just hasn't had the opportunity to learn good manners." She was not a stranger to the art of rejecting unwelcomed advances. Pouring water into a tin cup, she offered it to the man.

"Thank you kindly, ma'am." The Rebel accepted the cup, his voice dripping false sweetness.

Her stomach curdled, wondering what went on in the mind of a man like that.

She walked over to Johnson, who still lay unconscious from the bullet graze to his head. "How long until he wakes, do you suppose?" A niggling concern made her turn to James. "Shouldn't he be awake by now?"

"I am concerned. The injury was not terribly invasive, so I can only hope he'll come out of it soon."

A book lay on a stool near the cot. Augusta picked it up. "Poetry?"

"Yes, he carried it with him. I've been reading it to him, hoping it'll help bring him out of the coma." James smiled. "Quite a man, Johnson. I understand he was a schoolteacher before he volunteered."

Gus opened the book and read aloud:

> *"There be none of Beauty's daughters*
> *With a magic like thee;*
> *And like music on the waters*
> *Is thy sweet voice to me."*

James finished the recitation, his eyes squinting with recollection:

> *"When, as if its sound were causing*
> *The charmed ocean's pausing,*
> *The waves lie still and gleaming,*
> *And the lulled winds seem dreaming."*

Remarkable. Men like her pap memorized poetry, not Army doctors.

"Lord Byron," he said matter-of-factly. "I was nearly a professor of literature instead of a physician."

"Nearly? Did you make the right choice—about your profession?" Augusta set the book back onto the stool.

"I believe the answer to that question is as changing as a chameleon's skin." James turned to a ruckus at the barn door.

Melinda Jane stood bent over, gasping for breath, hands on her knees. "It's Will! She . . . she . . ."

Augusta hurried to put her arm around Melinda Jane's shoulders. "Just breathe." She waited while her friend took a couple of deep breaths. "What about Will?"

"She's in a tree. A bear has her trapped in a tree. I've never seen a bear that het up before, Gus. It just came out of nowhere and started chasing her!"

Augusta forced back a surge of panic. She had to think. She couldn't just bolt out the door. She needed a firearm. Relief washed over her when she saw James and Seamus already collecting their carbines.

James's face darkened. "Show us where."

Melinda Jane rushed ahead, leading the others to the edge of the pasture not far from Izzy's cabin. There, on the widest branch of a young elm tree, was Will, and halfway up the base of that tree, a black bear. The fur on his back was wet and matted.

"He's been shot." James exchanged an angry look with Augusta. An animal in pain was the worst kind of dangerous.

"What kind of fool leaves a wounded bear to run the countryside?" Seamus took aim with his rifle and fired. The bullet pierced the base of the bear's skull. The carcass dropped like a rag doll, hitting the ground with a heavy thud.

Seamus shaded his eyes as he looked up into the tree. "I know yer likin' to bide yer time in the trees these days, but if you care to come down now—" He paused, smiling. "Well, it doesn't matter to me one way 'tor another. You can take yer meals up there for all I care."

"Very funny," Will huffed. She dangled for a moment from the branch, then, just like before, dropped to the ground. She brushed off her palms and tugged up her britches. "Thank you kindly, but I was prepared to wait that bear out. He'd have tired, eventually."

"He was halfway up the tree, lass. What would you have done if he'd reached you?" Seamus shook his head, his mouth pulling to one side.

Will jammed her hands onto her hips and wagged her head. "Why, I would've done exactly what I just did and outrun him while he was making his way back down."

"And—" Seamus suddenly seemed out of words. "Oh." He looked at James and shrugged.

James kicked the bear with his boot. He reached down, dabbing his finger into the blood on the animal's back. "This wound is fresh. Whoever shot this old boy can't be far away."

"Are you thinking it could've been a Rebel? They're getting mighty bold around these parts of late." Augusta scanned her surroundings before starting for Izzy's cabin. "I'm going to check on Izzy."

"I'll go with you—just in case." James's gaze slid to the rifle in his hand.

Twenty-One

Fayete County

The *clip-clop* of hooves interrupted the familiar rhythm of the farmyard, drawing James's attention. He shook his wet hands and stepped off the pump platform. Water dripped from his beard, and he wiped more from his eyes. A vermillion sun rode low on the horizon as a lone Federal soldier drew his horse to a stop in front of the white clapboard house. Coot circled and barked as men emerged from the barn.

The rider lurched forward, gripping the mane. James and Seamus sprinted to the stranger and lowered him to the ground.

"We ran into Johnnies about a mile south of here." The young soldier gasped for air.

"How many in your party, Private?" James noted the paleness of his face.

"T . . . Twenty, sir." He grimaced with the effort. "They outnumbered us two to one. Came out of nowhere." He scrunched his eyes closed and drew a labored breath, then his chin dropped to his chest.

James lifted the man's head. "Stay with us, soldier." He patted one cheek. "Were there survivors?" *Please let there be survivors.*

"Don't know." Scratchy words jerked from his throat. "They ordered me on to alert you." His head lulled to one side as he lost consciousness.

"Seamus, keep one guard here with you to prepare for more wounded. The rest of us will take a wagon and ride out to meet that detachment." The words were no sooner out of his mouth when Mallory signaled two other men to join him in readying the wagon. James gripped the unconscious man under his arms, and Seamus lifted his feet.

Gus followed close behind as they carted the soldier to the barn. "Mind if I help out where I can?"

James didn't answer. When she pulled the blanket down on a fresh cot, their gazes met. Her eyebrows lifted, and those beautiful eyes commanded an answer. That uncanny confidence, swaddled in peace. Steadfast. Good thing she didn't know what that look did to his pulse.

"Would it make a difference if I said no?" He held her gaze, the urgency of the moment surrendering to a half-smile.

***

The wagon rolled at a steady clip behind him as James took the lead on the winding dirt road. By the side of the trace, two horses pulled up grass, their reins resting on the ground. One soldier dismounted long enough to collect the reins as two others searched the area.

Up ahead lay the carnage from the attack. Two Union soldiers knelt near a body—one of their own. James counted six dead Rebels, including the body wedged in the crook of an ancient walnut tree. Three more soldiers stood guard, visibly wary of another onslaught.

"Who is bleeding the most?" James asked, swinging down off his mount.

"Over here, Major." A soldier sat against a tree with a tear-streaked face. His muscled arms enveloped another man as one would hold a child. "Ya gotta save him, Major. Our mama said it'd break her heart if anything happened to one of us." He choked on a sob. "There's just so much blood—it's pouring from his gut. I can't see how there could be anymore."

James dropped to the dirt, his knapsack landing with a thud. He hastily threw back the flap, but a closer look at the man confirmed his fear.

The crumpled form in the soldier's arms spoke in a whisper. "It's all right, Luke. I'm not hurtin' none. Tell Mama I love"—he stilled; unfocused eyes aimed fully at his brother's face.

James clenched his teeth. Another mother's son. He hoisted the hospital knapsack and moved on to wrap a shoulder wound and apply a tourniquet to a badly injured leg.

A Union soldier's body lay unmoving, presumed dead. In the first battle, James had learned not to assume anything. He gently turned the body on its side. Sure enough, a spark of life flickered. One side of the man's head was caved in and matted with dirt and blood. Ragged flesh hung from his cheek and white bone glistened in the sunlight through the burnished gray mingling of soil and filmy ooze.

"Over here!" James examined the wound to find the bleeding mostly abated. Unless the man regained consciousness, he could do nothing until he reached the barn. He mourned the man's future, should infection not take him. The disfigurement of the scar would be significant.

He worked with the others to load the casualties. Duty trampled the familiar sprouts of gloom that could so easily grow into a strangling vine. A vine he'd chopped at for years, unable to dig out the root.

Injured and dead alike filled the wagon. Those who were able rode their mounts. One of the Rebels, still unconscious, had merely sustained a bullet to the shoulder.

As the wagon pulled up to the Dabneys' barn, Seamus and Gus emerged. Instead of her usual bright attire, she wore a dark dress with sleeves rolled to the elbows. A white apron covered her, neck to hem.

"We're ready for you, sir," Seamus said, looking into the wagon. His expression, sad at first, yielded to one of sober duty as he once again owned his role as a medic.

"Sergeant Mallory, there are bodies that need tending. Prepare the burial for first thing tomorrow morning." James was thankful for the quarter acre of land Jonathan Dabney had donated for use as a cemetery. A hastily erected fence of split rails cordoned off a relatively flat plot of pasture. A single birch tree would stand guard over the bodies of fallen soldiers of both sides.

James blinked against the sting of sweat as he worked among the injured. The clammy late July evening was oppressive—with the breeze commanded elsewhere, leaving swarms of gnats to hover at the barn's entrance. Resentment rankled as he willed the crickets to silence their song—to acknowledge this wretched station of humanity and mourn these suffering souls.

He excised a bullet from the shoulder of one soldier and stitched up the knife wound on another. Private Tipton lay on the table before him, still unconscious. Gus had meticulously cleansed the facial wound and sponged it dry of any fresh blood. He hadn't even asked her to. While James and Seamus had tended to others, she'd found tasks in need of attention.

"What are you thinking is to be done here?" she asked, appearing beside him.

James sighed. He imagined a tall glass of lemonade. The shade of a spreading oak. A blanket of cool grass. "Might I trouble you for some water, Gus?"

"Of course." She picked up the bucket. "I'm going for fresh," she said, darting out the door.

"This one's needing more for the pain, James." Seamus stood beside the soldier, Thibedeau, whose lower leg a Minié had shattered.

"Go ahead and give him more laudanum. We'll take care of him next."

Returning with fresh water, Gus ladled it into a tin cup for James. Its coolness revived him for yet another venture into the unknown. He'd not been trained for this kind of medicine. He felt little more than an educated butcher.

Hadn't he become a doctor to save lives, to ease suffering? Hadn't he chosen it for his penance? How many lives pay for the taking of one? He vowed he would not lift his hand to another. Never again. And yet, he'd sent men to their graves. He'd purposed to save the lives of Union soldiers who fought for a cause worth dying for—not be on the killing end of things.

He thought of Nan, and of the Orrs, and others like them. A showy, pillared plantation house. Rows of slave shanties. A tobacco drying house. Tears. Blood. *Ezra*. He struggled to reign in the wild reflections.

"James, are you all right?" Gus's hand rested on his forearm. Her emerald eyes darkened with concern as they searched his own.

He shook his head. "Yes, I'm fine."

"You looked so sad just now." Her timid smile faded as she looked down at Private Tipton, unconscious on the table. "Where do you begin?"

"You did an excellent job cleaning the wound. Now, at least, I can see what I'm doing." James used a scalpel to trim away jagged pieces of skin and muscle across the man's cheek. A bullet lodged just under the cheekbone. Since there was no tissue to retract, James easily removed it. A gaping hole in the bone revealed the sinus cavity.

"I'm afraid the only thing left to do is to cover this thoroughly. Then we'll change the bandage often, hoping he'll not succumb to infection. I expect he'll wake soon, if at all. There may be a head injury of which I'm not aware."

He had read of bone regrowth in certain instances and sincerely hoped this would be such a case. He rolled lint inside of bandages to create a sort of plug and placed it over the hole in the bone. Gus lifted the patient's head as James proceeded to wrap length after length around the man's skull to secure the patch.

They turned to a ruckus behind them. Thibedeau thrashed in the bed and had knocked over a stool, sending a tin cup clattering to the floor. Seamus wrestled his flailing arms to the cot.

"You're not taking off my leg!" the man screamed. "Not my leg. Not my leg!" His face was a mask of anguish, his eyes clouded and red-rimmed. Seamus called two men over to hold him down.

"Are you ready for him now?" Seamus looked hopeful.

"Yes, let's make the switch." James and one of the soldiers transferred Tipton from the surgical table to a cot while Seamus saw to the moving of Thibedeau, who bucked like a wild horse. James readied the amputation kit, needles, and suture material as Gus tipped the chloroform tin, guiding drips onto the paper cone.

Seamus grimaced, laying his full weight across Thibedeau's torso. Sergeant Mallory fairly sat on the private's leg while another man pressed the shoulders to the table. Within seconds, the patient calmed, surrendering to a drug-induced bliss.

"The boy's got fight, I'll give 'im that." Seamus moved to the foot of the table to assist.

James chose a knife and turned to take stock of his patient. He chuckled to himself as his attention settled on the bearded face of Private Thibedeau. "Deep sleep came down on every eye save mine—"

"And there it stood—all formless, but divine." Gus finished his words, her gaze intense and sparking of mischief, of intrigue.

For seconds on end, James was captive. Captive to her spirited gaze. Captive to the silence. He waited. Waited for *what*, he didn't know. He willed his eyes to turn from hers as the surroundings gained on his senses.

"Are we doing surgery here or are we to take a picnic?" Seamus's voice boomed into the moment.

Heat rose to James's jawline. He blurted in a too-gruff voice, "The sooner we're started, the sooner we're done."

Aside from requiring two different saws, one for the tibia and one for the fibula, James found this amputation to be less arduous than the one he'd performed on Jürgen.

He scrutinized Thibedeau's form as Seamus and Mallory transferred him to the cot. With this war rode a companion of lingering sadness, he'd discovered. But just now, after this surgery, he recognized a certain satisfaction. Thankfulness, even. At least, the educated butcher can now claim experience.

∞

James looked up from his reading, acknowledging Izzy with a nod. Ol' Izzy had taken to visiting the barn with regularity. Sometimes he'd sit with the patients, reading to them from the Bible. Other times, he'd make sure they had fresh water to drink. For those willing to listen, he'd stretch their ears with tale after tale, never admitting to truth or fiction.

"A good day for fishing, Doctor. There be some fine brown trout in that crick down by my cabin." Izzy ambled over to where James sat and placed a pitcher on the table. "Missy Gus done made you your own pitcher of boysenberry shrub. Can I interest you in a glass?"

James tossed back the last swig of coffee and held his cup out for Izzy to fill. "She's going to spoil us."

Izzy chuckled and began serving the boysenberry drink to the patients.

The old man had started a game of checkers yesterday with Johnson, but the private had grown too weary to finish. Izzy handed him a cup. "You figurin' on letting me beat you at the rest of this here game today, Private?"

"Izzy, you already beat me three out of three. Don't you think it's time you let me win?" Johnson still sported a bandage around his head, covering his temple. The graze he'd received wasn't deep, but he still suffered bouts of dizziness.

"I figure I'm helping you get well by working yo thinkin' muscle. If'n I let you beat me, you'll stop working at it so hard. I'll just see to these boys, and then we'll finish our game."

Izzy moved over to Thibedeau, then Jürgen, filling their cups with the cool, sweet drink.

Jürgen returned the old man's lazy smile. "Thank you, Izzy. You tell Miss Dabney how much we appreciate this, will you?"

"I surely will do that, I will." Izzy picked up a cup from an overturned box next to Miller, the Rebel found unconscious with the shoulder injury. James had managed to save the boy's arm, but with so much tissue gone, the healing would be slow.

"Can I offer you some of Missy Gus's fresh, boysenberry shrub?" Izzy asked.

Miller accepted the cup, started to take a sip, then tossed the cup and its contents onto the older man. The red liquid dripped from Izzy's white beard, down his clothes to the floor. "Fill it again, *boy*!" Hatred thickened the Rebel's voice.

James stood. His ire flared, and he thought to give Miller a piece of his mind. But Izzy's reaction gave him pause.

The old man pulled a frayed bandana from his back pocket and wiped his face. "I don't believe I be givin' you anymore of Miss Gus's fine shrub just now, son. Best to save it for them that are appreciative. But you just let me know if'n you change your mind and want to wet that parched throat you surely got by now." Izzy shuffled on to the next patient, filling another cup.

That benevolent expression never wavered. In the depths of those wizened eyes, James saw peace. Peace and something more.

Was it patience born of his long, knowing years? Or was it a soul anchored, not in the sorrow of *this* world, but in the tranquility of another?

He sat again, rolling his shoulders to release tense muscles. That stooped old man had indeed swelled in size in his mind.

The lazy afternoon stretched across the hours, a welcome lull in the often-chaotic arrival of new patients. The coolness of an afternoon drizzle was welcomed—the humidity it brought was not, and it hadn't abated all day.

James's eyes roamed over the patients. Most sprawled across their cots in sleep. He watched as Izzy stood and stretched his aged frame. After beating Johnson in another game of checkers, Izzy hobbled over to Miller. The Rebel had been holding a small picture when he dozed off, but now it lay on the floor beside his cot. The old man pulled a blanket over the boy's bare feet, up to his chest. Bending in slow motion, he picked up the Carte de Visite of a young woman. Izzy smiled as he looked at the photo before placing it on the box-turned-table.

James approached him. "He doesn't deserve your kindness."

Izzy smacked his lips. He spoke in little more than a whisper. "Well, Doctor, Massa Jesus loves them boys in gray just as much as He loves Ol' Izzy. Jesus say if'n we love *Him*, we gots to love others. Love 'em no matter how unlovable they be."

He looked hard at James. "When you was doctoring that poor boy, did you tell yourself, 'He don't deserve my kindness'?"

"I'm a doctor. I didn't think about it. He needed medical help."

Izzy turned to leave the barn. "Someday I'll tell you a story, Doctor. Yep, an old, old story, but right now I'm gonna fetch a fresh bucket of that cool Virginny well water for these boys."

"Oh, no you don't!" A woman's angry voice sounded from just outside the barn. "Get back, you. Right this minute!"

Twenty-Two

Fayette County

Melinda Jane studied the bucket of ripe tomatoes. She had meant them as a snack for the men, but something had to be done about this nuisance. Switching directions, she strode toward the chicken coop and hurled a tomato through the air. It connected with a thud to the shoulder of a burly raccoon.

"You get away from there this minute!" She grabbed up another, this time thumping the critter on the backside as it scurried away. With a huff, she looked around. "That hound is not doing his job. Where is he, anyway?" She searched the area. An audience of three stood fifteen feet behind her, sporting big grins. Irritation suddenly replaced her zeal to protect the eggs. So, she was the entertainment, was she?

"Whoo-wee. If'n I was that coon, I'd never show my snout in these parts again." Izzy elbowed James, shaking his head, his gap-toothed grin widening.

"Ay, nor would I. He'd be a fool to risk another onslaught of deadly tomatoes." Seamus walked up to her, grabbed a tomato, and took a bite. Juice trickled down his beard, and he laughed. "You may be a might small, but yer a force to be reckoned with, Melinda Jane."

"I was bringing these tomatoes for you and the fellers. But maybe I best deliver them one at a time?" She pulled back her arm, prepared to launch another tomato, this time at Seamus.

He raised his palms in surrender and cautiously took the pail from her. "Thank you kindly, miss. We're most appreciative of yer offering." He bowed, backing away as the other men laughed.

Melinda Jane sashayed up to Izzy and reached for his hand. She glanced at Seamus and James, then winked at Izzy. "I do believe since you're the finest looking man out here today, you ought to come get a piece of my cherry pie."

"Ooh boy! I see ya'll later." Izzy shuffled off, Melinda Jane leading him like a child.

"Hey, what about that cool Virginny water you were fetching?" James hollered after him.

Izzy didn't even turn. He stuck a hand in the air and waved.

∞

Augusta tightened the lids on each of the jars, lifted them into the canner, and lowered the rack. "That's the last of the cherries. Should be enough to see us through."

"I better check that other pie." Melinda Jane jumped up from the chair and used her apron to grab hold of the handle on the heavy iron door.

With the rush of heat came a heavenly aroma, adding to the other inviting scents that filled the kitchen. Augusta smiled to herself as she started washing up the dishes. She could almost imagine Mama standing next to her, teaching her how to lay out the lattice of dough atop a cherry pie.

"Gus, I'm wondering if you've even noticed how handsome that doctor feller is."

Augusta tensed and dropped a jar into the dishwater with a splash.

Melinda Jane snickered. "Didn't mean to rattle you none."

"I just dropped the jar, that's all . . . I didn't quite hear what you said." Guilt for the fib niggled at her. She dried her hands and untied her apron. "Anyway, I need to go check on Pap."

Izzy wiped the last of the cherry pie from his mouth with the back of his hand. "*I'll* check on Jonathan." He rose stiffly, his gaze connecting with Melinda Jane's, then headed to the bedroom.

Augusta watched him leave the room. "You don't need to gang up on me. There's *nothing* between me and James." She squeezed the water out of the dishrag. "Besides, there can't be."

"That's foolishness and you know it. You've backed yourself into a corner of your own making. You just don't wanna lift your head long enough to see the window."

Melinda Jane approached Augusta from behind, turned her around, and took Augusta's wet hands in her own. "Honey, you deserve to be happy. To find a man to love, to marry, to—"

"Stop!" Augusta pulled away. She crossed the kitchen and stood at the screen door, her gaze aimed at the garden, unfocused.

"Melinda Jane, I have a responsibility here. Bertie, Will, and Zander—they're my family. They need me. I'll be here for them until they're grown and on their own. And this farm will be here for them too. And I aim to make sure that happens. It's got to."

"But just because you're raising them doesn't mean you can't get married and—"

"I'm going out to the garden." Augusta grabbed a bonnet from a peg and pushed through the door with such force that the screen bounced shut behind her.

James exited the barn, squinting into the sunlight and wiping his hands on a towel. "What's the report, Sergeant?" Mallory dismounted and secured the reins. A half dozen soldiers followed suit.

"Not good, I'm afraid. The bulk of Cox's troops have gained on Gauley Bridge. There've been several skirmishes. Wounded are on the way from that direction and more are coming from some action not far north of here." Mallory lifted his hat and ran his hand through his sweat-drenched hair. "The woods are crawling with Johnnies. I managed to get to the post office like Miss Dabney asked, but I don't think we'll be getting another opportunity for a time."

He retrieved two letters from an inside coat pocket and slapped them into James's hand. "These are for the Dabneys." Mallory stuck his head beneath the pump and sighed as the water soaked his hair and collar.

"How far behind are the wounded?"

"Maybe a half hour, barring no trouble."

"We'll be ready."

Augusta emptied the basin of bloody water onto a patch of dried grass and headed to the pump to refill the bucket hooked over one arm. As the last of the water splashed into the bucket, she lifted her arms above her head, pulling on her tired back muscles. A gauzy cloud drifted across the face of the ocher moon, followed by two smaller ones—like a mother hen leading her chicks.

With all the cots in the barn in use, she had put Will to work making straw pallets, each covered by a blanket for the less critically injured. Bodies lay wall to wall in two of the box stalls, while cots lined the perimeter of the open area. Fin had hastily fashioned a second tall table for surgeries. In one corner, a guard watched over four injured Confederates on pallets.

All this death and suffering begot grief—a grief that was becoming too familiar to Augusta. The ease with which it found a place to reside in her heart was alarming. It was not a grief for the men she'd never known, but for the families they left behind. Two of the Union soldiers died shortly after arriving and would be buried in the pasture plot. She shivered with an unwelcomed thought—the plot would soon be too small to hold all these bodies of mothers' sons.

She continued her rounds, serving water to those who could drink and cleaning wounds so James could better assess them. Midnight had come and gone, and they had worked tirelessly for the past several hours. Many of the wounded slept now, but others groaned in pain, unable to claim the blessings of sleep. Only one amputation was necessary—that of a finger. Augusta poked stray strands back into her braid. What a mess she must look.

"I think that's just about the last of them," She smiled wearily at James and dropped a rag into the basin. "There's just these three left to tend." She pointed to a Rebel soldier. Dark eyes guarded a whiskerless face. Eyes that reminded her of a deer trying to decide whether to run or stand still. "It appears the bullet passed through his calf, and those two have knife wounds that need stitching, but I've got the bleeding stopped."

"Why thank you, *Doctor* Dabney. You've been quite thorough. Oh, I forgot—" James pulled two letters from his pocket and handed them to Augusta. "Looks to be a letter from your beau there."

Her curiosity faltered beneath the weary weight that pulled at her shoulders. Without even a glance at the return addresses, she slid them into her skirt pocket.

"Seamus and I can finish this." James gently pulled the basin from her hands, his tired smile disarming her natural inclination to resist his help. "Why don't you turn in for the night?"

Augusta started to protest, but a yawn surprised her, and she quickly hid it behind her fingers. "I'll just empty this on the way to the house," she said, pulling the basin from James's hands.

"Goodnight, Gus—and thank you for your help."

"Goodnight." Contentment warmed her through and through. Being needed was important. Sometimes she wondered if maybe it was unhealthy to aspire to be needed like she did. *What will it be like when Bertie, Will, and Zander are grown . . . and Pap is gone—and no one needs her?*

∞

The barn door creaked as Bertie leaned his weight against the weathered wood, holding it open for Augusta. Dawn's early haze lit a path to the cows, crowded into the stalls on the far side of the barn. She had made it a point to get to milking before the first cow could bawl its discomfort, not wanting to disturb the soldiers.

"Ma'am?" A timid voice caught Augusta's attention. "Ma'am, can I talk to you?" It came from the corner where the Rebels were bedded down.

She walked toward the guard, who was stretching his legs, a cup of coffee in hand.

"Good morning, Miss Dabney," he whispered. "Mighty early to be tending to patients."

"I came to milk, but I believe I heard someone calling for me."

"That'd be the little Johnny over there." The guard pointed to the corner. "I told him it could wait."

"It's quite all right. I'll see to him now, Private." She navigated the darkened barn, careful not to step on the bodies that carpeted the stall floor.

"Over here, ma'am." The voice was softer now. "I didn't want to wake no one."

"What can I do for you, soldier?" Augusta kept some distance between them, but knelt down near the wounded Rebel. She remembered this had been the one with the bullet wound in the right calf.

"I've got a problem, ma'am. I need to go to the privy."

"You'll just have to use the bedpan, I'm afraid, Private. You can't walk all that way with your leg like that." Augusta slid the pan closer to the patient.

"I can't use that. I just can't. Not here."

"I don't see why"—she froze. It all made sense. The small stature, the lack of facial hair. Why, even the soldier's leg had less hair on it than Bertie's. She pivoted to be sure the men lying nearby were sleeping.

"You're a woman?" Augusta whispered.

"Please, don't tell, ma'am. Could you help me to the privy?" The girl looked up at Augusta, her eyes pleading.

She had to think. Then it came to her. "I hope you can hold on for a few more minutes. I'll be right back."

Moments later, while everyone slept but the guard, Melinda Jane, and Augusta helped the Confederate soldier to the Dabney's necessary, and then into the house.

Twenty-Three

Fayette County

August, 1861

Hope tugged at Augusta's heart as she watched James listen to Pap's chest and then his back. His eyebrows sunk lower the longer he held the stethoscope in place. Weak spasms pulled at Pap's throat, and he tried to speak, but the ruckle stole his words.

She held a cup to his lips. "Just a little now, Pap." She set it down and searched James's eyes for some hint of his thoughts. His expression was at first grave, but then he smiled at Pap.

"I see you have quite the collection of literature, Mr. Dabney. Byron, Whitman, Dickens." James pulled a volume of *Moby Dick* from the ceiling-tall walnut bookcase. "One of my favorites."

He ran his hand over the darkened binding, then closed his eyes. ". . . 'and Heaven have mercy on us all—Presbyterians and Pagans alike—for we are all somehow dreadfully cracked about the head, and sadly need mending.'"

Pap's eyes widened, and something she hadn't seen for weeks shone in their depths. "'For all sinned and come short of the Glory of God.'" His voice was soft but clear. "A similar quote, from a greater Book."

"Yes, but were there a possibility for equity to abound regarding the greater sin, I'd expect that surely there'd be no rejection of forgiveness." James returned the book to its place on the shelf.

"Oh, but there is equity . . . Doctor," Pap closed his eyes as his features relaxed. "Firsss John, chapter . . . one."

"Verse nine," Augusta finished softly, then put her finger to her lips, motioning toward the door.

James followed behind her and noiselessly closed the door. "He's worse," he said. "He hasn't enough strength to produce a cough that will purge the build-up in his lungs. I'll bring you the paregoric. You mentioned that you have the syrup of wild cherry?" Sympathy shown in his eyes, and regret tinged his voice.

"Yes, I do. Just tell me what needs to be done."

So, the time had come. Nothing outside of a miracle would see her father returned to her in health. She would do everything in her power to see he didn't suffer. Right to the end. She'd been prepared for this. Really, she had. It's just that it had always remained at arm's length, and now, she would hold it to her bosom and once more embrace the pain of saying goodbye. She refused to be sad just now. There would be a time for mourning—later.

"Will you stay for supper? It should be on the table about now." Augusta was getting used to his presence. He was fast becoming one of the family, even though he insisted on eating with his men much of the time.

"Why don't I go ahead and get that medicine for you, then I'll be back. Whatever I smell wafting from that kitchen surely needs some sampling." James thumped his belly, then ventured toward the barn.

"Tonight's roastin' ears were from our first picking, and Melinda Jane made us all dessert from the first apple harvest." Augusta said, gathering empty plates from the table and signaling Will to do the same.

Melinda Jane set a platter in the center of the table. Fried apples, sprinkled with cinnamon and warm from the oven. Bertie reached for them first. Augusta swatted at his hand.

"Bertram Eliakim Dabney, you mind your manners."

"That looks so good. I was just thinking 'bout doing the same." Izzy winked at Bertie, whose pout transformed into a mischievous grin.

James passed the platter, and Zander heaped apples onto his plate. "You got any war news for us, James?"

"I suppose I do. Regretfully, none of it is good." James took a bite of the apples. "Over near Manassas, the Union took a beating. More than four hundred dead and over a thousand missing."

"What do you mean, missing?" asked Will, hanging her mouth open most unladylike.

Zander pierced an apple slice with his fork. "It means they're most likely taken prisoner, or they haven't found their b . . ."—his look bounced from Bertie to Gus—"them yet."

James looked at Augusta, a question in his eyes. She nodded, and he continued. "General McClellan's been appointed Commander of the Army of the Potomac."

"I thought there was just the Union and the Confederates," Bertie said. "What's the Army of the Poto-mak?"

"Potomac. It's just another name for the Union Army, Bertie. It appears General Lee is back this side of the Alleghenies attempting to retake some of the ground lost by Garnet. I don't suspect he'll make it down this far." James took a drink of milk, wiped his mustache, and stood.

"If you'll excuse me, I should probably look in on our special patient and then get back to the barn. Ladies, the meal was wonderful, as always. I look forward to more of that sweet corn again soon. And Melinda Jane, your culinary skills never cease to astound me."

"Well, if I didn't know better, I'd think you were trying to butter me up." Melinda Jane giggled and stood to collect the dessert plates. Augusta chuckled at the frown on Fin's face as he watched Melinda Jane carry the dishes to the sink.

James smiled. "Just practicing my gentlemanly manners. I can't very well do it with the company I keep in the barn, now can I?"

"This way, Doctor." Augusta led James to Will's room, where J.D. Hall lay, one hand chained to the bedframe. J. D. no longer stood for Jeremiah Daniel. Now she was known by the Dabneys and James as Juliana Delores Hall, Confederate prisoner. As soon as her leg was healed enough, she would be delivered to a prison up north.

"Let's take a look at that leg." James sat on the bed and unwrapped the bandage. Two large wilted leaves pressed into the wound. "What's this?"

"That's comfrey. It always helps heal a wound faster. Should I have asked you first?" Augusta gently pulled the leaves from J.D.'s calf.

"This looks better than I expected. I'd say this leg is healing at least a couple of days ahead of schedule."

J.D. propped her elbows under her, stretching her neck. "Now, just a minute here. You're telling me I'm a-gonna end up in that Northern prison sooner because of them leaves?"

Augusta patted the young woman's hand. "I'm sorry, J.D., I didn't think of it that way." Her compassion warred with the realization that this woman was a Rebel soldier. She'd probably even killed men. "Don't you concern yourself too much right now. You've still got a few more days here with us."

"Do you have more leaves?" James angled his head, meeting Augusta's eyes with a quizzical look.

She handed him a clean bandage roll. "I'll have to pick some fresh in the morning."

"Would you mind taking me with you? I'd like to use the comfrey for some of my other patients."

"Of course."

Minutes later, Augusta and James stood on the front porch. She glanced back toward the house. "I keep telling myself she's better off in a regular prison than with all the male war prisoners. But it still makes my heart sorrow."

"Yes, mine too. Not just for her, but for this whole ugly war." James pointed to the horizon. Hues of garnet washed the sky above the gilded line of the earth. "Beautiful sunset tonight."

"Indeed." She stepped to the railing. "'He appointed the moon for seasons: the sun knoweth his going down.'"

He moved to stand beside her. "The Psalms?"

"Yes, one of my Pap's favorite chapters."

"Your father—he has such a tremendous collection of books. Has he read them all?"

"Not only has *he* read them all, several times each, I suppose, but he's seen to it that each one of his children has read them, too. Well, all except Bertie, that is." She chuckled and faced him. "It may surprise you to know that my father is a Harvard man."

"Harvard. Is that so?"

"He attended before he met my mother. He had great plans for all of his children—if things had turned out differently. If my mother hadn't died. If Pap hadn't taken ill."

"I'm sorry."

A silence settled comfortably between them for a few moments as they watched the horizon.

James swatted at a mosquito and cleared his throat, seeming to do battle over his next words. But then his shoulders slumped in retreat. "I'd best check on things at the barn." His jaw muscle jumped before a smile lit his eyes. "Night, Gus."

"Good night, James." Her gaze followed his form as he walked away, nearly swallowed by the darkness. Just before he disappeared from the slice of lantern light at the barn entrance, he turned. Her breath caught as their eyes locked over the distance. Suddenly self-conscious, she turned and darted into the house, tripping over the hem of her skirt.

∽

The bright sun climbed its circuit, bringing the promise of another hot August day as James and Gus returned to the farm. He breathed in the woodsy fragrance, entertaining a silent chuckle as he remembered Gus's tutelage in the local flora and relative medicinal uses.

He followed her into the coolness of the barn, a basket of comfrey leaves cradled in his arm. Instead of the usual light bantering, a tranquil silence ensued. All eyes were on the white-haired man who sat on a stool, worn leather Bible in hand. Izzy's voice was strong and clear as he read:

> *"He hath not dealt with us after our sins; nor rewarded us according to our iniquities. For as the heaven is high above the earth, so great is his mercy toward them that fear him. As far as the east is from the west, so far hath he removed our transgressions from us. Like as a father pitieth his children, so the Lord pitieth them that fear him."*

The soldiers had grown used to Izzy's presence. Even the Rebel, Miller, now accepted Izzy's sincere, gentle demeanor.

James listened, entranced by the poetry of the Psalm. "What Psalm is that?" he whispered to Gus.

"The hundred and third." Her warm expression sparked something deep inside him.

Just as Izzy closed the old Bible, Coot's bark warned of a visitor. James was the first one out the door with Gus on his heels.

"Halloo to the house!" A scrawny man with an oversized hat turned his horse in a tight circle before heading their direction. "Am I ever glad you're here, Gus. Florence's time has come."

Gus waved. "That's our neighbor, Ned Meyers. He may look small, but he's big in heart. I've known him all my life, and I do believe he's worn that same old straw hat just as long."

She started for the house. "I'll get my things. Melinda Jane and I will be along real soon."

"You're not going without an armed escort," James cut in.

"I'm not?" She propped her hands on her hips. "I'll have my double-barreled escort right at my side."

"What I mean to say is—I would like to see you take a couple of my men along with you." He'd overstepped his bounds. What was he thinking? Gus wasn't some soldier to be ordered about.

She smiled. "I believe I *will* accept your offer of an escort, Major. Thank you." She dipped in a slight curtsy and hurried into the house.

Ten minutes later, James released his hold on the bridle of Gus's horse. "Please do as my men say, if there is even a hint of trouble. I'd go with you, but I can't very well be off delivering a baby if more wounded arrive. If there are any complications, send for me." Dash his station! He'd hold himself responsible if anything happened to her.

"I've delivered more babies than you have performed amputations, Doctor." She flaunted an enchanting grin, then snapped the reins.

His jaw dropped. Speechless. A glance his way carried that gold spark. She'd done it to him again.

"Keep a keen eye out, Mallory!" James's gruff order probably carried to the house.

"Yes, sir, Major." The sergeant kicked his horse to catch up to the women.

He shook his head, all too aware of a peculiar ailment that seemed to afflict his insides. And he wasn't sure he wanted to take the cure.

∞

As James made his rounds, glancing at the barn door now and then, even though experience reminded him that babies rarely make an appearance in such a short amount of time. He walked to the medicine pannier and back twice after forgetting whatever it was he needed to retrieve.

Activity had been light for a few days. Only one new patient had arrived from Camp Gauley—a picket who had been attacked and bore substantial knife wounds. Nevertheless, those roads aren't safe for anyone. Maybe he should ride up there and check on her.

"She'll be back safe and sound afore ya know it," Seamus said, lifting a bucket for James to dispense with the bloodied bandage he'd held in his hand for some time now.

"Who will?" James feigned ignorance.

"Doncha be thinking ya can fool Seamus McLaughlin. There's an old Irish Proverb: 'It's no use carryin' an umbrella if yer shoes are leakin'. Yer shoes are leakin', James. It's obvious you're frettin' over the lass. Why doncha tell her how ya feel?"

"My shoes are just fine, Corporal." James reached for a half-full pail of water. "I'm going out to get some fresh water."

He furiously worked the pump handle, staring off at the mountains peeking between lush hills and a carpet of treetops.

"I believe that there is the fullest bucket I ever laid eyes on, Doctor." Izzy said from the front stoop. The liver-colored hound lay with its eyes closed, its head resting on Izzy's foot.

James dropped the pump handle, abruptly aware water now flooded the wooden platform. He left the over-flowing bucket beneath the spigot and walked over to Izzy. "Mind if I join you?"

"You just set yourself down, Doctor. Babies tend to take a while. It's not something you can rush."

"Not you, too? First Seamus, now you." James dropped to the step, feeling more than a little foolish.

Izzy chuckled. "Yous tryin' real hard to hide your feelings behind that hang-dog face o' yourn. Just tell Missy Gus how you feel 'bout her."

"I'm not sure that's such a good idea." James tossed a pebble, and Coot opened one eye.

"Now what you say that for?"

"I've made some choices in my life, Izzy. Can't say I wouldn't do it again if I had the chance, though." James reached down and massaged Coot's floppy ear. "I don't deserve a woman like Gus. That's all there is to it."

"Ain't none that's righteous, Doctor. Not one that's deservin' of blessing."

James changed the subject. "You read very well, Izzy. I know it's illegal in some places for Colored folk to read. How'd you learn?"

"Jonathan taught me, he did. I'll always be beholdin' to him for that—and more so for his friendship all these years." Izzy looked off over the pasture and squinted.

"Were you born free, Izzy?"

Silence filled the space between the two men. James wondered if he'd crossed an unseen line. At last, Izzy grunted and sat straighter.

"I's from Kentucky, you see. Well, one day the massa took himself to a revival up in Logan County. A Brother James McGready was preachin'. The year was 1800. Yessir, the massa found Jesus at that tent meetin'. He come home, set all us slaves free, sold his land, and moved up North. Never did hear of him after that."

A lone cow bawled, and the muted cluck of chickens floated through the muggy air.

"I be a free man now for a lot of years, but I never forget the lick of the overseer's whip on my back or the wail of a mama when those white men pull her baby from her arms. Yessir, some things a mind never forgets." His mouth pressed into a hard line, then he scratched at his beard.

Some things a mind never forgets. James smoothed his mustache and stood.

"Doc? There's something I didn't say just now."

"What's that, Izzy?"

"I be free *before* Massa signed my papers. I be free when I let Massa Jesus set me free. The Good Book say when He set you free, you is free indeed. So, Ol' Izzy's been set free two times!" Izzy slapped his knee. Joy traversed his whiskered face by a dozen fine lines. "Yessir. Thank you, Jesus!"

James studied Izzy's white hair and age-bleached face, wondering about the years the old man had seen. A kind of light shown in the faded eyes, and a gap-toothed grin pushed lines of age into furrows on the old man's cheeks.

"Thank you for sharing your story with me, Izzy." He patted the bent shoulder and returned a smile of his own.

Coot raised his head, a growl climbing his throat. He trotted to the well and stood on the wooden platform. Hackles up, he barked frantically with his attention on the lane where it disappeared through the trees.

Twenty-Four

Fayette County

August 26, 1861

Sweat stung Augusta's eye, breaking her concentration. Rubbing her face against her upper sleeve, she forced her mind back to petitioning the Lord for His help, determined to ignore the bodily odors that mingled with the stifling air in the small bedroom.

Melinda Jane pressed a wet cloth against Florence Meyers's brow. "You're almost there, honey. You can do this."

"I can't. I can't do this no more!" Florence cried, tears coursing down her red face.

Augusta glanced up from the foot of the bed. "Yes, you can. I can see the head, Florence. One more push for me, please?"

Augusta ran a skilled, oiled finger around the neck of the womb, loosening the flesh restricting the baby's head. With a mighty growl, Florence pushed, her face contorting into a crimson mask. A blood-smeared head partially emerged, but the coloring—too dark. Augusta reached two fingers further until she could feel the cord around the baby's tiny neck. Gently, she maneuvered her fingers to slip the cord loop over the small head. *Thank you, Lord.*

"I'm sorry, Florence, but I think this really is the last push this time." When the baby's head pressed against her palm, Augusta released the breath she'd been holding.

One shoulder, then the other, came into view. With trained hands, she received the waxy infant, her heart swelling with emotion as the tender new life kicked and twisted within her gentle grasp. *Thank you. Oh, thank you, Lord, for the miracle of this child. The crowning glory of Your creation.*

Melinda Jane handed her a length of thread and Augusta went to work tying off the cord in two places, and then snipping it with the scissors. With a curled finger, she traced the inside of the tiny mouth, coaxing bits of mucus from within. Irritated at the entire process, the infant squalled up a mighty williwaw, igniting a burst of jubilant laughter from the women.

"You have a rambunctious little boy, Florence." Augusta wrapped the child in a soft square of cloth, then brought him to his mother's side for inspection.

"He's just beautiful. Thank you so much, Gus." The expression on Florence's face said it all—the unconditional love of a mother for her child.

When she passed the infant to Melinda Jane, she noticed new beads of perspiration across Florence's forehead. "Are you having more contractions?"

Florence nodded and bore down as Augusta returned to the foot of the bed. "We still have a bit of work to do here, honey. Just give me another push if you can, and we'll take care of the rest." *Please Lord, bless the rest of this delivery, and thank you for this healthy little boy.*

After a very few minutes, the afterbirth appeared, and Augusta placed it in a washbasin on a nearby chair. She hurriedly staunched the bleeding with rags and turned back to the basin.

No one had ever told her to, but it just made sense to make sure everything looked to be in one piece. She'd always done it with the farm animals. Why should this be any different? She turned the slippery mass over, checking for any rips or missing tissue. She breathed in relief, and an unquenchable grin took charge.

An hour later, Florence and a drowsy Baby Meyers lay beneath clean sheets. Both had been bathed, and the new little one introduced to his pap. The other children were content at the table, eating their fill of cornbread and honey.

"I've got you packed with rags now, Florence, and I know you know what to do. We'll send someone over later with some supper and fixin's for the next couple of days so you won't have to get out of that bed. If you have any trouble, just send Ned with word."

Augusta's eyes fell to the sweet cherub, resting in his mother's arms. "Mind if I hold the little angel to say goodbye?" The corner of her eye leaked some.

Florence nodded, and Augusta tenderly lifted the tiny bundle. Sleepy eyes, the dusky color of an early dawn sky, opened wide, then fluttered closed. "You are truly the purest form of love in this entire troubled world, sweet boy." She kissed the downy head and returned him to his mama's arms.

"I don't know how to thank you, Gus, Melinda Jane. I suspect this one will be just as healthy and ornery as my Billy you delivered year before last." Florence smiled down at her baby boy and reached for Augusta's hand. "Thank you again."

"It's the Lord who deserves the credit here, Florence." Augusta squeezed her fingers. "We'll be off now."

∞

James turned to the sound of a dozen blue-clad soldiers on horseback. A wagon trailed behind them bearing a green flag. Armed men approached from the barn as James descended the front steps.

Bertie was close on his heels, having become his shadow whenever the opportunity allowed.

"I'm looking for Major Hill." A towering soldier in the lead declared, clearly in command.

"You've found him, Captain. What can I do for you?" James's men had shouldered their weapons and were standing at attention.

The captain dismounted. "I'm Captain Robert Reynolds with Colonel Tyler's Seventh Ohio Volunteers. I've come from our camp at Kessler's Cross Lanes, eight miles northeast of here." He handed a folded paper to James.

"General Floyd's men attacked us this morning at five o'clock. I'm afraid we were caught a little off-guard—just as most were fixin' to eat breakfast."

James unfolded the missive, weariness settling into his muscles as his eyes followed the words on the page.

"They came in fast, outnumbered us by plenty, too," the captain continued. "We put up a fight for about an hour, then the colonel gave the command to abandon camp. While a few hundred of our men headed over the mountains toward Elk River, Colonel Tyler took about 200 with him. They should be arriving at Gauley Bridge just about now."

His eyes went to the wagon. "We grabbed up some of the injured as best we could and headed this way. There's a good many stragglers trying to make their way through the countryside to get to Gauley Bridge any way they can. The plan is to regroup at the fortification there." The captain looked down, shaking his head, his face pulled with the weight of the news.

"Casualties?" James asked. How he hated this war.

"We don't even know how many we've lost at this point. I'm afraid our retreat was so hasty that Floyd will have his hands full with our dead and wounded. Just from what I saw, I'd say the Confederates probably captured thirty or more of ours."

"You and your men help yourself to the water, Captain. We'll take care of your injured." James motioned to Seamus and Mallory.

At his suggestion, Will recruited her younger brother and rushed off to the barn to help ready more straw pallets. Buckets filled rapidly as Izzy manned the pump, allowing Zander to haul water to the barn while men were unloaded from the wagon. Even amid all the activity, James found himself wishing Gus was here. His frequent thoughts of her were unsettling. In some ways, he supposed, he'd come to depend on her.

He and Seamus conducted a hurried check of those needing medical attention to determine the most critical. One of the eight men had a bayonet wound to his abdomen, but thankfully the bleeding had slowed. James was hopeful the injury would heal, barring infection.

Another soldier was without a shirt as it was bundled tightly around the end of his wrist. Great drops of sweat poured from his face as Seamus unwrapped the bandage. Connected only by a thin sinew, a purple thumb dangled from the heel of his hand. It resembled a pincushion, splinters of bone in place of pins.

James exchanged a glance with his assistant. "Let's get him on the table." He gripped the man's shoulder. "We'll be leaving more than we're taking. Be thankful for that." He poured from a tin labeled *Spiritus Frumenti* and gave the soldier the cup.

"What's your name, soldier?" James poured a bit more into the cup.

"Ferguson, sir."

"I'm Doctor Hill. The next time we talk, you'll be minus a hand, but I'm hoping you'll be keeping your life."

While Seamus and Fin moved Ferguson to the operating table, James looked over the remaining wounded. After this amputation, he'd have to see to the bullet wound in the arm of a squatty sergeant. For now, the man seemed comfortable, having received some laudanum.

Seamus did double duty, dripping the chloroform into the cone and assisting James.

"Watch him carefully," James said, placing the spiral tourniquet high on the upper arm. Positioning the pad on the brachial artery, he tightened the metal screw. Selecting a scalpel from the wooden box, he proceeded to remove the shredded tissue and sloughing bone with a circular cut.

Seamus sponged up the excess blood, then quickly tended to the chloroform again.

Separating the skin, James pulled it up out of the way. He divided muscle with the metal catling, moving it aside as well. Concentrating on the even pull of the blade, he sawed the two bones cleanly through as Seamus held the hand and wrist steady.

He used the hooked tenaculum to draw the arteries into reach, then tied them off. The rest of the procedure—securing the muscles and affixing the skin flap—went as smoothly as he could hope.

"Let's get that sergeant with the shoulder wound onto the other table." James dropped the used instruments into a basin of limpid water that bloomed a murky purple. He rinsed his sticky fingers in a second basin and then turned to the other table.

"What's your name, soldier?" James asked the stout man.

"Johansson, sir." His words slurred. "Are you going to take my arm?"

"I don't believe so, Sergeant. We'll just try to retrieve the bullet."

Seamus administered the chloroform and within minutes, James could clean the wound. He worked the probe, searching for the bullet. "I think I found it. Just. There." He plunged his finger through the torn muscle tissue.

"Victory!" James brandished a slippery black chunk, holding it up to the light of the lantern suspended from the rafter. He curtailed a smile, surprised at his surge of humor.

After sprinkling morphine powder into the wound, he packed it with damp lint. He started to bandage it, but turned to Seamus.

"I'll let you finish this up while he's coming to. After that, we can clear both tables."

❦

Melinda Jane pulled the last pan of biscuits from the oven. She tipped her head, admiring the three large sheets of golden biscuits covering most of the sideboard. A familiar sense of satisfaction settled as she thought of the folks who would appreciate the fare.

"You reckon this'll be enough to last the Meyers a few days?"

"I think so." Gus stirred a tall pot of beans with chunks of onion and carrots, fresh from the garden. "Between the pies, biscuits, and beans, I'm thinking they won't starve." She smiled at her friend. "Did you ever see such a precious little soul? That baby is near perfect in every way. God's beautiful child."

"You say that about every new baby." Melinda Jane slid biscuits from the pans into a large basket lined with a gingham tablecloth. She bundled the fabric over the biscuits and set the basket on the table.

Using a towel for a hot pad, Gus pulled open the oven door. "Would you mind terribly taking Will with you to deliver these? I'd really like to get out to the barn now to help." She hoisted a large roaster of meat pie into the oven and closed the heavy door.

"Don't mind at all. If there're any problems with Mrs. Meyers, I'll send Will back here for you." Melinda Jane untied her apron, hooking it over a wall peg. She smoothed her dress as her mind went to Fin. Maybe she'd best check the mirror before she ventured outside.

"I was thinking we should round up some eggs to take to them," Gus said. "Extra will come in handy for easy meals the next few days. There are a few jars of beets and plums in the box with the pies, too."

"I don't especially want to take on Ol' Rupert this time of day. I'll tell Will you're wantin' those eggs. She thinks it's *fun* dodging those spurs of his." Melinda Jane chuckled and headed out the door.

Sitting on the front steps, Will cooed to a tiny kitten while stroking its soft neck. Melinda Jane leaned down and scratched the kitten's head with one finger. "You're going to the Meyers' with me, Will. We're taking them some vittles and making sure the missus is getting along well enough with that new babe. I'm heading to the barn for an escort."

"How about I'm your escort, and you can do the woman's stuff?"

"Now Will . . . like it or not, God made you a girl, and someday you'll be thankful for it. When you fall in love with that special man—and you have yourself a passel of young'uns." Melinda Jane smiled, gazing at the sky, her arms holding her elbows in a hug. Some days her dreams were bolder than others.

"You're just moonin' over Fin. I'm never gonna moon over nobody."

She relinquished her revelry. "I am *not* moonin'!"

"Sure, you're not. I'm gonna take this kitten back to the barn, then I'll meet you at the wagon." Will hitched up her britches, straightened her old hat, and struck out across the yard.

"You're supposed to fetch what eggs are out there to take along with us, too," Melinda Jane hollered. She chuckled at the exaggerated swagger that spoke of the girl's plucky nature.

Will spun around as she walked, the kitten nestled under her chin. "All right, I'll have a go at Ol' Rupert."

One day she'll be thankful she's a girl. *I know I am.* She pinched her cheeks and continued across the yard.

The barn door creaked open, and Melinda Jane savored the coolness inside. Izzy sat with his back to her, playing checkers with Jürgen. How he loved a game of checkers. Fin looked up from the halter he was tinkering with and sent her a warm smile. She returned a trace of her own, lifted her head, plucked up her hem, and sashayed over to Izzy. Wrapping her arms around him from behind, she gave him a little squeeze.

"Who's beatin' who?" she asked.

"Aww, child, now you know there is always a chance that Jürgen here might one day beat me, so I can't rightly be telling you who's winning."

Izzy moved a piece. "Crown me."

"Ja, looks like I'm going to get him this time. I can feel it in my stump." Jürgen roared at his own joke, then made a to-do of jumping one of Izzy's checkers. He plopped it beside the board with a flourish. "Just like that."

"The Lord giveth, and the Lord hath taken away," Izzy said as his leathery hand picked up a red checker and proceeded to jump three of Jürgen's, leaving him with only two checkers on the board to Izzy's six.

Melinda Jane felt Fin's presence next to her before he spoke.

"Who's winning?"

"Depends on who you ask, but I think we all know the answer." She turned her attention to him. "Will and I are taking some vittles over to the Meyers' place, and we need an escort."

Fin looked toward the ladder where Sergeant Mallory was slapping a harmonica against his palm. "I'll drive you in the wagon and talk to Mallory about some soldiers to ride with us."

She batted her eyes and waxed melodramatic. "Why, thank you kindly, sir."

∞

James watched the exchange with interest. He was mulling over Mr. Dabney's volume by Lord Byron when Melinda Jane made her entrance. It was nothing short of amusing—the way his patients followed her with their eyes. She was a beauty, that one. Her petite figure and that unique, dark golden hair. It was no wonder her every movement caught the eye of the men.

He grinned as another image filled his mind's eye. A spray of freckles on a reddened face, tendrils of gingered hair falling in disarray to frame the most vivid green eyes he'd ever seen.

"Ahh, tis that look of a heart gone for a holiday," Seamus said, startling James with his sudden presence.

"What?" Like a child caught with his hand in the cookie jar. "I don't know what you're talking about."

"Sure, and I'm the queen of England."

※

In a short time, Fin had loaded the food into the wagon. His cheek twitched with a smile as Melinda Jane scooted a bit closer on the buckboard seat. In the back of the wagon, Will had gathered a mound of small rocks to toss onto the road as they traveled to the neighbor's house.

He was thankful that Sergeant Mallory and two other soldiers accompanied them as reports of thievery and coarse treatment of the area farmers had increased in recent days. Confederates were reported to be deserting in droves as Wise's troops backed out of western Virginia. He'd heard talk that Rebel guerillas were engaging any Yankees they encountered on the roads.

This would likely be the last trip away from the farm for any of the Dabneys for some time.

Twenty-Five

Fayette County

September 1861

James unwound the soiled bandage while Gus held the man's arm in a firm grip. He coaxed the pink lint from the wound, drawing a string of pus stretching like a bridge to the red flesh.

"The wound is suppurating. I think we need to continue the quinine every few hours and change the bandage often." James sent her a knowing look then addressed the patient.

"How does your shoulder feel, Johanssen?"

"Somewhat worse than a bee sting, but better than a bear bite, I'd say." The man grinned and winked at Gus.

She smiled at him like a mother to a child and said, "I hope you've not had an occasion to endure a bite from a bear, sir."

"Oh, well . . . No, ma'am. It don't hurt much at all, really." He lowered his gaze, suddenly shy.

"You're a brave soldier, Private." She patted his hand, released it, and stood just as one of the men appeared at the barn entrance, rifle in hand.

"You better come and see this, Major Hill."

Gus shooed James off. "You go ahead. I can finish this up."

"Thank you." He smiled his gratitude and hurried out of the barn.

Sergeant Mallory accompanied several unfamiliar Union soldiers, each of which was leading a horse with a man either draped over its back or slumped in the saddle.

"One of our scouts came across these boys. Seems they were wandering around lost after being held prisoner up north of here by some of Lee's men." Mallory's eyes telegraphed concern.

"Let's get the wounded into the barn." James signaled for men to help.

One of the newly arrived soldiers leaned heavily on his saddle horn. "I'm sorry to say, Major, only three men are injured—and that happened when we met with a little altercation with Rebels up the road aways. Most of us are sick. Seems some sort of sickness is moving through Lee's troops like a brushfire." The man closed his eyes, drawing in a ragged breath to continue.

"Ol' Granny Lee is backing out of western Virginia real fast-like, givin' up on reclaiming what the Rebels lost this summer."

James shared a look of apprehension with Gus, who had appeared beside him. He approached a body draped over a saddle. The man groaned when James lifted his head. Red, circular spots dotted the man's face and hands. James could feel the heat radiating from his body, confirming his suspicions.

"This man has the measles." James moved to a second. "This one is dead."

"Can we put them in the loft to cut short the contagion?" Gus asked.

"That's an excellent idea." James continued his assessment of each of the new men.

∞

A short time later, Augusta scurried up the loft ladder with a clean cloth and a bucket of water, followed by a private with a stack of army-issued blankets. Until now, the haymow had been the sleeping quarters for James and all the Union soldiers appointed to the hospital. Their belongings had been removed, so she would do what she could to make way for the new patients.

She set upside-down crates about the space to act as tables. Then, with the private's help, fluffed the straw into pallets and covered them with blankets. One by one, soldiers were carried up the ladder on the back of a brawny private named Giles.

∞

James stepped from the ladder rung to the floor of the loft, where Gus stood with her back to him. "I don't want you up here with these men."

She whirled on him; her eyes wide. "James..." She put her hand to her chest as if to calm its rise and fall. "You startled me." A smile of understanding flashed. "All the Dabneys except Bertie have had the measles, so not to worry."

He nodded. "That is good to hear. How are we ever going to keep Bertie away from the barn, though? These men are showing signs of every stage of the disease. It will likely be a month before we can be sure it's safe."

She placed her hand on his arm. "We'll just have to make him understand." She paused and turned serious. "God is watching over us. I can feel Him."

He looked at her hand, aware of its warmth, and even a measure of peace. Dare he believe *he* could ever feel God? That God would give a thought for a man like him? For a long moment, her inquisitive eyes bore into his before she resumed tending to the newcomers.

∞

The hoot of an owl stirred the stillness, followed by the faraway yip of coyotes. James thought of the night creatures—scurrying, flying, hunting. Their lives went on as always, barely molested by this war. A war waged by human beings who deemed themselves more intelligent, more progressive, and more compassionate than those of the animal kingdom.

In an effort to remedy his insomnia with fresh air, James stepped outside and into the light of an almost full moon. He walked into the shadow of a yellow birch, allowing him a clear view of the yard. The Alleghenies rose off to the east, their charcoal outline awaiting the dawn. Near the corner of the house, Will's white mama cat, Sugar, crouched, stalking a tiny critter of the night.

A rustling in the hen house broke the quiet. He thought to see to the commotion just as Coot darted in that direction, barking for all he was worth. In a moment, the house door opened and there on the porch stood Gus, a robe cinched at her waist. One hand gripped the barrel of a shotgun, the other the stock.

Out of nowhere, a fox bolted across the yard, the hound fast on its heels. She raised the gun, following the chase with the barrel until Coot vanished into the night, his bark dying away. She released the hammer and leaned the gun in the corner.

James kept to the puddle of darkness as Gus stepped off the porch, his curiosity holding him prisoner. She tipped her head to the starry sky and stretched both hands heavenward; her robe aglow in the moonlight—an angelic vision.

She slowly turned in a circle. Moonbeams ignited her hair as the wavy locks flowed unrestrained. They reached to her waist. Never had he seen so much radiant hair—hair the hue of maple leaves in autumn. Of fire, aflame to a breeze. It possessed a life of its own as she tipped back her head and began to spin. She twirled around and around like a child, reaching for that state of unbridled delight. Stopping suddenly, her hands dropped to her knees. She staggered briefly, laughing aloud.

James realized he'd been holding his breath, utterly entranced by the scene before him. He breathed in, willing his pulse to slow.

After a few moments, Gus lifted her hem and walked toward the chicken house. Fearing he would be discovered, James decided it would be best to come clean.

He stepped out of the shadow, and hoping not to startle her a second time in the same day, he recited the lines of Lord Byron. The very words which had seized his thoughts since the moment he'd glimpsed her on the porch this night. *"She walks in beauty, like the night."* With a gasp, she pulled her robe tight and turned to him as he continued: *"Of cloudless climes and starry skies. And all that's best of dark and bright meet in her aspect and her eyes."*

"How long have you been standing there?"

He was certain a blush crept over her lovely face. "A while. I couldn't sleep." Guilt washed over him, as if he'd overheard a great secret.

The silence was deafening.

"It . . . it's a beautiful night." He was a schoolboy again. It's Gus. Just Gus. They'd been working together and eating together for months. Why was he suddenly speechless?

"It is lovely." She pointed to the starry sky. "Look, there's Vega, the falling eagle."

"It's in Lyra." James pointed lower. "And there's Sagittarius."

"It is breathtaking, isn't it?" Gus closed her eyes and poured forth the words of the Psalmist:

> *"The heavens declare the glory of God;*
> *and the firmament sheweth his handiwork.*
> *Day unto day uttereth speech,*
> *and night unto night sheweth knowledge.*
> *There is no speech nor language,*
> *where their voice is not heard."*

"Their line is gone out through all the earth, and their words to the end of the world," James finished.

"You are full of surprises, Doctor Hill."

"I am not completely unchurched, ma'am. It's just been a while since I read much from the Good Book."

He'd sat long hours in church as a boy. One day, within his father's hearing, he'd invited Ezra to church with the family. James's father had grabbed his friend by the shirt collar and shoved him roughly to the floor. *"Jesus does not care about the Colored, son."* James could still hear the poison in his father's voice.

"What are you thinking?" She angled her head to one side. "You looked so disquieted just now."

James shook his head. "It was nothing." He offered her his arm. "May I escort you to your door, Miss Dabney?"

"Why certainly, sir." She adjusted her robe and took the proffered arm.

"So, have you received any more letters from that beau of yours?" James asked, attempting a casual inquiry, but he feared his tone more resembled a lawman interrogating a suspect.

Their steps slowed in tandem.

"Now, you know there's been no mail made it through from Gauley Bridge in weeks. For another thing, my 'beau', as you call him, is none of your business."

He forced a gentlemanly smile, but his heart worked to recover from the unpleasant jolt. "Consider me put in my place, ma'am." James bowed slightly and searched for another subject, not willing to part company just yet.

"Tell me about Melinda Jane. She's obviously one of the family, but not by blood?" James delivered her to the front porch steps.

"Melinda Jane?" Gus turned, scrutinizing him with a raised eyebrow.

"Oh, it's not what you think." He scrambled, realizing his question may have given the wrong impression. "I see how close you two are. She seems very close to Izzy, too . . . uh . . . you both do, actually."

"You know why I love Izzy, but I guess I neglected to tell you about Melinda Jane. Her mama and pap died in a cholera outbreak three years ago. She's been living with us ever since." She picked up the shotgun and put her hand on the doorknob.

"As for Melinda Jane and Izzy, she's fiercely protective of him—as any girl would be of her grandpappy." She opened the door and slipped inside, leaving James alone on the porch with his thoughts. Another piece of the Dabney puzzle fell into place. Would this family ever cease to amaze him?

He strolled toward the barn. As he reached the door, he noticed Coot's silhouette against the side of the corncrib. Another shadow caught his eye. A man's shadow. James slipped through the barn door to retrieve his pistol. Keeping to the darkness, he headed to the corncrib.

"Hold it right there." James cocked the pistol. "Turn around nice and easy." The man raised his hands in a sign of surrender, then slowly turned.

"Can't sleep, Doctor?"

"Izzy? What are you doing out here?" James released the hammer and lowered the weapon.

"Ah . . . well . . . I just figured it be a near perfect night for a stroll, being I's having trouble sleeping, just like you." Izzy patted Coot's head. "I reckon I'll be gettin' on back to my cabin now. Goodnight, Doc."

"Goodnight, Izzy." James returned to the barn, baffled by the interaction. Hadn't he been standing in the shadows a short time ago himself?

Twenty-Six

～

Fayette County

Fin sauntered over to the birch tree near the barn where Will spread blankets on the ground. More wounded had come in, and space in the barn would soon be at a premium. As long as there was no rain, the less seriously injured could bed down in the tree's shade.

"Where did these boys come from?" Fin asked, a rifle in one hand and three rabbits in the other.

"I don't rightly know." She picked up two more sticks, clearing the ground for blankets. "Ask Sergeant Mallory."

"I'll do that." He glanced at his catch and headed off to clean them behind the barn.

"I see some rabbit pie in your future, Fin." Mallory said, dumping a bucket of bloody water onto the grass.

"Yep, looks to be. Where'd this new bunch of men come from, Sergeant?" He reached for a steel hanging from a leather strap on the barn siding and began sharpening his knife.

"Down off of New River. Seems Ol' Wise took it on himself to try to oust our boys from Hawk's Nest. Over a thousand men, General Wise had."

He'd already gutted the rabbits in the field, so he inserted the knife just above a bony ankle to start the skinning process. "How'd it turn out?" He caught up the first rabbit onto special nails.

They'd been hammered up long years before especially for hanging a carcass and stripping the skin.

It seemed every time he had the notion that altercations in these parts were slowing down, there'd be more trouble. He was fooling himself if he thought he could wait much longer—as if it was some family feud likely to burn itself out.

"Those Johnnies backed off after a spell. Yes sir, our boys were dug in real good and held that mountain just like kings. I'd better get back in there before they wonder if I've deserted." Mallory punched Fin in the arm and turned back toward the building.

The punch barely registered, and the rabbits were ignored as other contemplations claimed Fin's attention. He had a tower of sorts in his mind, built up with reasons for joining in this fight. It had a sturdy foundation now. And its walls were rapidly growing higher, brick by brick.

∞

James rolled his head, stretching stiff neck muscles. He stole a look at Gus as she worked with one of the injured men. A sergeant who had accompanied the wounded from Hawks Nest approached her, his saddlebag slung over one shoulder.

"Excuse me, Miss Dabney?" He retrieved a bundle of letters. "I believe these are for you, ma'am."

"Mail?" she said in surprise. "How ever did you come by these, Sergeant?"

"We intercepted a mail wagon a few days back. One of the men recognized your name, so we hung onto these until we could get them to you."

"I'm much appreciative for your thoughtfulness." Gus tossed the letters on a table and went back to bandaging a scalp graze on one of the new patients.

"Not bad news, I hope." Curiosity niggled at James, but he'd not embarrass himself by asking outright if the missives were from her beau. The letters splayed where they landed. At least three were addressed to Gus, and more to her father.

"I'll tend to those later. Did you check on the Andrews boy upstairs? He's the one with the arm wound." She frowned. "He's running a high fever. It looks like a blood infection has set in, and I'm not so sure his body can fight it—with the measles and all."

"I'll go see to him right now. After that, do you want to try your hand at stitching?" James selected a couple of bottles from the pannier of medicine. "Well?"

"I've done my share of stitching, but I would like to learn to do it like you do. I'm afraid mine is better suited for a quilting bee."

He chuckled. "Good, then. We'll get to that next." James grabbed his stethoscope and a few more items and tossed them into a bucket. Looping it over his arm, he scrambled up the ladder.

He knelt on the floor of the loft next to Andrews to unwrap the boy's arm. "Where are you from, son?"

"Charleston, sir."

The boy's sizeable brown eyes reminded James of J.D., their unusual patient-prisoner. She'd been young too, but not this young. He remembered how Gus and Melinda Jane had fussed and hugged her goodbye when Captain Reynolds took her away with the rest of the prisoners. Women!

Yes, that's what a woman does. She loves and mends and—more than that, she's tough. And strong. Strong enough to fight for a cause she believes in. She would devote her life to caring for her family instead of escaping to matrimony. And she would walk into the night alone, armed with a shotgun.

The arm was badly inflamed. James guarded his expression for the boy's sake. Streaks of red had traveled up to the boy's shoulder and crossed the deltoid in the back.

"How old are you, son—and I mean your real age? It won't leave this room."

"I told them I was eighteen, but if you ask my mama, I'm fifteen, sir." The boy grimaced as James sponged the raw area. He opened a morphine packet and sprinkled the powder into the wound.

"I see. And what do your parents think of you joining the army?"

"They're both dead, sir. There's no one but me and my older brother, Jeremiah. He volunteered right at the first. I don't know where he is."

Nary a trace of sweat glinted on his skin. His body radiated heat like a banked stove. James poured him a dose of laudanum.

"This should help you feel a better. I'll check back with you later today."

James watched as the boy drifted off to sleep. Anger and regret assailed him. Fifteen was too young to war, too young to love, too young to die. *Andrew's life has just begun, and now it must end.*

☙

Augusta looked over at the man bearing multiple knife wounds. He lay on the surgical table, blissfully unconscious. As she administered the chloroform, James threaded two needles with suture.

Although she was eager to expand her skills, the sheer amount of stitching that would be required here was far beyond her experience. Her confidence waned, but James was a good teacher. His easy way with patients extended to her likewise whenever they worked together. She'd learned a great deal under his tutelage and found nothing less than satisfaction in working by his side.

He handed one needle to her and began stitching with the other as he expertly squeezed the two ripped pieces of flesh together on the man's abdomen.

"I'm going to begin here, and I want you to begin on that cut." He pointed to the upper right arm. "Just imitate what I'm doing. I'll help you get started first, then again at the end."

Thirty minutes later, the man bore a great many stitches on his arms and abdomen. Augusta had insisted that James stitch the three-inch cut on the man's cheek, claiming, "His wife will appreciate it more than he will."

When at last she'd finished, she dried her hands on a towel, eyeing the letters on the table. She had procrastinated long enough. She scooped them up and headed for the house.

Standing in the kitchen, she set Jimmy Lee's letters aside. She'd written to him twice. That was before everything heated up around here. She could tell from the dates the letters were weeks old.

Trepidation slowed her fingers as she slipped a knife into the letters addressed to her father. Both were from the bank, apprising him of the past due payment. It seemed they were simply reminding Jonathan Dabney that he owed them money, but no amount was mentioned, nor was there a due date.

She sliced the seal on the two unknown letters addressed to her, opening the older one first. Her heart sank. The letter was from Edward Fontaine. Several lines of mundane camp routine were innocuous, but it was the last paragraph that set her on edge:

> *I've honored the deferment on your father's mortgage, as we discussed. I sincerely hope that you have considered my proposal, offered with a most altruistic purpose. I have confidence that you will choose what is best for your family and yourself.—Yours, Edward*

The second letter was much the same, with a warning added:

It would grieve me, my dear Augusta, to see you and your family in the poorhouse, wanting for sustenance when you could've prevented it.—Yours Still, Edward

∞

James watched as Gus struggled with the heavy water bucket. She gripped the ladder with her left hand and attempted to climb. A pulley system had been rigged to haul items up to the hayloft, but the rope had fallen loose to the floor at some point.

As she took a second step, he rushed over to stand behind her. "You know, there are plenty of strapping young men around here to do that for you."

"And would you be one of them?" She turned to make eye contact, but as she shifted, so did her grip on the ladder, sending her toppling backward. James reached for her waist, preventing her collision with the floor, but not before the water drenched them both.

He steadied her, catching his breath after the deluge. "That was quite refreshing!"

"Indeed!" Gus picked up the bucket, looking into it for an instant before dumping the rest over James's head.

Only when water dripped into his mouth did he realize it was hanging open. Before he could form words, she marched out the door, bucket in hand.

With the fallen rope over his shoulder, James climbed the ladder. He draped the length over the pulley once again. Maybe Gus would use it for the next bucket. He grinned as he replayed her expression when she'd emptied the bucket over his head. Amazing what that woman could say without uttering a word.

Most of the men with measles were progressing well. The disease had run its course with some, while others were still in the throes of fever.

He knelt down next to Andrews. His body still, the cherub face no longer glowed with the heat of fever. With a heavy heart, James pulled the cover over the boy's head.

He died alone. If James only had known Andrews would succumb so quickly, he would've held him. Yes, he would have. He would've sat right here on this floor and held him. So young. *Too* young. He swallowed a sob, burying his face in his hands. Movement to the right caught his eye. Two of the soldiers watched him.

His body tensed. Something erupted from the suppressed misery. "What are you looking at?" he growled.

He stood, feeling his blood pulse and muscles strain from his clenched fists. "He was fifteen!" The words thundered loud and gruff, but he didn't care. "That boy was fifteen years old, and I let him die!"

Exasperated. Furious. He struck out with his fist—crashing against the lantern hanging from the rafter. Glass shattered. Bedded men blocked their faces from the flying shards.

Standing there, his breath came hard and fast. He wanted to scream and not stop. He wanted to bawl like a child.

Movement caught his eye, and to his shame, Gus stood on an upper rung of the ladder, her sad eyes drawing him. She held out a cloth for him and motioned to his hand. Calm. Compassionate. "You're hurt."

As the rage shriveled, pain seeped into his awareness, and he looked at his hand. Blood dripped with an accelerating rhythm. A red pool spread swiftly across the floor. He imagined it must be dripping through to the level below. He took the rag from Gus's fingers.

"Are you coming?" she asked, her voice somehow offering him a measure of security. Her eyes shown with care, not pity. Understanding, not judgement. She offered a hesitant smile and backed down the ladder.

༄

In silence, James sat on a stool as Gus unwound the rag from his hand. His mind was numb, a sweet respite from the rage that had engulfed him earlier. He couldn't bring his eyes to meet hers. Not yet.

After pouring water into a clean basin, with practiced tenderness, she proceeded to wash away the blood. Though his eyes saw only the floor, he knew she wore her familiar composure as she retrieved morphine powder from the pannier and sprinkled it into the wound. Cutting a length of suture from a spool and pulling a needle from its leather swatch, she set to work, stitching the tender skin on the back of his hand in silence.

After a good deal of teeth grinding and refusal to make a sound, by the time the sutures were in place, James had relaxed some. "I'm sorry you saw that," he said, his eyes now on the fresh wound.

"I would be the pot calling the kettle black if I were to judge your outburst, James." With the gentlest touch, she tipped his chin and met his gaze. "You care for all these boys. I know you do. For you to not be enraged at the violence that takes a young man before his time . . ." She shook her head sadly, then dribbled carbolic acid onto a rag and wiped the needle, returning it to the leather swatch.

"Only God knows our hearts. Whether it's the tears on my pillow or the rage that begets your wound, God knows." Her eyes smiled behind a shimmer of moisture, sending a soft blanket of comfort over his battered spirit. "You're a decent, compassionate man, Dr. Hill

Gus lifted his hand to examine her handiwork. "Now, that will be a rather distinctive scar, I'd say."

"It rather looks like . . . an *H*?" James looked closer. "I believe you've forever branded me with my initial, Miss Dabney." He searched her eyes again for the truth of what she thought of him. What he saw in those green pools was serenity—and *affection*. Was it affection for James, the patient? Or James, the man? He could not be sure.

Her thumb stroked his as she cradled the injured hand in her own. The peace he'd seen but an instant ago melted to sadness. Her lips parted as if to say something, then closed.

He captured her gaze with some effort. What was it that tore at her heart so? He wanted to take away her sorrow. He wanted to fold her into his arms. He wanted to kiss those lips.

"I hear you got yourself in need of a little fixin', Doctor." Izzy hobbled toward them.

Gus gasped, softly. Rising suddenly, she strode past Izzy and out of the barn.

"I'm thinking I'm interrupting something. Sorry about that, Doc." Izzy motioned toward the door. "Missy all right?"

"She's fine Izzy. I . . . uh . . . had a minor accident, and she stitched up my hand." James presented Gus's handiwork.

"Most hurts around here ain't no accident, least not in the last few months." Sitting on a campstool, Izzy settled his elbows on the table and looked hard at James, wizened eyes inviting his thoughts.

James shook his head. "Some mornings I wake up and wish I was back in Charleston, setting broken bones or treating some old man's gout." He longed for the sheer simplicity of his former life. He missed the innocence of the ordinary.

"It's like I'm caught in the middle of a skirmish. On one side of me are the things that really matter"—he nodded toward the men sprawled in cots—"and on the other side there's the doctoring that just serves to make folks feel good about themselves."

Izzy pulled off his crumpled hat and set it on one knee. "When you was doctorin' in Charleston, didn't you feel like what you did was important?"

"Not most of the time—but there *was* Nan." James stroked his beard. "I tried to do right by her."

James told Izzy about Nan and buying her from that wretched Henry Orr. "I hope she's gotten word to Mrs. O'Donell that she's getting on all right."

"That girl has a whole new life because of you, Doc."

James sat straighter. "But there are hundreds of Orrs out there I cannot do anything about. Maybe, just maybe, this war will put an end to the likes of men like that."

"The way I figure it, Doc, is that we's all like Nan."

"How do you mean, Izzy?"

"That girl was in a situation—a prisoner to a cruel keeper. She wanted to get free, but didn't have no way to buy her freedom. Then you come along."

"So how are we all like Nan? I'm not following." James studied Izzy's face. The man's eyes never lost their sparkle. While the rest of his face hung rutted and sundried, his coffee-brown eyes fairly danced.

"We's all in bondage, James. We's born into bondage, just like I was all those years ago. Massa Jesus, he done paid the price to buy our freedom, just like you bought Nan's. Oh, He didn't pay with money, like you did. He paid with his own blood—his very life. Ain't nobody can say that wasn't enough." Izzy pounded the table once with his scaly fist. "'Cause Jesus didn't never sin. No, sir. Not once. He was perfect.

"He paid that price to buy us our freedom, so He picks us up, cleans our wounds, and sets us on a better path."

James was silent for a long moment, willing his thoughts to venture beyond the weary bog that seemed to suck him into the ground. He closed his eyes, massaging his forehead.

"Bondage comes in many forms, Doctor. Anger, bitterness, unforgiveness—they's all shackles—and Massa Jesus, He has the keys. It's Him who sets a man truly free." Izzy pushed up from the scarred table. "I best be gettin' to that checker game with Johnson over there."

Twenty-Seven

Fayette County

James leaned over the boy in silence, his ear to the stethoscope. Bertie slept peacefully, his chest and arms bare as Gus dabbed at the tiny beads of perspiration dotting his forehead.

"I'm sorry, Gus. I'd hoped to keep him clear of the measles." He tucked his stethoscope back into his bag. "He's young and healthy, so there's no reason to expect any complications. We'll have to let it run its course." He trusted his expression matched the encouragement he wanted to convey. Anything to dispel the worry lines marring her beautiful brow.

"Thank you, James. I feel better having you check on him." She pulled the light blanket up to her brother's shoulders, then cupped his red cheek in her palm and closed her eyes. "Father, please, oh, please protect this precious one from harm." James didn't miss a fat tear, though she quickly wiped it away.

"Care for a cup of coffee?" Her smile didn't reach her eyes.

"Not right now, thank you. I would like to check in on your pap."

They exited the room in silence, and Gus pulled the door closed with a click.

He followed her down the stairs and into her father's room. He listened to the man's ragged breathing and frowned. "Mr. Dabney?" He gently touched the smooth hand. First one eye, then the other opened. "Are you in any pain, sir?"

Mr. Dabney's easy smile spread across his pale cheeks. His eyes met James's, then shifted to Gus. His words halted and brushed the air. "I'm not in pain, but I don't like all this sleeping I'm doing." He scowled. "Bertie hasn't been in today." His look passed from James to his daughter. "What's wrong?" He attempted to sit up.

"Nothing to worry about, Mr. Dabney. Bertie has a case of the measles. He'll be fine in a couple of weeks." James smiled at his patient, but his gaze slid to Gus.

"Yes, Pap. Just as soon as he's up to it, he'll be in here pestering you again."

"I can read to you in his stead if you'd like, sir."

The Dabney family members took turns reading to their father. Sometimes they'd read from their pap's worn leather Bible. Other times, from a book off the shelf. And he had read from the volumes of Byron or Whitman's *Leaves of Grass* on his frequent visits. Bertie read from his primer though, since the school had not reopened this fall. Along with a lot of other folks, Miss Norris, the schoolteacher, had fled the county.

Pap raised his hand, and Gus grasped it. "What is it, Pap?" She leaned her ear closer.

"Could you please give me some time with the good doctor, honey?"

She glanced at James, who shrugged his shoulders. "Of course." She eased Pap's hand to his belly, then squeezed the pale fingers.

James waited until she closed the door behind her, then turned to her father. "You wanted to speak with me, Mr. Dabney?" His patient coughed weakly, and he offered water, lifting his head with one hand.

"I didn't say anything before, James, but I knew your father." He paused for a breath. "I didn't know him well, mostly by reputation."

James sat back, pressed into the chair under a weight of shame. Yes, he was ashamed of the type of man his father was. What he believed in. What he stood for. But just now—sitting here before Mr. Dabney, who was helpless and at death's door—a harsh truth came to him. He pitied his father. Yes. That was it. He pitied him. When had that changed?

"We don't choose our families, James. Nonetheless, they are the families"—Mr. Dabney wheezed, struggling for air, and James leaned forward to assist, but a trembling hand halted him—"the families God chose for us. I ran from my heritage, as I believe you have as well. Am I right?"

"Yes, sir." James fidgeted with the handle of his medical bag.

"I wasn't free from my past until Jesus gave me a future." Mr. Dabney closed his eyes, a sigh whispered from his upturned lips.

James stood silently and tiptoed toward the door. The floor squeaked, and he glanced back at the man.

One weepy eye opened, and he spoke. "She's a good woman, my Gussy. Just like her mama. Take care of her, James." His eyes closed again and his head lolled to one side. James watched for the rise and fall of his chest, then slipped quietly out the door.

He found Gus on the front porch. The dull staccato of rain on the roof vied for his senses, but Coot's bark alerted him from somewhere down the lane, beyond the bend.

"He won't make it much longer, will he?" She turned to him, resignation glistening in her eyes.

He thought to take her in his arms. To ease her grief. But forced his hands to remain at his side. "I don't believe so, but he could linger. At least he's not in pain." James nodded to the liver-colored dog galloping toward the house, his tongue flapping to one side. "I believe we have company."

The heavens opened, and water cascaded like a waterfall, so they remained on the covered porch, watching visitors splash across the yard to the house.

"Captain Reynolds, we meet again," James said, returning a salute. "Are you bearing wounded?" James looked over the contingent of more than a dozen soldiers accompanying the captain.

"Not this time, Major." Reynolds's eyes scanned the area. "May I have a word?"

"Certainly." James motioned to the front door. "Would you care for a cup of coffee?" He turned to Gus. "That is, if it is all right with Miss Dabney."

She smiled at the captain. "Certainly. Gentlemen, please come in, and I'll get you some coffee and apple pie." As she opened the door and glanced at James. A wrinkled brow betrayed her concern.

Captain Reynolds signaled his men to take shelter in the barn. He removed his hat and poncho, draping them over a rocker, then followed James into the house.

Gus set two plates of pie on the table and poured coffee. "Would you like some privacy, Captain?"

"That won't be necessary, Miss Dabney. I doubt you could be the woman of compassion I've witnessed *and* a Confederate spy."

"What's this about?" James wrapped his fingers around the warm mug.

"After General Floyd routed our men at Cross Lanes, he established a command on the bluffs overlooking Carnifex Ferry." Reynolds took a sip of coffee and shook his head. "He calls it 'Camp Gauley.' He's constructed extensive entrenchments along the bend in the Gauley River. That ferry crossing is one of a few places a troop movement of any size can cross the river. We aim to secure that crossing."

"What's General Floyd's current force in the area?" James took another bite of pie, but already the sweet apples were turning bitter in his mouth.

"Our scouts estimate about two thousand at the camp and several thousand more scattered in the area. Traveling this way from the East is a contingent of roughly fifteen hundred Confederates.

We assume their plan is to rendezvous with Floyd's troops at Camp Gauley."

James slid a glance to Gus, who stood at the worktable. Her lips pressed into a somber line. She fidgeted, then poured herself a cup of coffee.

Captain Reynolds took a long sip of the hot liquid. "Six thousand Union troops are marching down the Gauley Bridge-Weston Turnpike toward Camp Gauley as I speak, Major. General Wise is actively engaging our boys at Gauley Bridge at the moment, but we fully expect him to break away and head up to Carnifex Ferry."

"If that happens, there'll be thousands of Rebels marching right past our farm!" Gus had been listening in silence. Now she wrung her hands and looked toward the staircase. James knew she was thinking of her little brother who lay just up those steps, burning with fever.

He stood. "We'll be ready for the casualties, Captain."

The captain gulped down the rest of his coffee and stood. He pulled a folded paper from his jacket pocket and handed it to James. "I'm afraid you will have to leave men here to guard the wounded and to prepare for more, Major. General Rosecrans has ordered that you and your assistant report to the ferry crossing for field duty. The Union troops will attack Floyd's entrenchments tomorrow." His stern gaze softened as he looked from Gus to James. "I'll wait for you in the barn."

The captain turned to Gus. "Thank you for the refreshments, Miss Dabney." He saluted James, then strode from the kitchen.

"I guess that's that." James stood and refolded the paper, stuffing it into his pocket. He reached for Gus's hand as she approached. Cradling her fingers in his own, he studied their smallness.

His heart was heavy, but conflict did not lend to its weight. No. This was something he knew he must do beyond a doubt. He met Gus's gaze. Could this be the last time he looked into those captivating eyes?

"I'll pray for you every minute," she said, grasping his other hand. "I'll make sure everything is ready for you when you come back. And you *will* come back here, safe . . . and sound."

A fog of silence shrouded time as James imagined what it would be like to touch a finger to those freckles and caress those full lips with his own. His arms ached to hold her.

Without warning, she threw her arms around his neck. Surprised and delighted, he enveloped her, relishing the feel of her at last. But too soon, she pulled away and ran from the kitchen. With his arms abruptly empty again, a pang of regret he recognized all too well, constricted his heart. He could go after her. But if he didn't return, it was better this way.

Twenty-Eight

Nicholas County

September 9, 1861

While James prepared for what amounted to a vast chess game near Summersville, the playing pieces moved into position on the board. A five-mile-long ribbon of wagons snaked its way south, around the hills and curves of the Weston and Gauley Bridge Pike. A squadron of cavalry led the way, followed by the First Brigade under Brigadier General Henry W. Benham.

One regiment under his command was the 10th Ohio Infantry, Colonel William H. Lytle's mostly Irish regiment. They marched to the lilt of the melodies of their homeland, shouting their cadenced replies to the drum. This would be their first engagement since leaving Ohio as green recruits. Two more Ohio regiments, an Independent Battery, and two Virginia Cavalry units followed.

Next marched Colonel R. L. McCook's Second Brigade, comprising three Ohio regiments and Captain Frederick Shambeck's colorful company of Chicago Dragoons, armed as cavalry but expected to fight on foot as well. Behind them was the Third Brigade under the command of Colonel E.P. Scammon. Within his ranks marched two more Ohio regiments and Captain O.A. Mack's company of Fourth Artillery with his six-pound James guns.

Artillery, caissons, and wagons ladened with ammunitions creaked along, jostled by every mud hole. Gumbo-caked wheels and boots pressed forward through Nicholas County in an overall effort to open up Gauley Road clean through to General Cox's army at Gauley Bridge.

Weary soldiers made camp at Muddlety Creek, eight miles north of Summersville. Formerly a Confederate outpost, it provided a brief respite for the troops before proceeding to Summersville early the next morning to face General Floyd's forces.

∞

Summersville - Carnifex Ferry
September 10, 1861

Captain Reynolds laughed, clapping a tall Union officer on the back. "Major Hill, I'd like you to meet Colonel William Lytle. We attended Cincinnati College together."

"It's an honor." James grasped the man's hand. Mallory had mentioned Col. Lytle's Irish regiment. Now he had a face to connect with the name.

"The Major has set up a fine hospital in a barn just a few miles from here. I'm afraid I've had the unfortunate opportunity to deliver wounded to him more than once." Captain Reynolds nodded toward a congregating group of officers with an eyebrow raised in question.

"Ah, yes," Col. Lytle said. "General Rosecrans himself has laid all this out. We'll be getting briefed here shortly." The colonel turned to James. "Where do you hail from, Major Hill?"

"I have a medical practice in Charleston—at least I *had* a practice there."

"Charleston? Isn't that a hotbed of confederate sentiment? From what I understand, the entire Kanawha Valley is split down the middle as to where their allegiances lay." Col. Lytle stroked his distinguished, dark beard. The man stood taller than most and carried himself with authority as a veteran officer not unfamiliar with the forthcoming events.

"Yes, sir, it certainly is. Although General Cox's forces have swept through and nearly pushed General Wise from the Valley, there remains a presence of Rebel guerillas. There are camps of them scattered throughout most of these mountains, hidden in the thickly forested areas." Voices quieted as General Rosecrans raised a hand.

A couple of officers affixed a wide plank across two campstools. The general spread a map of sorts onto the impromptu table. "This is what we have before us, gentlemen. The Confederates have fortified a homestead with a house, barn, and a few other outbuildings on the north bank of the Gauley River. There is a parapet battery, three hundred fifty feet long, in the front and center. It's flanked by breastworks laid out here and here." He tapped the map with his forefinger. "The ends rest on these cliffs along the river."

James couldn't see the map, but no matter, he would go where the wounded dropped. He didn't need a map for that. Col. Lytle made his way close enough to see the parchment as the general continued to explain the situation in an animated fashion.

"A double line of breastworks on the left and this trench protect a battery, here." This time, he tapped the map with a pencil. "This deep ravine affords us some protection, but we need to beware of the cleared spaces on the right and left. However, you can see there are slight ridges protected by abatis. We'll count on the trees for cover, but expect the thick undergrowth to hamper your movements."

General Rosecrans stretched to a full standing position. He tossed the pencil onto the map. "Expect confrontation to most likely occur in that cornfield along the road."

"Let us pray for the outcome, gentlemen." The general removed his hat, and the other officers followed suit as he offered a heartfelt prayer. He passed a somber look across his officers. "Boots and saddles, men!"

∞

James waited with the Irish Regiment as Col. McCook's Dragoons headed down River Road to secure the ferry. Within minutes, as the skirmishers were engaged, musket fire sounded. As the rest of the First Brigade moved forward, Col. Lytle rallied his men to follow toward the Dragoons.

The Confederate detachment near the river fired upon McCook's boys but was routed when Col. Lytle's men arrived. No doubt they would double-time to their main camp. There would be no surprising Floyd. Col. Lytle managed to secure the ferry, and James moved with the rest of the troops down River Road to take up positions.

He found himself huddled beside Seamus with Col. Lytle and his men on the crest of a hill once they sighted the Confederate's fortified position. The air vibrated with a palpable anticipation, even while trepidation bore down on James's resolve. *So many Confederates!* Fieldworks of logs and fence posts did little to hide the twelve guns trained on the Federals as they entered the clearing.

The Irish Regiment, Col. Lytle's men, rushed forward as one, like a school of fish, following their commander's movements. Just as the front of his column reached a position to the center-right of the earthworks, a thundering barrage from the entire Rebel battery ensued. Grape shot and canister spewed forth in a cacophony of chaos as men fell to the ground in droves.

James watched in horror as gallant men's bodies exploded with the impact of the cannonade. A soldier attempting to reload looked into his breach, and in an instant, his hand and the rifle were gone from the force of a heavy shard of iron. Another man buckled and fell, his torso landing four feet from his legs.

The sordid scenes played before him in rapid succession—yet in slow motion—drawing out his own torturous, helpless state.

One soldier crumpled into a ball—his head buried in his hands. James started, muscles quivering to run to the soldier's aid. Only when the man lifted his head did James witness the soldier's eyeball hanging by a muscle, as he struggled to clutch it in his hands, blood flowing into his open mouth and down his chin. An instant later, he vanished in an explosion of dirt and grass.

Soldiers continued firing, bravely keeping their eyes forward, advancing amid the withering volleys of grapeshot and canister. Pride ignited within James's chest as color bearers stormed to the front, brandishing their flags heroically. Three of Lytle's companies rallied in a spirited push forward to within pistol shot of the barricades. In an undaunted assault, they fired into the entrenchment.

A bullet hit the staff of the state color bearer, breaking the pole, no doubt shattering his hand. With the injured hand pressed to his chest, he clutched the broken staff, bracing it under one arm, and continued to wave the colors with zeal. After one pass parallel to the enemy fire, the man collapsed to the ground. If only James could reach him. From his angle, he believed the color guard's thigh to be shattered. The poor man would lay there helpless, exposed.

A sergeant bearing the national colors boldly waved the flag directly in front of the enemy. He fell to the ground, but staggered to his feet and again shouted, brandishing the Union ensign. Never had James witnessed such bravery. He squinted through the smoke and the flying dirt. Where could he be most effective?

Thinking only of the wounded, James raised the green flag and, lowering his head, ran into the fray. Legs pumping, feet slipping on the mud-soaked ground, he pushed forward, knapsack pounding against his shoulder. One hand clutched the medic flagpole, the other his Springfield.

He stopped at the first man, who lay face down. Finding him dead, he moved on, zigzagging through bullets and grapeshot. James slid to a stop, dropping to his knees near a young man. His leg below the calf was gone but for a bloody stump.

"Where's me gun? I've lost me gun!" the soldier cried, frantically looking about.

His musket lay eight feet beyond. James stabbed the flag into the soft ground and crawled to retrieve it. As he lifted the muzzle-loader, his eyes fell on a worn brogan, the foot still inside. He handed the man his weapon, grabbed a tourniquet from his bag, and frantically applied it above the ragged stump.

James glimpsed his assistant directing stretcher-bearers near the rear of the action. Instantly, the ground exploded in front of Seamus, eclipsing the burly figure. James's gut clenched, and he forced his eyes wider, unable to look away. When the dust cleared, a ghostly figure staggered to his feet.

Relief burst from James's lungs. He turned his attention back toward the front just as his hat tugged to one side. From the graze of a bullet? A shiver coursed along his spine. *Too Close*. He touched his hat, settled it aright, and looking forward again, searched for his next patient.

Amazing. Even in the heavy exchange, Col. Lytle had remained on his mount, directing his men. He swerved as the ground erupted and his horse reared. But that didn't deter him. He shouted to his troops, and they seemed to drink in his courage and bravado, firing, trudging doggedly onward.

To James's right, a chaplain bent over a body and crossed himself. The man stood and deftly moved to crouch beside another of the many injured soldiers.

Dirt and rock burst into the fetid air. James dropped to the ground, heart hammering like a hundred flintlocks. He lay there for a moment. Were his limbs still intact? He willed his pulse to slow. A young corporal appeared and offered him water.

"Have a drink, sir." He handed James a canteen.

James tipped the canteen, not wanting more than to wet his dust-coated throat. "What's your name, son?"

"Sullivan, sir." The young man returned the lid to the blood-smeared canteen.

"Thank you, Corporal Sullivan." James watched as the boy ducked and ran through the daunting fire, only to kneel again in thirty feet to offer water to another fallen brother.

James shifted to his knees, looking for the next soldier to tend. A cheer to rally rang out to his left. In a flanking maneuver, Col. Lytle, reins slapping wildly against his horse's withers, emerged from the trees leading a bayonet charge. The volley swelled as he dashed forward. His men, yelling as one, rushed behind him with bayonets fixed.

James's breath caught as the colonel's horse screamed and reared. It pitched Lytle to the ground before dashing over the enemy rampart and collapsing to the ground. Lytle, visibly wounded, dragged himself a few feet.

If only he could get to the colonel. But how? Before James could formulate a plan, two Confederates grabbed up the colonel and dragged him into the barn.

On the opposite side of Ferry Road, four Ohio regiments advanced on the enemy line. Hope surged as James watched the new arrivals. He'd seen the ground they'd had to cover, hauling artillery across rugged terrain dotted with gullies and brush.

Part of the First Brigade held a line of battle. Col. McCook's Brigade maintained a position on a slope to the left, and farther up to the right was Col. Scammon's Brigade.

Four hundred yards from the earthworks, Federals positioned two rifled Union cannons. The sound was deafening as round after round of solid shot barraged the defilade, sending log and rail splinters high into the air. Shells whistled over the fortification, threatening the Rebels' stronghold with destruction.

James continued working his way among the wounded, offering liquid comfort to the dying, giving laudanum or morphine to the ones ravished by pain, applying tourniquets and staunching the bleeding where he could.

A burning sensation caused him to glance at his right arm. A Minié ball had grazed it just below the shoulder, leaving a wide tear in his sleeve. Even before the blood trickled from the wound, he could see a skid of blue fabric ground deep into his flesh. He hastily wrapped a bandage around the wound. Unable to secure it with only one hand, he tucked in the fabric edge.

More of General Benham's Brigade continued the fight, moving in among the fallen Irishmen of Col. Lytle's regiment. Soldiers dotted the pasture, some dead, and some likely wishing they were. James knew the Federals would hold this ground to protect their fallen.

He growled in frustration. Blast, but the hail of fire made it impossible for stretcher-bearers to retrieve the wounded. A handful crawled toward the rear, but most still lay where they fell. Brave fathers and brothers would die out there this night, just because he couldn't get to them.

Twilight had just about settled over the onslaught when James's attention was drawn to the front lines. A flanking maneuver, led by Colonel William Smith, penetrated the enemy lines. His command

and men under Colonel Augustus Moor and Major Rutherford Hayes had been working their way forward, scrabbling up the rocky, gully-laced terrain blanketed with a laurel thicket. Their mission was to surprise the Rebel lines.

A general advance had now begun. James stared in amazement, another rush of pride intercepting the surrounding atrocity, as an impassioned man in citizen's dress rushed back and forth along the lines, his frenzied shouts rallying the men forward to the enemy.

Despite the vigor that remained among the advance, the bugle called the Union troops back; the darkness preventing further assault. James called to the injured not to lose heart. Lantern light would only invite more casualties, so he vowed to be the first to reach them in the morning.

Before the heavy cloud cover doused the last of the day's light, he'd walked two of the men off the field, dodging craters, bullets, and the bodies of the fallen.

Twenty-Nine

SUMMERSVILLE - CARNIFEX FERRY

James twisted in his bedroll. All night he had endured the volley of angry words exchanged among the troops, venting their outrage at being pulled from battle. They'd been up since four in the morning, marched a grueling eighteen miles and fought hard for over five hours—only to be cut short by their own command. By the time nine o'clock struck, darkness had enveloped the woods and soldiers began to emerge. Now Union forces encamped dangerously close to the Rebel front—without supper.

The moon failed them all this night, refusing to push its way through the thick cloud cover. Sleep had failed him, as well. He lay on the ground in the blackness, his eyes searching the horizon for the first glow of dawn. He needed just enough light to see to his steps, then he would return to the battlefield to tend the wounded. Other regimental surgeons had worked at the rear of the fighting yesterday, helping those who could walk off the battlefield. Courageous soldiers carried many of their comrades from the forest. If only they could retrieve the injured from the field before commencing another clash.

As men stirred, James slung his knapsack over his shoulder, then checked his Colt. He set his face in the uphill direction. Stepping over still prostrate bodies, he trudged toward the battlefield.

Two soldiers trotted down the hill from the side of the fortification. The first one rushed by James and the second spoke as he passed. "They're gone. The Rebels moved out."

Gone?

The scouts delivered an animated report to their commanding officers. News spread quickly that General Floyd had fled Camp Gauley during the night. A victory shout rose among the troops, and soldiers began filtering up the hill. As relief seeped into his bones, James saw two other doctors, knapsacks on their shoulders, spreading out among the fallen. He remembered the wounded Lytle being dragged into the barn, and headed in that direction.

Col. Lytle's horse lay where it had fallen, its body free of any tack. The log barn sat in partial ruins. Cannon fire had decimated two of the walls, leaving the roof cocked at an odd angle and jagged wood splinters cluttering the ground. James needed a lantern. He stepped over shattered boards and scattered gabions the Rebels had used to carry the rocks for their ramparts.

"Colonel?" He squinted into the dimness. "Colonel Lytle, are you in here, sir?"

"I'm here. Did you bring breakfast, Major?" Despite his good spirits, the colonel's voice had lost its prior robustness. Most likely from blood loss. He lay half prone, a downed timber caught just above his head, protecting him from much of the fallen debris.

"I'll have you out in no time." James wrenched boards and implements from the pile in front of the colonel as he pushed his way through to him, clearing a path. Sharp log splinters and layers of chinking blanketed the floor.

At last, he reached the wounded man. "That was quite the theatrics out there—the way you dismounted and your horse took off over the parapet." He helped the colonel stand.

James coughed from the stirred-up dust. "Sorry about your horse, Colonel."

"He was a good one, my Ranger. I've become somewhat attached to the old boy. My saddle?"

"It appears the Rebels took everything off the horse, sir."

Col. Lytle swore, shaking his head. "Let's get out of here, shall we?"

The two men emerged from the barn to the sight of soldiers flocking up the hill. Many had already gone into the fortified area. Two men stood on the porch of the house with a trunk suspended between them. Farther down the hill, soldiers ventured into the woods in search of missing men while stretcher bearers and medics roamed the field tending to the injured.

James set a barrel on end and eased the colonel onto it. "Now, let's have a look at that leg." He used his knife to slice through the bandana the colonel had tied around his thigh.

"Looks like it missed the bone. No doubt went right through and into your horse."

After collecting supplies from his knapsack, James handed his canteen to Col. Lytle for a drink, then dribbled water over the wound, wiping away much of the blood. He sprinkled morphine powder into the gash, packed some damp lint into it, and wrapped the thigh snugly. As they picked their way through the debris, the colonel leaned heavily on him.

James looked over the high ground. Something wasn't right. Where were the Confederate casualties? He'd been so focused on getting to the colonel, it had evaded his attention until now.

Captain Reynolds stepped out from one of the outbuildings, a big smile on his face. "Major Hill, over here, if you please." An officer, which James recognized as Colonel Smith, appeared behind Reynolds.

James turned to Col. Lytle, settling him against a broken-down wagon. "There's nothing more I can do for you until I get you to a hospital."

"Go on, Major, there's wounded to tend to." He waved James off.

Snatching up his knapsack, James jogged over to the captain's position. "What is it Captain, Colonel?" James saluted.

Captain Reynolds motioned for James to precede him through the single doorway. Inside were over twenty men, many in a bandaged state. Most of them sat upright, though some sprawled on the floor in the tight quarters.

"Colonel Tyler's men. The wounded we had to leave behind at Cross Lanes." The grin on Reynolds's face spoke volumes.

Several of the men hailed the captain and exchanged greetings, while James did a preliminary examination on the ones that looked to be more serious. Apparently, the Confederates had rendered care for each of them, so James again prepared to leave.

"Thank you, Major. I can't tell you how it does my heart good to find these boys. We thought the worst when we had to leave them behind." Reynolds offered his hand to James.

One of Col. Tyler's men spoke up, "The Rebels loaded their dead and injured into wagons, sirs."

"That would explain why there are no bodies," James said.

Colonel Smith started out the door, then turned. "We are going to claim Camp Gauley for our own at this time, Major. See that the wounded are brought into the house and let the other medics know." He smiled. "I do believe General Floyd will come to regret that he tickled the belly of Goliath this day."

James worked most of the day, sewing flesh and removing bullets. The ranking surgeon of General Benham's brigade saw to the few amputations required. Miraculously, most of the injured sustained flesh wounds, and would soon rejoin their units.

Reports came in throughout the day of General Floyd's swift retreat. He'd taken nothing material with him except guns, part of his tents, and sufficient rations to allow him distance. The river showed evidence that the Confederates' crossing had not been without difficulty or casualties—a portion of Floyd's cannon was found in the water, along with the drowned bodies of his men.

Some of the Union soldiers took it upon themselves to fish the cannon balls from the river. James did not miss the irony—soon Confederate cannon balls would wound their own.

The Confederates had only recently constructed a trestle bridge over the wild, beautiful torrent that was the Gauley River. That same bridge, McCook's men discovered, was then burned by the Rebels after their retreat, making a quick chase impossible.

Troops continued to regale the fortification with stories of their discoveries. Union soldiers, searching the woods, returned with twelve Rebel prisoners. One of the Confederate officer's runaway Negroes, found hiding in the underbrush, reported fifty of General Floyd's men killed and more wounded.

As for the Union's newly gained *Camp Gauley*, they had inherited numerous Springfield muzzle-loaders, squirrel guns, powder, lead, cartridges, forage, and ample commissary stores. Horses and wagons remained fair game for the Federals to claim, too. Col. Smith claimed the abandoned personal baggage of General Floyd, along with the general's hat and haversack. The plunder also included his officers' parade stores.

James met with the other doctors and together consulted with General Rosecrans. By day's end, it had been determined that most of those needing medical attention would remain at Camp Gauley. Some of the Federal injuries had been from friendly fire, while units attempted to find their way out of the forest at nightfall.

Friday morning, the third day after the battle, James and Seamus loaded a wagon with the injured who could best withstand the ride to the Dabney farm. Captain Reynolds and a small contingent accompanied them back to Fayette County.

James found welcome relief from the tragedy of the last few days as his thoughts turned to the Dabney farm—and who was waiting just a few miles farther down the road. He allowed himself a smile as he dared to dream one minute—reigning in overly warm imaginations in the next.

Two miles north of the farm, the wagon and its escort met up with a company from General Cox's brigade with news. General Wise's Confederate forces had abandoned Gauley Bridge to retreat along the James River and Kanawha Turnpike to Big Sewell Mountain. This company was in route to transport prisoners from Camp Gauley to Camp Chase, outside of Columbus, Ohio.

The Union Army was now in control of the Kanawha Valley, as well as much of western Virginia. Despite the glad tidings, James did not hear the news that would bring him the peace he sought at this moment. According to the men's report, an obvious threat remained—Rebel guerilla units in the immediate area. The Dabney farm was still in a precarious situation. Gus was not safe.

Thirty

Fayette County

Every minute of every hour had stretched longer and longer with James's absence. When had he become a constant in Augusta's thoughts—consuming her daily duties, even invading her dreams? And commanding her prayers. Prayers that had not ceased since he rode off with Captain Reynolds. She dropped another handful of string beans into the bowl in her lap, absently plucking out a few more from the bucket. Would that God would allow her a snippet of those dreams and still provide for this family—a snippet named James Hill. She sighed.

"I think Bertie is just milking this bout of measles." Zander pushed his straight, blond bangs out of his eyes and filled a glass with water from the barrel in the kitchen. "Seems he's taken to asking every favor he can get out of me."

"Well, that's a sure sign he's feeling a might better." Melinda Jane set another peeled potato in the wooden bowl. "His fever's been down some yesterday and today."

"Maybe I should get sick just so people will wait on me," Zander said, in very much of a pout. A plate of molasses cookies sat on the sideboard, covered with a green cloth. He reached for one, but Melinda Jane swatted his hand.

"Those aren't for you. Well, leastways not just now."

"I suppose you made these for *Fin*." He fairly sang his brother's name, then snatched up the plate, lifting it high. "I might just have to take this whole plate outside and eat every last one."

"Zander Dabney, you give me those cookies this minute!" Melinda Jane brought her foot down on top of his boot. He howled, lowering the plate just enough for her to snatch it from him. One cookie hit the floor, cracking into two pieces.

Augusta chuckled. Why is it that every time Zander thought he'd gotten the best of Melinda Jane, she was faster or smarter or luckier?

"That one's yours." Melinda Jane huffed, glancing at the floor. "I reckon Bertie might like one of my fine molasses crinkles." She made a show of protecting the platter before flitting off toward Bertie's room.

Zander plucked the pieces off the floor and shoved them in his mouth. He smiled at his sister, cookie chunks pooching out his cheeks. "Mewinda Jane's Mowasses gookies," he said through the mouthful.

"Uh-huh. Do they taste better off the floor?"

He shrugged and drew a sleeve across his mouth before heading out the door.

"Would you mind carting in those other buckets of string beans from the porch for me? They're the last of the season. I'm going to use them for leather britches."

"And if I don't, you'll just say"—Zander put his hand on his hip mimicking his sister—"'Then you don't have to eat the stew I put 'em in come winter.'"

She snapped at him with a towel, and he scooted out the door, laughing.

Augusta continued appealing to heaven on James's behalf as she prepared a tray with warm broth and fresh water for Pap. If she could just get this down him, it would give him some strength. Pushing the bedroom door open with her hip, she smiled at the sweet sight.

Will looked up from the book she'd been reading to her father. "He hasn't looked at me once. Whenever he's awake, he just kinda stares at the ceiling."

Augusta set down the tray and sidled up to her sister. What are you reading to him? Her fingers combed through the mop of cropped hair as Will leaned her head into Augusta's apron.

"Walden."

"Maybe the Scriptures will catch his ear better just now, sugar." Pap's peaceful countenance drew a mixture of joy and grief to Augusta's spirit as he lay staring at the ceiling. Suddenly, his lips parted, and his eyebrows lifted. A wide smile broke across his face at something unseen. Her mind recognized what her heart fought against. She knew the signs. She'd doctored more than a few folks on their way out of this world.

"What's he seeing, Gus?" Will stood and grasped Pap's hand.

"I don't know, but it surely isn't something bad, judging by that smile. Would you mind leaving me alone with Pap for a few minutes, please?"

Will laid Pap's hand to his side. She turned awkwardly and buried her face in Augusta's collar. Tears said what words could not, and Augusta understood, holding her tight until Will let go and ran from the room.

Augusta sat close to Pap on the bed and stroked his ashen hand. "Pap, can you hear me?" She waited until the glistening eyes turned her way.

"Gussie." His voice was soft, gaze intense. "I don't have long, honey. The Lord is fixin' to call me home. I'll miss you children, but I surely am looking forward to seeing Jesus and your mama."

Try as she might, she could no longer stay the rivers flowing down her cheeks.

"You've been a mother to your brothers and sister for nearly six years now, honey. I know you feel it's so, but it doesn't all fall on your shoulders." He drew a slow, rattling breath.

"Don't you fret about such things now, Pap." She braved a smile and dabbed her apron to her wet face.

"Listen to me, daughter. It won't be but a few more years til Bertie and Will are fully grown. Don't you give up on a family of your own."

"But *this* is my family. I don't need another one, Pap. I'm happy. I love Will and the boys." The defensiveness in her tone rankled her.

"Allow yourself to love. I want for you what your mama and I had. She was my life, my heartbeat. Give James a chance, honey."

"James? Pap . . ." Her stomach tumbled. What was her father saying, exactly?

As several weak spasms claimed his chest, Pap closed his eyes. When he opened them, she saw a hint of brightness before a single tear escaped. "James loves you, Gussie. Are you *truly* blind to his feelings for you?" Little twitches curved one side of his mustache.

"But, Pap . . ." Augusta shook her head, fighting a fresh onslaught of tears. Silence betrayed her heart.

"I've prayed for a helpmeet for you, honey. I have peace that James is the answer to that prayer." Pap's words faded away, and before she could force a thought to a whisper, sweet sleep commanded him rest.

Augusta bolted for the door. Racing across the yard, quick breaths puffed in rhythm with her pumping legs. She couldn't reach her *thinkin' spot* soon enough. A torrent of tears burst, filling her nose and coursing down her cheeks as she flattened her chest against the rough bark of the giant cedar.

She wept for the years behind her, when her mama had been her rock. She collapsed to the ground in a heap, burying her face in her apron and sobbing in great, gasping bouts for the years ahead, without Pap. A knife twisted in her heart, the physical pain sucking the air right out of her. Her belly heaved as she coughed, choked, unable to breathe through her nose. A person truly *could* die from a broken heart—and maybe she was. What about Bertie, Will, and Zander, and the years ahead without a father's hand to guide them? She wept for that, too.

Just when she felt her tears had run dry, James's image pulled her back into the arms of turmoil and her heart wrenched anew. *James.* The war. Was he even alive? What if she never saw him again? The deluge refreshed, flowing unabated. Lost between logic and longing, her mind swirled. She pressed her hands to her ears, thoughts churning in an eddy of uncertainty.

"*James loves you.*"

Words that, until now, she'd believed to be meant for another world—a world that lay beyond a door, the key to which she had long since thrown away. A foreign grief, new and raw, lurched from her anguish—as if her heart's very rhythm relied upon something she couldn't reach.

I love him.

A sprouted seed of revelation. Beyond all reason, somehow, she knew that seed would grow. Grow and bear fruit. She didn't understand the how of it all. Only God could weave her future and dreams together in such a way—one that would intertwine her commitment to her family with the desires of her heart.

Father, please, oh please, bring James back to me! The plea arose like a swollen river, overtaking the banks of her heart, coursing its torrents of yearning through every pore.

It felt like hours, but surely it must've been less than one when Augusta wiped her face and smoothed her hair. She seized the swing and lifted herself onto the board seat. For long moments she swung, her eyes drawn to the leaves above. The green cedar feathers washed the amber light, making her eyes ache, but she couldn't look away.

"They're back!" Will's not-so-lady-like holler arose from the direction of the house, likely heard clear to the Myers's farm.

Leaping from the swing in mid-air, she grabbed her wadded apron, clutched the skirt of her dress, and ran. *Please, God, let James be with them!*

※

James, astride his dun gelding and Captain Reynolds at his side, led the small envoy up the Dabneys' lane. Followed by Union troops, a full wagon swayed under the weight of its passengers as the wooden wheels met each dip of the ground.

Tension drained from his stiff shoulders when the white and black clapboard house came into view. Everything was as he'd left it. His eyes went to the front porch in anticipation, expecting—no, hoping—to see her step out and wave. Since leaving Camp Gauley, his mind had been hard pressed to think of anything but Gus. His thoughts jerked like a fishing line—one minute hoping she was thinking of him, the next knowing someone with his past didn't deserve a woman like her. Women like her don't fall for men like him.

Will stood near the barn, her hands cupped to her mouth as she yelled something he couldn't make out over the rumble of the wagon. Izzy, Zander, and Sgt. Mallory appeared from inside the barn, and Melinda Jane stood at the corner of the house, shovel in hand.

What of Bertie? He was confident the boy would pull through just fine with his sister watching over him.

Jonathan Dabney. It would not surprise him to find the patriarch had met his Maker. The sense of peace that permeated his very nature was powerful. Never had James known such a strong and admirable personality—unless it was Izzy. It was clear why their friendship was so strong.

Guiding his horse to the hitching post, James dismounted and looped the reins over the rail. He turned to address Captain Reynolds, but a vision in a blue dress rushed at him, arms outstretched.

"You're safe! Thank you, God, thank you." She hooked his neck in an enthusiastic embrace, squeezing tight as James's arms encircled her waist. What did it matter that he couldn't breathe? For as he held her in his arms, the delightful warmth that sluiced through him was heavenly. He closed his eyes, savoring the feel of her so close to him.

Too soon, she let go and tried to step back, as if just discovering the audience of soldiers and family. James kept his hold on her, feeling like a schoolboy, refusing to wipe the grin from his face.

"Sure'n I'd like a homecoming of me own like that one, I would." Seamus broke the awkwardness of the moment. He rolled his eyes and set the brake on the wagon. Two of the soldiers chuckled, sobering with a stern look from Captain Reynolds, who then sported a smile of his own as he dismounted.

James reluctantly released Gus, but couldn't look away from her blushing face and emerald eyes.

She frantically tucked loose hair into her braid. "I . . . I'm just glad you're home. Bertie . . . is still sick and . . . and Pap . . ." She took a deep breath and let it out. "We can talk about Pap in a little while. I've readied some of the empty cots for more men. I wasn't sure if you'd be bringing any back with you, but I meant to be prepared." Her eyes fell to the ground. She fidgeted with her dress, fingers smoothing wrinkles from the skirt.

"Thank you." His voice had gone raspy.

He cleared his throat and motioned toward the pump. "Refresh yourselves, men." He turned back to her, lowering his voice again. "I'll see my patients for a bit, then I'd like to see Bertie and your pap."

She lifted her head and gasped. "You're wounded!" She touched the white bandage that peeked through the tear in his sleeve.

"Just a graze. It's nothing. Seamus took care of it for me. Merely my memento from Carnifex Ferry."

"Still, I should take a look at it—just to be sure it's healing properly."

"Of course, Doctor." He chuckled, trying to read her thoughts. Was it *only* the wound she fretted over?

Her cheeks bloomed a rosy hue. "Do you need me to help you in the barn?"

"None of these men are critical. I'd just like to see them situated. How are the prisoners? Have they been any trouble?" He kept his voice low, not wanting to lose the intimacy of the moment.

"No trouble. They're pretty much all on the mend. Your men are very protective of us."

"As am I." He searched her gaze. Perhaps he wanted to glimpse the gold he'd seen earlier. Perhaps he hoped to find a hint of the same ardor that seized his own soul just now. *Do you know you've beguiled me?*

Thirty-One

❦

Fayette County

Augusta pushed aside the flowered curtain below the worktable, searching for another skillet on the hidden shelf. Already, a heady aroma filled the kitchen. It was surely a sign that fall peeked around the corner when the supper menu changed from fresh garden fare to the heartier soups.

Steam rose as Melinda Jane lifted the lid on one of the tall pots of chicken and dumplings. She poked through the bubbles with a fork. "Looks to be nearly there. Can you keep an eye on this? I'm gonna hunt down Fin and have him round up some help to haul these kettles out."

"I'll watch them. I think we made enough to feed an army." *Army*? Augusta glanced at Melinda Jane. Unbridle, unlady-like laughter tumbled out.

"Well, that's pretty nearly what we're doing, isn't it?" Melinda Jane clapped her hands. "The men are gonna be so happy to be eating home cookin' tonight. I bet those new wounded boys from Ohio haven't had a decent meal all summer."

Augusta waved her hands in the air, shooing her friend toward the door. "Go on with you now and find that brother of mine. If you can't find him, maybe Sergeant Mallory or Seamus will help."

Glorious odors escaped the hot oven as Augusta snuck a peek at the blackberry cobbler.

"Uh oh. There's that man." Melinda Jane stood in the open doorway, wagging her head. "I best get while the gettin's good."

"What man?" Now what's she going on about? Augusta puffed a wisp of hair from her eye.

"Hello, Doc, glad to have you home. We're cookin' up a storm. Special treat for you and your men tonight—and your patients too, of course. I'm fixin' to give them the good news. If you'll excuse me." Melinda Jane winked at Augusta, and with wide eyes above a broad smile, sashayed past James.

"Well, she certainly knows how to make an exit." James pulled at his collar. He took off his hat and motioned toward the stairway. "I'm going up to look in on Bertie." He hesitated, as if to say something, then continued toward the bedroom.

Augusta smiled to herself and sighed. The lid on the front pot of chicken and dumplings rattled, pulling her attention back to the task at hand. She slid the heavy pots to the side and closed down the damper on the fire. Maybe she'd just peek in on James and Bertie.

Keeping mostly to the hallway, she stood at the edge of the threshold. She wasn't *exactly* spying on them. Bertie was propped on a pile of pillows, covers scrunched into a pile at the foot of the bed. Still blotchy and a little achy, his fever was down and he had returned to his normal talkative self.

"Did you kill any Johnny Rebs?" You'd think he was asking for ice cream, the way excitement grabbed hold of the boy.

"I don't believe I did, Bertie. Anyway, I went there to save men, not to kill them." James ruffled the boy's hair. "It looks to me like you're on the mend. I wouldn't be at all surprised if you're up and out of here by this time next week."

"A whole nother week?" Bertie slammed the back of his head onto the pillow. "I'll have bed sores by then."

"Now, how do you know anything about bed sores?"

"I heard Gus say something to Melinda Jane about Pap and bedsores."

"I see." James stood. "If my sniffer is working right, I'd say we are in for one dandy of a feast tonight. *Maybe*—a big *maybe*—you can come out to the barn for a little while if we wrap you up real tight in this quilt."

"Gus's been making me stay in this bed the whole time you was gone. She made me use the slop pot every time I had to go!" Bertie screwed up his face.

Gus pressed a finger to her lips to stifle a chuckle.

"You've been quite ill, Bertie. If you want to get well and run and play outside with Coot again, you're going to have to do what your sister tells you." James bent close to Bertie's ear. "Even *I* do what Gus tells me."

His mock whisper warmed Augusta's middle. *That man.*

"Excuse me, gentlemen." She dismissed the grin that gave away her eavesdropping as she leaned into the room. "I'd like to borrow the kind doctor, if I may, Bertie."

James's throat bobbed. "I didn't know you were standing there." He turned to Bertie. "I'm going to go check on your pap now. You rest up for later." He grabbed the boy's toes through the quilt and gave them a squeeze.

Augusta listened to James's steps following behind her. Down the stairs and through the hall, she thanked God for those steps, remembering her prayer for his safe return. God had heard her. He'd heard her every thought, too.

Her hand paused on Pap's bedroom doorknob. "I don't think he'll make it through the night," she whispered, meeting his somber eyes.

The blankets rustled when James sat on the edge of Pap's bed. "Jonathan, can you hear me?" He tapped the back of one pale hand.

Pap turned his head in a lethargic motion, his watery eyes peeking beneath heavy lids. "James," he whispered. Then a little louder, "You're back."

"Yes, sir, I'm here. Billy Yank scared those Johnny Rebs so bad they all ran off during the night." James smiled, and Augusta hoped the levity would coax one from his patient as well.

"That so?" Pap's eyes searched the room until they found her. Only then did his lips ease upward. She smiled back, but her chin trembled as she moved to fold Pap's hand into hers.

Tipping his ear to the stethoscope, James listened closely to Pap's chest. "Are you up for a visit from the family after supper, Jonathan?"

Pap nodded. A silent knowing colored those hazy eyes—a meeting of determination and resignation. She loved this man so. Would heaven hold him as dear as she did this moment?

"We'll let you rest now so we can all visit with you later." She tucked his frail hand beneath the covers and rose, blinking hard to stay the flow of tears a few seconds longer.

James motioned for her to go ahead of him, then closed the door with a soft click behind them. "I agree with you. His heart is very weak."

"After supper, I'll tell the family. We'll all say goodbye together." The words carved her throat raw.

He opened his arms, and she went to him. His embrace swaddled her like a blanket, warming the chill of sorrow if only for a moment. She tried to focus her emotions—to concentrate on Pap's home-going instead of the goodbye that had loomed ever nearer these past weeks.

"I know it sounds silly, but suddenly I feel like a little girl." Her voice caught, guttered with the aching. "That's my pap in there. I just want him to bounce me on his knee again and tell me everything's all right." The dam broke. His arms tightened, and he pressed his head to hers.

"It doesn't sound silly at all. I believe, if you were to ask your pap, he'd tell you that you are *still* his little girl." He pulled back, seeking her eyes. Rivulets careened down her cheeks, and he tenderly brushed them with his thumb. "You're still his *beautiful* little girl." His eyes caressed her hair, brow, lips.

The crash of the screen door shattered the spell, and she pulled from his arms.

"Everything's ready in the barn. Gus?" Melinda Jane turned to them. "There you are." She cocked her head in silent question. After a brief pause, she continued in her animated fashion. "We set up some tables and even got the boys in the haymow down for the feast." She pointed over her shoulder to Fin, Seamus, and Mallory. "These strapping men are carryin' out the food."

Seamus lifted a lid on the dumplings, closing his eyes as he breathed in the steam.

In a short time, hearty food laded the makeshift tables in the barn. Hungry soldiers—Yankee and Rebel alike—calmed their growling bellies, calling a truce for the occasion. Only four patients stayed to their beds, but Augusta made sure they each received a plate.

Izzy stood and removed his hat, pressing it to his chest. Silence descended as others followed suit. "We are humbled by Yo love for us, Lord, even though we's sinners. Thank You, Massa Jesus, for setting us free from this wicked world. Thank You for Yo blessings, Lord. Thank You for the hands that have labored and prepared this here food before us. We welcome You, Lord, to be our guest this evenin'. Amen."

"Amens" peppered the table, some hardy, some mumbled.

Melinda Jane dished out the chicken and dumplings from the kettle as each plate passed from hand to hand. With more yet to serve, Fin lifted the empty pot off the table and set a full one in its place. The cacophony of voices soon quieted while the men filled their stomachs.

"This cooking beats the swankiest hotels in Cincinnati," one of Rosecrans's men mumbled around a mouthful of food. "Thank you much, ma'ams." Grunts of agreement and bobbing heads brought to Augusta's mind the scene of Indians and pilgrims sharing a feast. That's it. This was like Thanksgiving. She'd have to work at being thankful today—work harder at it than most days.

"I've got a little gift for you, Gus." Fin pushed a small bundle of cloth across the table toward her. A piece of twine encircled it, tied into an oversized, floppy bow.

"For me?" Suspicion couched her acceptance, born of long years of experience. "What do you want, Fin Dabney?" Her eyes narrowed.

Fin raised his hands in defense. "Can't a brother give his sister a gift?"

"Mmmm." Fake sincerity if ever she saw it. Was that a twitch in his grin? She pulled her mouth into a straight line, then plucked the twine loose.

"It's not like a snake is gonna jump out at you, Gus. Just open it!" Bertie sat bundled in his robe between her and James, a quilt drooping off one shoulder.

Augusta chuckled, then laughed louder. She lifted two sharp, three-inch, boney-looking objects. "Are these what I think they are?" She looked to her older brother for an answer.

"Yes, ma'am. That's all that's left of Ol' Rupert. Nothin' but his spurs."

Melinda Jane clapped her hands. "That's one rooster I won't be missin'. Not one bit!"

∽

The faint odor of death permeated the room. Augusta ignored her nose and sought the only One who could ease the pain crushing her heart. Bertie sat Indian-style on the soft mattress near Pap's feet. The rest of his brothers and sisters, Melinda Jane, and Izzy, circled the bed where Jonathan Dabney lay. His ashen skin paled against the quilt, and his chest hardly lifting with each ragged breath. James stood nearby, yet apart from the family.

Pap endeavored to lift his head, and Augusta promptly rolled the pillow behind his neck so he could see everyone. Deliberately, one-by-one, he made eye contact with each of his children.

"Water." The weak croak sounded like a stranger. She held a glass to his mouth.

His lips curved upward, a tremble latching onto his chin. "I am a blessed man." He cleared his throat. Then, much louder, "I am a blessed man. My quiver is full and so is my heart."

With that, Augusta looked at James. But he'd fixed his gaze on Pap. A gleam shimmered in his eyes, and he stood tall, his shoulders pulled back.

She glanced at her brothers.

Zander's attention seemed drawn to his shoes. He wiped his nose on his shirtsleeve. Fin's red-rimmed eyes were intent on Pap.

"I've done my best to see that each of you has come to the truth." Pap's words were softer now, but amazingly clear. "To know Christ and Him Crucified, to believe in the resurrection, and to accept God's forgiveness." He inhaled through his nose, pressing his mouth into a quivering line with an arduous blink.

"I couldn't be a prouder father." He looked at Melinda Jane. "I do consider you a daughter, Melinda Jane." She raised her hanky to her nose, nodding. She leaned into her grandpappy's arms. "And Izzy—you know my heart better than anyone this side of heaven. Thank you, old friend. I 'spect I'll be seeing you soon enough." Izzy smiled and nodded, his droopy eyes sparkling with unshed tears.

Pap's gaze connected with James, and he solemnly nodded once with slightly pursed lips. Augusta didn't miss the knowing look that passed between them. James's face was inscrutable as his head bobbed subtly in response.

"This life I've led—here on this soil—is but a vapor. When I step through this threshold of death, don't you be grieving for me. I'll be just on the other side. I'll be sitting at the feet of my sweet, sweet Savior; your mama right beside me." His cracked lips splayed in a rapturous smile.

"Don't go, Pap!" Bertie's pleading voice broke. He stretched out beside his father. "Don't go, Pap!" Tears careened down his face. He ground them into the quilt, wadding the fabric in his fists.

Augusta squatted beside the bed, encircling Bertie in her arms, her own silent tears washing her shaky smile. She whispered to her brother, "You'll see Pap again, sweetie. He'll be waiting for you."

Pap's attention seemed drawn to the ceiling, his eyes focusing on something unseen as he'd done earlier that day. His mouth opened, then lifted into a serene smile. His eyes closed and an invisible hand smoothed away every crease of pain and concern.

She held her breath, staring hard, watching for the next rise of his chest.

It didn't come.

James stepped to the bed and placed his fingers under Pap's ear. His kind eyes met hers. Holding her gaze, he mouthed, *"I'm sorry."*

Melinda Jane's mellow voice cut through sniffles and Bertie's ragged sobs. She sang out slow but strong, *"Jesus, lover of my soul, let me to Thy bosom fly."*

More quaking voices joined in:
"While the nearer waters roll,
While the tempest still is high,
Hide me, O my Savior, hide—
Till the storm of life is past.
Safe into the haven guide—
O receive my soul at last!"

Thirty-Two

Fayette County

Augusta soaked up the barn atmosphere, thankful for the chance to be busy and useful. A Camp Gauley soldier drew a length of dark thread through the fabric of his uniform sleeve. His jacket lay across his lap, and an army-issued sewing kit set on the stool next to him.

She hummed to a familiar tune that floated through the barn and smiled at Johnson. The teacher-turned-soldier nodded, his fingers encasing a harmonica. His head wound had healed up nicely, and he had reluctantly resumed his duties.

She worked loose the clingy bandage from the shoulder of Private Lynch, a graying man about her father's age. He was shorter than most, and plump. She wondered if he might even be a grandfather.

"Do you have a family back in Ohio, Private Lynch?" Her practiced fingers washed away the pink ooze.

"I sure do. My wife, Meaghan, and three grown daughters. Two are married, just this summer, so no babies yet." He cringed as she sprinkled Dover's powder onto the wound. "What about you, ma'am—you and your husband have children?"

"My . . . husband?"

"Yes ma'am. The doctor."

Heat climbed her neck. It was all she could do to keep from fanning herself like some swooning society lady. "Oh, he's not my husband. I'm not married, Private Lynch."

"Well, if you're not, you ought to be. I see the way the man looks at you when you're not looking at him."

She dropped the new bandage, catching it before it tumbled from her lap. "Oh . . ." The word escaped on a breath. Unwilling to meet his gaze, she circled the fabric around his arm.

"I know the look of a man in love, missy, and that man has it bad." He chuckled and shook his head. "Ah, love. I'm pining for my Meaghan myself."

"There now. You've got a clean bandage, and you look to be healing real well, Private." She tossed the used bandage into a bucket and set the brown bottle on the table, knocked it over, and righted it again in her haste to put distance between herself and the private.

Zander's head poked around the edge of the barn doorway. "We got company."

Four riders steered their mounts into the yard. Fin walked confidently forward to meet them, a recently acquired Sharp's carbine in his hand. Augusta trailed him by a few lengths. All four men wore gun belts.

Frock coats hung long on the two strangers in front. The others followed, unkempt in raggedy jackets and crumpled slouch hats. One spewed a string of brown juice over a five-foot swath of ground.

"That's far enough. What's your business, gentlemen?" Fin's fingers flexed, one hand on the barrel, the other on the gun's stock.

One of the lead riders doffed his tall hat. "Allow me to introduce myself. I am Jeffrey Hampton, and this is my associate, Mr. Richard Stratton. We've been on the trail of some runaways from down in Mercer County." The man drilled his gaze into Augusta, then Fin, as if trying to read their thoughts.

"Have you seen any unusual activity around these parts? Maybe heard dogs barking more than usual? Seen signs of folks camping in the woods?" The man's associate, Mr. Hampton, didn't hide the fact that he was taking a thorough look at his surroundings, even with a half dozen armed Union soldiers trickling onto the scene.

James had appeared from behind the barn bearing a rifle. He stood near enough now for Augusta to see the muscle in his jaw tighten.

Fin took a step closer to the strangers. "You are on Dabney land, and I suggest you leave the way you came before I decide you're trespassing." Fin raised his gun. James followed suit and Sergeant Mallory fingered the handle of his colt.

"We'll be leaving, Mr. Dabney. But I'd like to remind you that harboring a fugitive slave is punishable by a $1,000 fine or two-year incarceration." With a last scan of the yard, he turned his horse to leave, and the others followed. Craning his neck, he fixed his black eyes on Augusta. "Good day, ma'am." He donned his hat and trotted off.

∞

James turned to the staccato of gunfire in the distance. Earlier in the day, a contingent of General Cox's men had loaded up prisoners, then left for Camp Gauley. They'd been gone too long to be a party to this recent ruckus.

When Mallory rushed into the barn, James followed him through to the rear stalls. "That sound close to you, Sergeant?"

"We'll ride to investigate." Mallory and two of the men were already grabbing saddles.

"There may be wounded. I'll come too." James hoisted the medical knapsack over his shoulder and turned to Seamus. "All right, if I borrow your horse? Mine's in the paddock."

"Am I to stay here, then?" Seamus scowled.

"Somebody has to." James clapped him on the back. "Thanks, old man."

James and the men spotted Federals a quarter mile south. Several mounted soldiers trained their weapons on one unfortunate Confederate. The Rebel stood, hands in the air. A crimson stain had enveloped his left leg from the thigh to his shoe. Another Rebel lay curled in a fetal position on the side of the road.

None of the Federals looked familiar to James. "I'm Doctor James Hill. I have a field hospital just up the road." He dismounted, and grabbing the knapsack, rushed over to the soldier standing. "Sit down," he ordered. "Unless you want to bleed to death."

The soldier lowered himself awkwardly to the ground, and James applied a tourniquet.

"Your femoral artery must have been nicked."

A glimmer of recognition flashed in the stranger's eyes. "So, you're a doctor now?" The soldier grimaced. His eyes closed and head lulled to the side.

James thrust out his hand in time to cradle the Rebel's head as it struck the ground.

For an instant, a hazy thought reached for his attention, but he shook it off, moving to check the other injured man. This one was gut shot. Chance of survival slim. The man was stirring, so James administered enough laudanum to put him out.

Two more Federals galloped out of the trees. "The rest got away."

James looked at the ranking soldier, a sergeant. "Any of your men injured?"

"Not a one. I think we just surprised these boys. Got the jump on 'em. Probably got a camp not too far. Every day, our scouts are having run-ins with these guerillas."

"Let's get these men up to the barn." After they secured the leg wound over a Confederate mount, James steadied the other Rebel in front of him.

∞

The bloodstained pant leg fell to the floor as James finished snipping the fabric from the still unconscious Rebel. Gus handed him a threaded needle, then dribbled water into the wound to clear away the blood. They worked in silent tandem. As James tied off the artery and released the tourniquet, she wiped down the leg and monitored the chloroform. He pinched the slug of lead between two fingers and held it up for her to see.

"Completely missed the bone." One side of his mouth shifted into a crooked grin. "Would you like to close?"

"I'd be happy to, Doctor." The look she gave him flipped his insides. She chose a different needle and threaded it while he prepared the wound.

He marveled at the confidence with which she worked. Her fingers moved with the deftness of a seasoned surgeon. She paused and looked up from the sutures. Their eyes locked. He found himself greatly amused by the blush creeping up her neck.

"Sponge, please." she said, yanking his thoughts back. He dabbed at the edges of the torn flesh, and she resumed stitching.

James dropped the spent cloth into a bucket. "I'm going to see to the other patient. I don't think there's much hope for him, but I at least want to keep him comfortable." The severely injured man lay on his back. Unseeing eyes fixed on the rough-hewn ceiling. James's gut tightened. Another he couldn't save.

He hated this sense of helplessness. It reared its mocking head more and more of late. He'd not slept last night for dreams of the past taunting him. He looked at his hands and remembered them swollen and bloodied, a result of his escaped fury so many years ago.

When James closed the eyes of the dead Rebel, he noticed a small book in the man's pocket and pulled it out. A New Testament. And inside the cover was an inscription: *For my Frederick. Come home to me. Love, Mother.*

James combed fingers through his beard, and setting the Bible aside, he called for Sergeant Mallory to form a burial detail. *Another mother's son who won't be coming home.*

"I'm done here." Gus wiped down the needle and replaced it in the leather holder. "Do you want to look at this before I bandage it?"

"The other one didn't make it." He shook his head, defeat tugging him lower.

"I'm sorry, James. There's nothing you could've done. You must know that." She stepped aside so he could review her handiwork.

"My intellect knows, but it's never a good enough reason for the rest of me, I guess."

He allowed his gaze to meet hers. "At Carnifex Ferry, the wounded lay on the field throughout the night. How many of the dead might have survived if only we'd been able to tend them?" His attention dropped to the floor as he massaged his temple. "It feels like it's all an ugly game—'You win some, you lose some'—like a hawker at a carnival."

She touched his arm, and he looked up. "You can only do so much and leave the rest in God's hands."

A groan rose from the man on the table.

"I'd better get his leg bandaged." Gus picked up the roll of torn cloth and uncoiled it as James held the limb up off the table.

He watched her slender fingers and their practiced movements. Even red and rough from hard work, her hands were beautiful. She undoubtedly still shed tears for her father, but in the secrecy of her room. At night. Night always holds sway over matters of the heart. This he knew too well.

"I'm finished." Her voice jarred his thoughts as his hands still held the limb aloft. He released it abruptly, offering a sheepish grin.

"I'll get Seamus to help move him to a cot," he said, departing in search of his assistant.

∞

Seamus set a tin cup of broth on the short table near the wounded Confederate. "If you're feeling up to a bit of sustenance, there's broth here for you. And don't ya be trying anything funny, 'cause those two Federals have their eyes on you—and their guns, if need be." He cocked his head toward Johnson and Hanley, standing no more than fifteen feet away.

"Where am I?" The Rebel wiped at one eye. His head jerked upright. "Do I still have my leg?"

"Don't ya be panicking, now," Seamus said. "The doc managed to save it for you. You'll be taking it with you to a Union prison as soon as yer able."

The Rebel stiffened, eyes wild as they combed his surroundings. "A barn?"

"A Union field hospital north of Gauley Bridge." Seamus turned away, his mind already on his next task.

"Wait, please. Who owns this farm?" The soldier twisted on the cot, grimacing.

"Now, what difference does that make to the likes of you?"

"I have kin around these parts."

"You do, have you? Well, I'm not from around here, so best I not be the one to answer that question." Seamus lifted one eyebrow and passed a look to Johnson. He'd mention the prisoner to Fin just as soon as he finished his work. If he didn't forget. Between the inventory and the patients, he'd be lucky to remember his name by nightfall.

∽

Fin fiddled with the latigo in his calloused hands. If only life was like this leather—long and smooth, no tears, bumps. Adam and Eve sure enough messed it up for everybody, that's for certain.

"You don't really want to fight those Rebels, Fin. You could get killed!" Melinda Jane propped her chin on the top rail of the corral fence.

"All I'm saying is that I been thinking on it for a couple of months now. I haven't made up my mind." One day he was sure he'd head out, then the next, he knew he had to stay. He'd wrestled this bear long enough. He had to decide. Soon.

"But you're needed here, to look after your family"—her anxious smile saddened—"now that your pap's gone." Melinda Jane picked at the fence with a fingernail. "*I'd* like for you to stay."

"It's not that I *want* to go, Melinda Jane. It's just that I feel a duty. A duty to protect my family, this land—to keep this side of Virginia out of the hands of the Confederacy." Pride swelled inside him again. It always reared when he thought about this land. This farm.

She crossed her arms and pooched out her bottom lip. "While you're off—probably gettin' yourself killed—what are the rest of us supposed to do? There's no telling how much longer these Union soldiers will be here watching over us."

Fin vaulted the fence, landing on his feet. He faced Melinda Jane, his hands on her shoulders. "I want to raise a family on this farm someday, Melinda Jane. I want to be able to tell my children that their pap fought for their home in the War of Rebellion."

"Well, if you go gettin' yourself killed, you'll never have a family of your own, then they won't be needing this farm—and then there's no use of you going to fight . . . and—" A tear trickled its way down her cheek to her jaw. When she turned her back, he knew she was wiping it away.

Another thought came to mind. "If I remember right, King David got himself in trouble when he let everyone else go fight a war while he stayed behind."

She whirled on him and planted her hands on her hips. "Oh, now you're sayin' that just because I'm wanting you to stay, I'm leading you into sin like that Bath Sheba? Pooh. That makes about as much sense as a square wheel."

"That's not what I'm saying at all."

"The next crazy thing you'll be saying is that you want me to wait for you."

She stopped her fussing and tipped her gaze, those caramel eyes of hers drilling a hole into his very soul and kindling a fire in his belly. Her full lips quivered, beckoning him. Luring him. Mercy, but she was beautiful.

He froze. Confound it! Why couldn't he just kiss her?

"Uh . . . well . . . I . . ." Fin shoved his hands into his pockets, the connection between his brain and tongue suddenly severed.

"I declare. Fin Dabney, you have less pluck than a nekked hen!" She grabbed up her skirt and marched off to the house.

He snatched off his hat and flung it to the ground.

Women!

Thirty-Three

Fayette County

The sweet scent of hay and tang of manure brazed the air as Zander curried Rampart's chestnut-speckled withers. "Good ride, huh, boy?" He leaned against the warm shoulder, pressing into a quiver that swelled beneath the sleek coat. Seemed like his world was turning and twisting so fast these days.

Since the Rebel presence across the countryside made it too dangerous to leave the farm alone, he'd been exercising Rampart in the pasture, a lacking situation for both of them. "Fin said we'd get a little hunting in this week. You'd like that, wouldn't you?" He switched to a brush and followed it across the gelding's back with the palm of his hand.

"That you, Zander?"

"In here, Seamus." Zander snatched the currycomb from the top of the rail. "Night, boy." He closed the gate to Rampart's soft nicker.

"Are you heading up to the house soon?" Seamus's head popped into view around the end stall.

"I reckon."

"Would you mind taking a couple of things up to the house when you go?"

"Won't be a problem. I'll be there in a minute." Zander set the pail of brushes inside the tack room and headed for the hospital area.

"Here you go." Seamus handed him a pan loaded with a half dozen bowls and spoons.

"Looks like somebody's been eating Gus's sweet potato pie." Zander grinned at Seamus.

"I washed those dishes, boyo. They're clean as a slate. How'd you know what was in those bowls?"

"I'm thinking you're savin' some for later." Zander eyed an orange mess nestled in Seamus's beard. "Actually, it blends in real nice with that hank of fur you got there."

Seamus scowled and wiped his whiskers. He grumbled as he turned and headed toward the loft. *"Savin' some for later,"* he mimicked, wagging his head. "Wiseacre!"

The newest Confederate patient leaned up on one arm. "You live here, boy?"

"I do," Zander turned to the soldier.

"I don't reckon you know a Jonathan Dabney around these parts."

"Why you asking?" He narrowed his eyes and took a step closer to the man.

"He's kin. My father's brother. I know he lives somewhere around here."

Zander set the pan of dishes on the table and stepped closer. He glanced at Johnson, standing guard duty. The private shook his head slightly, then repositioned his rifle.

"Jonathan is . . . *was* my pap, I'm Zander Dabney."

"Well, what do you know? I'll bet you were just a sprite when last I saw you. You have an older brother and sister, don't you, cousin?" The Rebel dropped the back of his head onto his cot. "If that don't beat all! Here I lay, all shot up in my own cousins' barn."

"What you'd say your name was?"

"I didn't, but it's Carter. Carter Dabney."

"I'll be back. I'm gonna find Gus and Fin." *Carter?* And a *Rebel*. They'd never believe it. Zander trotted halfway to the door, then remembered the dishes, grabbed them off the table, and headed out of the barn.

"Gus! Gus!" Zander barged through the back door and set the pan of dishes on the table. "Gus!"

༄

Augusta made her way down the stairs, peeking around a pile of pillows and quilts.

"What is that boy up to?" Melinda Jane grunted, following with her own stack of linens.

"I'm right here, Zander. You can stop hollerin' now." She walked past him to the back porch, where they dumped the quilts and pillows into a heap. Melinda Jane proceeded to hang the quilts on the clothesline to air out.

"Gus, that new Confederate in the barn—apparently, he's our cousin. His name is Carter."

The fluffed pillow slipped from Augusta's hand. "Carter Dabney is in our barn?"

"That's what he said."

"Why don't you see if you can round up Fin? Would you do that, please?" He vaulted over the last three porch steps and jogged off.

She shook her head, trying to settle on the truth of it. It was a lot to take in, but it *did* make sense. "Our own cousin—and I tended him!"

Melinda Jane returned to the porch for another quilt. "What's this about a cousin?"

"Well, if what Zander says is true, my Uncle Bertram's son, Carter, is a Rebel soldier, and he's lying wounded in our barn." She fussed with her flyaway hairs and inspected her work dress. "I'm not very presentable."

"You ever meet this man?"

"I was just a girl. It was . . . must've been about eight years ago. I was Will's age. Our family made a trip back east to visit Pap's family. Carter was a few years older than Fin and me."

∞

Augusta smiled as Carter Dabney wiped the last of the soapy lather from his face. "That looks a bit more like the cousin I remember," she said, taking the mirror from his hand.

"I'd forgotten what my face looked like." Carter's fingers kneaded his smooth chin.

"I know I wouldn't have recognized you if you hadn't said something." Fin pulled up a barrel and sat down. "So, when were you home last?"

"Not since July. A whole slew of us enlisted together." He looked around. "The boy I was brought in with?"

"I'm afraid he didn't make it." Augusta frowned, saddened for her cousin at the loss of his friend.

"Too bad." Carter shook his head. "I suppose I should write a letter to his mama and daddy. They were neighbors of ours back home."

"You know you'll have to go to a Union prison just as soon as the doctor says you're able." Fin's eyes moved to the man's bandage.

"He doesn't need to worry about that right now, Fin. We'll take care of you while you're here, Carter. You can even write to your folks and tell them where you are so they'll know." She handed him a bowl of sweet potato pie and a fork. She meant her smile to ease him, to reassure him. But it felt like *she* was the one sending him to a Union Prison.

∞

James and Sgt. Mallory, with two of his men, neared the Dabney turnoff with a wagon of supplies. They'd come from Camp Gauley, the former Rebel stronghold, now stocked and manned by the Federal Army. In the distance, a wagon and Union soldiers crested the hill to the south.

"Let's wait for them here. They may have wounded." James recognized the ranking officer as Captain Guthrie, one of General Cox's men.

"Afternoon, Major Hill. We've brought some men for you." Captain Guthrie saluted James and signaled his men to a stop.

"Where did this happen?"

"We were bringing you three injured men from a run-in with some guerillas on the other side of the bridge. Next thing you know, we found ourselves smack dab in another cluster of Rebels a couple miles farther up Gauley Road."

"Follow us on up to the hospital, Captain." James motioned to Mallory, who rattled the traces to guide the team up the lane.

Once in the yard, James looked over the six Federals and three Confederates in the crowded wagon bed. Two lay prostrate. He took a preliminary look at the wounded and eyed his assistant, who peered over the side of the wagon.

Seamus nodded as if reading James's mind. He turned and headed for the barn to prepare cots for the new patients.

∞

Blinded by the barn's shadowy interior, James paused at the entrance. But no amount of blinking could erase the sight. Or ease the lightning that thrummed through his stomach and limbs, at once sickening him and coiling his fingers into fists. All these years he'd worked to leave his past behind, and here it was, bedded down right in front of him.

Carter nodded in a silent, sober greeting.

Ignoring him, James gruffly ordered the placement of the new patients. "I want that one and," he pointed, "this one on the operating tables. The rest can wait their turns."

The next two hours passed in a haze of memories that charged at James with acridity. He sliced, stitched, and bandaged without thought, limiting his speech to the necessary. He avoided looking toward the cot with the new prisoner, whose stare felt like a bayonet in his back.

"James, are you all right?" Gus slipped the morphine bottle into his hand.

"I'm fine." His voice was less than polite, and he hated himself for it. He found her eyes. "I'm sorry. I guess I'm just distracted."

"When you're done, I have a surprise for you." Her cheerful voice—the antithesis of the one that droned in his head—failed to douse his sour mood. She stepped around him, retrieving the soaking surgical tools, pouring carbolic acid over them. Wiping each with a clean cloth, she returned them to their respective holders.

Nine new patients tended to and situated; James drank deeply from a dipper of cool water. Fin's hand clapped over one shoulder, and James turned.

"We have someone we want you to meet. Come with me."

James followed Fin—his dread sharpened by an iron-hard attitude. Would that he could spend the next twelve hours in surgery rather than face this specter from his past.

Gus motioned to a cot. "James, I'd like you to meet our cousin, Carter Dabney."

Carter flashed a toothy smile and extended his hand. James stared at the proffered hand. Finally, he raised his hard gaze to meet Carter's.

"We've already met," James said, his voice flat.

"Now Jimmy, is that anyway to greet your old friend." Carter looked from Gus to Fin. "Jimmy and I grew up together. Why, his family's plantation was pretty nearly right next to ours."

Gus crossed her arms, lips tight. She silently grilled James for an explanation. Now he knew how Bertie felt.

"What?" Fin's attention jumped from Carter to James and back to Carter. "What plantation?" He narrowed his eyes at James in confusion.

"That was a lifetime ago," James said at last. "Excuse me, I have things to tend to."

James strode out to the pump to splash water on his face and neck. Seeing that Captain Guthrie and his men were preparing to depart, he quickened his pace. "Did you and your men get something to eat, Captain?"

"We've been well taken care of, Major. Miss Minard saw to that." He patted his belly. "I'd like to leave two more men with you since I've just increased your prisoner count."

"Thank you, Captain. Most appreciated. I was hoping for some sort of update. We hear little unless it comes by way of visitor."

Guthrie reached into his saddlebag. "I nearly forgot." He handed James three letters. "With Wise's Legion out of this area, there should be near regular postal service again in Gauley Bridge."

James glanced at the letters. One was for him and two for Gus. From the mystery man again, no doubt.

"You probably heard that Lee's Rebels had a failed attack on General Reynold's forces at the Cheat Mountain Summit. Forced to retreat." The captain collected the reins, preparing to mount.

"I did hear some mention of that this morning up at Camp Gauley."

"Last I heard, Ol' Granny Lee holds a goodly force up on Sewell Mountain. I expect to see trouble real soon."

James nodded his agreement and hung the dipper over a pin near the pump handle.

"Seems the Confederates are still trying to lay claim to the Coal River Valley. Down at Kanawha Gap, Cox's forces sent the Rebels running with their tails between their legs." Guthrie chortled and shook his head. "They hightailed it out of there so fast they left their wounded, prisoners, even horses, in the trenches. Not long after, we took Chapmanville back from the Rebels. They'd been using it for a headquarters and such." He hooked a canteen to the saddle and mounted.

"Appreciate the update, Captain. And thanks again for the extra men."

James squinted at the dust as the soldiers urged their mounts back down the lane. If he had his druthers just now, he'd choose to ride out with them. He was in no hurry to face the music that Carter Dabney, no doubt, would insist on playing.

∞

James pulled out the letter from Mrs. O'Donell. Inside, she had folded a stamped letter into one handwritten page. Curiosity got the better of him and he read the mystery letter first.

Dear Dr. Hill and Mrs. O'Donell—Mrs. Ford is writing this letter for me. I am working as a cook for the Cooleys. They are friends of the Fords and a fine family with two young boys. They pay me fifty cents a day, and I've already saved enough money for a store-bought hat! The Fords are very kind to me, just like you said. My arm has healed up real good. I hope you will come visit me when this dreadful war is past. The good Lord keep you both.—Forever Grateful, Nan

He warmed, smiling at the memory of her. *Good for you, Nan.*

After reading Mrs. O'Donell's letter, he stuffed them both into his pocket and headed into the house for supper.

∽

Stars glittered, diamonds against black velvet. James marveled at the beauty amid so much heartache. Hat clutched in one hand, he stood on the porch, relishing the silence until the door spring whined.

Gus moved to his side. "Beautiful night, isn't it?"

Her presence emanated questions, disapproval, even hurt. He could feel her gaze upon him, but he avoided it, wondering how he would untangle this knot between them. "Yes, it's one spectacular sight, all right."

"You didn't say more than 'please' and 'thank you' at the supper table tonight." She leaned her forearms on the porch railing. "You ready to tell me about you and Carter?"

Motioning for her to sit on the top step, he claimed the space beside her. He drew in a long breath through his nose and exhaled. Procrastination he could do. She could not.

"Like I said—that was a lifetime ago."

"I'm listening." She hugged her knees and tipped her head to look at him.

"Carter was nearly my best friend growing up. From diapers on, our families were close."

"You're the son of a plantation owner." It was a statement, not a question. She shifted her gaze to the night sky. He didn't blame her for not wanting to look at him.

"Yes. I despised the way of it all, Gus." He hung his head and steepled his fingers. His voice was slow, deliberate. "Their hubristic lives and their shiny fortresses chinked with the sweat and blood of slave labor."

He stood. He wanted to reach for her hand and place it on his heart so she could feel it beat with the injustice he'd witnessed—and the turmoil that drove each pulse toward the next.

"The peremptory attitude that a man is less than human because his skin bears a different hue. The very idea, were it not so wretched, would be deemed imbecilic." He clenched his fists, redirecting the emotion threatening to erupt. He couldn't bring himself to tell her more. Not yet.

"We don't choose our family, James. God does."

He chuckled. "Someone else told me the same thing." At the thought of Jonathan Dabney, he smiled through the sadness that squeezed his throat. How different his life would've been had the man been his own father.

"How long has it been since you were home?" Gus stood, folding her hand over James's forearm.

"March the third, 1855, more than six years now. I left and never looked back." He remembered that windy afternoon. Ezra's eyes. Barnes, the overseer. So much blood.

"Please excuse me, Gus. I need to check on the patients." He pulled from her touch, avoiding her eyes, and strode across the yard. The dark hollow within him couldn't bear the light of her presence just now.

Thirty-Four

Fayette County

"Morning, cousin. I brought you some fried cornmeal mush and bacon." Augusta set the plate beside Carter's cot.

He lifted one eyelid and groaned. "You're up early." A corner of his mouth jumped at the sight of the plate, and he eased himself upright as Augusta stuffed a rolled blanket behind him. "The family has already eaten. I saved some out for you."

Carter picked up the fork and cut a piece of the mush. He smiled his thanks. "Much obliged, Gus. Is Fin hereabouts?"

"He took off hunting with Zander before sunup. Mostly it's been the soldiers posted here doing all the hunting because of the Confed—" An awkward silence settled for a moment until Carter laughed.

She pointed to a tin cup on the table. "There's fresh coffee too." He rolled his eyes in delight after a cautious sip. "That maple syrup is from our trees down by the crick."

"I haven't eaten this good since I left home. I don't suppose my leg is requiring several months of mending?"

"Afraid not, soldier. Speaking of your leg, as soon as you're done with your breakfast, I need to see to that bandage." Patient or not, he *was* her cousin. "Maybe it'd be better if Seamus did it."

"What about the *Doctor* Hill?" He shoved the last morsel of bacon into his mouth.

"I don't think that's a good idea, Carter."

"Why do you say that?"

"James told me about his past—how he feels about all that." She looked down at her fingers, then picked at her apron.

"He did, did he? About Ezra?"

"Ezra? No, I don't think so. Who's Ezra?" Augusta's smile tightened.

"Maybe you should ask *James* that question yourself." Carter handed her the empty plate.

"I believe I will." She paraded out the door, tapping the empty plate against her hand.

∞

Fin hoisted the whitetail carcass up to the beam by a rough rope. "We'll let it hang a few days, then *you* can skin this one. I skinned the last three, Zander. You're the one who needs practice, not me."

"I will, I will." Zander tied off the end of the rope while his brother held it taut.

"Well, just don't you go disappearing when it's time to do it."

Coot's staccato bark drew their attention. "Someone must be here." Fin picked up the rifles and handed one to Zander as they headed out the door.

Four riders halted their horses in front of the house. Fin nodded to a few Union soldiers, drinking their fill near the pump. He recognized the newcomers, and it made him extra thankful for the soldiers' presence. His grip tightened on the firearm. "I thought I made myself clear the last time you stopped by here, Mr. Hampton."

"You did. Indeed, you did, Mr. Dabney." The man turned his head as the front door opened. Gus walked toward them.

"I've simply stopped as a courtesy to let you know we found the guilty party that's been hiding runaways. I do hope our business here is concluded." The man tipped his hat to Gus and reined his horse into a tight turn, disappearing down the lane with the other three.

Melinda Jane stepped out of the house and watched as the riders disappeared. She looked at Fin. "What was that all about?"

"Those slave hunters came by the other day looking for some runaways."

Her eyebrow arched. "Did they find them?"

"I reckon so. They said they found whoever was hiding them."

Melinda Jane gasped and stumbled forward. Her fingers tore at her hair and her beautiful face cringed in horror. "No, no, no, no. Please God, no, no—" Her desperate cries sliced the air as she tore off running.

"Melinda Jane!" *What is . . . ?* Fin glanced around for something he'd missed.

Gus's trembling hand covered her mouth, and her eyes widened. She clutched at her skirt and bolted after Melinda Jane. "Izzy!" Her hoarse scream trailed behind as her legs carried her frantically down the incline. "Izzy!"

Fin sprinted after the women, rifle still in hand—across the pasture and over the hill, overtaking Gus. Izzy's cabin popped into view, and just at the edge of the grove, Melinda Jane dropped to her knees.

Her fists pounded the ground. "Nooo!" Great sobs convulsed her body.

Fin stood, paralyzed, a nightmare playing out before him.

Gus caught up to her, heaving for breath. She threw her arms around her dearest friend, as Melinda Jane wailed, rocking and rocking in her agony.

A shadow tinted the dried grass, its shape stirring the dappled sunlight as it moved. Izzy's limp body, suspended by a hangman's noose, swung in a slow circle from the branch of a tall maple. An eerie stillness settled. No breezy whispers or birdcalls. No woodland chatter. The creak of the limb—the only accompaniment to the women's grief.

Two soldiers trotted up on horseback, followed by James and Will on foot. Will's hands flew to cover her face before she turned into James's embrace.

Fury sprouted roots as Fin's insides quaked. He pulled his hunting knife from the sheath strapped to his leg. "Help me get him down!" A soldier started toward Izzy's body, but Fin grabbed the horse's halter. "I'll do it." The soldier nodded and dismounted.

※

Augusta's muscles ached from holding her sweet friend. Tears and snot had matted hair to her face and soaked her bodice—trivial compared to her gouged insides. She struggled to stay upright. She wanted to throw herself down and let the ground swallow her up.

The ache numbed her senses, and she watched the movements around her like a play. A show on a stage. A wretched scene in a wretched play. It couldn't be real. She drew the inside of her arm across her face. The tears were real. Nausea about overwhelmed her, but she'd not loosen her hold on Melinda Jane. She glimpsed James's boots on the grass beside her and felt his hand on her shoulder before Will dropped to the ground beside her, clinging to her side.

∞

Helpless again. James yearned to comfort Gus. A walnut-sized lump burned as he sucked in air. His temple pounded from the steel clench of his jaw. The familiar rage, from which he'd failed to part ways, rattled his chest.

He watched as Fin swung onto a horse and rode to where Izzy hung. He stood in the saddle and wrapped one arm around his friend's waist. James jogged over to help. *Maybe, just maybe, there's a chance . . .*

Fin reached up to cut the rope, and James settled Izzy carefully on the ground. He felt for a pulse. *A miracle, God. We need a miracle.* That instant of hope made the truth more bitter to taste.

He looked up at Fin and shook his head. "We're too late."

Fin turned. "Zander, get up in that tree and get that rope off of there. I don't want any trace of it left!" Fin slapped his hat on his knee, hard. His eyes flashed with the force of a geyser.

Gus's arms encircled her friend, and they rocked as one—Gus sobbing and Melinda Jane keening to her Maker for the loss of her last family member. Will lay her head on Melinda Jane's back, her body shaking in silence.

"Seamus said he'd corral Bertie and keep him up at the house." James said.

He looked down at Izzy's body. Emotion so strong it tipped his senses and reared in his chest. He loved this man. The admiration, respect, and affection he held for Izzy blanketed his spirit even as grief raked his insides. *But he's with you now, Lord. Of that, I have no doubt.* The thought brought a surprising measure of comfort.

Gus approached with Melinda Jane. As he moved aside, they settled on the ground, and Melinda Jane pulled her grandpappy's head into her lap. Indiscernible words tumbled as she stroked his white hair and washed his face with her tears. Gus wrapped Izzy's weathered hand in her own, her blotched face a veil of heartbreak.

Silence bonded their grief as time tip-toed around the circle of mourners.

At last, James raised his head and took in the surroundings. The cabin. He caught Fin's eye and indicated the open door. They drew their weapons and approached the hovel.

Inside was a single, upended table and three toppled chairs. A shelf hung crooked on the wall and tin dishes littered the puncheon floor. A rag rug lay wadded against one wall and an opened trap door exposed a space under the floorboards.

"I'll go down." Fin stepped around James and lowered himself into the opening. He stood in the pit, his shoulders even with the floor. "There's not much space down here."

Disappearing for a minute, Fin reemerged and shoved two dirty quilts onto the floor. His hand clutched something—a rag doll—made from worn black fabric, its pink calico skirt gray with dirt. He stared at the doll, his eyes rimming red before climbing out of the hole and heading out the door without a word.

∞

Fin strode directly to Melinda Jane, pulled her to a standing position, and handed her the doll. Recognition dawned in her swollen eyes. She squeezed them shut and wilted. He caught her limp body even as his own trembled. A cauldron of hatred and grief rose to a boil, its steam seeping into his lungs, filling his breath with reckless intentions.

Long after the other men had lifted Izzy's body onto the back of a horse and started for the house, Fin held Melinda Jane. Long after James had walked Will and Gus up the hill, still, he held her.

Thirty-Five

Fayette County

James busied himself, ignoring the unwelcomed patient. If only he didn't have to be in the same room with the man. He was sure Carter's eyes followed him. Out of the corner of his vision, he watched Carter struggle to a standing position, leaning on the crude crutch Zander had fashioned for him.

After hobbling to the operating table, Carter rested. "Looks to me like this doctorin' suits you just fine, Jimmy. Doesn't pay much though, does it?"

James kept his head down, noting the bottled medicine levels on the supply list.

"You broke your folks' hearts, you know . . . when you left." Carter hobbled a little closer. "It wasn't good manners—not saying goodbye."

"What would you know about manners?"

"I know they're highly overrated. Cabbage turns far more heads than manners, *Doctor*."

He ground his teeth like a caged animal. Fin walked in, hailed Carter, and headed their way. Seizing the chance to distance himself, James traversed the room and pretended to take inventory. Anything to avoid that pompous annoyance.

"Hey Carter. I see you're getting around pretty well." Fin motioned to the crutch. "Zander's handiwork, I understand."

"Sure is. Works real fine, too."

"I suspect anything beats just sitting around all day long."

Carter pressed his lips together and shook his head. "Real sorry to hear about your Negro, Fin."

James looked up in time to see Carter slam into the operating table, the crutch clattering to the floor. He cursed, rubbing his jaw. Eyes flashing, he growled out the words, "What was that for?"

Fin whirled and stomped out of the barn without a word.

James grinned, imagining the steam that surely rose from Fin's collar. He watched Carter stagger to his cot, and for the first time, he saw him for what he was—a pathetic excuse for a man. A wisp of sympathy touched his conscience, then disappeared like a vapor.

James found Fin at the pump, sluicing water from his beard. "That's some right cross you got there."

"He had it comin'—cousin or no."

"You just beat me to it. Carter always did have a problem running off at the mouth."

Fin wiped his hands across his shirt. "How long you figure the Union Army to be using our barn?"

"I can't say. I understand your eagerness to get things around here back to normal."

"No, that's not why I ask." Fin glanced over his shoulder toward the house, then pinned James with a grave expression. "I'm gonna volunteer. But leaving the family in danger . . . If you and the soldiers are here, I can rest easy knowing they're in good hands."

"I wish I could give you an accurate answer, Fin. Near as I can figure, so long as the Rebel guerillas are roaming these hills, there'll be need of a hospital here."

"I appreciate your honesty." He sucked in a breath and extended a hand. "I'll be leaving in the morning."

James gripped Fin's hand and nodded. His thoughts shot to a certain redheaded beauty whose heart would be broken, yet again.

∽

The bay gelding stomped and nickered as Fin tied the leather strips of the saddlebag. Turning to face his family for what could be the last time, he'd not dwell on the *what-ifs*. Nor would he admit to the emotions grinding in his gullet. He just needed to get through the goodbyes.

"If Pap or Izzy were standing here with us right now, I know they'd have something wise to say." Gus opened a small, worn Bible and read:

> *"I will lift up mine eyes unto the hills, from whence cometh my help. My help cometh from the Lord, which made heaven and earth. He will not suffer thy foot to be moved: he that keepeth thee will not slumber. Behold, he that keepeth Israel shall neither slumber nor sleep. The Lord is thy keeper: the Lord is thy shade upon thy right hand. The sun shall not smite thee by day, nor the moon by night. The Lord shall preserve thee from all evil: He shall preserve thy soul. The Lord shall preserve thy going out and thy coming in from this time forth, and even for evermore."*

Closing the Book, she handed it to Fin. "He'd want you to have this."

He took it, wrapping her in an embrace and kissing the top of her head. "I'll be back, don't you fret. You're in good hands." He jerked his head toward the barn. "You've got the Union Army watching over you."

She laid her palm aside his cheek, her watery eyes taking him in for several seconds before stepping aside.

Fin opened his arms wide, and Will and Bertie ran to him. "I don't want you to go, Fin," Bertie sniffled.

"I have to go, Bertie. You just pray for me every day I'm gone. I need you to be brave now, and watch after the girls."

Snot trailed from the boy's nose, and he wiped it with the back of his hand. "I'll be brave . . . and I'll pray for you every day. But you better not go gettin' killed, or I'll be mighty mad at you."

He ruffled the boy's hair. "That's not something I aim to let happen, Bertie."

He kissed Will on the cheek. "I'm gonna miss you, little sister. Maybe when I come home, you'll decide that wearing a dress ain't so bad after all."

Her mouth gaped, then snapped shut. A frown slid into a sad smile. "I'll miss you too, Fin."

Zander stepped up, his back rigid, and thrust his hand forward. Fin offered a bemused smile and shook his hand. "I'll miss you, brother," Zander said, his voice deeper than usual.

"You're a man now, so you watch over the family." A jerky smile lit Zander's face for an instant, before Fin pulled him into an embrace. "I'll miss you too."

Gus collected her brothers and sister as a hen gathers her chicks, and headed to the house.

Melinda Jane dangled a tied flour sack. "I know you've already got lots of vittles for later, but this is for sooner."

Fin lifted the sack to his nose and breathed in a sweet, buttery aroma. "Cinnamon buns?"

She nodded. "And I put a couple of ham sandwiches and boiled eggs in there, too."

He worked the top of the sack into the tie holding his bedroll.

She slipped something from her pocket. "This is a carte de visite I had taken in Charleston the summer of last year. I want you to have it so you don't forget me."

He smiled at the likeness and his blood warmed. Even her image was beautiful. "This picture and Pap's Bible—they're my two most prized possessions. Thank you, Melinda Jane." He slid it into his shirt pocket, right behind the Bible.

"Fin, I—" She looked up at him, her eyes red. A single tear slid down her cheek and before she could wipe it away, he brushed it with his thumb, holding her soft cheek in his palm, memorizing her face.

"Don't cry. I'll be back, you'll see." He wrapped his arms around her, and for the second time in as many days, held her close. Her delicate body trembled against him as wetness seeped through his shirt. He pressed his face into her hair. Breathing in her scent, he vowed to remember its sweetness. To recall it for the long days ahead.

At last, she pulled away. Wiping frantically at her tear-streaked face, she attempted a trembling smile. She thrust her hands onto her hips and scolded, "You'd better come back to me, Fin Dabney!" She clutched her skirt and raced up the steps into the house.

Thirty-Six

◈

Fayette County

October, 1861

Augusta tucked the letter to Jimmy Lee into her apron pocket. In her endeavor to lift his spirits, she'd promised him some of her shoofly pie if he came home safe. She included some scripture for inspiration and was careful to sign it, *your friend, Gus*—just in case he was imagining their relationship to be anything more. She'd walk out and slip it into the mail sack. Surely, one of the soldiers would be heading into Gauley Bridge soon.

Harmonica music floated down from the loft as she entered the barn, settling a sort of calm over the patients. As they stood guard duty, Johnson held Hanley spell bound with a history lesson. One of General Cox's wounded men worked his knife, flipping slivers of wood from the bowl of a freshly fashioned pipe.

Augusta walked to the ladder, recognizing the polished melody. A few others played the mouth organ, but only Mallory could play it so skillfully. "Sergeant Mallory, is that you up there?"

Mallory's salt-and-pepper beard popped over the edge of the loft. "Yes, ma'am. What can I do for you?"

"I have a letter here to be posted. Are you aware of anyone heading into town?"

"If not today, I'm sure somebody will go soon." He climbed down the ladder and held out his hand. "I'd be happy to put it into the mail pouch for you, miss. That way, it will go out with the next batch of mail."

"Thank you, that's most kind of you." She pulled the letter from her pocket, handing it to him with a smile.

She spotted two soldiers playing checkers and her eyes misted, recalling the long hours Izzy sat with Pap playing checkers over the years. A familiar ache rose to her throat. Experience told her that eventually the pain would succumb to bittersweet memories, but for now, she determined to put one foot in front of the other and lean on Jesus. *When I am weak, You are strong.* Do not cry. She stilled her quivering chin with a touch and strode toward the barn door.

※

James waited as a detachment of Union soldiers halted their horses. A sober-faced sergeant reached into a courier pouch. "I have orders for Major Hill."

"You've found him, Sergeant." James unfolded the missive. Not a task he would've chosen. "Please tell General Rosecrans I will report to Gauley Bridge first thing in the morning."

The Federals turned their horses, trotted down the muddy lane and out of sight.

He squared his shoulders and chewed on the inside of his cheek. An irrational apprehension niggled at him.

"Well, you going to tell me what's in those orders, or am I to have a guess?" Seamus scratched his beard and folded his arms across his chest.

"General Rosecrans's troops are taking up a position to oppose Lee at the summit of Sewell Mountain. He wants me there to set up a field hospital."

"What about me? Am I to stay here and play nursemaid?"

"It would appear so."

A growing sense of protection, even commitment, had staked its claim on James's heart, so far as Gus was concerned. Fin's departure had only driven the stake deeper. If only he could—An idea took hold. He strode toward the barn. Yes, he'd write Mrs. O'Donell promptly.

The buckskin gelding pawed at the wet ground as Sergeant Mallory saddled up to head for town. When he swung the mailbag up to its usual place behind the cantle, James quickened his pace. "I've got something for you before you leave, Sergeant. I won't be but a few minutes."

He retrieved paper from his portable writing desk and hastily penned a letter, hoping Mrs. O'Donell would receive it within the week.

∞

James's gaze settled on Gus, seated across from him. She grinned and whispered something in Bertie's ear. The boy returned her smile with one of his own, complete with a milk mustache. Pap's and Fin's chairs sat empty. James stared at the back of the oak chair next to Melinda Jane. For a moment, he pictured his wise friend, Izzy, sitting there—shoulders rounded with age, his snowy beard quivering with his easy laugh.

He looked at the petite young woman whose stunning eyes sparkled with mischief, just like her grandpap's. Likely, Fin would one day come to his senses and marry the girl.

"What do you find so amusing, *Major* Hill?" Gus's smile curled up on one side. Her fork held a bite of potato above her plate.

"I . . . uh. I am simply delighted to partake of such savory victuals, Miss Dabney. My sincere compliments to the cook," he nodded to Melinda Jane, "or, *cooks,* as the case may be." He lifted his coffee cup in a toast.

Melinda Jane beamed and dipped her chin. "Why, thank you, Major Hill. I believe I will graciously accept your compliment."

Gus chuckled and pulled the potato morsel off her fork in slow motion. Her unblinking gaze met his. His breath caught. Heat spread across his chest. He'd missed his mouth and coffee was trickling through his beard onto his shirt.

Will covered her mouth, a snort erupting from her suppressed giggle. Bertie howled, slapping a hand to his forehead as Gus rushed to get a towel.

She handed it to James. "I hope you aren't burned." Her compassion eased his embarrassment until Melinda Jane found it necessary to add her two-cents-worth.

"Why, I'd be surprised if he felt a thing, as I reckon his mind was elsewhere."

Snickers fluttered around the table. His face burned as Zander joined in and the amusement climbed to lofty heights at his expense. He stood, swiping at the brown stain on his shirt before tossing the towel onto his chair. A meal with the Dabneys was its own kind of battlefield. The only casualty being his dignity.

"I believe this is my exit. Thank you for the splendid meal and the . . . uh . . . *fine* company." Glancing at Gus just long enough to fuel her amused expression, he snagged his hat from the rack and exited the front door.

After checking on his patients, James ventured out to the yard. A sliver of moon struggled for notice behind drifting clouds, and the evening sky still glowed its farewell to the day. Light shone bright through the kitchen window, so he claimed a place on a front porch rocker.

He considered going around to the back door. Maybe he would find Gus just finishing up in the kitchen. Before he could devise a plan, the front door opened.

Gus backed out of the door and gasped. "You startled me—I didn't know you were out here." She glanced at the blue shawl draped over one arm. "I thought I'd take a little stroll."

"May I?"

He draped the shawl around her shoulders and stepped closer as he drew the edges together. Her demure smile only kindled the ever-present spark inside him.

"I believe it would be wise if I accompanied you on that stroll, Miss Dabney—as your protector, of course." He held her gaze as the few seconds of silence fanned that spark into flames, distracting and desirous.

"As my protector. Yes, of course, Major Hill." She slipped her hand through his arm and lifted her skirt to descend the steps.

"Dinner was wonderful tonight."

"So, you said."

"I seem to have been the evening entertainment, I suppose."

"Perhaps."

They walked in quietude, their steps a lazy rhythm of crunching leaves. The crisp fall air held its own special scents of wood smoke, dust, and chill.

"I miss Jonathan and Izzy." James had spent hours replaying their conversations with him in his head. So many questions he could've asked them. *Should've* asked them. "I didn't realize how much I had come to admire them . . . until they were gone."

She turned to him. "I miss them too." Her eyes reflected grief. "I will always miss them."

"Forgive me. I didn't mean to make you sad. I grieve for them too, in my way." He patted her hand and continued their stroll. "In a brief time, they each became more of a father to me than my own father—in all the time I lived under his roof."

"Tell me about Ezra."

He stopped, inadvertently tugging her backward. "Where did you hear that name?"

"From Carter. He said I should ask you about Ezra."

James resumed walking in silence, pulling her hand around his arm again. How much should he say? Could he even make her understand?

"Ezra was my friend. My very *best* friend. From the time I was Bertie's age until . . . until I was twenty. We were practically inseparable. Played together every day, and later we hunted together. Raced the horses. Fished. We did everything together. Well, nearly everything. Ezra was the one person who knew me better than anyone."

James swallowed hard, willing his words more audible. He needed her to know, but he wasn't ready. Not yet. "Ezra died just before I left home. I haven't been back since."

"Few people ever have someone like that in their life. You were blessed to have his friendship as long as you did." She squeezed his arm to her side. "Sometimes I wonder what life would be like without Melinda Jane. I can't even remember a time when she wasn't around. I remember our first year together at the schoolhouse. Well, it was a barn back then, where the students met. She was a mite small for her age, and the other kids picked on her. I threatened to have Fin wallop anybody who was mean to her." She chuckled. "After that, she called me her guardian angel. We still laugh about it from time to time."

They reached Gus's *thinkin' spot*, and she lifted herself into the swing. James pushed her from behind. The cooler weather had stifled the tree frog serenade, and a calm infused the crisp air.

He let the swing slow to a stop and circled to face her. "I've received orders. I'm leaving at first light for Sewell Mountain. The Army has plans to take on General Lee. Most of the Confederate force this side of the mountains is dug in at the summit."

"Tomorrow? So soon?" Her sweet face dipped, and her disappointment seeped through the evening's shadows. He'd give anything. *Do* anything to keep her from another minute's sadness. But his life was not his own. Blast this war!

He set his hands on her shoulders, memorizing her features. "Gus, if anything happens to me. If there are no more soldiers here to guard you . . . I've written to Mrs. O'Donell. She's a dear friend and a motherly sort, watching after my house in Charleston. I want you to go there should circumstances change. I don't want you here at the farm without protection." He could feel her tense, sensed an affront.

"I believe I can take care of my family, Major Hill. I—"

He pressed a finger to her lips. "I couldn't live with myself if anything happened to you. I want you to promise me you'll go to Charleston if the Army moves out of here." He handed her a folded paper. "This is the address of my house."

She stood, slipping the paper into her dress pocket. Her eyes pierced his own, a question coloring their darkened pools. "What did you say?"

"I said I want you to promise me—"

"Before that."

A giddiness worked its way to his lips, pushing them into a timid grin. "I said I couldn't live with myself if anything happened to you." Shadows played across her barely visible freckles. She swallowed, and her Adam's apple bounced briefly against her ivory neck, screaming for his fingers to touch its softness. To caress the hollow of her throat.

Her lips parted, and irresistibly drawn, he met them with his own. Her arms encircled him and he drew her closer, relishing the feel of her, willing the moment to carry him through tonight, through his tomorrows—such was the desire, the hunger that surged through him. He moved his mouth to her ear and murmured her name, raising an ache inside he'd never known. His lips traveled of their own accord, to her cheek, her mouth, her ear, her throat. A moan sighed from her lips, and he covered them again with his own.

Time, held captive by their embrace, shattered at last with the *yip* of a coyote.

A mountain of reluctance weighed on him as James walked her back to the house, his arm protectively holding her close, her head tucked against his shoulder.

She turned to face him at the door. Her fingers stroked his cheek, rekindling the fire. She probed his eyes with her own, misted and lovely. "God go with you, James Hill." She stood on her tiptoes and pressed a sweet kiss to his lips, lingering but for a moment.

"Come back to me," her voice rasped, sad and uncertain. She whirled, disappearing too soon as the door closed behind her.

Standing there, arms aching to pull her back, a painful realization blazed its way into his brain—he was helpless to alter or command a single moment of his own life.

He turned away from his dreams and strode toward his destiny. But never had his steps been heavier.

∞

James stepped into the low light of the barn. Carter, the only patient awake, sat on his cot, a book in one hand, and his bandaged leg propped on a wooden crate. A single lantern burned on a nearby table, shedding just enough light by which to read. He looked up when James closed the door. Hanley stood guard duty, his Springfield in hand.

"There's only two things that keep a man out this late, Jimmy." Carter threw the book on the cot. "That'd be women and a coon hunt . . . and you don't look to be dressed for no coon hunt."

James glanced his way and ground his teeth, determined not to engage the man. He shook off his jacket and draped it over the back of a chair.

Carter stood, free of his crutch, and walked toward James. "If you know what's good for you, *Yankee*, you'll stay away from my cousin. It wouldn't do to have *yeller* blood mixing with the Dabney pedigree."

Hanley repositioned his weapon, and James stayed him with an upraised hand. "Why don't you give us a minute, Hanley?"

"Yes, sir." Hanley glared at Carter and stepped outside.

He could only keep silent for so long. "What business do you have talking to Gus about Ezra? Huh, Carter?"

"I just figured if she knew the *real* Doctor James Hill, she'd know enough to run the other way."

James took a step closer. "I'd like to remind you that you are a prisoner here. You'll be heading to the prison camp in a couple of days, so don't be causing any trouble."

"We used to be friends, Jimmy. You'd send your friend to a Yankee prison camp?"

"There's a war going on, Carter. Friendship and kinship are of no matter where this brand of bloodshed's concerned."

James picked up his haversack and the canteen he'd filled earlier. He walked back to the stalls where he'd piled his belongings. Striking a match on the wall, he lit the lantern hanging outside the tack room.

"If it was Ezra instead of me standing here, you'd be cookin' up the fatted calf. Isn't that right, Jimmy?" Carter had followed him.

"Ezra was my friend," he growled.

"*Ezra was my friend*," Carter mimicked. He slammed his hand against the wall, then took a step closer and sneered. "Ezra was your *Negro*, Jimmy! Your *Negro*!" He drove a finger into James's chest to punctuate his words.

His face contorted. "Every time I wanted to do something with you growing up—just me and you—*Ezra* had to come too. 'I want *Ezra* to come,' you'd say. 'I'll ask *Ezra* if he wants to.'" He whined out the name.

Eyes narrowing, Carter tipped his head to one side, an exaggerated smile painted across his face. "Well, I finally found a way to get your attention. A way to put that Negro in his place—because you weren't man enough. Even after we were grown, you weren't man enough."

James gripped Carter's arm, his fingers digging into the muscle. A horrible truth burned its way to his senses. "What are you saying?"

"I'm the one that let that stallion out of the stall that night. I told old Barnes, the overseer, that I'd seen Ezra leave the gate open."

"You—" The blow of an invisible sledgehammer stalled his breath.

"It had to be done, Jimmy. Ezra didn't know his place anymore. He was gettin' too uppity because you never knew how to handle him. I saved you from disgrace. A man's gotta be the master of his slave, not his *friend*." He spat the word.

Growling, James wrenched on Carter's collar. Rage blistered and vented as it had on that night so long ago. A frothing geyser. Scalding. Dangerous.

Carter gasped for air, clawing at James's hand. "How was I supposed to know Barnes was gonna whip him to death?"

James's fist exploded into Carter's jaw, dropping him onto the hay-strewn floor. He jerked him to his knees, repeating the act, and once more Carter crumpled to the ground.

"Get up! I've got a mind to—"

"What? What, Jimmy? You got a mind to leave me here to die—like you did Ol' Barnes. You beat him senseless. Left him for dead. And you ran. You ran away like the coward you are."

Fury thundered beneath James's ribs. Muscles trembled. He stilled, waiting for the rage to loosen its grip on him, his fingers flexing and fisting. "I never meant to kill Barnes. I've had to live—"

"Kill him? You didn't kill him. Oh, he was crippled up some. Died a few months later in a card game gone bad. You ain't even man enough to kill that old drunk, Jimmy!" Eyes still wild, he spat a stream of blood and wiped his mouth.

"But all this time, I thought I'd killed him." His mind swam. All these years he'd lived with the guilt. Was Carter telling the truth? How could he trust him? Especially after this.

James turned and walked down to the end stall, where his horse stomped uneasily. Suddenly, two hands gripped his neck from behind, cutting off his wind mid-breath. He fought the panic and threw his elbow behind him, knocking a pitchfork to the floor. Grappling with his fingers, he found a fistful of fabric and yanked Carter close. He slammed his head back, butting Carter's face. The crunch of cartilage told him he'd hit his mark.

Carter dropped his hold and wailed, clutching his face.

James whirled on him, landing a blow to the midsection, doubling Carter over for long seconds. Carter snatched up the pitchfork, swung it wildly, and in a blur, the lantern crashed to the ground. Glass shattered, throwing kerosene into the hay. Flames scattered across the floor, licking at the dried fuel, gathering momentum.

"Fire! Get the men out!" James left Carter still heaving for breath, the pitchfork in his hand.

He raced to open the stall gates. "Hiyah! Hiyah!" Horses screamed, bolting to the paddock, eyes white, nostrils flaring.

Soldiers in the haymow slid down the ladder, some jumped from the loft, boots in hand. Already the fire had spread to the main part of the barn and timbers groaned.

James yelled to Mallory, "I've got the patients. Get this fire put out!"

He motioned to Seamus, and they each grabbed an injured man. Most of the wounded scurried about, making their own way out. Debris littered the floor as sparks rained from the ceiling, just before the timbers erupted into flames. He heard a voice over the roar of the inferno.

"James! James!"

"Gus, get out of here!"

She pulled from a soldier's grip and ran into the smoke. When he lost sight of her, panic roiled in his gut. Daggers sliced his eyes, but he cracked one open and kicked his way across the floor, dragging his charge with him.

Stumbling on a chair, he pitched it from his path. He handed off the patient to someone near the door and turned again into the conflagration. The black smoke blanketed his vision, but he could just make out Carter several feet away—trapped under a fallen beam.

James gripped the charred timber, searing his hands. His legs and arms shook with the weight, only to suspend it a few inches. "Get out! Get out!" He couldn't hear his own words—his mouth formed them, but his hoarse voice bucked against the noise. Carter crawled free and hobbled toward the door.

"Jimmy, come on!"

"Gus is in here!" James staggered, throwing himself in the direction he'd last seen her.

He crawled on his hands and knees, shoving furniture and burning debris out of the way. A thousand knives sliced his hands and legs as he crawled through the embers with his only thought of Gus. He had to find Gus.

A loud crack sounded to his right, and he turned his head. Crushing pain.

Blackness.

Silence.

PART THREE

*Hope is faith,
holding out its hand in the dark*

Author Unknown

Thirty-Seven

FAYETTE COUNTY

Voices.

Across an ethereal expanse, echoed voices seeped into Augusta's hearing. She willed her eyes to open, strove to work the muscles of her lids, to no avail. When she tried to speak, razors sliced at her throat. The weight of a damp cloth brought a cool relief to her aching eyes.

"You waking up, Honey?" Melinda Jane's voice. "You just lay still now. It's likely to take a few days to get back your voice."

Augusta lifted her hand to her forehead. She fingered a bandage, touching off an explosion in her head that took her breath away.

A gentle hand pulled her fingers away from the bandage and covered them, patting them like a mother would a child's. "You don't want to be doing that now, Gus. That gash is going to pain you for some time to come."

Melinda Jane heaved a sigh. "I reckon you've got some questions. Do you know who this is? Just nod if the answer is yes."

She nodded gingerly.

"Good. I don't think you've got amnesia."

Augusta thought hard. She remembered the barn burning. Soldiers with buckets of water. Men staggering from the barn, coughing. She didn't see James. She went into the barn to look for him. Then she woke up here.

"You remember the barn fire?"

She nodded.

"Seamus carried you out, then he and Carter pulled out a few more. Seamus was in pretty bad shape himself. Sergeant Mallory and his men hauled him and the rest of the injured up to Camp Gauley in a wagon." A soft rap on the door interrupted Melinda Jane's account.

"We're about to leave with the prisoners, ma'am. This one's wanting to have a word with Miss Dabney. He says he's her cousin."

Melinda Jane's steps clicked across the floor to the door and the hinges whispered as it opened. "Oh! Your hands are tied. Well, you are a prisoner, after all. Aren't you?" Melinda Jane's voice wavered, then resumed her usual bravado.

"Can I talk to my cousin alone, please?" Carter's voice. A rustle.

"I'll give you privacy, but you're not leaving my sight." A soldier's gruff voice. The familiar clatter of the musket. The soldier must still be in the room.

"I'll be right outside the door if you need me, Gus." Melinda Jane, always protective of her family. "She can't talk yet, you know, and her eyes are still swollen shut." Her friend's punctuated steps clicked on the bare floor as she left the room. Melinda Jane was clearly not happy about Carter's visit.

Uneven steps crossed the floor, then the mattress gave as Carter leaned close.

"I'm real sorry all this happened, Gus. Real sorry."

She raised her head, opened her mouth to speak. A single, excruciating grunt. She dropped her head back to the pillow, grimacing at the hammer strikes beneath her scalp.

"James was a good man. I'm sorry he didn't make it. You'll heal up real fine, and life will get back to normal . . . someday. Goodbye, cousin." She heard him stand.

He didn't make it? James is dead?

"I'm ready now, Private."

The men's departure barely registered. A tumult of questions and broken dreams roared in her mind—only to be dwarfed by the earthquake in her soul.

∽

Melinda Jane waited until the men left. She found Gus thrashing her head from side to side, her face twisted in tearless agony. What had Cousin Carter said to upset her so?

Laying her palm against her friend's face, she whispered, "Shh . . . I'm here, sister." She prepared a cool cloth, humming and whispering words from the psalms as she pressed it to the fevered cheeks and eyes. Gus dozed after a time, and Melinda Jane dropped to her knees next to the bed to lift her dearest friend in all the world to the Father.

∽

Augusta woke to Melinda Jane's familiar, sweet voice in another part of the house:

"Gin a body meet a body,
coming through the rye.
Gin a body kiss a body,
need a body cry
Lika body has a body,
ne'er a one ha'e I,
But a' the lads they loe one weel,

and what the deuce care I?"

Again, Augusta tried her voice. Now, it seemed, she could manage a whisper, but only a few words at a time. Her eyes didn't ache as much, and she imagined them less swollen, though crusted shut as they were. The soft squeak of the door intruded on the silence.

"I figured you'd be waking up soon. Let's see if those eyes of yours are gonna open today."

Warm water trickled over her face, soothing her eyes and cheeks. Melinda Jane tenderly massaged her eyelids with a soft cloth.

"The swelling is down a lot. Yesterday you looked like a wasper stung you in the face."

"Thank you," Augusta managed a painful whisper.

"Well, listen to you! You'll be talkin' in no time."

She imagined the smile on her friend's face. *I'll never smile again. James is gone.* She was a fool to think they might have a future. A slit of light interrupted her sorrow.

"Are you crying, honey?" Melinda Jane's voice dripped with concern. "You're wetting those eyes from the inside, aren't you?" She dribbled more water onto Augusta's eyes, blotting up the runoff with a towel.

"That's probably enough for now. You might be peekin' out from those lids of yours by supper time. I'll just leave you a cool cloth over them to help with the swelling."

The bed lifted as Melinda Jane stood. "I bet you're just full of questions and yearning to talk to the kids. They been asking to see you, but I thought it best if I waited until your eyes were open. If you want to see them now, though, you just nod, and I'll bring them in."

Augusta shook her head and rolled to her side, facing the wall. Grief wrapped its calloused hands around her shoulders and squeezed. Squeezed until she willed herself to sleep and never wake.

Thirty-Eight

○∞○

Fayette County

Augusta coughed, swallowing back more spasms as dust filtered through the air while Zander swept smaller pieces of debris into a pile. The barn lay in sooty ruins, all but the largest timbers and stone foundation burned to ash.

"What's that?" Augusta pointed to a glint in the rubble.

Zander stooped to pick up a small round stone. He frowned. "It's the stud from the browband of the bridle I made for Rampart. He shoved it into his pocket and continued sweeping.

Her arm slid around her brother's waist. "I'm so thankful they saved the horses and livestock."

"Yeah. I've told myself that a hundred times, but I still got this sick feeling in the pit of my belly. I'm glad Pap can't see this. He and Izzy built this barn together. It's like it was the last part of them here. Now, even it's gone."

They stood in silence. Her gaze roamed over the area that once served as the hospital. All that remained of the cots were the metal hinges scattered here and there. She recognized a lantern, and what she assumed was part of the medicine pannier. The once polished oak box lay smashed and charred, its glass bottles shattered on the ash-covered ground. Beside a piece of the burned table sat a large, blackened washbasin, overturned and dented.

"Maybe this is worth a rescue." She turned it over and gasped. There, beneath the basin, were the wadded remains of a Union jacket. She choked back a sob as her fingers caressed a green strap, its embroidered leaves and *MS* badly charred. She slumped to the ground, the billow of her dress scattering plumes of ash.

As if her own life were being siphoned away, she clutched at the physical pain pulsing through her, convinced there could be no more sunrises. Wasn't it in the Bible where folks suffered such agony that they wanted the mountains to fall on them? Another day of living was impossible.

How could she ache so? For Mama, Pap, Izzy, and now James . . . and what of her brother? Was he even alive? Her shattered heart was surely ground to powder.

An arm squeezed her shoulders. "Let's get you cleaned up, honey." Melinda Jane pulled her to her feet. Augusta clutched the medical insignia to her chest, following her friend. Numbness dared each foot to shuffle onward.

Just as they started up the steps to the house, the staccato of musket fire punctured the air. Melinda Jane's body stiffened. "That sounds close."

Jerked from her sorrow, Augusta looked over the barnyard. "We need to get everyone into the house."

"I'll check the shed and the chicken coop." Melinda Jane raced off, yelling for Will and the boys.

Within minutes, they all gathered in the house, curtains pulled, with two pistols, a shotgun, and a Springfield single shot musket that had belonged to one of the dead soldiers. Coot paced the floor, his tail rigid. The gunshots grew louder for a time, then faded away.

"Thank you, Lord," Melinda Jane whispered, squeezing Bertie until he wiggled from her grasp.

Zander removed the percussion cap and released the hammer of the musket. "We need a plan, Gus. If any of those bushwhackers show up here at the farm, it's just us."

"You sure you know how to use that thing?" Will asked.

"Of course, I do. Fin had me practicing with it before he left. Who do you think shot that last buck we snagged? Anyway, it's our best protection against anything that's off aways. I can rest it on the windowsill and take a good clean shot at—"

"That's enough of that kind of talk." Augusta pulled Bertie to her and pushed his hair out of his eyes. "Zander is right. We need a plan."

Will piped up, "How about if we use the supper bell?"

"I don't know, maybe that's kind of like announcing we're all here. I was thinking more along the lines of all of us hiding in the cellar." Augusta raised her eyebrows, trying to gauge her family's response.

"We can't fight them off from the cellar, Gus." Zander rubbed the back of his head.

Will stood beside her brother. "I'm with Zander. I say we whup them Johnny Rebs if ever they come on our property!"

"Willamina Dabney! That is no way for a lady to talk." Augusta handed the shotgun to Zander. "I'll think and pray on the matter, but right now, I'm going to change my clothes and start supper. If you hear any more shots, you get yourselves into this house, though. Is that clear?"

∽

Augusta pitched the quilt to the bottom of the bed. She'd fought sleep most of the night. Each time she closed her eyes, she saw the flaming barn, felt the scorching smoke in her lungs. It had been two weeks since the soldiers departed. Three times they'd heard the popping of musket fire, fearing at any minute the Rebel guerillas would ride up their lane. Or worse—surround the house without warning.

She slipped her feet into the moccasins Izzy had made her for Christmas when she was fifteen. Pulling her heavy shawl around her shoulders, she felt her way downstairs in the darkness. The low fire she'd banked in the woodstove kept the kettle hot enough for tea, so she opened a tin of dried peppermint leaves. Coot circled the kitchen table, whining.

"What is it, boy? Can't you sleep either?" She massaged the loose skin around his neck.

The dog's head turned to the back door, a rumble purling from his throat. He padded over to the screen, hackles raised. His growl grew louder. He pawed the door and barked.

She feared for Coot if she let him out. Oh, he was smart enough not to take on a bear or wildcat, but it was the human animal she was concerned about.

Zander stormed into the kitchen, fully clothed, his musket in hand. "What is it, boy?" Will wasn't far behind, followed by Melinda Jane.

Pulling back the curtain, Zander stood beside Augusta as she focused on the darkness outside. Two shadowy figures moved at the edge of the stand of corn.

"I can't see if there's any more than two," he muttered.

"Just let them take what they want, then maybe they'll leave us be." Melinda Jane bounced on her bare feet, wringing her hands. "Ooh, I don't like this."

"I'm just going to take a closer look." Zander opened the inside door a few inches and reached to open the screen.

"Zander, don't!" Augusta lunged, too late.

Coot saw his opportunity and charged out the door, his furious bark trailing in his wake. Zander started after him, and Augusta caught his arm. "Zander, no!" She yanked him back and slammed the door.

Loud male voices. Yelling. Barking. Two shots rent the night, then silence.

"Now what?" Melinda Jane whispered. She'd plopped into a kitchen chair, her eyes wide with fear.

"We wait," said Augusta.

"But Coot could be hurt." Zander's jaw muscle worked back and forth.

"We wait!" She said again. The sternness in her voice broke no argument.

"Coot probably scared them off." He paced for several more minutes.

She met her brother's pleading eyes, her resolve dwindling.

"They're probably into the hills by now, Gus."

"All right, but first we pray." She stretched her hands out and her family circled. "Father, we ask for Your continued protection. In the name of our Lord Jesus, Amen."

"I'm going with you." Augusta grabbed the shotgun off the wall, positioned the cap on the nipple, and followed Zander out the door.

༄

"Help me clear the table." Augusta said as Melinda Jane joined her in a rush to remove the few dishes and lantern from the middle of the table. Zander laid Coot on the oak surface, slipping his blood-stained arm from beneath the hindquarters.

As the dog lay unconscious, Augusta worked quickly. A Minié ball had gone clean through the thick muscle of his back leg. She blotted the bleeding and used a straight razor to shave away some of the fur so she could see the wound more clearly. Melinda Jane had already fixed a needle and thread. How Augusta wished for the medical equipment and anesthetics that had burned up in the fire.

"Zander, you hold his head in case he wakes up."

She stitched the inside of Coot's leg, then turned him over and sewed up the wound there. After more than an hour of tending and cleaning up the blood, Gus's concern rose when the brave dog still lay unconscious.

A sleepy voice invaded the hushed kitchen. "Hey what are you—?" Bertie ran to the dog. "What happened to Coot?" He looked from Augusta to Zander to Melinda Jane. Tears coursed down his cheeks. "Is . . . Is he dead? Like Pap and Izzy?"

Augusta stooped to look into his eyes. "No. No. He's not dead, Bertie." She took hold of his shoulders. "He was a brave soldier and took a bullet protecting his family. He's just resting right now. We'll pray for him."

She took Bertie's small hands in her own and asked Jesus to make the dog well again. Well enough to run with Bertie, and well enough to chase wild turkeys. But she also mentioned the most important thing was that God's will be done.

"But what if God's will *is* for Coot to die?" He blinked his wet eyelashes and frowned at his sister.

"Do you believe God causes all things to somehow work together for good, Bertie?"

"I suppose so." He dragged the sleeve of his nightshirt across his wet face.

"We have to trust in God's love for us, even when we don't understand." James's face appeared before her, and she suddenly felt weak. Weak in body and weak in spirit. *I need your strength, Lord.* She held her little brother tight. *I need your strength.*

"I'll make Coot a nice pallet over by the stove, Bertie. You can just bed right down here with him if you want—that is, if it's all right with Gus." Melinda Jane was already moving the butter churn and a chair to make room.

"I think that's a wonderful idea." She pushed Bertie toward the stairs. "Go fetch your pillow and quilt."

Thirty-Nine

Fayette County

Augusta stared into the darkness. Golden fingers of dawn had yet to touch her window. Of late, the sun had merely run its circuit each day—casting no warmth on her spirit. The gloom of her heart smothered even hope's dimmest rays.

After returning to her bed in the wee hours of the morning, sleep had refused her, so she took out her Bible. The last words she'd read before closing her eyes returned to her: *If any of you lack wisdom, let him ask of God, that giveth to all men liberally, and upbraideth not; and it shall be given him.*

Her nightgown gathered on the cold floor as she knelt beside her bed. *I need wisdom, Lord. Show me what to do and give me Your peace so that I know it is You. And Lord, in Your great mercy, please bring Coot through this. Bertie has born so much loss already—and I fear I am too fragile myself to weather one more storm.*

She rose and pulled aside the curtain to peer across the barnyard. The purple mist of early dawn unveiled the blackened ruins. The tool shed provided a temporary shelter for the horses and the corncrib protection for the milk cows at night. This was only a temporary solution. Winter would be upon them before long.

Soldiers had assisted with the harvest. Even so, stores would run low without Fin's extra income from his leather business. And as of two days ago, the smokehouse was empty, thanks to bushwhackers. Her mind buzzed, a mishmash of solutions rising, only to be dashed. And what of the danger? Were they to remain prisoners in their own house? She would continue to be fearful every time one of the children stepped outside or a knock sounded at the door.

Augusta shed her gown and stepped into a muslin work dress. She opened the drawer of the small secretary desk near the window. A letter glared up at her. She had received another communication from Edward Fontaine, firmly urging her to consider his offer of marriage. Each word on the paper punctuated the raw truth—she held no affection for the man.

But circumstances had changed since that letter arrived. How would she ever find a way to rebuild the barn? What was left here for Zander, and Bertie—even Will—to build a future? If her family lost what remained of the farm, it would be *her* fault.

She lifted the letter from the drawer, and her eyes fell on a folded paper. *James*. She opened the note with his Charleston address. Her finger caressed her name, penned in his hand.

"He's awake! He's awake!" Bertie's shouts could've rattled the windows. "Hey everybody, Coot's awake. He's going to be all right!"

Augusta stuffed both papers into her dress pocket and rushed downstairs. There, by the stove, Bertie lay on the floor, his head next to Coot's. The music of his giggles filled the kitchen as the dog's tongue washed his face. The more the giggling, the more the licking. Coot appeared just as happy to see Bertie as Bertie was to see his best friend, alive and well.

"Thank you, Lord!" Augusta knelt beside the pair, and the rest of the family soon surrounded her.

"This calls for a celebration breakfast, I think." Melinda Jane scratched at Coot's chin.

Augusta felt the smooth insides of the dog's floppy ears. "Doesn't appear to even have a fever. That's a hopeful sign, but we'll have to watch him close." She stood, stretching her back, stifling a yawn.

Zander stuffed the revolver in his belt and pulled his coat from the peg. "I'll get to the chores. I'll do yours this morning, Bertie. You stay with Coot." He donned his hat and headed out the back door, snugging up his collar to ward off the morning chill.

"Thanks, Zander." Bertie ran his hand down the length of the dog's body, massaging ample folds of the furry neck. He smiled up at Melinda Jane. "Does Coot get a celebration breakfast, too?"

"Do you think Coot would like some buckwheat cakes and blackberry jam?"

"I believe he surely would—and if he doesn't, I'll eat his." He planted a kiss atop the dog's head.

"I'll see to the chickens," Will said, shrugging into a favorite old jacket of Fin's.

Melinda Jane pulled the damper hook on the stove. Lifting the burner, she dropped some kindling onto the smoldering fire. She blew on it until it flickered to life, then added a few twigs.

"The Lord truly protected Ol' Coot last night, Bertie." She grabbed the black iron skillet with two hands and set it over the burner. "The Lord will protect us, too. We've just got to trust that He's watching over us."

"Why do I have a feeling that you're talking to yourself just as much as to Bertie?" Augusta scraped a solid glob of bacon grease out of the tin and let it drop into the skillet.

"That's 'cause I reckon I am. Things are getting more unsettling around here all the time." She glanced at Bertie, then Augusta. Her mouth turned down. "Sorry."

Crisp air rushed into the kitchen as Will handed a basket of eggs across the threshold. "I'm going back out to help Zander." As the door closed, Melinda Jane angled a look toward Augusta, an unspoken question in her eyes.

"*She's* mighty obliging this morning," Augusta said, shooting a grin at her friend.

"Couldn't have been something in the food. She hasn't had breakfast yet."

While batter sizzled in the skillet, Augusta broke an egg into a bowl and set it in front of Coot. Just that quick, he lapped it up, tail thumping in delight. "Now that's the best sign."

A leaning tower of flannel cakes claimed a blue porcelain platter in the middle of the table. Melinda Jane added a spoon to the freshly opened jar of jam. "Well, the table's set. Where is everybody?"

"I'll see what's taking those two so long." Augusta lifted her shawl from the peg. When she pulled the door open, her sister plowed into her.

"We can't find the bull calf, Gus!" Her pink cheeks puffed as she tried to catch her breath. "Zander is still out looking, but we searched everywhere."

"You sit on down and eat. I'll find Zander." If they'd already looked everywhere, where was Zander now? She lifted the shotgun from its pegs and rushed out the door, fearful she'd find her brother lying dead on the edge of the pasture, a Rebel's bullet in his chest.

"Zander! Zander!" Panic clung to her words and rose to her throat like bile as she ran faster and farther from the house. Izzy's cabin came into view, and a wisp of chimney smoke caught her eye. She stopped and crouched low. *Bushwhackers? What if they had seen her from the window?*

A movement caught her eye, and she turned to her right. Zander leaned against the bark of a sugar maple, out of sight of the cabin, the pistol tucked against his chest. He motioned for her to back away and stay low.

She hesitated.

He urged her again with a nod, then backed away himself, skirting the grove of trees until he was over the crest of the hill. When he caught up with Augusta, they both ran to the house in silence.

The kitchen door slammed behind them. Blood hammered in Augusta's temple. She leaned her hands on her knees to catch her breath. *Wisdom. I need wisdom, Lord.* Her hand dropped to her dress pocket, grazing the papers she'd put there earlier this morning.

"There's somebody in Izzy's cabin!" The words tumbled as Zander worked to catch his breath.

"Somebody? Who?" Melinda Jane stood, throwing her napkin on the table. The scowl on her face matched her indignation.

"I found the entrails—where they slaughtered the calf. No doubt they're eating our beef and our corn for breakfast." He paced the length of the room. His face, already red from the run, grew taut in a deeper shade as his temper flared. Of all her siblings, he was the most levelheaded. For the second time in as many days, the boy was being tested.

Augusta slipped out the folded paper and read the address James had written. Her breath slowed. Peace resounded in her spirit, urging her to move forward—to have no fear. To trust.

Her voice was calm. "We're going to be leaving for a while."

"Leaving?" Will shoved her plate away and stood. "Where is there to go?"

"Can we all just sit for a few minutes? I want us to talk, as a family." Augusta pulled out a chair and sat, motioning for the others to do the same.

Melinda Jane fidgeted, and Will drummed her fingers on the table. Zander stabbed a fork into his stack of flannel-cakes until it looked like a sponge. Bertie tossed morsels of his breakfast to Coot as if he thought no one was looking.

"This is my plan. If any of you have thoughts, I'd like to hear them." Augusta paused, her gaze bouncing to each sibling. She laid the paper from James on the table and smoothed it with her fingers.

"We have no way to keep the horses safe. If a group of Rebels came riding in here right now, we'd be nearly defenseless." She looked to Zander, expecting an argument, but his eyes drilled an invisible hole into the back of his hand.

"I think, for the time being, it'd be wise for us to stay at James's house in Charleston." She tapped the paper. "He left me the address. He wanted us to go there to be safe if need be."

"What about Coot? Can he come too?" Bertie shifted to the floor and crawled on his hands and knees to his friend's side.

"Of course, Coot can come."

"And the milk cows?" Will's shoulders drooped.

"We'll have to sell them. Or if we can't sell them, we'll loan them. I'll talk to the Meyers or the Dortons—see how much of our stock they'll take."

"I'll gather our food stores. There's no telling what will happen to whatever we leave here." Melinda Jane stood, then sat again. "Sorry, Gus. You're not finished, huh?"

Augusta patted her friend's hand. "Zander and I will ride over this morning to talk with the neighbors. We'll lead the cows over on faith that they'll take them."

"What if you run into trouble?" Will stood. "I can go with you."

"If we run into trouble, we'll just offer up one of the cows as a peace offering."

"Let's hope it doesn't come to that." Zander stood. "I say we offer to trade the cows for any tack folks can give us. We lost most of what we need in the fire."

"That's a fine idea." Augusta smiled at her younger brother. He was growing up before her eyes. It seemed like such a short time ago that Fin was his age.

"Whatever we can't get in trade, I'll try to rig from some pieces in the shed."

"Thank you, Zander."

"When do you want to head out, Gus?" Melinda Jane stood, then started to sit again. She froze when Augusta stood, too.

"The sooner the better. Tomorrow morning."

༄

Augusta set the last of the dried plates on the shelf. Her mind flitted in a myriad of directions. She took in the warm kitchen and breathed deep of the familiar yeasty smell that clung to the walls, calling to mind the family chatter of happier times.

Melinda Jane dried her damp hands. "I believe I'll get to collecting food and bedding for the wagon. Are we packing clothes in the carpet bags?"

Augusta wrapped her arms around her dear friend. "You are truly my sister. I don't know what I'd do without you."

"Well, I don't like to think about where I'd be without you and your family. I'd be an orphan living who knows where, doing who knows what."

Melinda Jane pulled back, gripping Gus's hands. "Far as I'm concerned, this *is* my family, and I am truly your sister. Now, you've got a heavy load on you right now. Don't you hesitate to let me know what you need me to do. We're a team, you and me." Her eyes danced with an undaunted optimism Gus had always envied.

"No need. You'll just read my mind, anyway. You always have." They both chuckled.

Melinda Jane disappeared up the stairs. Augusta wandered into her pap's room, closing the door behind her. She walked to the bed and drew her fingers across his pillow. Pap. Her eyes swept over the tall shelf of books he'd treasured. She could almost hear his voice reading to the family in the evenings.

She dragged the heavy oak chair to the bookcase, scraping it across the floor. Standing on the chair and reaching above her head to the top shelf, she pulled out the faded green tome of *Gulliver's Travels*. In the exposed space, her fingers searched for and found a worn leather satchel.

"Thank you, Pap," she whispered.

She untied the cord and opened the bag. It was not enough to save the farm, but it was enough to see the family to safety.

Forty

Fayette County

With a heavy heart, Augusta surveyed the only home she'd ever known, memorizing the lay of the buildings and the welcoming front porch with its old twin rockers. Regret trembled through her as she remembered her goodbyes at the family plot earlier this morning. If only there was some other way. Some way they could stay here. If only James hadn't died.

For whatever reason, God had not chosen to spare her this grief. Nor would He allow her the future she desired. God is sovereign. Isn't that what Pap had taught her? God's will is best. *But, Father—it just hurts so much.*

Will cranked her head, watching the chickens scratch in the dirt. "You sure that Mamie's pap is coming to get the chickens?"

"That's what he said. He seemed fairly pleased about it, too." Augusta fingered the two reins she held in each hand. "Before we go, would anyone like to offer up a prayer?" She looked from Melinda Jane to her siblings. Silence. Then Zander cleared his throat.

"I'll pray," he said, snatching off his hat. "Lord, we ask that You go with us and protect us. Watch over our farm, please. We trust You, Lord. Amen."

Pride swelled in her heart. He reminded her so much of Pap just now. "Thank you, Zander."

She gave the reins a jerk, and the matched pair of Morgans stepped out. Zander rode bareback on Rampart, keeping pace beside the wagon. Bertie reclined on a pile of quilts with Coot's front legs folded over his lap. The dog's head pivoted, as if taking in the farm for the last time.

Feather pillows padded heavy crates of canning jars, snuggled behind the wagon's seat. They had stacked bulging grain sacks and four carpetbags against the backboard, covering them with an oilcloth for their night on the road. And hidden beneath the wagon bed against the wooden frame, Zander had wired the worn leather pouch.

Silence ensued but for the creak of the wagon and the rumble of the wheels as they rolled over the uneven ground. Augusta took comfort in the daylight, since Union soldiers still traveled Gauley Road between Summersville and Gauley Bridge.

Clothed in the spectacular attire of a Virginia autumn, the trees waved farewell, casting amber and scarlet leaves over the trace before them—a bittersweet reminder that even in death, there is beauty. She inhaled the crisp, dusty air, summoning her courage—Melinda Jane would have to cry enough for both of them. To everything a season.

The Gauley River crossing was slow, adding to their travel time. Confederates had burned the bridge back in July, so military and locals alike depended on the keelboats to ferry the wagons across the river. Gone forever was the grand covered bridge that marked their little town.

"Whoa." She halted the horses, and Zander tied Rampart in front of Jackson's Mercantile.

He lifted Melinda Jane and Augusta down from the wagon, then led the horses to drink. Planks covered the store windows, but the watering trough was full.

Bertie frowned at the shuttered windows. "I forgot it was closed. I was all set to talk you into some licorice for the trip."

"You can just pick that lip right back up now. I packed a few treats for you to have along the way." Melinda Jane patted the covered basket on the floorboard.

The town's small population had dwindled. Federal uniforms appeared here, but no familiar faces.

"I'm going to check in at the post office." Augusta stepped away from the wagon.

Melinda Jane hurried after her. "Maybe there's a letter from Fin."

"Wouldn't that just brighten this day?" Augusta looped her arm through her friend's.

The tiny post office wasn't much more than a lean-to off the side of old Mr. Pritchard's house, just down from the mercantile. Augusta pulled on the rickety door and a bell rang. They waited until the postmaster shuffled his way through the door connecting house to post office.

"Morning, Mr. Pritchard. How are you doing today?" Melinda Jane spoke loud since the old gentleman was hard of hearing.

"Can't complain, Miss Minard, but things would be a mite better if these Yankees skedaddled on out of here."

Augusta offered her kindest smile. "Do you have any mail for the Dabneys, sir?"

"I sure do. This one come just yesterday." He handed her a letter bearing a familiar script, and her heart sank. "I'm real sorry to hear about your pap passing and all the trouble you've been havin' up that away."

"Thank you, Mr. Pritchard. If anyone asks, the Dabneys are going to visit a friend in Charleston for a spell." She handed him a piece of paper. "This is our forwarding address."

The old man nodded before sliding the piece of paper into the Dabneys' slot. "Safe travels, Miss Dabney, Miss Minard." He held the door for the ladies, then shuffled back into the house.

"Are you going to tell me who that letter's from?" Melinda Jane asked the moment Mr. Pritchard was out of sight.

Augusta slowed her pace, and making sure her family wasn't within hearing, she discreetly told Melinda Jane about Edward Fontaine and his insistent proposals.

"I can't believe you've kept this from me." Melinda Jane crossed her arms. "A man proposes marriage, and you don't tell your best friend."

"It's more like a business proposition than a proposal. Some might even call it blackmail."

"Well, I'm sure you put him in his place."

Augusta pressed her lips together, her gaze falling to the ground.

"You *did* put that man in his place, did you not?" Melinda Jane scooped her head lower, trying to meet Gus's eyes. She scowled and propped fists on her hips. "You're not considering marrying this man just so you can keep the farm, are you?"

"It's not that simple. October is near gone and—Well, it's up to me to make sure that everything Pap worked for is there for Fin and Zander and Bertie—and Will, if she wants. Now don't you say a word to anyone about this."

Melinda Jane twisted her mouth right and left.

"Promise me, Melinda Jane Minard." She faced her friend, turning her back to Zander, who was fast approaching. Her eyes drilled into Melinda Jane's until she finally relented.

"Oh, I won't tell," she whispered in a huff. She caught up her skirt with a swish and marched to the wagon.

∞

Charleston

The long, uncomfortable journey that had begun with such somberness yesterday was almost at an end. Heavy rains the last two months had flooded Charleston and left the river still running high. Thanks to the breeze, road dust coated Augusta's face and filtered through her dress. She imagined the gray color of her once yellow bonnet.

After stopping twice for directions, Zander pulled the team up in front of a neat, white house. Framed by black shutters, the windows added a welcoming touch to the house, and a white railing encircled the porch along the front left side. An extra little square of window high on the right side revealed a third story. Hanging beneath the porch filigree, a white shingle quivered in the breeze. Painted words in black calligraphy read: DR. JAMES HILL, PHYSICIAN.

Augusta wanted to run to the sign and trace her finger along each brush stroke of every letter. A familiar wave of grief washed over her. It pressed into her heart and burned her throat.

"I do believe we are here," Melinda Jane said, straightening her bonnet and brushing at her dress.

Zander helped the women down. "Maybe you'd better go knock first. She's not exactly expecting us, this Mrs. O'Donell, is she? Mayhap the lot of us will scare her."

"I hope not. From what James said, she's like a mother to him." Augusta could still hear his voice.

She started up the brick walkway and paused to examine the shingle. *Oh, James*. Filling her lungs, head high, she stepped onto the porch and turned the bell in the center of the varnished door.

Seconds passed like minutes. The door opened, and a round middle-aged woman stood, her graying hair pulled into a tight bun. She smiled, then squinted. Her mouth dropped. Her hands flew to cover her ruddy cheeks.

"Are you Mrs. O'Donell?" Augusta asked.

"Saints be praised! Ya needn't say another word, child. Come in, you and yers. You'd be Augusta Dabney or my name isn't Maggie O'Donell." Her voice fairly sang with the lilt of the Irish. The woman stepped onto the porch, taking Augusta's hands into her own and giving them a squeeze.

She waved to Zander and shouted, "Ya can take the wagon around to the back! We've a small carriage house and barn there. We can unload yer belongin's through the back door."

"That's very kind of you, Mrs. O'Donell. This is my dear friend, Melinda Jane Minard."

"Truly a pleasure, Miss Minard. I hope ya don't mind me callin' ya Melinda Jane. I feel like I know the lot of ya from James's letters."

Warmth crept its way into Augusta's chilled heart for the first time in a long while.

∞

Zander hupped the team, steering to the alley behind the house, and Rampart ruckled from his tether behind the wagon.

Will scurried into the spot next to him on the hard seat. "She seems nice." She wiggled back and forth, coaxing a squeak from the wagon seat. Zander nodded in agreement, too hungry and tired for conversation.

A sleepy Bertie rubbed his eyes. "I hope she lets Coot in the house. I'd hate to leave him outside, all wounded as he is." Coot lifted his head at the mention of his name, and Bertie ran his hand over the dog's smooth coat.

"Don't you worry, Coot. If you have to sleep in the barn, I'll sleep out there with you."

∽

Augusta stretched her stiff arms and shoulders. Standing in the cozy kitchen, she was plum tired—not just from the long ride, but from being alone with her thoughts for too long.

Mrs. O'Donell set a platter of bread and cheese on the table next to a jar of apple butter. Zander added two more chairs from the dining room-turned-waiting room to accommodate the crowd around the table.

The older woman waved her hand over the food. "This is just a snack, mind ya, now. Ya must be road weary after the long trip. We'll have a hearty meal before yer head hits yer pillows."

"You are too kind, Mrs. O'Donell. Thank you so much for your hospitality." Augusta continued exploring the inviting home with her eyes. This was where James lived. Where he saw patients. Where he slept and ate. Her appetite, ravenous a few minutes earlier, gave way to the heaviness she'd come to know as grief.

The touch of a hand drew her attention. Mrs. O'Donell tipped her head to the side, her wrinkled brow sheltered concerned eyes. "I know you and yers wouldn't be here were it not that something has put ya in danger. Can ya tell me what it is, las? And how goes it with James?"

Augusta forced a smile. Dropping her gaze to the veined hand, she covered it with her own. Unable to meet the older woman's eyes, breath trembled through her body.

"The barn at our farm—there was a fire. Everything was lost. James"—she swallowed hard—"is . . . dead." She stilled her quivering chin. *I will not cry. I will not cry.* Oh, how she was tired of the tears.

Mrs. O'Donell walked to the stove, her back to Augusta. In a voice that betrayed her sorrow, she said, "Why dontcha all rest a bit? I'll let ya know when the meal is ready."

An enameled bed frame set in the corner of the cheerful room. Rose-strewn wallpaper and a bright rag rug hugged her battered soul, making Augusta feel less a stranger. Next door, Melinda Jane's room, decorated in yellow toile, was just as welcoming.

The rest of the Dabney family would sleep in the hospital beds that lined one wall of the large room downstairs. And in her kindness, Mrs. O'Donell had allowed Coot a spot on the floor in the kitchen beside the coal cookstove.

Augusta's gaze fell on the letter atop the ornate oak commode. Drawn against her will, she picked it up. From Edward. The deferment on the farm's note had expired. Somehow, she felt leaving the missive untouched would hold off the inevitable. At last, she broke the seal on the letter:

Dearest Augusta—I am writing to ask you to come to me. I have been wounded and am being kept at the Wheeling Hospital. Although I am a prisoner of the Union Army at this time, the nuns here are providing excellent care. I am confident I will be accepted for a prisoner exchange as soon as I am able-bodied. As you have failed to give a clear response to date, you must consider this my last request for your hand in marriage. Such is the case pertaining to the security of your family's property. Please know, Augusta, that I am a humbled man at this juncture, and it would warm my heart immensely if I were to wake in this place and find you by my side.—Yours, Edward

She pinched the bridge of her nose and squeezed her eyes shut. She imagined herself in a closed coffin, staring into the darkness, the ominous sound of dirt splattering across the top of the tomb. No panic. No scream. She just lay there, numb—waiting for the end.

∞

Augusta let the carpetbag drop to the floor with a thump. As she had packed her bag, every effort had felt like pushing a boulder uphill. Her only option was obvious. Augusta straightened her bonnet ties and turned to face her best friend.

"You don't have to do this, Gus. God will make a way." Melinda Jane's hands gripped Augusta's in desperation. "A marriage should be for love, not financial security."

"You don't understand. I can't lose the farm. Some arranged marriages turn out quite successful, even happy. This is no different."

Melinda Jane lifted an eyebrow. "You look me in the eye and tell me that this Fontaine fella is the kind of man you could fall in love with." She thrust her head forward like a chicken, but her eyes grew watery as the sternness melted away.

Will and Bertie ambled in from the kitchen, each with a cookie. Mrs. O'Donell apparently dealt with her grief by baking. The last two days, the oven had hardly cooled. Mountains of cookies, three pies, and enough potatoes and meat to lend toward gluttony added to an endless river of food.

"Not a word, Melinda Jane," Augusta whispered. She forced a smile and turned her attention to her brother and sister.

"I still don't understand why you have to leave us here, Gus. Why do you have to go clear up to Wheeling?" Will—always the suspicious one.

"It's just to tie up some loose ends with business dealings. Nothing for you to worry about." She hugged her sister, then stooped to look into Bertie's eyes. "You mind Melinda Jane, now."

"I will." Bertie pooched out his lip.

"Maybe I'll have the chance to pick up some of that strumpet candy you like so much."

"Promise?"

"I won't promise, but I'll do my best." She planted a kiss on his cheek.

Mrs. O'Donell moved behind Bertie and set her hands on his shoulders. "Safe travels to ya, Gus."

"Thank you so much, Mrs. O'Donell. Thank you for opening your lovely home to us."

"Tis James's home. Tis yers too, las."

Augusta embraced the kind woman, sharing a kinship of love and the grief it bore.

"If I'm delayed more than two weeks, I'll send you word as to my progress." After a last embrace, Augusta strode out the back door to the carriage house, where Zander waited with the wagon to take her to the docks of the Kanawha River.

She would board the river steamer *Kanawha Queen*, and travel northwest to Point Pleasant. Then she would continue her journey on the *Cincinnati Queen*, following the Ohio River all the way to Wheeling. All the way to Edward Fontaine.

Forty-One

WHEELING HOSPITAL

Strong hands lifted his limp body from the tepid water. Despite the laudanum stupor, he cringed as his attendants placed him on clean sheets, propping him in an awkward position partially on his back and not quite on his right side. His arms extended into the aisle—a ridiculous, helpless pose. The now familiar process of soaking cloths and then spreading them across his scorched skin resumed.

The constant cough had abated some, but rawness still clawed at his chest and throat. He'd lain in a coma for the first week after he arrived. How he wished for the oblivion of unconsciousness just now as a soldier cried out in pain somewhere beyond his scope.

Night and day bore little difference. But night was preferable, sparing him the interruption of his self-loathing and the bothersome dunk into a vat of warm water. Bandages still required moistening, but they left him to himself more often—left to the pain, an inseparable companion for weeks now.

Gauzy, damp bandages covered his left eye and the side of his face. His left hand, a soggy white mitten, rested on a towel, and a single wrapping of bandage encased the fingers of his right hand. More gauzy wet strips swathed his left arm and lower left leg.

Weakened from the agony of the cleansing process, James could only lie with his one eye staring into the darkness once night finally fell. The wanderings of his mind proved a different sort of agony altogether.

He'd told himself he was too wretched for Gus—what he'd done to old Barnes—to know of what he was capable. Hadn't his penance these last years been to help those in need? Why hadn't his self-imposed sentence lifted the guilt that dogged him? She deserved a better man than he'd proven to be.

Ignoring various rank odors, for just a moment, he allowed his thoughts to turn to the light.

No wonder people use the word *fall* to describe love. Fall, he did. His grip had torn from the jagged edge of his own bitter existence and fallen desperately in love with her.

A prisoner in his body, he lay there, powerless to help anyone, not even himself. Izzy's words floated through his mind: *"Bondage comes in many forms... anger, bitterness, unforgiveness—all shackles—and Massa Jesus has the key. It's Him who sets a man truly free."*

Yes, he was in bondage. His physical pain bowed to a more real agony that gored his soul. He squeezed his eye shut. Bitterness had gnawed a hole in him. A wretched, ragged hole.

He'd found relief in the discovery that he hadn't killed Barnes that miserable day, but something vile inside him wished he had. The blood on his hands was still just as real. Just as haunting. For it told him who he was, deep inside—where no one else could see.

Startlingly, he envisioned another set of hands—nail-scarred hands. His breath caught. *Forgive me.* For so long, he'd carried this hatred. *It's so heavy. It's all too heavy.*

"... He picks us up, cleans our wounds, and sets us on a better path."

His body shook. His insides clenched. The reality of who he was and what he needed overwhelmed him. He pressed his mouth against his pillow as tears flooded his eye. Muscles screamed as he tried and failed to stop the torrent. Within his soul's crushing blackness, a light flickered. A single flame in the blackest of nights.

Forgive me.

"*What do you want, my child?*" The voice spoke into the shadows of his mind.

Something he'd never known crashed over him like an ocean wave, driving him to abysmal depths—lost, yet not alone.

Change me, Father. I don't want to keep walking this path. I don't like who I've become. Set me on a better path—one where You walk with me. I don't want this embittered life.

The misery he'd worn like a second skin ebbed, assuaged by a keen sense of peace. He wiped his clogged nose with his bandaged hand and lay there in the darkness. Soon his breathing slowed, and he slept a deep, painless sleep for the first time in weeks.

∞

"Good morning, Major." Sister Mary Feeny's voice called from far off, a mere echo. "Good morning." Louder this time.

James pried open his eye. The heaviness he'd owned for so long was gone. He smiled at the sister. The shock registered on her face, and she smiled back.

"You've had the best sleep yet. I'm sorry to interrupt it, but I fear I've waited too long with your bandages. We'll soak them off in the bathtub."

He nodded. The unfamiliar lightness in his heart reminded him of the war he'd waged before sleep had claimed him. "Sister Mary, would you be kind enough to find a Bible for me?"

"I'd be happy to, but how will you hold it?"

James glanced at his hands. "I'll manage."

Henry and Mason, the two attendants, lifted him into a wheelchair, then rolled him to the bathtub. Warm water would soak off the bandages, then a gentle, but painful scrubbing process would remove the dead tissue from his charred skin.

James tensed as Dr. John Frissel gingerly removed and replaced several of the moist cloths. "I believe we have moved forward enough to begin a less aggressive treatment, Major... Dr. Hill." The tall man's compassion betrayed his rugged appearance.

"That's worthy news."

"Yes, I believe you are on the road to recovery. You gave us a healthy cause for concern for a while. Of course, I don't need to tell you what to expect, but suffice it to say, the sooner we get you moving, the less restrictive the scar tissue will be as it is forming."

"Dr. Frissel, I do have a concern I'd like to address."

"What is that?"

"The laudanum dosing. I'd like to discontinue it."

Dr. Frissel raised his eyebrows. "That's a new one. Usually, these boys want to smuggle out a month's supply when they leave."

"The sooner I learn to live without it, the better."

"You are a wise man, Dr. Hill. I'll write the order up to step it down over the next few weeks."

"Thank you."

Dr. Frissel motioned to Henry and Mason. "This patient will need to be transferred to the B Ward sometime soon. Please find out from Sister Mary when a bed is available." He turned to James and smiled. "It's good to see a glimmer in your eye, Doctor. I'll check in on you this evening, after you're settled in your new surroundings."

When Sister Mary arrived to moisten the bandages, she placed a black leather Bible on the edge of the bed, its cover worn and curled from use. "It's just a New Testament. The War Department leaves them for us."

"That's fine, thank you." James tried to maneuver the Bible between his forearm and his chest with little success. When a bout of coughing seized him, it slipped off the bed.

Sister Mary rolled a towel and used it to prop up the Bible. "There, you can at least read two pages until I come back and turn it for you."

"Thank you, Sister."

James read every word of the small print. Sadly, some disappeared into the binding. He recognized the words of the Lord's Prayer. The first time he read, he skimmed it, but the second time—*"But if ye forgive not men their trespasses, neither will your Father forgive your trespasses."*

He had to forgive Carter. Even forgive Barnes. He couldn't do it on his own, but somehow, he knew if he purposed to forgive, God would help him.

Just as twilight seeped through the windows, Henry and Mason moved James into the new ward. A Confederate patient lay in the second bed over, a thick gray bandage encircling his rib cage. A telltale lump on his chest revealed the extra packing of a chest wound. Experience told James this patient would not survive.

With the transfer to a different ward, came the new burn care regiment over the next several days. The medical staff soaked cotton cloths in a water-carbolic acid solution and laid them over the worst of the burns. Vaseline-coated bandages covered the lesser wounds. As had been the case for weeks, he still resembled a giant wet sponge. The dousing was necessary to keep the dressings from sticking to the healing and dead flesh.

"I have a surprise for you." Sister Mary sat in a nearby chair, a bowl of bean soup in her hand. "The doctor said you can have proper food again."

"Now this day just keeps getting better and better." James chuckled at the rumble in his stomach.

"Speak for yourself."

James recognized that voice. He tipped his head toward the speaker. He was getting used to seeing the world through one eye—an eye that seemed clearer today, thanks to the smaller laudanum dose. *The banker, Edward Fontaine.* At some point, James would make himself known, but for now, he wasn't up to a conversation.

"I expect my fiancé to show up any day now. That's the only thing that will improve my day. That and a prisoner exchange." Fontaine, a mite loopy from the comfort medicinal, slurred his words like a drunk.

James obliged Sister Mary as she deftly spoon-fed him the hearty soup. "Thank you, Sister. That was delicious."

"You're welcome, Doctor. I'll be by every hour to moisten those bandages."

"I'll be here." He dropped his head back, closing his eye. Fontaine had mentioned a fiancé. His thoughts turned to Gus, and for the hundredth time, he relived their kiss the night of the fire. She'd never been far from him, between his fuzzy head and trying to deal with the pain. Would that God permit a miracle and heal his body so he, too, could spend the rest of his days with the woman he loves.

James deliberately avoided a mirror. He knew what burn scars looked like. The side of his face would pucker and discolor. His left hand could well be deformed. Clothing would cover the burns on his leg and arm, but a wife would see them. What woman would want to look at that? His young patients would recoil in horror at the scarring on his face.

Help me, Father.

Forty-Two

WHEELING HOSPITAL

James strove to get comfortable. The lower dose of medication would take some getting used to. He still had the option of morphine, but the addition of baking soda solution to the burns seemed to help with the pain. He had enjoyed a bowl of watery oatmeal this morning, and even some warm coffee. Swallowing was tolerable now, but an impossibility at first.

"You have a visitor, Captain." Sister Mary was standing over Fontaine's bed.

"Who is it?" Fontaine's voice betrayed the high dose of medication.

"A very nice young woman. She says you are expecting her."

"H . . . help me sit up. M . . .my fiancé." He grimaced as Sister Mary folded over his pillow and stuffed it behind his back.

James noted the pallor of his skin, the beads of perspiration that dotted his brow. *He doesn't have long. Poor soul.*

In a short time, Sister Mary led in a woman attired in a matching pale green dress and bonnet. They crossed in front of James's bed as the woman removed her bonnet. James's heart lurched. *Gus.* The vision before him was Gus!

With a jolt, everything fell into place. The letters she'd received. Her unwillingness to talk about a beau. Didn't Fontaine introduce her to him at their first brief meeting? How could he have been so thick-headed?

He sucked in a deep breath. A coughing spasm tore at his throat. Sister Mary hastened to his bedside with a glass of water. He sipped it, plummeting into self-pity.

"Better?" she asked, setting the glass on the small table by his bed.

He nodded. Tortured by Gus's presence, but yearning to set eyes on her once more. He turned his head to the side, better able to view Fontaine and her profile.

"Hello Edward." At the sound of her voice, an arrow pierced his heart.

"Augusta, you came." Fontaine's raspy voice, barely audible.

"Were you shot in the chest?"

"Yes, but I'll be out of here in . . . no time." He hesitated, his lids sinking.

"I don't wish to tire you."

"Nonsense . . . I'm strong. Just need . . . time." His eyelids fluttered.

"You need to rest."

James twisted his head further, for they were to his left, the side with the bandaged eye. Now he could drink in her face. But what of her sweet smile? A dullness shaded her once-vivid green eyes. Where was that sparkle? *My Augusta*.

No. She was his no longer.

Looking at the ceiling, he breathed deep to scatter the remorse, but again, a spasm seized his throat, racking his wounds. He closed his eye in concentration, trying to catch his breath.

"Here, sip this." *Gus*.

After downing the proffered water, he opened his eye. He couldn't bear her nearness. With his right hand, he clumsily pushed the glass away.

She gasped.

The glass threatened to slip from her fingers as Augusta's world tilted. She used both trembling hands to set it on the table. *Dear God, is it possible?*

She reached for his right hand. He started at her touch, jerking his head to the side with a grimace. She lifted the hand, lungs paralyzed. *But, how?* Tears blurred her vision as her finger traced an H-shaped scar.

"James?" Her throat ached with the sweet word. "James?"

His eyelid fluttered. A tear escaped. She touched the rivulet with her thumb, brushing it from his cheek as a sob stole her breath. She battled the tremors that threatened to pull her apart. A torrent flowed like a creek, filling her nose, wetting her neck. So, so many questions.

Her head pulsed with the reality of it all as she took in the thick wrapping on his left hand and the bandaged leg protruding from the flimsy sheet. The gravity of his injuries almost buckled her knees as her senses recognized the stench of dead flesh. An unfamiliar ache squeezed her chest. *My darling James, how you've suffered.*

"I . . . I thought you were dead." Tears dripped from her jaw, and she wiped them away, drawing a shaky breath. Joy eclipsed her shock at last, overwhelming the dark depths of her broken heart. She smiled through the tears as laughter bubbled over.

"Why did you think I was dead?" He brushed at her wet face with his best hand. The lines where his eyebrows sprouted anew, abruptly carved a deep furrow.

"Carter told me you died in the fire."

His eye flamed. "Carter's always had trouble with the truth." He turned his head away, avoiding her gaze. His visage grew dark, and his lips pressed into a hard line. "Fontaine—you're going to marry him."

How . . . ? She shot a look at Fontaine and whispered, "I came here to tell him I'd marry him."

James let out a breath, carried on a soft moan.

"*But* I decided I can't."

"But you've been engaged all this time." His eye bore into her, his voice accusing, yet broken.

"We're not engaged, James."

"Wh . . . what do you mean you can't—You're not?"

"The bank was going to call in our mortgage. Edward said he'd pay it off if I married him. I couldn't lose everything Pap worked so hard for."

His face softened, and an uncertain smile crept across it. He blinked several times and a familiar fire kindled in his eye. "Why didn't you tell me you could lose the farm? I would've helped you."

"It's *my* responsibility. That doesn't matter now. I did some soul searching on the long river ride here. God's ways are not my ways, but I can't imagine He'd want me to marry a man for money. I was going to tell Edward that I won't marry him—because I don't love him."

"Have you ever loved him?"

"No." She kept her voice low, wary of the slumbering Fontaine. "I didn't even like the man. I was foolish to think I could go through with it."

"Never would I call you foolish." His sincerity hugged her bruised soul.

She lifted his right hand to her lips and pressed a kiss to the scar.

"You seem to fancy your handiwork, Miss Dabney." His boyish smirk quickened her pulse.

"It *is* a rather fitting monogram, wouldn't you say?"

"Indeed, it is." His lip twitched. He chewed the inside of his cheek as he seemed to scrutinize her. "Would you consider making it your own—for, say, the next fifty years?"

Her breath caught. She pinned him with her gaze. Only in her dreams had she imagined this moment. And only God could have made it possible. Warmth spread from her toes to her bursting chest.

She caressed his cheek, his chin. Leaning in, she tortured him with delay before capturing his lips with her own, conveying her answer with every beat of her heart.

THE BEST WAY TO THANK AN AUTHOR . . .

If you enjoyed *WHEN THE MOUNTAINS WEPT*,
please consider leaving a brief review
on social media and wherever you
buy your books.

See more places to post your review at

kendypearson.com

WANT A SNEAK PEEK?

Keep reading for a Sneak Peek of the next book in this captivating
series by KENDY PEARSON.

West Virginia: Born of Rebellion's Storm 2

WHEN HEAVEN THUNDERS

KENDY PEARSON

Heart of History
an imprint of
PEAR BLOSSOM BOOKS

December 1861

"Shake a leg, Hicks. The call of nature wasn't hollerin' from the next county, ya know. A pie-eater like yourself oughta know not to dally." What was taking so long? They only had a four-day pass, but Fin Dabney meant to make the most of it.

He tucked the poke of sowbelly into his saddlebag, stiffening as a too-familiar wisp of cool air brushed the back of his neck. Setting his jaw, he inched the Colt from his gun belt, snugging it between his chest and the bay gelding.

Steadying his breath in a practiced rhythm, he called louder, "You keep lollygagging, you'll find yourself working to catch up to me and Duke." One hand stroked the horse's sleek withers as his trigger finger twitched on the other. His eyes scanned the dense woods pressing in on the narrow trace.

The snap of a twig. Another.

The brush parted, and a shoeless boy prodded Noah Hicks forward with an ancient musket. "You best leave that horse be and step over to that tree, Yankee." He jammed the gun harder into Noah's back. "No tomfoolery, now."

A fierce expression—more fear than menace—glared from the shadow of the boy's ratty kepi. One eye disappeared behind a hank of straw-colored hair. A threadbare havelock draped over his collar, its edge snagged in a frayed rope tied to his britches.

Fin turned three quarters to the bushwhacker, pistol out of sight. "You don't want to do this, boy. Why, I bet you're no older than my little brother. Reckon Zander would be seventeen now." Holding the young Rebel's gaze, he scrubbed his beard with his free hand. "What do you plan on doing with the two of us?"

"I . . . I'm gonna take them horses. Our band has need of 'em."

Noah raised his thick eyebrows, grilling Fin in silent communication as he lifted his hands higher in a cagy surrender.

Fin offered a half-smile to the boy. "What's your name, son? You from around here?"

"Ain't none of yer business. Just step over there, or I'll sh . . . shoot this 'un. Right here and now." His attention darted from Fin to the prisoner.

"I'm pretty fond of 'ol Duke here. If you're insisting on taking him, you don't leave me too many options."

"In case ya haven't noticed, I got a gun in yer friend's back." Despite the frosty day, a single glistening trail crept from under the boy's hat, angling its way across a dirt-streaked cheek.

"I see that." *He's so young. Give me true aim, Lord.* Fin gave an apathetic shrug. "Aww, just shoot him. He eats too much anyways."

Hicks played along. "Dabney, I oughta—"

In an instant, Noah dropped to the ground. Fin fired, propelling the boy's cap three feet into the air. He snagged the musket from the Rebel's hands. The boy's eyes gaped wide in shock; his face paled, falling slack as the truth of the moment sank in.

Noah stood, brushing the dirt from his britches, a grin twisting his wheaten mustache. "Took you long enough, Dabney." He yanked the pistol from the boy's waistband. "I reckon this'd be mine."

Fin holstered his Colt. "Gonna have to take you into Gauley, son. Who you with?"

"I ain't talkin'." The boy spat on the ground, scooped up the smoking kepi and crammed it back on his head.

"At least tell me your name."

"Marrs. Seaton Marrs." He drew back his shoulders and pinned a defiant look on Fin.

"You Claude Marrs's boy?"

"What if I am?"

Fin grumbled, slapping his hat against his thigh. He'd been taking on the irregulars down on the New River of late, and this was the closest he'd made it to the home place. Holding Claude Marrs's son at gunpoint was not the homecoming he'd imagined.

"Your pap fightin' for the Confederacy?" Sadness twisted his middle like bad meat. Most of the folks he'd known all his life were siding with the Secesh. And here he was, back in his own neck of the woods—in a Union uniform, no less.

"No, sir. The Yankees took him away. Said he was a political prisoner." Seaton gave his leg a shake and shifted his weight.

Fin hated this nasty business of war, but if he didn't trust he was in the right, he'd have a hard time living with himself. And sending this boy to a prison camp . . . "We're gonna take you to the Federal encampment at Gauley Bridge, just like any other prisoner, Seaton." He snatched the grungy hat off the boy's head and tossed it into the scrub brush. "But they'll let you go if you and your pap take an oath of allegiance to the Union. Maybe your pap is still there."

He tugged a length of rope from his saddle strap and tossed it to Hicks. "Tie his hands."

∞

A grin tugged at Fin's cheek as he took in the familiar sights. A smattering of white on the upper ridges of the hills, like frosting on a birthday cake, hailed recollections of his growing-up years. Naked sugar trees waved hello, and the roar of the river welcomed him home. Here, the Gauley and New Rivers converged to form the mighty Kanawha, the watery pike of western Virginia.

"Nice to be home, ain't it?" The words sank to the ground, glum as the look on Noah's face.

"Aw, now. You paid a visit to your home place when we made that run through Greenbrier, didn't you?"

"Yep. I'm a-kinda wishin' I hadn't, though. Seems since I left the holler, Bubba Cletus and my cousin both joined up with them Rebel bushwhackers. It'd be a mercy not to meet up with a body I know in *this* county. I'd be coddlin' the mully-grubs for sure." Noah's sigh was forlorn as they come.

Regret and melancholy swirled together like a river eddy. What an intolerable thing to come up against your kin. He heard tell many a story thus far in all his three months of soldiering. Stories of brothers hugging one minute, then taking up arms against each other the next. It stuck in his craw like a spiny bone. Try as he might, he couldn't wrap his thinking around it—a family warring amongst themselves, a mother broken-hearted even before a shot's fired. A father taking up arms against his son.

He yanked off his hat and combed his fingers through matted hair. He'd cut off both his legs before he'd take on his brother or his pap, God rest his soul. Jonathan Dabney had been a force to be reckoned with in his day. He'd held the respect of the entire county and always had a knack for figuring the right way through a trouble. *I miss you, Pap.*

And what of Jimmy Lee? His best friend was somewhere off fighting for the Confederacy—most likely far from Fayette County. Least ways, he surely hoped Jimmy Lee was far from here. And still alive.

Seaton Marrs growled from the end of the rope lashed to Noah's saddle. "How much longer we gotta traipse down this road? Seems to me we oughta be there by now."

"It always seems longer when you're the one walking, sonny." Noah slowed his horse on a cue from Fin. "Need a little break, do ya?"

Even with bound wrists, the boy caught the tossed canteen and plopped to the ground. His Adam's apple bobbed with a long draw of water.

Fin shifted in the saddle. "Almost there, Seaton. I sure hope you find your pap. Albeit you're prisoners, best you be together."

Seaton stood, capping the canteen. "You a Dabney?"

"I am."

"Thought so. I recollect you helped with our harvest a couple years back." The boy kicked at the dirt as his tongue tripped over the words. "I wanna thank you for that. Mama took to her bed that summer. She died just after harvest. It was a real hard time for all of us."

Fin remembered. Just neighbor helping neighbor. Now it's folks fightin' folks. He snugged his canteen back into place. "Let's get on to the camp." Nudging Duke into the lead, he continued ahead, his mind already on the farm and his family. He'd surprise them for an early Christmas.

His attention bounced back and forth between vigilance and imagination for the rest of the journey into Gauley Bridge. Try as he might, visions of family and home crowded his thoughts. He could almost smell the steaming platters of ham, onions, cornbread—and Melinda Jane's cookies. It was so clear in his mind. His brothers' and sisters' faces. And Melinda Jane's enticing grin.

He ached for it all. The inviting kitchen with its grand stove. The sitting room and Mama's settee. He'd have to check the woodpile. Maybe work with Zander to lay up some more. No such thing as too much firewood.

He reached back and patted the saddlebag with a measure of satisfaction. He'd picked up a few small gifts passing through Charleston, including a pretty hanky for Melinda Jane, folded into a neat square. What a misery it was choosing just the right one to buy.

Now to figure out how to give it to her. He'd like to do it in private, but if he didn't give it to her with the family, they'd all wonder why he didn't get her anything.

"Dabney . . . Fin! You off wool gatherin'?"

Fin straightened in the saddle and studied the rows of tents through a haze of wood smoke.

Noah dismounted and untied the rope from his saddle. "I'm gonna find out where to deliver this boy."

Fin nodded to their charge. "You take care now, Seaton. Give your pap my best."

The boy dipped his chin in a tenuous nod. Pale blue eyes, void of their earlier fire, spoke more than words before he stared at his feet and shuffled off. Young Seaton Marrs was now a prisoner of the United States Army.

Fin struck out on foot for the command tent where a flag on a tall post drooped for lack of a breeze. After tying Duke, he retrieved a thick envelope from his saddlebag and stepped up to the lean, beardless private standing sentry. "I have a package from Ceredo. From Colonel Lightburn for Colonel Moor."

"Send him in, Private," a throaty voice boomed from inside the tent.

He pushed the flap aside. Cigar smoke hung in the warm air, lingering just in front of the short, black stove in the middle of the spacious tent. The camp commander's private quarters formed a nook to the left. A hinged trunk, square table, and a quilt-covered cot took up much of the space. Books overflowed two stacked crates.

Fin saluted and handed the envelope to the sturdy, graying colonel. "From Colonel Lightburn, sir."

"Ja, thank you. He wired ahead that you would be coming. You have a pass also, I understand." His words rode up and down in a crisp fashion.

"Yes, sir. My farm is only five miles down the road, so Colonel Lightburn issued a pass for us. The other courier is taking a prisoner to the stockade."

"You brought a prisoner with you as well?"

"A young man wanted to borrow our horses, and we weren't too obliging, sir." Fin cleared his throat of smoke, refusing to cough.

"Well done, then. What direction are you headed, Corporal?"

"Up Gauley Road, sir."

"We are still having run-ins with bushwhackers in that area. Probably best if you head that way tomorrow. Not a lot of daylight left. Seems those nasty creatures like to come out just as the sun disappears." He jabbed the cigar into one side of his mouth. "I hope you find your family well, Corporal. Godspeed."

"Thank you, sir." Fin saluted and turned about.

As he watered Duke, troubled thoughts rolled over him. *Bushwhackers.* He quickly snuffed out the notion. Federal soldiers guarded his family and farm. No need to borrow worries. But he'd head out right away just the same.

༺༻

The horses took the bend in the road at a healthy lope, and Fin swallowed a lump in his throat at the twilight-washed sight. The graceful weeping willow stood watch, guarding the rocky path that led home. *Home.* It had consumed him from the minute Colonel Lightburn gave him this mission.

"This is our lane," he said, gesturing ahead.

"Good thing, too. Don't fancy meetin' up with them critters the Colonel bespoke." Noah stretched, arching his back. "Don't s'pose there's a possibility of sleeping in a proper bed tonight? A body forgets what a mattress feels like after a time. Mayhap you got one of them plush feather mattresses?" His eyebrows wiggled like fat, yellow caterpillars.

"I think I can oblige you. Pretty sure Gus won't mind tossing Zander out of his bed. He'd just as soon sleep in the barn with his horse, anyway."

"Gus sounds like a tough fella."

"Gus ain't a fella," Fin laughed. "She's my sister. Given name's Augusta."

"Au-gu-sta." Noah drew out each syllable. "Mmm. Sweeter than cornbread and honey. She purty?"

"I reckon so. Strong too. Mothered the younger ones since Mama passed six years ago. But Melinda Jane—now, she's the real beauty."

"I seen her likeness in yer Bible. How can ya live with a woman that comely that ain't yer kin? Don't seem right. Likely there's many a tongue wagging at both ends 'bout all that." Noah shook his head like a wet dog. "Tsk . . . tsk."

"You know it's not that way. We took Melinda Jane in when her folks passed. Shoot. I've known her all my life."

They rounded the switchback and Fin squinted, unwilling to believe his eyes.

What?—No!

An iron hand gripped his gut. He kicked Duke into a sprint, pitching dirt and rocks into the air. "Hyah! Hyah!" Scorched lungs begged him to breathe, but he couldn't. He skidded to a stop at the pump and slid from his saddle, numb.

He staggered forward, shock twisting to anger. Debris lay scattered among charred remnants of the once-magnificent barn—a barn that housed Union soldiers and wounded men when he'd joined up. Not a wall stood, a ghostly reminder of some unknown violence.

He crouched and scooped up a handful of the stale, black crumbles, stirring a hoary powder that seared his heart and nostrils. All the years, all the memories, rendered to...this. He shook his head, trying to vanquish the ache that glutted his throat. Standing, he let the grit fall through his fingers, then wiped his hand across his thigh. He stared at the streak it left—dark as the notions spiriting through his mind.

A troubling silence hung in the air. No barked greeting from the old hound, Coot. No hurried steps, rushing to give a welcoming hug. No hollered announcement of his homecoming by seven-year-old Bertie. His innards churned like river rapids as he whirled, charging from the grisly sight toward the house.

Seeing the front door ajar, Fin pulled his Colt and scrambled for the back door. Questions assaulted his mind like angry hornets, and he swallowed down the horror of what he might find.

Instead of fodder shocks, rotted cornstalks lined the garden fence like defeated sentinels. Gus never would've let those spent stalks go to waste.

He nudged open the screen door with the toe of his boot, heart thumping wildly with each metallic groan. Footfalls silent, he entered the back porch, then the kitchen. He touched the stove. Cold. Ears straining for the creak of a floorboard or the snap of a flintlock, he inched forward.

A chair lay on its side near the once-polished oak table, its surface now gashed and blotted with dark stain. Broken jars, emptied of the women's labors, littered one corner. The carved sideboard stood gap-toothed, drawers ajar or missing, contents strewn across the floor.

He winced at the crunch of dried corn and beans crumbling under foot. After a pause, he continued, this time sliding the sole of his boot along the floor, moving on through the debris before edging his way to the parlor.

The dimness of the room and shadowed corners drew him forward until the faintest of sounds cut the silence. A familiar groan of the floorboard—*the one beneath the hall rug, just inside the front door.* Slipping into the shadows, Fin waited. Could be Noah. But why was he sneaking around?

Just as he considered moving from the corner, a figure crept into the room. Rifle ready, it advanced slowly, tracing the room's perimeter, body rotating, wary.

Fin saw his chance and emerged from the shadow. He slammed his pistol grip into the base of the man's skull. Catching the limp body before it crashed to the floor, he lowered the man noiselessly to the rug.

He slipped back into the kitchen, checking to his right, his left. Before he could take another step, the unmistakable snap of a hammer froze his movement.

"Turn around nice and easy there, Yankee. I like to look a man in the eye when his light goes out."

He turned, met with a wooly chest on a human mountain of greasy, rank flesh.

A mouth spoke, buried beneath a grizzled beard. "We leave for a short spell and all kinds of varmints invade this nice place we got here."

Fury gripping his voice, Fin snarled, "What happened to the family that was living here?" Possibilities tore through his mind like demons rising from Hades.

The Rebel chugged out a rough snicker. "Ain't none of yer concern." A sneer bared yellow teeth as he leveled the gun barrel. "Goodbye, Yankee Bill."

Fin dove at the bulky arm, sending the revolver clattering to the floor. It discharged, raising an acrid fog. He landed a kick to the man's shin. The Rebel bent with a grunt, and Fin brought his twined hands down like a sledgehammer onto the man's neck. With a mad-dog growl, the bushwhacker jerked upright and drew back a meaty arm intent on squashing him like a gnat.

He snatched up a chair and crashed it against the side of the tree-trunk leg. The big man wavered like a drunkard as spittle and foul words sprayed the air. To Fin's dismay, his foe managed to stay upright.

Diving for the worktable, Fin pulled at the curtain covering a shelf. *Please be there!* His fingers curled around the handle of an iron skillet.

The Rebel groaned and bent to pick up his gun. Before he could straighten, Fin brought the heavy skillet down onto the back of his head with a *THUNK*. The giant dropped, sending the floorboards to bouncing. Fin waited, chest heaving and skillet poised for another strike.

"I'd pay good money to see all that again." Noah stood in the doorway, a trickle of crimson slithering over one ear. One fist gripped the arm of a scraggy Rebel and the other pressed a pistol to the man's head.

"How long you been standing there?" Fin sidestepped the motionless heap on the floor.

"Long enough, I'd say. Got knocked silly takin' a drink at yer pump, and when I come to, I found this one sneaking in the door real quiet-like. Then I had to come see to all this clatterment." His mouth pinched lop-sided as he perused the room. "Got any rope around here?"

"I'll get it." Fin retrieved a length from the back porch, and before long, the three prisoners were situated in a neat little row against one wall, trussed up like hogs on a spit.

"Too bad one of them buzzards got away. Had a face likened to an eight-day clock—all scarred up like a splittin' stump."

"Scarred?" It couldn't be. "Just one side of his face? Long, gray hair?"

Noah scowled. "That'd be him. You know him?"

Fin swallowed hard as an old fire flared in his belly. The only man on God's earth he'd imagined killing with his bare hands.

Maybe he'd get the chance.

AUTHOR NOTES

I taught the American Civil War many times in my years of teaching school. Three thoughts caused me the most angst: What would it be like to have your home, town, or county become a battlefield? 2) What would it be like to fight your own neighbor, maybe even a relative? 3) What would it be like to send your husband or son to fight this kind of war? I address each of these considerations in the first three books of this series. I chose western Virginia because it was the most contested piece of real estate in the U.S. at that time.

When writing historical fiction, I first immerse myself in research for several months. After a time, ideas emerge for the foundation of a novel. I then weave a story of fictional characters through the maze of factual events on a historical timeline. The characters undergo their various journeys inspired by the lives of people who actually lived during that period. While the main characters in *When the Mountains Wept* are fictional, they interact with real historical personalities, events, and settings. Here are some examples from the pages you have just read:

- Preacher Coulter's sermon (Chapter 7) was modeled after an authentic sermon script preached in that day by a member of Confederate-leaning clergy.

- My mother-in-law had a cantankerous rooster named Rupert with long spurs. Her uncle later gifted her those spurs by mail after the rooster's demise.

- Regarding the female confederate soldier, J.D. Hall (Chapter 23): There were, in fact, several accounts of women masquerading as a man in order to fight. When captured, these females were generally incarcerated in Civilian prisons instead of P.O.W. facilities.

- A measles epidemic indeed moved through General Lee's troops. In the fall of 1861, 1,800 confederates in Western Virginia were incapacitated with the disease.

- The Captain George Patton, Sr. mentioned in my story headed up the Kanawha Riflemen at the war's onset. He was granddaddy to General George S. Patton of World War II fame and great granddaddy to Major General George Patton IV, who died in 2004.

- Dr. John Frissell and Sister Mary Feeny were real historical personalities at the Wheeling Hospital. (Chapter 41)

- The maps I used were images from the mid-19th century. Some roads and names have changed since those days, so if you are a Mountaineer and don't recognize a place or street name, that may be why.

Regarding the various battles, I strove to portray related incidences with accuracy:

- **Battle of Barboursville** (7/11/1861): James's first altercation was fought between the Wayne and Cabell County militia under Col. Ferguson and the Second Kentucky under Col. Woodruff. (Chapter 15)

- **Battle of Scary Creek** (7/17/1861): Gen Cox commander, "Brigade of the Kanawha" and General Patton collided at Scary Creek, where General Patton was wounded in the shoulder. (Chapter 16)

- **Kessler's Cross Lanes near Carnifex Ferry** (8/26/1861): CFS General Floyd's successful attack against Captain Robert Reynolds of Colonel E.B. Tyler's Seventh Ohio Volunteers—200 men escaped to Gauley Bridge and 400 escaped through mountains to Elk River, then to Charleston and Gauley Bridge, leaving many stragglers through the forest to arrive in Gauley Bridge. (Chapters 24, 27, 29)

- **Battle of Carnifex Ferry** (9/10/1861): When 6,000+ troops under General Rosecrans marched down the Gauley Bridge-Weston Turnpike toward "Camp Gauley," attacked the confederate troops, and fought all day. This battle was ripe with fascinating action, which I had fun recreating in detail. (Chapter 28)

- **In the fall of 1861**, the day before the fire, James was ordered to report to the Sewell Mt. area of Fayette County, where both armies had been fortifying the hills for several months. For two weeks, the two forces opposed each other until Rosecrans withdrew, and Lee's troops were recalled to Virginia.

I sincerely hope I've sparked your interest in this tumultuous, heart-wrenching era of our nation's history. Sadly, it is no longer taught in most public schools. At one time, I had a large sign on the wall of my classroom:

THOSE WHO CANNOT REMEMBER THE PAST ARE CONDEMNED TO REPEAT IT.
       —George Santayana, 1905

ACKNOWLEDGEMENTS

I am indebted to many people who deserve much credit. This series, "West Virginia: Born of Rebellion's Storm" has been a labor of love. Foremost, I am thankful to Jesus Christ, my Lord, and Savior, Who reminds me He chose me to bear fruit (John 15:16). For over a decade, writing has been fruit-bearing for me. I want to thank the following for helping me bear that fruit:

Present/past members of my critique group, The Encouragers, who have faithfully offered support and true encouragement over the last ten years. A special thank you to Melody Roberts, my ever-vigilant critique partner throughout three novels.

My hero husband who advised me on a variety of technical issues and sacrificed many a home-made meal while I worked away on this book. And to my four (now adult) children, whose tastes in entertainment spurred the viewing of a plethora of war movies over the years. (It's a guy thing.)

Kara Starcher of Mountain Creek Books LLC for her lovely book cover, expert recommendations, and patience with my unending questions.

Sarah Forster and Joan Anderson—proof-readers extraordinaire. Rachel Williams, Publicity Assistant extraordinaire.

Terry Lowry, historian at the WV State Archives Library for his expert recommendations, reading of my battle scenes, and sharing numerous maps and images with me.

West Virginia State Historic Preservation Office for answering a myriad of questions about architecture.

Donny Jones, reenactor with the 13th West Virginia Infantry (aka "The Uniformed Historian") for his expert advice and patience, answering my many questions.

Andrew Potter, reenactor with the Western Federal Blues for his generous spirit and his Frock Coat photo for the cover.

RECOMMENDED READING – Fiction

Do you enjoy clean and Christian Historical fiction set during America's Civil War? Here are some books I'd like to recommend:

- The "Rescued Hearts of the Civil War" series by Susan Pope Sloan: *Rescuing Rose, Loving Lydia,* and *Managing Millie,* https://susanpsloan.com

- These three novels by Tara Johnson: *Engraved on the Heart, Where Dandelions Bloom,* and *All Through the Night,* https://tarajohnsontories.com

- The "Accidental Spy" and "Ironwood Plantation" Series by Stephenia H. McGee https://stepheniamcgee.com

- *A River Between Us,* and "Heroines Behind the Lines" Series by Jocelyn Green https://jocelyngreen.com

- The "Belmont Mansion", "Belle Meade Plantation", and "Carnton" series by Tamera Alexander https://tameraalexander.com

- "Refiner's Fire" Series by Lynn Austin https://lynnaustin.org

RECOMMENDED READING – Non-Fiction

If you are interested in further reading, I recommend these books to learn more about the Civil War in West Virginia:

- *The Civil War in West Virginia*: A Pictorial History: Cohen, Stan

- *Bullets and Steel*: The Fight for the Great Kanawha Valley, 1861-1865: Andre, Richard, Cohen, Stan, Wintz, William D.

- *The Atlas of the Civil War*: McPherson, James M.

- *Civil War in Fayette County West Virginia*: McKinney, Tim

- *The Coal River Valley in the Civil War*: West Virginia Mountains, 1861 (Civil War Series): Graham, Michael B.

- *A Banner in the Hills*: West Virginia's Statehood: George Ellis Moore

More from Kendy Pearson

West Virginia: Born of Rebellion's Storm series

∞

Fall 2024

WHEN HEAVEN THUNDERS

Book Two

∞

Winter 2025

IN TEMPEST WINDS

Book Three

ABOUT THE AUTHOR

When Kendy Pearson discovers a pocket of American history omitted from the schoolbooks, she enjoys digging in and turning that pocket inside out. Her novels weave fictitious stories through historical events, places, individuals, and timelines. Every story is a journey through tragedy, secrets, regrets, and God's undeniable grace. She is the recipient of three Cascade Awards, two Genesis Awards, and a Crown Award.

Kendy is an accomplished musician, worship leader, music instructor, and veteran high school teacher. She relishes ice cream, snowy days, fireplaces, and Maple trees. Learn more about Kendy at kendypearson.com

Find Kendy on Social Media:

- facebook.com/kendy.pearson.author
- instagram.com/kendypearson
- twitter.com/kendypearson
- linkedin.com/in/kendy-pearson